EMISSARY

D1510584

BY FIONA MCINTOSH

The Quickening
MYRREN'S GIFT
BLOOD AND MEMORY
BRIDGE OF SOULS

Trinity
BETRAYAL
REVENGE
DESTINY

Percheron
ODALISQUE
EMISSARY

FIONA McINTOSH
EMISSARY

PERCHERON: BOOK TWO

www.orbitbooks.net

ORBIT

First published in Australia in 2006 by Voyager,
HarperCollins*Publishers* Pty Limited
First published in Great Britain in 2008 by Orbit
Reprinted 2008

A CIP catalogue record for this book
is available from the British Library.

ISBN 978-1-84149-461-6

Typeset in Garamond Three by Palimpsest Book Production Limited,
Grangemouth, Stirlingshire

Printed and bound in Great Britain by
Mackays of Chatham plc, Chatham, Kent

Orbit
An imprint of
Little, Brown Book Group
100 Victoria Embankment
London EC4Y 0DY

An Hachette Livre UK Company
www.hachettelivre.co.uk

www.orbitbooks.net

For Mum and Dad . . . 50 years!
Amazing

Acknowledgments

A trip to the Gulf this year allowed me to ride a camel into the golden sands of the desert on the outskirt of Dubai, as well as to learn more about Bedouin settlements, to experience belly dancing under the stars surrounded by the shifting dunes, and to explore a traditional spice souk, filled with sensory goodies. It was a boon for the story of Percheron and my thanks to Dubai's Dept of Tourism for its help in making the trip so enjoyable.

Many people make a vital contribution to my books but suddenly there's so many of you that I'm hoping a simple list will suffice. So . . . my deepest thanks to: Pip Klimentou, Sonya Caddy, Gary Havelberg, Judy Downs, Matt Whitney, Trent Hayes, Apolonia Niemerowski, William Fougerai, Bryce Courtenay and Robin Hobb. Plus, of course, Darren, Tim, George, Gabby and the team at Orbit, and to my agent Chris Lotts for his ongoing partnership and support.

My thanks to all the wonderful librarians who have involved me in their communities this past year and encouraged their readers to give fantasy and specifically Percheron a go and the nomination for the international literary award in Dublin is a most unexpected surprise.

And special thanks to the booksellers, at the coalface, who do such a terrific job of handselling sf to an eager community.

Finally, heartfelt gratitude to Ian, Will and Jack for their endless patience in losing me to other worlds.

Fx

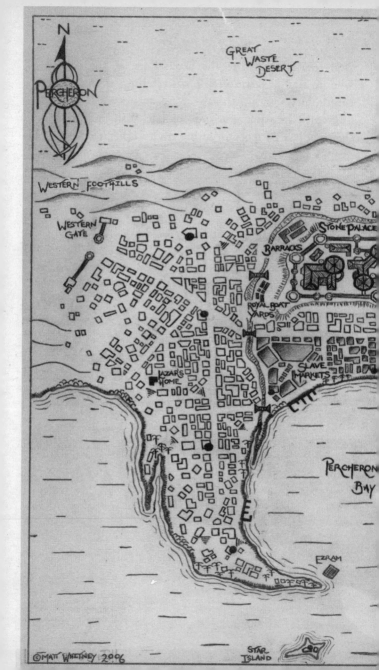

THE FARANESE COASTLINE

❦ PROLOGUE ❧

The slave held a painted silk parasol above the woman's head as she glided along, her face turned out towards the glistening Faranel. It was still only early spring but the women of the harem preferred to keep their complexions pale, unblemished by the harsh Percheron sun. This woman was slim, taller than she had been when the slave first remembered seeing her, and so much more curvy, but her hair – loosely plaited today – remained its familiar brightly golden colour. The eunuch slave had come to know her well these past eleven moons and so could sense her wistfulness this morning.

'Are you in good health today, Odalisque Ana?'

'I am, Kett, thank you for escorting me.'

'You seem sad. Is there anything I can do for you?'

She smiled. 'Dear Kett. I have always felt that is the precise question I should be asking you. After all you—'

The emasculation of Kett had always hung between them as an unspoken grief of an evening both had shared much despair over. On the night that Kett had been made a eunuch, Ana had also been sold into the care of the palace and both had become instant prisoners of the harem. 'Don't, please, that was nearly a year ago and I am recovered and almost fully resigned to my situation.' He shrugged. 'It was never your fault.'

She knew this but it didn't stop her feeling connected to him, sad for him. She stopped walking, pausing to stare out towards an island that was beyond the harbour but still under the watchful protection of the giant statues, Beloch and Ezram. 'Why is my gaze always drawn there?' she wondered aloud. 'What is that place?'

Kett looked out to sea. 'It is a leper colony, Miss Ana, and although I have never visited it, I gather it is very beautiful. Perhaps you are drawn to handsome, rugged, windswept things?'

In spite of her mood, she giggled her soft amusement at his words, and in touching his arm briefly, felt how his skin shivered at her small show of affection. 'You make me smile, I'm fortunate to have you in the harem.'

'But, Odalisque Ana,' he exclaimed softly, 'everyone loves you. You are the most popular of all the women.'

'Not so popular with the Valide and the Grand Master Eunuch, I fear, although, Kett, I am really trying to fit in. I have not raised either's ire in many a moon.'

'And yet you stare out across the water, Miss Ana, searching to escape – in spirit perhaps, if not in body? This is dangerous.'

'Ah, Kett, you know me better than anyone,' she said sadly.

'Only because I feel the same as you do. It is why I am only *almost* resigned to my situation. We both wish we could escape this place – am I right?'

'Yes, although I could admit that to no-one else. I have given my word to those who care about me and made an oath to myself that I must not attempt to leave the harem again. I have learned that the repercussions often stretch painfully to others.'

'You refer to Spur Lazar, I think?'

She flinched at the mention of his name. 'The Spur is dead because of my irresponsible actions. I can never forgive myself.'

'He would never blame you, Miss Ana. He wanted to protect you, that's why he claimed Protectorship, took your punishment.' Lazar's story had spread like fanned flames through the harem, firing the hearts of the young women searching for romance in their lives whilst secretly knowing they would probably go to their graves and not find it in the harem.

'I know but still I killed him,' she said, unable to mask her pain. She changed the subject from the former Spur, still very much alive in her mind . . . and her heart. 'And you, Kett, how do you cope with being a member of the harem? I suppose at least you have some small measure of freedom.'

'I run errands for Grand Master Salmeo on occasion, yes.'

'Do you ever think of running and never coming back?' she asked, forcing brightness into her tone.

'Always.' He looked back at her, his wide-eyed look intense. 'But on each occasion I have returned.'

Disappointed, Ana returned her gaze to Star Island, still wondering what magnet drew her attention there. 'I wonder why?' Ana said absently, finally turning to continue her journey into another part of the palace. She did not see the look on the eunuch slave's face; did not appreciate the subtle message he had tried to pass to her. 'I'm sure if I had your opportunity I might be tempted to break my word and my oath, for despite my strong words, the faith behind them is hollow, dear Kett. I think I am a liar to those around me and to myself.'

He hurried to dispel these notions. 'Please, Miss Ana, do not utter such harsh rebuke against yourself.'

'But it is true,' she said, passing the sherbet rooms and waving to one of the girls who stared out from behind the latticed windows. 'I want to believe I would keep my promise – really I do – but as I consider a whole lifetime stretching before me here as a prisoner of the harem, I think I would take any chance that came my way.'

'And risk death?'

'Yes,' she answered without hesitation. 'For this is a living death for me anyway,' she added softly.

'There is a story amongst the Elim about an odalisque who did escape from the harem once.' Kett hadn't meant to share this but it had spilled from his mouth anyway in an attempt to amuse her, to lift her spirits, or indeed anything that brought her out of her maudlin mood.

As she slowly walked Ana turned her head to stare gravely at her companion. 'You jest, surely?'

Kett shook his head. 'Only yesterday I watched the Grand Master Eunuch laughing at the tale – no-one is old enough to know if it's true – that she persuaded one of the bundle women to carry her out in the bundle itself. The young odalisque escaped that way.'

'For ever?' she asked, halting, incredulous.

'Hush,' he said, eyes frightened, gaze searching for eavesdroppers. 'Let us continue, Miss Ana.' He guided her forward once again.

Ana persisted. 'Do you mean she was never returned to the harem?'

'Apparently. Salmeo said it would never happen under his keep.'

'How did the odalisque do it?' Ana demanded in a tight whisper. 'What did she offer the woman?'

'She stole something and used it to bribe the bundle woman. The older Elim didn't say what it was. Sounds as though it was many years ago,' he said, wondering whether he might live to regret sharing this tale of escape, for he could see in her eyes how it fired her imagination. 'Come, Miss Ana, you cannot be late for His Majesty.'

'Forgive me for dawdling, but I am intrigued by your tale, Kett.'

'Not too intrigued, I hope. I would hate to lose you,' and then he added hastily, 'so would all the girls of the harem.'

'You're very kind. Here come the Zar's men,' she said, noticing the two Elim approaching. 'I would be lying if I said I didn't enjoy these meetings with Zar Boaz. He is a very good conversationalist. We even talk in different languages sometimes. I test him on his Galinsean.'

'Are you better than him?' Kett asked, impressed, still holding the parasol aloft until he was formally relieved of his duty by the mutes.

'A little,' Ana admitted conspiratorially. 'I have a natural tongue for language I'm told, although linguistic skills are of little use to me here,' she added.

'You never know,' Kett said. 'I imagine the Zar will choose you soon, Miss Ana. It is obvious how fond of you he is.'

'Not too soon, I pray,' Ana replied before fixing her veil across her face. 'Thank you for the story of the odalisque, Kett. I know you told it to cheer me up and it has.' She smiled softly, reassuringly at his trusting eyes before she turned to address the mutes, who were upon them now, with a gentle nod of her head. 'Farewell, Kett. Think of me when you roam that bazaar.'

He grinned and handed the parasol to the mute, Salazin, who would now escort the odalisque into the private chambers of the Zar.

As he watched her petite figure retreat, dwarfed by the special mute warriors who formed an elite guard for the Zar, Kett wondered when his former childhood playmate, Boaz, would take Ana for his Favourite. He suspected it wouldn't be long now, for the Zar was nearing seventeen and Ana had emerged from beautiful child to an exquisite woman. He sighed as he realised he would very soon be forced to love this woman not just from afar as he had this past year, but as another man's wife.

↜ 1 ↝

Three moons later . . .

It was Pez's idea but it was Zafira who had found him, had seen the potential; still it came as a shock to appreciate how skilled he was. She feared for the young man but his uncannily calm manner and quiet confidence convinced her. His reward was not even money, which made it harder for her, and when she did press him for his reason for taking on such personal risk he had staggered her by confiding that all he wanted to do was serve the Goddess. At his tender age what could he know about Lyana and yet he had impressed upon her that he was called to this dangerous task and Lyana had brought them together.

She had been lost for words and now Pez seemed to echo all the same anxieties even though it was his plan and she simply the expediter of the audacious concept. She had hoped he would ooze the usual confidence – needed him to – but it seemed he was as unnerved as she by this youngster.

They sat in a small room stirred gently by a soft breath of wind that had made a journey halfway up the hillside of Percheron from the sea. They could see the harbour from here. The massive giant statues of Beloch and Ezram gazed out across the Faranel, ever watchful for the long-feared raid that hadn't come in centuries.

'How does an orphanage command such a view?' Pez wondered aloud.

'I gather the palace gave it over to widowed Percherese Guard women. Down the decades those families were given better care; housed separately, given a stipend from the royal coffers and this building became defunct until one Zar gifted it to the orphans of Percheron. It's still known as the Widows' Enclave.'

'It's wonderful.'

'Yes, although there's talk of that magnanimous act being revoked now.'

'Surely not?' Pez frowned, unable to imagine Boaz making such a claim.

'So the sisters quietly claim.'

'What would the Zar want it for?'

'Not the Zar. I think his newly intimate adviser has designs on it.'

Pez pulled a face of disgust. 'Tariq is certainly carving a new role for himself.'

'Well that is his role, of course. But according to what you've told me in the past it sounds as though our last Zar never chose to have his close counsel.'

'And who could blame Joreb? The odd thing is that Boaz always despised the man as much as his father did.'

Zafira nodded. 'I saw Vizier Tariq the other day—'

'That's Grand Vizier Tariq, Zafira,' Pez interrupted, grimacing. 'It's amazing what nearly a year's worth of constant ingratiation can achieve,' he added bitterly.

'What is it, Pez?' she enquired gently. 'Has Boaz cast you aside?'

The dwarf shook his great head. 'No, but he doesn't look to me for all of his companionship now.'

'He's coming up towards seventeen; he had to grow up some time, my friend. You've been his confidant for many years. He's just spreading his wings a little,' she reasoned. 'He has a man's job to do – little wonder he had to cast off childhood so fast.'

'True.' Pez sighed. 'I just wish it wasn't Tariq's arms he walked into though,' he complained, adding with a tone of frustration, 'the man's undergone some sort of metamorphosis.'

'Well how odd that you say this,' Zafira said, leaning forward eagerly. 'I was telling you that I saw him the other day. We passed each other around the main fountain in the market and I hardly recognised him – not that he would know me from a goat.'

Pez didn't appreciate her soft jest. He was still frowning, deep in thought. He aired them now. 'Curious, isn't it?'

'Am I deceiving myself?'

Pez gave a derisive smirk. 'No, I've noticed it too. Younger, straighter, more . . . what is it?' he said, searching for the word. 'More presence. The old Tariq was weak and his greatest weakness was craving attention from the royals. This newly invented Tariq exudes absolute confidence. He needs no endorsement from anyone, it seems. I swear he all but treats the Valide Zara with disdain.'

'Well, so do you,' she reminded.

'But I'm mad, remember . . . and rude to everyone, especially Herezah whenever I can find the opportunity.

Tariq has all of his faculties intact and he openly does not suffer fools gladly.'

'Are you saying the Valide is a fool?'

Pez gave some semblance of a rueful grin. 'Far from it, but I sense she's as baffled as I by this relationship that seems to deepen by the day.'

'And you? How does he regard you?'

'Tariq? I sense that he's suspicious of me. He watches me carefully. He thinks I don't notice but I am aware of his constant attention.'

'What is he suspicious of?'

'He can't know the truth of my sanity, I'm sure of this, but it's as if he suspects there's more to me than meets the eye and so he keeps watching for some sign.'

'Iridor?' she posed, her voice a whisper.

Pez shook his head. 'He wouldn't even know who he is. Why would he suspect that?'

She shrugged, still kept her voice low. 'If you have magic, why not others?' she suggested and then moved on to more logical argument. 'Perhaps it's more that he's jealous of your relationship with Boaz.'

'It could be. That would make sense and yet I feel as though I'm in a contest as to when I'll make my mistake and whether he'll see it. He is searching for any slip, any small sign that I am not what everyone believes me to be.'

'That does sound paranoid if you don't accept that he knows something.'

'How can stupid Tariq know anything? It doesn't add up, but then neither does his behaviour over the past year. I need to be more attentive.'

'Then I understand your curious idea.'

Pez moved restlessly to the window to watch the children playing a boisterous game of pigball in the courtyard. 'Are you sure about him?'

'He's astounding, Pez. He can do it but can you do it to him?'

'There are bigger things at stake than individual lives, Zafira.'

'Except, lose enough individually and you can lose a nation,' she counselled softly.

'Don't preach to me,' he said, but without any heat.

'I just need to be sure that you understand the stakes. His life is what you're gambling with, not yours.'

'I'm aware of it, priestess, no need to remind me.' There was a spike of irritation now.

She responded in kind, angry that Pez wasn't helping assuage her own guilt. In truth Zafira was angry at herself for agreeing to this madness. 'He doesn't want your money, either!'

'Pardon?' Pez said, swinging around to face her. This was entirely unexpected. 'What does he want?'

'Nothing we can give. He serves Lyana apparently.'

Pez's expression changed swiftly from confusion to incredulity. 'And you accept this?'

'He made it clear that she had called upon him and asked this gift of a life from him.'

'Do you believe him?'

'I believe in her — that goes without saying. But I believe he's true, yes. It occurred in a dream when he was very small. She has come to him frequently since, he says, and he knows the name Iridor but not what it signifies.'

Pez now looked deeply troubled. 'I'd prefer him to accept the money,' he admitted.

'I imagine it would ease your conscience. A fair exchange you could say.'

'Zafira—' Pez began and this time there was a tone of angry exasperation.

She interrupted him, equally frustrated. 'I'm sorry, Pez, but I am fearful for this boy. What he is prepared to shoulder is frightening. We both know that should our clever plan be discovered he will not be given an easy death.'

The dwarf's irritation dissipated. His head dropped in resignation. 'I know it.'

The priestess heard such depth of emotion in those three words that she hurried to soothe her friend's troubled soul – and her own as well, no doubt. 'You have equipped him well, Pez. I would be lying if I told you that he's not ready.'

'I hope so.' He found a sad smile. 'Tell Lazar I shall visit later today. We have things to discuss. How is he?'

'Oh the usual. Angry, distant, scowling, handsome, exasperating. Need I go on?'

Pez smiled genuinely for the first time during their meeting. 'Sounds like the old Lazar.'

She nodded, reflecting his smile. 'I think he is recovered physically, yes.'

'Not emotionally, though.' He said it for her.

'Ana has scarred his heart. There are times I could wish the two had never met.'

'And none of this would have happened? No, Zafira. This is Lyana's work. She is manipulating all of us. Lazar and Ana were meant to meet but I don't understand why or the purpose of such a brief meeting and one so marked by such pain and suffering on both sides.'

'The Goddess works in mysterious ways, Pez. Let that be a comfort.'

'It's cold comfort but I'm glad our man is back. Now we have to discover his purpose.'

'He may have already served it by nearly dying.'

Pez shook his head. 'No. Lyana has more in store for the former Spur. We just have to be patient.'

2

Maliz, the demon, masquerading as the newly promoted Grand Vizier, approached the Zar confidently. The young ruler was in his private courtyard with its wide verandah overlooking the Faranel. Alongside the slim Zar stood the monstrously large form of Salmeo, Grand Master Eunuch of the harem.

Maliz smiled. He was supposed to vie with Salmeo at every turn but Maliz shared no history with the eunuch – unlike Tariq, the man whose body he had stolen. Tariq had hated the black castrate and the feeling was so intensely mutual that none of Maliz's genuine attempts at repairing past damage was welcomed with any warmth by the suspicious head of the harem. History prevailed, hate reigned. Maliz found it amusing, as much as wise, to keep trying, though.

He bowed, 'Zar Boaz,' before nodding his head in a far more polite gesture than Tariq could ever have mustered for the eunuch, 'Grand Master Eunuch. Please forgive my interruption.'

The Zar nodded. 'We were just finishing, Tariq. Salmeo has agreed to organise the boating picnic I promised the women many moons ago.'

'Oh, how charming,' Maliz replied, and meant it, but it was obvious Salmeo thought he was being sarcastic.

'It is the Zar's desire,' the black eunuch reminded softly and there was intent in the firmness of his voice that Tariq should not challenge the head of the harem in front of their Zar.

'But it is you the women will remember for this idea, Salmeo,' Maliz said in a conciliatory tone.

Salmeo blinked, slow as a lizard, as if weighing up carefully what the Vizier was saying, testing it for guile. As it was, he was entirely confused by the Grand Vizier who had appeared to have experienced some sort of epiphany. Certainly an immense change had come over the man since Joreb's death. Salmeo was quite sure he preferred the old Tariq, the witless, obsequious, self-serving Tariq who was so transparent it was easy to manipulate him. This changed Tariq was opaque and very hard to read, and he had discussed this at length with an equally confused Valide but neither was in a position to do much more than talk and observe, for the Grand Vizier had ingratiated himself so slyly into the new Zar's life that to try and undo him now was far too dangerous. 'I shall take my leave, Majesty,' he said finally without another glance to the hated Vizier. 'I have many arrangements to make. Would you like me to inform the women, Highness?'

Maliz heard the soft lisp in the black eunuch's speech and wondered how many had been taken in by that affectation, not knowing what cruelty this man was capable of.

'By all means,' Boaz said, 'although I would appreciate it if you would advise the Valide first and seek her participation,' he suggested, finding a hesitant smile, and again

Maliz noted how uncomfortable the Zar was around the massive eunuch. He noted that the royal worked hard to hide how much he disliked him, but Maliz was too sharp not to notice all the silent signs that Boaz's body gave of not wanting to spend a moment more than he had to in the private company of his head of harem. It intrigued the impostor as to how many different strained relations struggled but somehow survived within the palace walls.

'Thank you, my Zar,' Salmeo lisped and bowed before gliding away, curiously light on his feet.

Boaz sighed. 'How does such a huge man tread so softly?' he mused, then turned to his Vizier. 'It would be so much easier if you two liked one another,' he said, glancing back to the glinting sea.

Maliz, unfazed by the power of the man who stood before him, gave a wry smile to the Zar's back. 'I could say the same to you, Majesty.'

Boaz swung around and any lesser individual might have quailed in fear of retribution for such a bold comment but Maliz, relaxed and almost allowing a mischievous grin to crease the corners of Tariq's mouth, awaited the Zar's response. Boaz watched his Vizier intently for a moment. 'I wish my father had known this new Tariq who stands so brazenly before me. I believe he would have liked you, Vizier.'

'No, Highness,' Maliz said, knowing it was important to find any way to stop adding fuel to the fire of specu-lation that burned constantly in Boaz's eyes at the strange personality change that had claimed the Vizier since the old Zar's death. 'I think even I might have disliked me in your father's day. It is only since you have come to power that I've realised how important my role can be. Previously

I searched for gratification, reward, power . . . oh dear, the list of cringing need feels endless sometimes,' he said, shrugging in a self-deprecating manner.

'And now?'

'A change did come over me at your father's death, Majesty. There's no denying it,' he said, constructing the pathway with great care before he led the Zar down it. 'I realised that as soon as you took the Crown of Percheron you could have had me executed, Majesty. You and I were never what could have been termed friends.'

'I hated you,' Boaz replied, determined to be candid.

Maliz nodded. The Zar had matured much in these past few moons, growing strongly into his role, accepting its burden. His directness was refreshing in comparison to the usual politicking around the palace. 'And I understand why. I had so little autonomy, my Zar. I could have been a good Vizier to your father – may Zarab keep him – but he was headstrong and fiercely independent. He didn't want advisers and he did not like me from the outset.'

'Neither did I. I'm still not sure I do.'

This surprised but privately amused the Vizier, who had no real interest in the Zar's success – this relationship with Boaz was simply convenient and, if he was honest, mildly entertaining. His own agenda would set the palace alarm bells ringing if anyone knew or understood what was truly at stake here.

Only one other within the palace knew, but that person remained elusive. Maliz was now sure that Iridor had not only risen but was roaming these corridors somewhere. He could feel him. The ancient enemy was near and that meant Lyana, too, was close as well, as he suspected. He would exercise patience and he would find and destroy them both as he had in every battle, over millennia.

'I appreciate your candour, my Zar, and hope I never offend you.'

'I hope so too, Tariq,' Boaz said softly, but there was a threat in his tone and Maliz realised that, for all his careful work, the Zar remained suspicious and hesitant to give his trust. He actually admired Boaz for his reluctance and considered Percheron fortunate that it might enjoy two Zars in a row who were worthy of their status.

Boaz interrupted his thoughts. 'You wanted to talk with me?'

'Yes, Zar Boaz, I do.'

'Walk with me, then. I was going to take some sea air on the high balcony.'

'It would be a pleasure,' Maliz replied, knowing that walk would take Boaz past the sherbet rooms where many of the members of the harem liked to relax after their long morning, which he understood was spent simply bathing. Boaz was obviously maturing if he was beginning to parade himself past the girls. It wouldn't be long now, Maliz thought, before those same girls, quickly turning into young women, would be called upon to offer a new kind of homage to their Zar. Sometimes his strange life could be fun. Maliz imagined how much sport it was going to be to observe these delicious girls, whenever he was permitted, as they set about their single-minded business of attracting the Zar's eye. If only they knew what it was like to be a young man, his wits challenged by the fierce new drive of sexuality, they would understand that they would have to do very little in fact to win his attention. The mere suggestion of the rise of breast behind their robes, the glimpse of a nipple beneath a silken sheath, the very outline of a nubile body moving gracefully, was enough to send any hot-blooded youngster into a frenzy of desire. And if the Vizier enjoyed the opportunity to see all this beautiful, virginal flesh on offer – even though it was so subtly shrouded – then Maliz was certainly not going to complain at this potential for vicarious thrill.

He smiled slyly. 'Perhaps we should send a runner ahead to let others know I accompany you, Zar Boaz.'

'No need,' Boaz replied nonchalantly. 'That's what I was talking to Salmeo about. I'm relaxing some of the rules attached to the harem. I see no reason why the Zar – and whomever he chooses as his companions to enjoy the palace surrounds with him – should not be permitted to walk alongside certain buildings without permission.'

'Indeed, Highness,' Maliz said, surprised and delighted, enjoying also the thought that this new rule must have caused the sour look on Salmeo's face. 'Is the Grand Master Eunuch comfortable with this . . . relaxing of the old rules?'

'What do you think?'

'I imagine he believes it's an encroachment,' Maliz answered truthfully.

'Yes, that's precisely what he believes. But I know Salmeo considers it an encroachment on his personal status rather than on tradition. He cares not for the old ways so much as his territory. I don't intend staring into windows or hunting down the women. I just don't see that I must avoid them.'

'It's part of your role as a ruler to modernise life,' Maliz encouraged.

'Salmeo believes I'm stomping on tradition.'

'It's what I'd expect him to say.'

'You think it's appropriate then.' Boaz did not make it a question, more of a statement.

Maliz was sharp enough to appreciate that the Zar was not asking his permission but the young ruler was nevertheless gently searching for endorsement. 'I think it's wise, Majesty. Each Zar will surely introduce his own modern thinking to his reign. Your father made many changes — some were fought by the traditionalists, but had he backed down, then good things such as your great education might never have happened. Your grandfather did not believe in his heirs being educated as broadly. Your father learned the arts of warfare and diplomacy, for example, but taught himself how to read and write as well as he did.'

'I never knew that,' Boaz commented, surprised by this information, especially as he'd considered his father so literate. 'He was so creative too.'

'This is true but that was your father's inherent talent. He had the soul of an artist. We can see his influence all over the city, certainly in the palace. And how much poorer would the citizens be had he not exercised his right to change things? You are not doing anything that Zars before you have not already done. It is fitting that you make subtle improvements wherever you see the need.'

'It seems so archaic to separate the women to the point of imprisonment.'

'Ah, now we touch on something else,' Maliz warned, enjoying the conversation as he strolled by his young charge.

'Not really. I don't see it that way.'

'Others will. If you don't mind me offering humble advice, then may I suggest you move slowly, my Zar.

Don't try to change too much at once. Small leaps will still cover the same distance as big ones . . . it just takes longer, but it makes it easier on those who feel the effects of change.'

'Salmeo, you mean,' Boaz qualified.

Maliz gave a gesture that said Boaz could reel off a dozen names. 'Salmeo included, definitely. The Valide might also feel that you are undermining her status if you grant too much freedom to the women. You must remember, my Zar, if I dare be so bold as to guide you here, that the harem is your mother's power base. Erode that and you will destabilise her influence over the other women. If you implement too much change in a short time, they will soon be looking to you to override not only Salmeo but also the most powerful woman in the realm. She sits atop a throne in the harem; I know you understand this because you were raised in it, so I don't mean to give you a lecture.' The older man bowed slightly in deference as they walked.

'I understand. Please continue,' Boaz commanded.

'You don't want your mother as an enemy,' the Vizier said directly.

Boaz paused and Maliz wondered if he'd made an error in judgement. 'What is that supposed to mean?' the Zar asked.

Maliz was in too far to pull out now. Not that he cared much for Boaz or how his reign turned out, but he rather enjoyed the role as Zar-maker. 'The relationship I've noticed between you both is strained. It is none of my business, of course, and I realise it is neither the fault of your mother nor yourself. Circumstances of the harem will almost always put this sort of pressure on the golden couple, which is how I like to think of each slave mother who rises to this position and her precious son that claims the throne.' He paused, ensuring that Boaz was not taking offence. Boaz said nothing but his stare was intense. Maliz continued. 'Her future is in your hands. Whatever power you grant her is all she gets and she must feed off your status at all times. She is nothing without you.'

'I have heard such advice before,' Boaz replied steadily, recalling now a similar conversation with Pez – which reminded him that he had not seen the dwarf in a few days.

'Then forgive me for being repetitive. The Valide is a weapon that you can use, my Zar. I would caution against alienating her by undermining her authority over the other women. The more freedom you give them, the less mystery to her role and her access to you.'

Boaz considered the wisdom of his Vizier's words. He was mindful of his mother's role, which was why he'd instructed Salmeo to direct the boating trip with his mother's involvement in the first instance. However, he had to silently admit that he was not necessarily considering her seat of power and how it might be eroded by the changes he had in mind. Perhaps Tariq's caution was worthy.

'I shall consider your advice, Vizier,' was all Maliz got for his careful guidance. 'As you can see,' Boaz said, waving in the direction of the pale, ornate building known as the sherbet rooms that they were now approaching, 'Salmeo seems to have my measure anyway,' referring to the ring of red-robed Elim guards who stood against each tall window that might give the women a chance to eye their Zar at too close range for Salmeo's comfort . . . and vice versa, of course.

Maliz permitted himself a smile. 'It seems he does.' It was the right thing to say. Boaz gave a grudging grin, as if acknowledging that they both shared a common dislike for the man. Maliz decided it might just be easier to maintain the hate that Tariq began. It seemed more useful in terms of remaining closer to the Zar.

Boaz inhaled the sudden fresh breeze blowing off the Faranel that rolled like a restless animal before them. He laid his hands on the stone balcony and raised his face to the sun to accept some of her early-season warmth.

Anyone looking at the Zar could be forgiven for thinking all traces of childhood had disappeared this past year but Maliz, well attuned to Boaz now, could still sense faint echoes of the boy. He would have to rely on their presence to help him manipulate this young Zar.

'What did you want to speak to me about, Tariq?' Boaz asked, not opening his eyes but knowing he was being scrutinised.

'About your security, my Zar,' Maliz replied, without missing a beat.

Now the Zar did open his eyes and turn to his Vizier. 'That's a regular haunt for you, isn't it?'

'It is part of my greater responsibility, Zar Boaz. Did you know that less than a century ago we did not even have a Spur? The Grand Vizier was responsible for the entire realm's security.'

Maliz deliberately mentioned the Spur, making his words, though softly spoken, re-open the wound of loss that perhaps the young Zar had tried to ignore. But the Vizier knew this was impossible. Boaz had admired Lazar, probably loved him, Maliz realised; those wounds would never heal, especially since the Spur's death was shrouded in such mystery. It was time to turn the screw a little on the Zar's pain.

'Yes, I knew this from my history lessons,' Boaz said evenly but not without a hint of sorrow.

'I just think these are more dangerous times, my Zar. The fact is if Percheron's head of security can disappear, without a trace, then we have a problem in our city. Now I accept that he invoked the law of Protectorship and was punished on behalf of Odalisque Ana. It is also clear that his flogging was savage, mishandled badly enough to speed him to an early death.' He watched the Zar's jaw silently working with tightly held emotion. Oh yes, those wounds were not just seeping blood now, they were gushing. He continued, 'But to have to trust the word of an old woman regarding the corpse, that it was properly dealt with according to the Spur's wishes, and so on,' he added a note of weariness to his tone, suggesting it sounded too far-fetched for his liking, 'well, it doesn't sit comfortably with me, Highness. You are my responsibility after all, and in the absence of our Spur, I feel moved to make suggestions to improve your safety. One tragedy in our palace is one too many; you must not allow our people to suffer another loss of similar or even higher magnitude.'

Boaz nodded. 'You mentioned a change in the guard not so long ago. I presume you now have an idea to share?'

'Yes, Majesty. I am proposing an elite group of strong young men who will permanently be at your side, so to speak.'

'How many?'

'At least a dozen on call so I can ensure a ring of men in and around your chambers or wherever you are, every minute of the day.'

'This began as food tasters in the kitchens, Tariq. Now you're suggesting they all but live with me? I fear I will find your measures claustrophobic.'

Maliz nodded sadly. 'At least one will sleep near your bedside, Highness.'

'No!' Boaz said. 'Absolutely not. How uncomfortable will my life be if they can hear everything I say, repeat it to their colleagues and—'

Maliz raised a hand gently but the smile on his face had a malevolent quality to it. 'Hear me out, Majesty.'

Boaz's expression suggested he couldn't imagine what the Vizier could possibly say that would change his reaction to this idea.

Maliz continued. 'I am proposing that this elite corps will be highly trained and very capable of killing whoever might overstep the cordon without permission.' He paused somewhat dramatically. 'But they will also be deaf-mutes.'

Now Boaz looked startled. 'To a man? How do we train them? How do we instruct them? How do we find that many brilliant warriors?'

Maliz tutted, irritating the Zar, and the Vizier quickly realised he must be on guard at all times against his own impatience showing through. He must never reveal too much of himself and should constantly remember that he was still Tariq to all who met him. He bowed. 'Forgive me, Zar. I did not explain this well. The men will be hand-selected for their fighting prowess and ability to follow orders using signals. Once we have selected them, and trained them fully in their roles, they will be made deaf and made mute.' He stressed the final five words.

Boaz opened his mouth to say something but closed it again. He clearly had not anticipated such a chilling explanation. He took a moment or two to gather himself. 'You will maim healthy men for this role?'

'Yes,' the Vizier said simply.

'But that's barbaric.'

'I care not for how we make them, Majesty. I care only that we have a supreme fighting ability in place to protect your life. I know if Lazar were sharing this conversation with us now, he would agree in principle to what I'm proposing.'

'Then that shows how well you did not know the man, Tariq,' Boaz countered firmly. 'I assure you Lazar would never condone such injury to a warrior.'

Maliz was unfazed. He was enjoying the banter. 'Lazar would not allow his Zar to be under any threat,' he replied.

'Well, am I?'

'Pardon, Majesty?'

Boaz frowned. 'Has a direct threat been detected?'

Maliz wondered whether he should lie in order to achieve his desire. He opted not to. 'No, Highness, but these are different times to the ones your father lived through. None of your enemies could know how capable you are. They imagine a youth, seemingly vulnerable, capable of being more easily killed or deposed than his father. Perhaps spies have reported the death of your Spur. It makes you even more at risk. Furthermore, Percheron has never been more vital as a critical trading point between east and west. I suspect that if we are ever going to be attacked, it will happen during the early years of your reign, Highness. We must think ahead, be prepared.'

'All speculation,' Boaz dismissed.

'But that's my job, Zar Boaz. I must anticipate all scenarios in connection with our ruler. And without the

Spur, I feel even more compelled to offer higher protection than we currently have.' He could see Boaz tiring of the conversation so he pushed once more. 'I shall keep it to just a few men if that makes it easier on your conscience, my Zar.'

'Then I insist they must take their roles willingly.'

Maliz couldn't help Tariq's expression changing to one of bemusement. 'To be willingly made deaf and mute?'

'Or I won't allow it. Offer them and their families gold in exchange for the maiming. Be generous. If you insist upon this course, then I will set the parameters. I will also approve each before the maiming takes place.'

Maliz smiled inwardly. He had won. 'As you wish, my Zar,' he said obediently and bowed his head, revelling that he could now have the Zar permanently observed and, more importantly, that he could keep a constant spy on the dwarf.

3

The Valide sipped her fruit infusion, which she took habitually each morning, maintaining it kept her complexion unlined and unblemished. 'And what did he want to see him about?' she asked her guest as she put the porcelain cup down beside her. She was simply making conversation, for she couldn't trouble herself with every discussion that her son had with the reinvented Tariq.

'I don't know, Valide,' Salmeo admitted. 'I thought you might,' the eunuch enquired, always inquisitive.

'Boaz doesn't include me in his decisions any more – certainly not in recent times. He looks like a man now. Thinks like one too,' she said, and he heard the not so well disguised sorrow.

'Then he'll be acting like one soon,' Salmeo replied and knew the Valide missed nothing of the innuendo in those words.

'He'll choose her first,' she warned.

It was not something the Grand Master Eunuch needed to be told. 'We can't stop that.'

'She's dangerous, Salmeo. I made a mistake in selecting Ana. I should have let Lazar have his little girl,' she snarled.

'I'm not sure anything used to simmer in Lazar for

anyone,' he commented, always glad to be reminded of the Spur's demise.

'If you were a woman you'd understand,' she replied caustically. 'He didn't just simmer for her, he was feverish, but he arrogantly thought he hid it. From me!' She shook her mane of hair that had lost none of its black glossiness, even though she was now past her third decade. 'I'll never understand why he ever brought her through those palace gates if he was so infatuated with the child.'

Salmeo understood instantly that none of the Valide's own fiery infatuation with the long-dead Spur had cooled.

It surprised him that even after all this time she burned so fiercely for the soldier, or at least the memory of him. She had not mentioned Lazar's name to him since the day his 'murderer', Horz, had been executed – accused of poisoning the whip used to flog and ultimately kill the Spur. Horz was dead and forgotten, but not so Spur Lazar – it seemed his memory would never die, and certainly not for the Valide. He stored the thought away.

The Valide was not an enemy but she could be. That accepted, Salmeo had long ago realised that his fate was tied up with Herezah. There would never be any opportunity to ingratiate himself with the new Zar – it was all too obvious what the young ruler felt towards his keeper of the harem, but as distant as Boaz might have made himself from his mother, he was still of her blood and would see no wrong done by her.

If I can remain her ally, Salmeo thought, I might buy my own protection should the truth of my involvement in Lazar's death come out. He didn't think it could. Having successfully blackmailed Horz into taking the blame and with Horz's corpse long since rotted on the impaling post outside the palace, his secret felt safe. But Salmeo knew in his heart that the Zar believed that he was at the root of the mysterious death of the Spur, so the royal's suspicious nature where Salmeo was concerned could never be discounted. Boaz would be looking for anything that might connect Salmeo with wrongdoing, so staying close to the Valide, pandering to her needs and making himself indispensable to her machinations might be that extra insurance he needed. He deeply regretted that rare moment of spite when he had impulsively allowed his anger to overtake his sense. Poisoning the whip that would ultimately flog the Spur was effective but ultimately perilous. Yes, it killed the proud, arrogant soldier who had become such a thorn for Salmeo's plans to dominate Odalisque Ana, but was death really necessary? No, he thought, it was stupidly reckless, and although blame had been laid through some swift manipulations of his own, it had almost found him and wrapped itself about his own shoulders. The Zar surely wanted him to wear that mantle and it was only a stroke of genius that he had found the weakness of Horz, the one brave person he could count on to be the victim and go to death with courage, knowing his family was preserved from persecution. He suddenly realised the Valide had been watching him whilst he mused. She required a response to her grumbling over Ana.

Herezah watched the eunuch's tongue flick out and lick his lips in an obscene habit that revolted most, but one she had become used to over the years. She regarded the shrouded eyes too. Both signs that Salmeo was plotting.

It was still a surprise for her, though, when he spoke his thoughts, and so directly. 'I could just have her killed,

Valide. She could accidentally slip or mysteriously drown – the boating excursion provides a marvellous opportunity. I can even manufacture a culprit if you ask this of me.' His tone was sly and he did not look her in the eye, simply waited patiently for her response.

He guessed the suggestion brought a flare of hope that would torch through Herezah's body. The thought of the young odalisque, who was rapidly shaping herself as the Zar's Favourite, disappearing from the harem echoed a daydream he suspected the Valide permitted herself. Ana was a threat to her. The Valide had not anticipated Boaz taking on the challenge of being a Zar quite so swiftly. She had hoped he would accept the role in title only and then return to his more studious pursuits, giving her free rein to essentially run the realm. Her intention had been to always involve her son, probably holding meetings over supper each evening to discuss the day's affairs as though she was consulting with him. Herezah was too clever not to factor in male pride, and Salmeo understood that she was more than happy to allow everyone in the palace to continue the pretence that a new Zar was confidently on his throne whilst she herself pulled all the strings of the puppet ruler.

But it was not to be. For all her cunning and clever ways, Herezah simply hadn't counted on her once shy, slightly withdrawn son actually embracing his new role, shouldering it with dignity and now living it with a real sense of purpose. That potential had slipped by her sharp senses and now she was paying the price of raising a well-educated son who had never been allowed to shirk a sense of duty.

All of this taken into account, Herezah could struggle

to live with this mature Boaz in her life and carve out new powers for herself. It would be enough. But what she couldn't abide, Salmeo knew, was Ana and the profound effect this young woman was having on her son. Ana and her speedy rise in the Zar's estimation threatened to kill off any aspirations that the Valide still held for herself.

Nothing had occurred sexually between them yet, he knew this, but there was a bond, for certain. It had formed when the girl had first been brought to the palace – she had been lonely and vulnerable, whilst Boaz was uncertain and fearful of his new role as Zar. Herezah could only blame herself for having not paid sufficient attention to her son's emotions at that time. Boaz had genuinely grieved for the loss of his father, whilst Herezah had expected him to get over the death quickly and find a similar excitement as she had at their new status – Valide and Zar.

Of course her mistake was imagining that ambition would somehow naturally override Boaz's love and grief for his father, and her expectations of her son had been interpreted by him as heartlessness, Salmeo deduced. The eunuch appreciated that Herezah was right to expect Boaz to show no weakness, to pick up his father's mantle – overnight – in order to establish his rule. But from what he could tell it remained an unspoken rift between the Zar and his mother.

Salmeo slipped one of the violet tablets he habitually sucked into his mouth. The flowery fragrance wafted towards the Valide and she pretended to ignore his soft sigh as he awaited her answer to his offer.

'Too risky,' she said finally. 'Any number of things could go wrong. No, Ana needs to be entrapped by her own doing.'

'I don't follow, Valide,' he said, lacing his fat, bejewelled fingers together, a sure indication that he was intrigued.

She picked up her cup again and sipped, waiting for the explosion of citrus flavours on her tongue, before she spoke. 'Ana is by far the smartest odalisque in the harem, wouldn't you agree?'

'I would. Most of the others seem to look to her for leadership, I note.'

Herezah did not like hearing this. 'Hmm, you see that in itself is a declaration of her intentions.'

Salmeo disagreed. 'To be honest, Valide, I think Ana would be happier if she had less attention. She's a strange sort of a girl – very contained, seems to need no-one and yet she's the very person most of them seek friendship or comfort from.'

'Is it just the younger ones?'

He shook his head. 'I'm afraid not. She's a natural leader. I would be lying if I didn't admit that the entire harem adores her.'

Herezah smirked. 'That will change.'

Salmeo's mind moved quickly with the Valide's. 'When Boaz begins choosing his sexual partners, you mean?'

'The moment my son starts singling out girls for his romantic attention, they'll be the target of hate from all the others.'

'Then Ana will be despised, for I have no doubt that she will be Absolute Favourite.'

Herezah slammed her cup down and Salmeo wondered if he didn't hear it crack with protest at such treatment. 'This is my very point! She must be undone before she attains such a position.'

Salmeo stifled the smile he was privately enjoying at the Valide's insecurity. Herezah might consider herself powerful but she was not feeling terribly powerful right now, with her son so independent and a slip of a girl about to claim the most important position in the harem, save her own, and one that would ultimately threaten the Valide's future. 'You were telling me how we might undo such aspirations,' he said, calming her, pouring her a fresh infusion.

Herezah took a breath to quell her anger. 'We agree she's clever so we must use that intelligence against her. I'll wager she is bored?'

'Senseless,' he confirmed. 'She hates the harem, as you would guess. She is not interested in anything it offers, from its decadence to its pampering or its riches. She couldn't be less interested in any of it.'

'Good. Let's keep her bored and frustrated then.' The Valide sipped her drink, taking a few moments to organise her thoughts. Salmeo knew to remain quiet during her pause.

'This boat trip you want my involvement with, when is it planned for?'

'Soon — in several days, I imagine,' he replied.

'Even better. It will give her a taste of freedom. And her imprisonment back in the harem afterwards will feel all the more smothering. Let's plan some tedious training in the meantime, shall we?'

'Embroidery?'

She groaned, remembering the hours of soul-destroying boredom spent learning how to work on a piece of silk. 'Precisely. And letters. No swimming or outside walks. Keep it all indoors, especially now whilst the sun is shining with its promise of summer.'

'And?' He knew the crux of her plan was yet to be revealed.

'We'll make it easy for her to try and escape.'

Salmeo made a soft sound of disbelief. 'Do you really think she'd disobey the most important rule of the harem?'

'She did it once before,' Herezah replied, tapping her teeth with a blood-red painted fingernail . . . a habit she now couldn't help when in deep thought.

Salmeo wasn't convinced. 'She had hardly arrived then and we'd just inflicted the Test of Virtue.'

'She's a year older, a year bolder and a year more bored with her life. She's ripe to make another attempt. She just needs a push.'

'You speak with knowledge, Valide,' Salmeo commented.

'I fought the urge every day of my life, eunuch; I sometimes think I still do,' Herezah said, unable to disguise a slightly wistful note in her tone. 'But Ana believes she has the ear of the Zar and his indulgence. She'll risk it, I promise . . . and just in case, I might sow the right seeds in her mind.'

'Oh?'

'Send her to me today. I think I'll be giving her some responsibility in the harem. It's timely anyway that the girls take on some special roles but I'll endow Ana with the most trust . . . confide a few things in her.'

'Let her think you might be friends?'

Herezah shrugged. 'I wouldn't go that far. Ana's too much of an island but perhaps some fragile bridges might be built.'

'And then what, Valide?'

'I'll tear them down and expose her. What is the harshest punishment for leaving the harem?'

'Lashes . . . you'd remember that from Ana's previous attempt at escape. But this time there'll be no Spur Lazar to twist the rules to claim Protectorship and take the strokes on her behalf.'

'Is that the best we can do?'

'Well, being caught unveiled, perhaps in the company of a man, would certainly increase the punishment,' he said, enjoying where this conversation was headed.

'To what?'

'Death.' He said it coldly, without hesitation, and saw how the word appealed to her by the involuntary twitch at the corner of her mouth. The Valide was planning murder, it seemed. He loved it.

'Mandatory?'

He nodded confidently. 'Drowning in the Faranel is the easiest. I'm not sure anyone could save her then, bar an extraordinary set of circumstances.'

'Such as?' Herezah demanded.

Salmeo shrugged his huge shoulders as he considered. Then he held his great hands out, his palms shockingly pale pink against his black skin. 'I simply can't imagine what, Valide.'

And that was good enough for her. If Salmeo couldn't bend his mind to a situation that might save the girl's life, then no-one could. 'Excellent. That's what I want you to arrange, Salmeo.'

'You want me to bring about her death, Valide?' he queried innocently.

Herezah knew what he was doing. She understood he was making it unequivocally clear between them what was being planned and who was giving the orders. 'I want you to ensure she is somehow found in that unforgivable position you suggested and cannot be saved from the consequences. The rest is up to the laws of our harem.'

'And the Zar, Valide. What of his interests?'

She frowned, not understanding. 'What do you mean, Salmeo?'

'Only that if he was on side it would be easier to manipulate the law in our favour,' he said gently, his eyes heavy-lidded, intrigue spicing his tone.

She smelled the nauseating fragrance of violets on his breath again, reminding her of the dangerous plot she was designing and the even more dangerous individual she was hatching it with. 'Boaz, unfortunately, will not be our pawn. As I have said, he has become a man these past thirteen or so moons and he will not be manipulated easily.'

'He need not know, Valide,' Salmeo said softly and she recognised his habit of looking down at his fingers, not giving eye contact. This was Salmeo at his best, slippery and cunning.

'You want to use my son without his knowledge?' she stated, determined to avoid all innuendo.

Salmeo nodded but still would not meet her gaze. 'He need not be in on our plan.'

The word *our* was not lost on her. She knew from this moment she had tossed her future in with that of Salmeo. Her grand notion to align Tariq with herself and keep Salmeo at more of a distance, but still under her authority, had not unfolded as she had hoped. The Vizier was now Grand Vizier and far more powerful, and he had so cleverly ingratiated himself with her son, it was sickening. Even now she couldn't quite grasp how it had happened, under her nose and with such speed. At the old Zar's death he was a snivelling, obsequious adviser with no-one's respect and only her lukewarm patronage to save him. Within weeks of the new Zar being crowned, Tariq was a changed man in many respects. His demeanour, even the way he presented himself, had undergone some sort of transformation. The man was suddenly interesting, pithy, dry-witted and downright clever – aspects she had not once previously appreciated in the Vizier. And, damn him, he looked somehow different. Oh, it was Tariq all right, no-one could claim otherwise, but gone was the stooped carriage and all the vulgar adornments he so favoured, including jewels in his beard and on his sandals. A few moons back she couldn't spot a single item that sparkled on his person, and his clothes were no longer ostentatious. All of a sudden he was wearing subtle colours and simple lines, more befitting a man of his appointment as Grand Vizier. Herezah could swear he now had a roving eye for women too, something that had never occurred to her before. Tariq had seemed almost sexless in the years gone by and she knew he lived alone, took no women casually and certainly had no long-time lovers. This much Zar Joreb had confirmed directly with her on one of their cosy nights together. But this new Tariq all but flirted with her, winked at some of the serving girls, and, in the rare company of the veiled members of the harem, gave them lingering appreciation.

It was Tariq who was now seemingly closest to the Zar – him and the despised dwarf, of course; how could she overlook Pez? She realised Salmeo was watching her and drew herself back from those thoughts that irritated her so much.

With her next words she knew she was not just aligning herself with Salmeo rather than Tariq, but also risking her fragile relationship with her son, the Zar. 'And so now please explain this mystery to me as to how we use my son without his consent,' she said. 'But first, I need a fresh brew of my tea. Would you organise it, please, whilst I change out of my silk robe.'

Salmeo gave instructions to a eunuch servant and Herezah disappeared into her sleeping chamber, which led into her dressing-rooms. She emerged at the same time as Salmeo was dismissing the servant who had laid out fresh crockery.

'You look very lovely, Valide,' the chief eunuch commented.

She nodded, not really needing to be told this. She knew how splendid she appeared today. There was work to do and she needed to be at her dazzling best.

'May I pour for you?' he added.

'Please,' she replied, settling herself by the window. As she stared out into the gardens she contemplated, not for the first time, how often she stared at garden or sea, as all in the palace did, with inextinguishable longing to be elsewhere.

'We're all prisoners of this beautiful place,' she said, speaking her thoughts aloud.

'Privileged prisoners, Valide,' Salmeo commented from behind as the steaming citrus brew swallowed up a slice of lime that he had slid into it. He lightly stepped towards Herezah and delicately handed her the tall, exquisite cup that stood on an equally beautiful saucer. It was her own design, commissioned by Joreb when she was pronounced wife and Absolute Favourite. Its colours were bold and daring, reflecting Herezah's personality, Joreb had told her.

She sipped, making a soft sound of pleasure at the warmth. 'All servants dismissed?' she checked.

'We are alone, Valide.'

'Then I am all ears, Grand Master Eunuch. Tell me your cunning plan.'

❧ 4 ❧

The man, hunched like a sack of grain in the chair, stared intently out to sea. Hair, once black as the famous velvet from Shagaire, now curiously golden, blew across his face, unnoticed.

The wind was refreshing rather than cold, for summer had begun to lay its new warmth over the land. Nevertheless the man's bones seemed to rattle from a constant shivering that had nothing to do with any chill. The goat-hair blanket hung loosely from his hollow frame, ignored and as unwanted by this wearer as any other form of comfort that tried its healing qualities but failed. This one wanted to suffer, for in suffering there was life.

The day itself had been sublime, its brightness almost painful on the eyes, but the man's gaze was distracted neither by the sparkle of the first season's sun nor the glistening Faranel Sea it lit and ultimately warmed. Instead all focus was riveted on the far distance and the glowing outline of the city of Percheron, blushing fiercely in the late-afternoon sunlight. High on the hill that overlooked the magnificent horseshoe-shaped bay was the Stone Palace, and it was to its quiet hallways and chambers that his thoughts fled. And although the twin giants who kept guard over Percheron captured his attention from time to time, as though trying to distract him from the lonely vigil, that gaze was always quickly drawn back to the dominating presence of the Zar's palace.

'You should move inside now,' the old woman who had limped up urged gently. 'And it's time for your medicine,' she added.

'For whatever good it will do me,' he replied.

She didn't mean it to but her tone still came out bitter. 'It's no good staring towards the palace, Lazar. She cannot see you but she is safe. Let that be enough.'

They both knew that was simply her opening gambit for an old argument. He bit. 'Don't lecture me, priestess. At least you can go into the city freely. I am stuck here, as much a prisoner of this leper colony as Ana is of the harem.'

'Well, blame yourself! You took too big a risk and set yourself back moons with a journey you were not well enough to make.' She made a sound of disgust. 'Attending Horz's execution was madness.'

'I told you, I needed to get the note to Pez,' he replied, his anger stoking.

'I could have taken the note to Pez, but of course you wanted to see Ana again. What good are you to us if you insist on speeding your own death?'

'My life is my own,' Lazar growled. 'It does not belong to you, not anyone!'

'Is that so?' she said in a manner suggesting the opposite, but this time she had heard the fury and could feel only relief, for it was a good sign of his recovery. 'You can try and fool us but I suspect you can't fool yourself with such hollow words. Your life is already given – she owns it,' she said, her crooked finger pointing angrily towards the palace where Ana lived.

It was a cruel jibe but Zafira needed anger from Lazar. Where there was anger there was fight, and where there was fight there was surely life, for if his crushing despair won through – and it still could – they were lost. She hoped there might be something equally cutting spat in reply but there was only an echo of her own sigh. They both knew what she said was true, but they also knew the stakes of this strange battle they were now engaged in were high, and in truth risks were all they had to choose from.

'I shall be in shortly,' finally came the response.

'Let me help you.'

'No. I will manage.'

'Lazar, you must forget her,' she cautioned softly. 'I suspect—'

'Just a few more minutes, Zafira,' he said, cutting her words off.

He didn't deny that it was the sad memory of the loss of a woman that was so destructive to his healing, and yet Zafira knew it was because of this woman that Lazar still lived, still bothered to wake each day and breathe, eat if she could get much down him, hobble around keeping his limbs supple, if not strong. It was so ironic. Opposing emotions pulling him apart, both good and bad for his health.

His perilous trip into the city was seemingly to let Pez know that he lived and to summon the dwarf to come to Star Island immediately. This was his pretext for slipping away from Zafira, risking his life just hours after being revived from the unconsciousness that had followed the flogging and poison, when he was not nearly strong enough to make the journey across the water. But the note was his excuse – anyone could have delivered it for him. No, his true motive was that one final glimpse of Odalisque Ana. And that effort had nearly taken what little life had been left to this man.

He had barely clung to existence after the poisoning from the whip that opened his back so badly. Blood loss, drezden poison and a deep sorrow all conspired to kill him. But love sustained him. His fragile hold on life was there, Zafira knew, only because it might mean he would see her once more. And so he had fought death this past eleven moons, fought it so hard he was left a living wreck, but mend he would, if he took his rest and medicine.

Lazar now understood that the drezden brought with all its evil intention a dark gift. A legacy. He knew from the curious woman known as Ellyana, who had effectively saved his life, that this gift could not be given back.

'It will stay with you forever,' she had counselled when he was sufficiently recovered to focus on words, and on living. 'It will lie dormant within you and then like a sickness curse you all over again on a whim.'

'What is my warning? How will I know when it comes?' he had asked, when he was strong enough, his throat raspy from lack of speaking for so long.

'You won't. It simply attacks when it chooses.'

'And how can Lazar protect himself then?' Zafira had asked on his behalf.

'With the drezden itself. You must always carry a vial of it with you. Put a drop of the concentrated poison on your finger – no more than a single drop, mind – and put that on your tongue. It will take some hours but it will restore you.'

'But it hasn't restored me on this occasion.'

'Lazar, you were as good as dead from the whipping alone. I defy any physician to have brought you back from the brink of the abyss with their modern potions and notions. Trust me. If you were at the palace or under the care of the male doctors, you would have been given up to your god. Drezden saved you. It will again and much faster now that your body can cope with it, but only . . .' She stopped, shrugged.

'For a while,' Lazar finished what Ellyana had not said.

The woman had simply nodded. Not long after, she had disappeared. Zafira still found it unsettling that the woman had come into their lives at a time of such high drama and then left so soon with no warning, no farewell, and no further instructions . . . except for a caution; she had told Zafira that Iridor, the demi-god in his owl form, would rise, and once that occurred, then the battle of the gods, which she had spoken about, would have begun. She had counselled that Lazar was integral to the success of the Goddess but wouldn't, or perhaps couldn't, explain why. Zafira hadn't really understood much of it at all but Ellyana was not one to be pressed, and then she had disappeared. They hadn't seen or heard from her in almost a year.

Zafira had suspected who Iridor might be but had no idea of what his rising meant. She was none the wiser now, although her suspicions of who the Messenger of Lyana the Goddess was had been confirmed on the night after Horz of the Elim had died. It had come as no surprise in truth, but despite her easy acceptance she experienced an intense feeling of awe every time she saw the beautiful snowy owl.

She returned her thoughts to the present, realising that she had remained standing there beside the former Spur.

Lazar reminded her. 'Please, Zafira.'

His plea tugged at her heart. He had suffered enough, now needed encouragement.

'You are mending, Spur. I have been hard on you, perhaps not as honest as I should be. I know you feel weak but your back is healed and I've watched you exercising. I see you have some strength back.' He nodded, remained silent. 'Allow yourself to be well. The medicine can only do so much. Now it's up to you.'

'I realise this. Now please, just give me a few more minutes alone.'

There was such a plaintive note in his voice that the old woman could do little more than shake her head and oblige. Turning, she hobbled away towards the small hut that served as home nowadays, wincing at the snag of pain in her hip that constantly reminded her she was well past her best years, and yet never had she needed strength and health more than she did now.

Ana bowed low and gracefully. 'You wished to see me, Valide?'

'I did, child. Come, walk with me in the courtyard. This mild weather is too delicious to waste,' Herezah replied, noting with surprise how different Ana appeared since she had last paid her any close scrutiny. Herezah detested the girl so much she had deliberately ignored her, had in fact had so little to do with the girls these most recent moons that she had allowed Ana – and no doubt some of the older odalisques – to suddenly blossom into womanhood without noticing. That was a mistake and most unlike her but then no-one understood how the death of Lazar had personally affected her. For all her outward goading of him, her public rebukes and the hardships she could force upon him, this was the one man over her lonely lifetime who had made her otherwise cold heart burn.

She had never loved Zar Joreb but she had admired and enjoyed him. Without his favour she shuddered to imagine what would have become of her, and Boaz would have suffered the hideous death his brothers had. In truth, love was something she had never experienced, so whether she loved Lazar she could not say. But did her lust overflow for him? Yes! She had never wanted any other man with that kind of intense passion but he had ignored her advances, denied her even simple pleasures – a kind word, a smile. Since Ana had arrived in their lives, his polite shunning of Herezah had crystallised into hatred, she was sure of this. He despised her for denying him access to Ana. Still, Herezah's heart could jump at the mention of his name after all this time, could also ache when she allowed herself space and time to think about his loss. And so, very unwisely, amidst her most private sorrow and her desire to improve her relationship with her son, she had permitted the harem, her seat of power, to essentially function without her closest supervision. Here she was paying the price for that error as she watched Ana approach. It was never too late, though; striking woman or not, Ana was still just an odalisque and far beneath the Valide's status.

'And how are you, my dear?' Herezah asked, not at all interested but keen to appear as friendly as possible.

'I am well, Valide, thank you,' Ana answered as she followed Herezah into the small, private garden.

'Come and stand in the light, Ana, so that I may look

at you,' Herezah suggested. She watched the girl glide towards the column of sunlight that cut through the cypress pines and warmed the stone flagstones beneath her sandals. She felt instant envy at the way the girl's hair blazed brightly beneath the golden rays, glinting as she tossed that free-flowing hair without knowing what effect it could have on the onlooker, particularly a male one. 'You have changed, Ana.'

'How so, Valide?' Ana asked politely.

Herezah considered. 'You are taller, you have an eye for costume, I see, and fuller of figure too – which is a good thing, for you were on the narrow side.'

'I try not to eat too many of the sweet dishes that the kitchens tempt us with, Valide,' Ana replied but not defensively.

'I don't think you have to worry too much, my dear. At your age I could eat a camel for a snack and not put on so much as a sheld. It's after childbirth that you have to observe new eating habits. You wouldn't have been acquainted with the old Zar's harem,' she said.

'It was disbanded just prior to my arrival.'

'Well, you'd have seen a queue of fat women waddling out of the palace, I assure you,' Herezah said, more viciously than intended.

Ana betrayed no recognition of the insult on her expression, which remained somewhat frustratingly serene under Herezah's gaze. 'I was once told that roundness of body meant prosperity, Valide.'

Herezah blinked in irritation. The girl was far too forward in presenting her own thoughts. 'That may well be, Ana,' she said, instantly regretting her jibe at the old harem's women and wives, 'but no Zar is going to choose a corpulent woman over one whose body is voluptuous but still trim.'

It was as if Ana ignored the Valide's comment. 'I was also told that beauty is in the eye of the beholder, Valide. Perhaps each Zar has different ideas of what is attractive in a woman. Zar Boaz may find a woman's mind beautiful and not lay so much store by her figure.'

Herezah couldn't stifle the gasp of indignation that escaped her.

Ana realised her error. 'Forgive me, Valide. I meant no offence. I am merely posing an idea.'

'You offer your private thoughts too easily, Ana, for one so young.'

'I apologise, Valide Herezah,' Ana tried again, this time going to her knees. 'I am trying to teach myself not to.'

Herezah looked at the kneeling figure and it was as though she were looking at herself from fifteen years ago. Elegant, headstrong, beautiful on the outside and a sharp intelligence held within. Herezah had fed the fire of ambition that burned so brightly inwardly – that was all that had got her through the years of destructive boredom. But ambition did not burn in this girl, she deduced. It was something completely different and yet still it gave off the similar heat, simmering constantly but invisibly.

'What is it that you want?' Herezah said, the words slipping out before she could stop them.

Ana looked up in surprise. 'I want nothing, Valide. I just want to be,' she answered, not explaining anything.

Herezah again felt the twitch of exasperation. 'To be? Whatever does that mean?'

Ana shrugged, 'Pardon me, but I'm just not sure how I must respond.'

Again the evasiveness and lack of anything but cryptic responses.

'You say you want nothing,' Herezah repeated, clutching at the only thing Ana had said that made sense, 'and yet you have all the girls in the harem eating out of your palm.'

Again Ana looked down and Herezah knew the girl understood. 'It is not from choice, Valide. I do not encourage it.'

'And still it happens, Ana. Are you dangerous for the harem? You may stand.'

Ana rose in a fluid movement and once again Herezah was struck by the golden beauty and grace of this young woman. She certainly had filled out in the past few moons and looked ripe for the plucking, as the Grand Master Eunuch had observed. He was right, Boaz could be used unwittingly to bring this threat to Herezah's status to an end.

'Dangerous?' Ana queried.

'Your innocence is always convincing, Ana, but it does not fool me,' Herezah commented, again carefully covering her rancour with a soft tone as though she were merely making an observation rather than an accusation. 'It will serve you well. I'm sure the Zar will love it.'

Now Ana dared to raise her depthless green eyes and regard the Valide, her gaze serious, and Herezah felt impaled by the stare.

She affected a coy laugh as if embarrassed. 'Oh surely you realise that my son will want to bed you soon, Ana?' Not all of the mockery was disguised in the tone. She wanted Ana to hear it. 'And I for one will be delighted when he takes his first virgin between his sheets,' she continued.

Ana stammered some sort of reply but although the words were lost on Herezah, the effect of her baiting the girl was not. She smiled inwardly. This was where she wanted Ana — unsure, hesitant.

'Anyway, let's not talk about that,' she said in a more friendly manner, waving away the previous conversation. 'I brought you here today to discuss Zar Boaz's picnic for the harem.'

'Oh?'

'Yes, you see, I imagine some of the younger girls are going to be a little fearful of being taken out of the harem. They've been here now for a year so this is where they feel secure.'

Ana had regained her composure to some degree and answered without thinking. 'No, Valide, I think everyone in the harem is very excited. I sense no fear.'

Herezah blinked slowly, as if talking to someone too dull to understand. 'Nevertheless, while you may think most are looking forward to it, I assure you some will be reluctant.'

Ana nodded, quickly appreciating her lack of tact in answering back so quickly.

Once again Herezah found and fixed a friendly smile to her face. 'I am hopeful, Ana, that you will counsel the youngsters, dissuade any hesitation, and especially show them not to fear their Zar.'

'How do you mean, Valide?' Ana asked, frowning.

'Let's take a tour of the garden,' Herezah suggested, even linking arms with Ana, and despising the feel of her young and unblemished silken flesh next to her own. Herezah could sense her anger rising at the unfairness that this beautiful creature had so much going in her favour.

The Valide understood that she, too, had once enjoyed similar qualities but that freshness and vitality had gone now. Oh yes, she remained a beautiful woman but she was an older woman now, a Valide no less. No man was going to come looking for her these days – no man would dare – but she missed being able to use her body to render a man helpless. It was such a powerful feeling, one Ana had not yet known . . . or had she?

Lazar had been totally in Ana's thrall; Herezah had seen it in his hungry, desperate gaze when he was lying through his back teeth to save the girl from the harem's imprisonment. During the Choosing Ceremony when all the purchased girls were first presented to the Valide, he had argued persuasively for access to Ana. Herezah suspected it was a lie that the mother in the foothills had demanded as part of the sale that Lazar act as some sort of ongoing mentor – he made it sound credible – but nevertheless, adroit though the Spur was, he could not hide . . . not from her anyway . . . the helpless ardour he possessed for Ana. Her hackles rose just thinking of this fact. Not only did Ana seem to have Boaz focused on her but the girl had somehow managed to win the heart of the only man Herezah had ever desired and yet never so much as touched.

She remembered now Lazar half-naked, standing tall at first against the whipping post in the Courtyard of Sorrows, but it didn't take too many bites from the Viper's Nest to savagely open up his back and for precious blood to flow all too freely out of Lazar's hard, proud body, to leave it slumped and lifeless by the end of the twenty strokes. She felt a keen pain as she allowed the frustration and anger she normally kept so securely buried to have free rein in her mind that this man had never laid a finger on her, hated her in fact, not that she could ever have fully told what he was thinking.

What she would have given for one night with Lazar. She knew he paid prostitutes for their services and that riled her. She would have given him all of herself for free; risked everything for a single night. And Ana had had several nights with Lazar at Herezah's expense; from travelling with him from her home in the foothills to a carefree evening the girl had spent with him in Percheron prior to Lazar presenting her at the palace. Herezah had discovered that on this final night of Ana's freedom, she and the Spur had wandered the bazaar – hand in hand, no less! – had shared a meal and sat close together around a fountain. Her spies reported laughter, tenderness and even sorrow when the time came to leave the alley of gold – where he had bought her a present – their last call prior to wending their way to the palace. Her fury, a year on, still burned.

Herezah had only two men in her life, two men on her mind and Ana laid claim to both of them. It hurt like a savage wound and it took all of the Valide's willpower not to pull her arm from the young woman walking carefully beside her.

The silence between them had lengthened. Herezah pointed to a bench seat beneath a fig tree. She swallowed her despair and her voice came out bright and steady. 'Let's sit, shall we?'

Ana did as asked, maintaining her silence, unsure of what was coming.

'Do you ever think of Spur Lazar, Ana?' She felt the involuntary movement next to her, knew she had hit a nerve.

'I do, from time to time, with sorrow that he is no longer striding around the city.'

'Is that how you remember him?'

Ana hadn't meant to shrug but she did. 'I don't really know how I remember him. My time with him was limited,' she said carefully, her intuition serving her well. She had long ago sensed the Valide's unhealthy interest in Lazar.

'But you admired him?' Herezah prompted, unable to help herself.

'Yes, I did. I thought he was a fine man and a loyal one to Percheron. It was not right, what happened on account of my indiscretion.'

Herezah heard the pain in the girl's voice as she tried to shape well-chosen words into something less revealing than they actually were. 'No-one could know that Lazar would be quite as gallant as he was, child. He was very protective of the youngsters he brought in and it was a terrible thing, I agree, but no-one's fault.'

'Someone's fault that the whip was tipped with poison, Valide, surely?'

Again Herezah felt the breath catch in her throat at Ana's audaciousness in answering as she did. 'And he paid the price.'

'My uncle Horz would never do such a thing, Valide. I did not know him as well as you, perhaps, but I knew him to be a faithful and proud servant of the harem. We were distant relatives – I'd met him only twice in my life before I was brought to the palace and it is coincidence that two of the same family lived here. He never treated me any differently and he was loyal to the Elim.'

'And still coincidence that you both became embroiled

in the drama that led to Lazar's death?' The Valide watched Ana nod unhappily.

'Then who, Ana?' Herezah asked innocently, interested to hear what the girl might say. 'Who poisoned the whip?'

Ana turned now and worked hard to stifle the glare she levelled at the Valide.

Zarab save us, Herezah thought, *she thinks I contrived it!* 'What does that look mean?'

Ana hung her head. 'I . . . I mean nothing by it, Valide, my apologies. I just thought you might know something more than has been explained.'

You lie well, Herezah thought, *but not well enough to dupe me.* 'I know only what you do, odalisque,' the Valide replied in a rare moment of honesty. 'He cannot be brought back no matter what the truth is.'

'He should never have gone, though, Valide. It is my fault and I can never forgive myself.'

'Perhaps you have learned your lesson, then?' Herezah asked, not quite believing the lovely pathway in conversation that Ana had led herself towards.

'Definitely,' Ana replied unequivocally.

Herezah was not yet satisfied. She would remind Ana of this conversation in time to come. 'So nothing could persuade you to escape again?'

Ana held the Valide's gaze defiantly. 'Nothing.'

Herezah smiled. It was too perfect. 'Thank you, Ana. I appreciate this. You know, I chose you as the finest odalisque of the exquisite selection of girls on offer. I have high hopes for you. Perhaps you see yourself as a Favourite? Possibly Absolute Favourite, as I was?'

'No, Valide,' Ana answered gravely. 'I have never thought about such things.'

'Well, you should, my girl. You have the intelligence and there is no doubting your suitability as a mate for the Zar. Doesn't producing heirs to the throne of Percheron excite you?'

Ana shivered, despite the warmth, and shook her head. 'I know what happens to spare heirs, Valide. No, I would not wish that on any mother. I will happily remain barren to avoid such trauma.'

Now Herezah did gasp. 'You must not talk like this, Ana. You have a role now in the harem. Even if you can't see it, we can. You are the most likely first choice of the Zar. I can't speak for him but I can see what he sees.'

'Beauty is not everything,' Ana whispered.

'So you've said, but it is vital as an odalisque. You have little else to recommend yourself to the Zar.'

'It will not matter to me if he does not choose me, Valide. If you'll forgive my candidness, I think this is where you and I differ.'

The courage of the girl to speak so forthrightly to the most powerful woman in the palace had to be applauded, and Herezah forgave her the couched insult – for Herezah had never made any secret of her own ambition – and quietly admired Ana her spine. It reminded her painfully of her own determination, even though they seemed to want different things. If Herezah was honest, she had still not clarified what it was Ana would want if she could have it. Freedom probably – what every odalisque would take over all the riches and pampering.

'I'm pleased, Ana, that you will stay faithful to the harem and not test us again, with any further escape attempts from the palace. Your dash for freedom from the harem after the Choosing Ceremony was gravely ill-advised, as you've now discovered in the harshest possible way. I put it down to a fearless nature combined with your immaturity. It must never happen again, though. Let that fearlessness manifest itself in positive ways in your duties as odalisque. You have led a blemish-free existence these past thirteen moons, as I understand it.' Ana nodded, staring at the ground. 'This is wise,' she reiterated, wanting to get back on the track of her plan. 'Which is why I am asking you to take charge of the picnic next full moon. The girls are still very frightened of me so they will find it far easier to follow your lead.'

'I understand,' Ana replied.

'And, as a reward for your help, I am recommending that you be allowed to visit the Grand Bazaar.'

Ana looked up sharply, her eyes wide with consternation. 'Leave the palace?' she asked, her tone filled with disbelief.

Herezah smiled again, indulgently. 'Fully veiled, and with Elim escorts, of course.'

'Valide . . . I . . . I . . .'

'It's all right, Ana. I know what you're trying to say. I think you forget that I, too, have been a prisoner of the harem as a young woman and wanted nothing but to escape its smothering ways. I still am a prisoner. I still yearn for freedom but I have learned to accept, as you will. But I don't want you to suffer as I did. If I can allow you to enjoy some rare moments of independence – such as the boat picnic but, more importantly, such as this trip into the city – then I will allow it. I feel it will keep you less troubled, shall we say.'

'I really don't know what to say, or how to thank you,' Ana stammered, truly shocked at the indulgent gift being given to her by someone she thought held only hate.

'Thank me by being true. Keep your promise not to try anything silly and help me to give these girls a good time out on the water. Help me in the harem itself by being co-operative, less sullen, not so withdrawn. This is your life now. I want to try and make it easier to live but I can't save you completely. You must accept, as I did, embrace your role as odalisque and do the very best you can. Ana, you're so bright, I'd like to see you studying more. Is there anything you really enjoy?' Herezah already knew the answer to this.

'Well,' Ana began, 'I believe I'm good at language, Valide. Perhaps I can concentrate fully on that.'

'And not embroidery?'

Ana actually smiled and Herezah could see how any man would be instantly captivated at the way her eyes sparkled when she was happy. 'I don't care much for sewing,' she admitted wryly.

'And who could blame you,' Herezah replied, arching her eyebrows, feeling the fragile bond forming between them. 'All right, I think focusing on language is an excellent idea. We always have a need for translators. Any particular one?'

'Galinsean,' Ana gushed, then reined in her enthusiasm. 'And of course, Merlinean.'

Herezah really was amused now. 'Galinsean! It's an impossible tongue, child! And we don't need Galinsean.'

'Since losing the Spur I would suggest that we do, Valide. He was the only person who spoke Galinsean fluently as I understand it. And although I know he was Percheron's army head – and I'm merely a slave – it may be handy to have someone, other than the Zar, who understands the language. I must admit to you that I've actually been teaching myself the language for the past year. But I'd like to devote more time to it; perhaps a tutor can help with my accent?' This last suggestion about a tutor was a lie. Ana needed no help with her accent but she'd far prefer to just keep working in language than show she had time for anything as tedious as sewing or dancing.

The Valide gave a sound of surprise at the girl's claim. 'Taught yourself?'

Ana nodded, embarrassed.

'How?'

'The library, Valide.' Ana failed to mention that Pez had guided her in this, found all the right books and secretly aided her learning, even introduced her to a shy slave – an old man who had suffered the misfortune of being captured by slavers twice in his life. He was originally from the north, where Lazar's great friend, Jumo, hailed from. Jumo had disappeared since Lazar's death but he had known the slave in the library and had suggested him to Pez as a mentor for Ana's learning of the tough language from the west. After his second capture by the Galinseans, the slave was sold to the aristocracy because of the man's skill in painting portraits. The librarian had learned both the language of the streets and the higher language of the wealthy. Finally taking his chance to flee from slavery, he had risked an escape with a caravan across the Great Waste Desert in an effort to reach his homeland but had been captured by Percherese slavers and sold to the palace where he now worked in the library assembling a contemporary history of Percheron in pictures. He had taught Ana well.

'And how well do you speak Galinsean now, Ana?' Herezah asked, unable to hide her shock.

Again Ana chose not to admit that she was fluent. 'You are right, it is a difficult language,' came the diplomatic reply.

Herezah had to admit that talking with Ana felt like she was conversing with a peer. The girl still looked too young to have anything much in her head, save expensive gowns and glittering jewels, but it was obvious that all the perfectly normal traits of being young and female and spoiled were completely lost on this one. Even her manner of speaking was so mature. 'Not even Boaz can master Galinsean and he has been studying it most of his life.'

'I would like to try, Valide, if you'll permit it.'

'I'll permit it, Ana, but I see no use in it. I'll recommend to Salmeo that you be given tutoring but I would like you to learn Akresh as well, which is far more useful for visiting dignitaries and the like.'

'I'm happy to do so.'

'Good. So, we'll both help each other – that is agreed. You have only days to get the girls prepared for their boating picnic. I will recommend the trip into the city to pick out some fabrics and some jewels for you. It's time we started dressing you to show off your lovely figure and to present you as a potential Favourite for the Zar.'

At this Ana's eyes clouded again but she maintained her eager expression. It was obvious to Herezah that all mentions of bedding the Zar were causing fear for Ana but, like most things, after the first time it all got easier. Ana would survive as every fearful odalisque down the centuries had. 'I shall start helping to plan the picnic festivities now, Valide.'

'Excellent. And I'll inform Salmeo of our bargain.'

Ana excused herself and in her hurry to depart missed the sly smile of the Valide, well pleased with how adroitly she had manipulated the young woman. Herezah reached for her bell to summon a runner. Salmeo must hear that their plan was now in play.

5

Pez found Ana sitting with most of the other odalisques in the divan suite. Here couches were laid out around the walls and across the room at well-spaced intervals so the young women could lounge, relax, take some iced tea or sweet pastries if they chose, but, importantly, where most could inhale the fumes of the burning garammala.

This oil, yielded by squeezing the leaves of a tree that grows only on the fringe of the desert, was headily expensive, yet most of the rich of Percheron enjoyed it occasionally. Pez had tried it only twice and both times had been violently ill, so he had never grasped the attraction, although watching others, he realised it had a completely different effect. It appeared to relax users to a state of calm whilst somehow keeping them alert, as if all their senses were heightened. Unlike other relaxants, garammala did not make the user slur, drowse or hallucinate. It simply put them into a gentle mood and one that was happy, bordering on mildly euphoric. It apparently made the inhaler feel almost instantly erotic too, for Pez remembered wandering into this room when the previous harem had made good use of the pipes and noting that all inhibitions were dropped. It seemed the women were quite happy to spend their newfound erotic currency with anyone who'd pay attention, hence many a eunuch found himself in a compromising position, and it eased amorous relationships between the women themselves. Knowing how they were left longing and lonely and sexually frustrated for years, he could feel only pity for the women who escaped their demons through garammala.

Only Herezah, he recalled, never took the oil, and just as the Valide had resisted it all those years ago, now sat Ana, contriving similar symptoms of joyful mood. She, too, as the Valide did before her, ignored the pipe by her side, knowing no-one would notice . . . no-one except him, of course. He winked at Ana and she gave him a soft smile as she swung her legs down and stood to greet him.

'I've missed you,' she said, hugging her friend. It didn't look out of place. Pez was popular amongst the harem; he had long ago stopped frightening the youngsters with his terrible tales and now worked hard to keep them entertained by his antics. 'Where have you been?'

Pez gave her an equally gentle smile but tinged with regret. 'I'm sorry,' was all he said, pulling at his hair, as if it were crawling with nits. A couple of girls nearby laughed. 'What have you been up to in my absence?' he added more brightly in a whisper.

She took a breath and arched her eyebrows as if to say plenty had occurred. 'The Valide requested a meeting with me today.'

Pez expressed his surprise, despite the foolish little hops and jumps he performed to conceal his intelligence from the others present. He burped. More of the girls giggled. 'And?'

'Shall we walk?' she asked.

'Cartwheel for us, Pez,' one of the youngsters beseeched.

He did so, happily spinning around the room and expertly avoiding collisions with furniture and beautifully attired women. He enjoyed warranted applause before pretending to be dizzy and staggering out onto the pathways outside the room. Ana duly followed and no-one took much notice of her departure, save a few eunuchs, and none would have thought it a curiosity for one of the odalisques to take a stroll. Pez carefully sat on a small wall and studiously picked his nose, staring at the sky as if uninterested in the person who had followed him. Ana spoke in a low voice as she strolled by him very slowly, pretending to enjoy some sun on her face.

'She made a bargain with me.'

'Tell me,' he whispered.

'I'm to co-operate, help her with the other girls, especially on this boating trip.'

'And?'

'And if I promise not to try anything that breaks the harem rules, she's going to let me out for a few hours of freedom.'

'What's that supposed to mean?'

'I'm to be permitted into the city alone save an Elim escort.'

Pez stopped picking his nose and resisted the urge to stare at Ana in his anxiety. 'She's up to something.' He watched the beautiful odalisque do an unhurried circumference of a pond.

'Such as?' she asked as she returned to pass by him.

'I don't know,' he answered, worried. 'What else?'

'I'm to be given a tutor to study Galinsean.'

'You didn't tell her you were fluent, did you?'

'Hardly,' Ana replied, once again returning and passing

him. 'I didn't give away much at all other than that I've been teaching myself.'

Pez leapt down from the wall and took her hand, pretending to walk alongside her like one of the strange monkeys from the Zar's zoo. 'Ana, you have a gift of tongues.'

'Like you.'

'No, better than me,' he whispered amongst the hooting noises he was making. 'You speak Galinsean already better than any tutor – I hope you can lie your way through the lessons.'

She sighed. 'I will. It makes me feel closer to him.'

Now Pez stopped, both from sorrow and the guilt of knowledge he did not share with her. He knew precisely to whom she referred. 'This does not do you any good, Ana.'

'Keep lurching beside me, Pez, everyone is watching us and enjoying your antics,' she cautioned. He did so. 'Galinsean could be useful anyway,' she continued.

He snorted. 'What possible use could it be?'

Ana shook her head in gentle capitulation. No-one could understand how much it meant to her to hang onto every last reminder of Lazar. She regretted now not discovering whether he spoke any other languages and asking him directly where he was from. She answered Pez. 'None, I suppose. She wants me to learn Akresh as well.'

'Now that is a practical suggestion.'

'I wonder why she's being nice?'

'Herezah will always have a reason for everything she does. Be suspicious at every turn, Ana. She fears you.'

'Why?'

Pez made a clicking sound of exasperation with his

tongue. 'Because Boaz adores you. Isn't that obvious? The two of you meet often enough. You forget I'm usually there and hear you laughing with him.'

'I have asked him not to single me out,' she countered.

Pez decided it was time to career around the courtyard like an angry monkey now. When he charged near her, his back to the divan suite, he replied, 'But still he does, whether you like it or not. His admiration is obvious . . . and he's near enough seventeen, Ana. Old enough. You must be ready for where his thoughts head now.'

She scowled. 'I love another,' she said, truly shocking him into being still, his expression betraying his complete understanding.

He waddled over to where Ana stood and took her hand, heedless of any eyes watching, although grateful that they could not be heard. 'This is not about love, child. This is about duty. An odalisque's duty. As for the person you refer to, it is hopeless.' That was all he could say without revealing the terrible secret.

'He's dead, I know, but that doesn't stop my heart aching for him, my mind remembering every single little item it can about him, my conscience reminding me that I am the reason he is no longer alive.'

'Ana, stop!' Pez said, knowing tears were next, and then raised eyebrows should anyone notice. The other girls would then have to come outside to find out why she was crying. He dropped his voice. 'This is foolhardy.' Pez cartwheeled away and then, back on his feet, he ran from the courtyard.

'Are you all right, Ana?' someone asked. 'Did Pez upset you?'

Ana turned. It was an exquisite girl called Sascha, from

the region of Akresh, a hilly realm to the east of Percheron famed for its sapphires. Her hair was the colour of burnished copper and she had become something of a friend these past moons. Ana knew Sascha could see the tears in her eyes. It was best to go along with the idea that Pez ultimately upset everyone for one reason or another. 'Yes, he was threatening to stone the monkeys in the zoo.'

Sascha gave a pained expression. 'Don't believe him. You know he says stupid things all day long.'

'He sounded so determined, I feel as though he's rushed off to do the stoning now.'

Sascha took Ana's arm. 'Pez is mad, Ana. Everyone knows that. He says anything and everything that comes into his head. Most of the time he's amusing, I'll admit, but sometimes he can be quite vicious . . . but I don't think he even knows it himself.'

Ana found a watery smile. 'You're right,' she said, squeezing the girl's arm. 'I shall ignore him.'

'That's the right way to treat him. Pez hates to be ignored and I'm sure to be ignored by you will wound him terribly.'

'Why do you say that?'

Sascha gave a soft look of exasperation. 'Everyone can see how he loves you. You're definitely his favourite.'

Ana was tired of hearing that word. 'Come on, we have to make preparations for our boat excursion,' she said, determined to keep her promise to the Valide.

Iridor flew. Pez was risking much in this flight, having received a request from the Zar to meet with him for the midday meal. Boaz was used to Pez's unreliability but as they hadn't seen each other for many days it might make the Zar suspicious and if Boaz mentioned anything to the nosey Vizier, then Tariq might take still more interest in the dwarf.

But he had to speak with Lazar as promised. This was becoming a detestable situation. It was not so bad for Zafira – she did not have daily contact with Odalisque Ana. But Pez did, and the situation of blatantly lying to the girl was well past the point of discomfort.

He also needed time to think about Herezah's latest move. What was she up to? It would be best to share this with his friend.

He found Lazar in the small copse behind the cottage.

'There you are,' he said, in his dwarf shape once again.

'Greetings, Pez. Zafira said you planned to visit. Join me on my walk.'

'Is that what you call it?' Pez asked and grinned at Lazar's crease of confusion. 'More like lurching.' It wasn't true, of course. He was genuinely thrilled to see his friend moving so easily once again.

'Be quiet, dwarf. You can hardly make fun with that strange waddle of yours,' Lazar replied. It was the first time in a year that Pez had heard Lazar say anything that was even remotely lighthearted. This was a great sign that the strong man they were counting on was returning to them. Considering that even as recently as three moons ago the man had not been able to concentrate for any length of time, other than when gazing forlornly across the water, he had made stunning progress suddenly. 'You'll take into account I don't use sticks any more,' he added, a note of triumph in his voice.

'I do. I'm impressed, Lazar, truly,' Pez said.

'One day I shall run again. I'll even be able to overtake you,' Lazar said, warming now and the hint of amusement in his tone made Pez's heart soar.

'You fail to appreciate, friend cripple, that I fly with such grace I would leave you in my wake.'

They both grinned. It was a special moment in a year of bleakness. It felt to Pez as though they were crawling out of a dark tunnel. Because Lazar had been so ill they hadn't even had the right opportunity on the two brief occasions they'd seen each other to talk about all that had occurred since Lazar had returned from the foothills with a young girl in tow. Perhaps today was the day to have that discussion.

'It's good to have you back, Lazar,' he said.

The former Spur sighed. 'I made a decision last moon that I either give into this affliction and hope the next attack kills me, or I fight back fully to health. I'm almost there.'

'I gather it will still attack, though,' Pez said, never one to observe diplomacy.

'According to Ellyana, it will. But it will have to attack a fit body rather than a frail one. That's my only defence.'

Pez nodded, moved by the change in his friend's mindset from brooding, angry silence to this new optimism. He had always known it would arrive but as the year had drawn on, the dwarf had begun to question his faith in Lazar's resilience. 'That's the spirit. And your hair is now its true colour, I assume?' he said, amazed at the difference but also keen to continue the lighthearted banter.

'Yes, just as yours is,' Lazar replied tartly, referring to the strange line of white hair that ran down one side of Pez's head.

'Ah, my change makes me look even more odd than I ever did. But you, my friend, you look more handsome than ever.'

Lazar gave a soft self-deprecating snort, knowing how gaunt he truly appeared.

Pez continued, waving his arms theatrically. 'Now you look truly like a Galinsean prince.'

Lazar impaled him with those light eyes that gave him away as a foreigner. 'It's a relief not to have to colour it any more,' he said and the sigh that followed said so much more about secrets and family, pain and grief.

'Such lengths to hide an identity.' Pez gave a sound of admonishment.

'We are not so different, you and I,' Lazar reminded Pez. 'You've feigned madness for decades to hide yours.'

'Not to hide my identity,' Pez corrected.

'Just your sanity, right?'

Pez nodded. 'And something else.' Despite his need to be back at the palace swiftly he had promised today was going to be one in which all of his secrets were shared.

This captured Lazar's attention. 'Oh? What else have you been hiding from me?'

Pez took a deep breath. 'I have the Lore.' Lazar stared at him for what felt like an eternity. 'Say something,' the dwarf added, uncomfortable in the silence.

His friend shook his head in wonder. 'I thought I had you worked out but you are full of surprises. I also thought the Lore was make-believe.'

'It's not.'

'What does it mean for you?'

'It means secrets, Lazar. It means hiding and constant anxiety at being found out. It means denying the call of the magic that is at my fingertips, which I refuse — most of the time anyway — to even acknowledge.'

Lazar had never seen Pez upset before. It stopped him in his tracks. He sat down on a tree stump. 'Most of the time?'

'I relented and used it twice recently. Until those two moments, I have resisted being seduced by it during all of my years in the palace.'

'What happened?' Lazar asked.

This was going to be the hardest bit, Pez knew. 'Remember Kett?'

Lazar's eyes narrowed. 'How can I forget?'

'I was there. I was in the corridor with him when he was captured.'

'What?'

Pez nodded. He needed to tell it all. 'So was Boaz.'

Lazar stood and Pez could see the effort it took. He watched Lazar lean against a nearby tree. 'Tell me.' It was an order — just like the old Lazar.

'I needed to divert Boaz's attention. It was an impulsive decision. I thought he might like to see the girls being chosen for him.'

'Wait,' Lazar interrupted. 'Pez, I've known you a long time and I know you do nothing on a whim. Tell me the truth, all of it.'

Pez sighed. Lazar was right. He should hear everything. 'I can't explain it, Lazar, and I know you won't want to hear this, but I felt a calling towards Ana. I'd never met her, I didn't know of her existence. But from the moment she entered the palace I became aware of her. It was not knowledge so much as a sensing of the arrival of some sort of force or power.'

Lazar looked bewildered. 'Ana is enchanted?'

'No,' Pez replied emphatically, then he relented, somewhat confused. 'Well, in truth I don't know. I sensed her. I needed to know what the pull towards whatever this thing was. Until I saw her I had no idea it was a young woman. Anyway, I was telling the truth that I needed to divert Boaz, so I killed two birds with one stone, you could say. Sadly, we stumbled upon Kett and, without going into the details, suddenly all three of us were in the forbidden area. But if Kett hadn't sneezed we'd have been safe.'

'And when he did?'

'I could only shepherd Boaz and myself.'

'Shepherd?' Lazar knew he sounded like one of the Zar's parrots in its gilded cage, repeating what it hears, but this was an extraordinary revelation from Pez.

'I made us invisible,' Pez explained coyly.

Lazar had nothing to say to this. It was too incredible. He stared at Pez open-mouthed.

Finally he said: 'And the next time?'

'To aid Boaz in facing Horz's death. I simply channelled some strength to him.'

'Strength?'

Pez shrugged. 'Courage. He was nervous, terrified that he would let us all down and not be able to face the execution.'

'I hear Horz was incredibly brave. Zafira tells me the city was abuzz that he died without murmuring so much as a sound when they impaled him.'

'He was a good man. He did not deserve to die badly and for a crime we both know he did not commit.'

'And so you helped him too,' Lazar replied, the pieces of the jigsaw slotting into place in his mind.

'Not using magic. I used the Lore on Boaz only. Do you believe me?'

Lazar clamped his jaw shut, studied Pez before answering. 'Of course I believe you. You can change yourself into a bird, why not become invisible?'

Pez felt the bite of familiar sarcasm but didn't react. 'The bird business is something entirely different. It has nothing to do with the Lore,' Pez assured.

'But that's just it, isn't it, Pez? It's probably because of the Lore or because of what you possess that you have been chosen to be Iridor. I can't believe I say that so blithely. Iridor! Messenger to Lyana!' He shook his head. 'And your connection to Ana is real – we know that now. It is not coincidence.' He made a sound of disgust as he banged the tree trunk with his open hand. 'I feel as though we're pieces in some grand game, being manipulated towards some final goal.'

Pez nodded. 'That's a very good analogy, Lazar. I used to think I had complete control of myself and my life. The deception of madness was all part of that control. But ever since Ellyana appeared to me and my clever disguise was suddenly seen through – by her anyway – I've felt as though someone else is orchestrating things.'

It was Lazar's turn to nod. 'Ellyana knows,' he said sagely. 'She just didn't bother telling us before she vanished.' He sat down again. 'What news from the city?'

'Plenty. It's why I'm here unexpectedly.'

'So tell me.'

'Who first?'

'Ana.'

No surprises with that answer. It was time for truth, Pez had promised himself. 'She's more beautiful and graceful than ever. She's also still filled with sorrow about you and not getting past the notion that she is to blame for your death. You know this but it's getting worse rather than better. It is unbearable to be around her, I have to tell you. A year on and none of her grief has eased.'

Whatever small sense of optimism had put Lazar into a good humour this day now evaporated. 'You did not—'

'No, I didn't!' Pez replied. 'There are times when I wonder why we are keeping this charade going, and then find myself agonising over the thoughts of what it will do to her to discover that you aren't dead.'

Lazar looked pained and Pez could tell the former Spur was as uncertain about this decision as he himself felt. 'Hopefully she will never learn the truth. Ellyana wanted to preserve the secret.'

'Ellyana wanted a lot of things but she gave no clue why,' Pez returned caustically. 'Why is Ellyana in charge of us? Why does she still command us? She's not even here.'

'Pez, you yourself admit that she was touched by a powerful magic. Do you remember saying that to me?' The dwarf grimaced and kept a grumpy silence. 'Well, do you?' Lazar prompted.

Pez relented. 'I do.'

'Then you and she are inextricably tied – you both possess enchantment and I've seen it with my own eyes to know I'm witnessing fact. She was definitely the same woman that Ana and I met in the market that first night in Percheron. And I maintain that my eyes did not deceive me, I saw a chain as the item being negotiated for money. Ana did too. But when we ended purchasing the piece, it turned into the statue of Iridor. You tell us she visited you in the harem: one moment an old crone, the next a fresh-faced young woman.'

'All true.'

'And now you have a new and happy knack of transforming yourself into an owl – Iridor, no less – and I go along with it as though it's the most normal thing in my day.'

'Magnificent, aren't I?' Pez said.

'Annoying as well,' Lazar said.

'There's nothing normal about your days,' Pez retaliated sulkily.

Lazar ignored Pez's gripe. 'As I was saying, you and she are linked, there is no doubt. We are all unwittingly linked through both of you. We being Zafira, Ana and myself. We're the pieces in Ellyana's game, you might say.'

Pez nodded in agreement, his heavy brow creased in thought. 'There is another.'

'Another pawn?' Lazar asked, and Pez nodded. 'Who?'

'I don't know but I feel him and he's no pawn.'

'Him?'

Pez shrugged. He wasn't ready to discuss this. 'I think it's a him. When I was talking with Boaz after Kett's unfortunate capture I felt a disruption in the Lore. Someone was eavesdropping on our conversation and that person was not around in the flesh.'

'Magic?' Lazar asked, gawping.

Pez nodded. 'I believe so.'

'What did you do?'

'Took instant precaution. Fortunately my seeming madness is my best protection and of course Boaz is very used to me suddenly acting the lunatic. I wrote him a note telling him to hold his tongue, that we were being listened to.'

Lazar made the leap, understanding that Pez had revealed the truth to the Zar. 'You told Boaz about the Lore.'

'I had to — he wasn't going to let me get away with the shepherding trick without an explanation. But although he might have forgotten my caution over the eavesdropper, I haven't.'

Lazar sighed. 'Pez, you know something and you're not telling me. Either be direct or stop alluding to a threat I don't understand.'

'I'll stop, then,' Pez said, frowning. 'I'm not ready to say more until I myself understand more.' He gave Lazar a look to beg his trust. 'Suffice to say, his name is Maliz.'

Now Lazar looked incredulous. Maliz was a name he recognised from ancient myth surrounding Percheron and many of its older, more exquisite carvings. 'The one who turned Beloch and Ezram to stone? Lyana's nemesis?'

The dwarf nodded unhappily.

'You think *he* was watching you?'

'I told you, I don't know!'

Lazar could barely give voice to his shock that they were talking about Maliz, the warlock . . . the man turned demigod. He shook his head in confusion. 'All the more reason to trust Ellyana perhaps,' Lazar finally said in an effort to settle Pez's rising frustration. 'If we accept that she is our guide and trusts us, then we shall all have to trust one another.'

'We don't have much choice.'

'So we must listen to her advice. She was firm about not letting Ana know that I was still alive. She obviously chose not to even let poor Jumo in on this, which probably explains his disappearance and us having no knowledge of his whereabouts,' Lazar said, scratching his newly golden hair.

Time for truth, Pez reminded himself. 'Lazar, I do know something about Jumo,' he said, feeling awkward, and at the look of hope on Lazar's face he decided to wait just a little longer before his friend disowned him. 'But let me finish my report first. I must return to the palace swiftly or I run the risk of being missed.'

Lazar looked anxious to hear about his former manservant but nodded. 'I will remind you of Jumo, though.'

'I'm sure you will. Ana has had a meeting with the Valide.'

At this the former Spur looked back at his short friend sharply. Pez told him everything that Ana had told him.

'Herezah's plotting something.'

'My thoughts exactly.'

'You have to find out.'

'I intend to.'

'How?'

'That's my concern. The fact is I came here today to tell you that Ana is vulnerable and her weakness for you is not helping her to be strong when she needs to be. I'm sure I don't have to remind you what an odalisque is required to do should the Zar's eyes fall favourably upon her?'

Lazar scowled. 'No, you certainly don't.'

'Well, that time is rapidly approaching, Lazar. And I can't change that – Lore or not.'

'I don't expect you to.'

'No? Then why do you lose hours staring at the palace, or—'

'Don't, Pez,' Lazar warned.

The dwarf ignored the warning. 'Lazar, Boaz is going to choose her, you know this!'

'And there's nothing I can do about it,' Lazar roared, 'so why keep rubbing it in my face!'

Pez decided not to point out that this was the first time he had mentioned it. But he knew full well that Lazar probably thought about little else. 'Forgive me,' he said instead.

Lazar stood and walked away a few paces, his emotions raw. 'She was his from the moment I paid forty karels to her grasping mother,' he groaned. 'She was always going to be his,' he added softly.

'But she is part of this "game" as we call it.'

'Because Ellyana singled her out with the owl statue.'

'That as well, but I think it was the other way around. I can't shake the knowledge that I was drawn to the power that Ana gave off long before I even knew of her existence. And now that I do know her I can feel it emanating from her. I believe Ana chose Ellyana; Ana is the power, not Ellyana.'

'What makes you think this?'

'Because whenever I hold Ana's hand or inadvertently touch her I feel a thrum of some sort of powerful force pass through me. I don't think she's aware of it and I'm now so used to it I don't flinch each time. She recognises nothing in me as far as I can tell, so it appears we are not sharing our secrets.'

'But it's not the Lore that she has?'

'Definitely not. I wouldn't even term it magic. It is a force all of its own and I can't access it. I've tried. All I can do is sense its presence.'

'A bit like you sense the "him" you spoke of?' Lazar reminded.

At his friend's words it was as if a dawning had occurred in his mind. Pez couldn't believe he had been such a dullard in not bringing the two together until now. It took Lazar's sharp observation to cut through his misty thoughts. 'Of course! I'm so stupid,' Pez exclaimed, hopping around. 'That's it, that's precisely it, Lazar!'

The former Spur had to smile even though he didn't feel in the mood for humour. 'Nice jig, Pez. Are you going to explain?'

'I'm not sure I can. But I'll try.'

But before he could speak further, Zafira hobbled out of the shadows. She realised immediately that she'd interrupted something.

'Forgive me, gentlemen. I came to offer quishtar?'

At the intrusion of the priestess, Pez was reminded of the urgency of his return to the palace. 'I don't have time, Zafira, but thank you. The Zar has not seen me in days and he will begin to question my absence. Although it is very hard to refuse your quishtar.' She smiled and nodded.

'What about Jumo?' Lazar asked.

'We have much to discuss. I will do my best to visit often now that I know you are well enough to see me at length but for now I must go.' He grinned apologetically at his jest, but his mind had already fled to the danger waiting for him. 'Forgive me,' he murmured distractedly to them both.

6

The Zar had invited the Valide to meet the young men being presented.

'They are primarily for my protection, mother, but I would like to put them at your service as well.'

Herezah felt a stab of joy. So her son hadn't forgotten her. 'Me?' she said, all innocence.

'Of course. Mother to the Zar? I cannot have you under any threat.'

Now the Valide smiled at her son. 'Thank you, Boaz, although I cannot imagine any danger to me within the harem.'

'It's Tariq we owe gratitude to,' Boaz admitted and Herezah's joy turned sour.

'Oh?'

'This is his idea. He wants all-day, all-night protection. He suggested this morning that I should include the Valide in this special ring of security.'

'I see,' Herezah said, trying to disguise the chill in her tone with a forced smile. 'I must thank him. Is there a threat to concern ourselves with?'

Boaz reached for one of the huge redberries piled on a silver platter. He dipped it into the glistening bowl of honey nearby before putting the fruit in his mouth. Finally he answered her. 'No, I don't believe so. Tariq just wants to ensure that we tighten up our security generally.'

'He fears what?'

'Well,' Boaz began, licking his lips free of the sticky honey, 'he feels that the Crown of Percheron has never been more vulnerable. Our enemies might think now is a good time to take advantage of a new Zar, a young one,' he said.

'He is right in principle. But who does he believe might make such a move?'

'The Galinseans, I suspect, although he's not coming out and saying as much.'

Herezah arched her eyebrows. 'Perhaps Ana is right,' she murmured.

'Pardon?'

'Oh nothing, my beloved. One of our odalisques wants to learn Galinsean. I was surprised to hear it but perhaps she has a point. A translator – now that Lazar is no longer with us – may be valuable.'

Boaz gave a snort. 'Are you talking about Ana?'

Herezah bristled at the familiarity. 'The odalisque known as Ana, yes.'

He laughed again. 'She speaks Galinsean with ease. Her command of it is amazing and it sounds very different to the Galinsean I know. She says it is more a pidgin version of the streets used by foreigners but I suspect she's being diplomatic.'

Herezah pursed her lips before replying, calming her rising irritation, knowing that time with the Zar was precious and should not be spent in snarls. She felt as though she were living her early life all over again, waiting for the Zar's favour to fall upon her. Except this time it was wrong. This Zar was her son! She deserved better than having to yearn for time with him and then feel as though she were subservient in his presence. It was never like this in her daydreams. She was the Valide, the most powerful woman in Percheron. She should be ruling, not discussing boating trips for the harem! An expert in guile, Herezah showed none of this inward turmoil on her now serene expression. 'She did say she had begun to teach herself.'

The Zar was eating another redberry. He chuckled as he chewed, irritating her still more. 'Well, I'm hazarding she speaks courtly Galinsean as though it's her mother tongue, and now she's moved on to mastering it at the colloquial level.'

'Has she indeed? And how do you know this, Boaz?'

'I've spoken to her about it. She used to practise now and then with me but, as I say, I became useless to her after a while. She has found a new teacher, one of the slaves, a Merlinean.'

'You seem on very friendly terms with Odalisque Ana?' Herezah probed. 'I should tell you that I approve. I met with Ana yesterday to discuss her taking a more leading role in harem life. She has a fine mind and the innate knack for leadership. I shall reward her if she rewards me with honesty and trust,' Herezah added, keen to ensure he understood that the harem was her seat of power.

She could tell Boaz hadn't expected this, could see by his hesitation that he wasn't sure how to respond. 'I intend to be on very friendly terms with all in the harem, mother. You know I am relaxing some of the more archaic rules.'

'I'd heard.'

Boaz gave a sly sneer. 'I imagine Salmeo shares everything.'

Herezah was not to be treated with disdain by her own child. 'Need I remind you that's his role, my son. He and I run the harem.'

'No, you don't need to remind me,' Boaz replied, glowering now. 'But perhaps I should remind you that this is the same man who taunted and persecuted you for a great deal of your life. The same man — if you can call him that — who tested your virginity at eight years old and then viciously destroyed it at barely thirteen, no doubt smiling that gap-toothed grin of his the whole time. Perhaps I don't understand women well enough yet, but it strikes me that all of this might leave a lasting memory on someone like you, who bears grudges.'

Herezah's fury had gathered during this tirade. She knew he hated Salmeo, having lived under his rule for so many years of his childhood, and she knew that Boaz would not forget her own endless nights of weeping at Salmeo's harshness. But she would not let him turn his years of hate for the eunuch on her. She had worked too hard for Boaz to have this position and status, which he now enjoyed because of her alone.

Her voice was icy when it came. 'Salmeo did for your father, Boaz, precisely what he will do for you. And I am the one thing standing between his sharp fingernail and Odalisque Ana's virginity. When the time comes — and it will, my son, trust me — and I see it in your eyes that she is your first choice, it will be only because of me that Salmeo is forced to be gentle. I would counsel you on taking a less disdainful approach with the chief eunuch and a less authoritarian approach with me. I am your mother. I demand respect.'

At this Herezah rose, bowed low and elegantly to her Zar and took her leave.

Boaz was still stunned at the reprimand. It made him feel like a child again, and reminded him of yet another aspect of his mother – when cornered she was at her most dangerous. He had to admit she was dazzling, and he could once again appreciate why his father had been so smitten by her.

He was intrigued by her discussion of Ana. Obviously something was playing on her mind, and her suggestion that Ana would make a good Favourite made him smile inwardly. Having seen his mother's reaction to Ana from the moment she met her, it was obvious that Ana was a prime choice. He had even gone so far as to enquire of Ana whether his mother had had much to do with her, and Ana had surprised him with the news that she had barely glimpsed his mother in the past few moons. He had expected Ana to be under his mother's watchful eye constantly. However, the Valide's distance didn't necessarily mean that Ana was not being observed. Herezah and Salmeo were more than capable of spying effortlessly on someone as naive as Ana, he decided. And yet his mother's mention of her had come out of nowhere, her surprise at Ana's education in Galinsean was genuine and the Valide's offer to reward Ana in return for her loyalty was amusing, for Herezah never acted with such simple motivation. There would be more to this move of his mother's, he was sure. It was also reassuring, though. Boaz wanted his mother to get on well with Ana. They'd had a rocky start with Ana's escape from the harem and then all the business with Lazar had clouded the early brightness of his mother's intentions for this particular girl. But that seemed to be behind them, Boaz decided. If his mother was making an attempt to forge a relationship with Ana, then this could only be a good thing . . . for the harem, for himself and indeed for the Crown. Boaz had every intention of making Ana his Favourite. With every sighting, every opportunity to talk with her, every chance to eat with the girls, as he tried to at least each new moon, it was Ana he was most interested in.

She was always courteous and gracious around the other girls, making sure as many as she could involve were brought into their discussions. But on the rare occasions that he could speak with her privately, Ana showed herself truly. She was a marvellous mimic and could impersonate the voices and mannerisms of Salmeo . . . and even more dangerously, the Valide, with hilarious precision. That she would risk sharing this with him warmed him.

He felt gladdened that she seemed to adore Pez. The other girls, especially the younger ones, were a bit scared of Pez and his unusual looks. They laughed at him rather than with him but Boaz could see that Ana, by contrast, cherished Pez. It occurred to him now, as he sat here waiting for Tariq to appear, to wonder whether Pez had shared his secret of sanity with Ana. Boaz suddenly straightened, his brow creasing in thought. That was it! Of course! Ana surely had such a deep relationship with Pez because he'd shared his great jest with her. The Zar felt a prick of intense jealousy but it lasted only a moment. If Pez had shared his secret, then it gave Boaz all the more reason to get closer to Ana. Pez trusted her as much as he trusted the Zar. That had to be worth something, Boaz reasoned.

He summoned Bin, his secretary, to give instructions to find the dwarf. It had been far too long since they'd spoken.

After nodding that he would find Pez immediately, Bin delivered his own message. 'Zar Boaz, Grand Vizier Tariq has conveyed that he is ready to escort you now. The Making of the Mutes is about to begin.'

Boaz felt his belly twist, answering the nagging fear that had been with him all morning and probably the reason for his baiting of his mother. His natural inclination was to avoid what was clearly going to be a horrific ordeal to witness. And it would be so easy just to say no. He did not even have to give a reason, but Tariq and Bin and then many other palace servants no doubt would sense the cowardice. And that would not do. He could all but hear his mother saying it.

As he thought this he wondered whether his mother would care to attend such a ghoulish event. Although he'd invited her, he hadn't anticipated that she would want to be present for the actual ritual itself that turned healthy men into mutes. But then again her inclination was always towards the cruel – she would no doubt accept whether she was still seething or not. He could make amends for mocking her slightly today.

'Inform the Valide that a special event, the Making of the Mutes, is imminent, Bin,' he said, glad to note his voice was steady. 'Invite her to join me if she cares to, but please inform the Valide that the Zar will not be in the slightest offended if she chooses to decline. And find Pez.'

Bin bowed. 'I shall do this before I find Pez, my Zar. The Elim will escort you to the chamber.'

'Where is this being held?'

'Grand Vizier Tariq has chosen the Chamber of Silence, Majesty.'

'Appropriate,' Boaz murmured.

'Yes, he thought so too, Highness,' Bin added, before bowing again. 'May I tell the Elim you are ready, my Zar?'

Boaz shook his head. 'I shall be ready when I'm ready,' he replied, not intending to be so sharp, but the threat of blood and shrieks at Tariq's upcoming showpiece unnerved him. He could use some of Pez's strengthening Lore magic right now. It irked that Pez had been so elusive and his absence had now begun to play on the Zar's mind. On top of this, did he detect a high-handed tone in Bin's voice? He hoped not. 'They can wait.'

'My Zar, forgive me but—'

He glared at the servant. 'Begone, Bin. I'm not sure why you're still here and not conveying the message I expressly asked you to deliver to the Valide,' Boaz said, his frown actually saying far more.

'I am gone, my Zar,' Bin said very humbly, bowing as he withdrew.

There was a sound of clapping behind him as the door closed on Bin and Boaz turned. 'All hail the Zar and his mighty power.'

'Pez!' Seeing the dwarf and recognising an easy target for his surging emotions, Boaz struck. 'Were you hiding?'

The palace clown leapt nimbly down from the sill of the open window. 'Absolutely not,' he said, sounding indignant.

'That's a mighty fall beneath the window. What are you doing here?'

'I've come to see you,' Pez's voice was mild.

'I realise this,' Boaz said more pointedly. 'But where were you that you could appear at my window so many shevels from the ground? Where were you this high that you could sneak up on me and eavesdrop on my private conversations?' It was too late to change this path now. He secretly wished he hadn't taken it but he was picturing proud young men waiting to have their tongues torn out. And for some reason all he could think of was Lazar and hearing his old friend sighing with regret that Boaz had already sunk this far that he was maiming healthy Percherese in the archaic manner of the Zar's forebears.

'Well, I can see I'm not welcome,' Pez grumbled, still not outwardly offended. 'And there was I thinking you might have missed me.'

'Stop it, Pez. Were you using your Lore skills?'

Pez hesitated. His large forehead creased. 'Are you upset about something, Boaz?'

It wasn't patronising but the Zar chose to take it that way because it suited his suddenly stirred mood. 'Don't take that attitude with me, Pez. Remember your place. You may have the ear of the Zar but you remain his servant and servants should not miss luncheons with their royal.'

Pez looked at him with an expression Boaz struggled to read; it was a mixture of deep disappointment and shock. He watched with private regret as the small man gathered himself, cleared his throat. 'My manner of arrival was just a jest, my Zar. A surprise,' he said and bowed, his hand touching his heart in the formal manner used for everything from salutations to apology in Percheron.

'I've missed you,' he added with a slight tone of injury and it sounded genuine to Boaz, as did the swift move into attack that followed, so unexpectedly. Pez was certainly no coward. 'You don't seem to really need my company these days, Highness, not now you have your grovelling Grand Vizier to play with.'

Boaz bristled. 'You know he's not grovelling. Quite the opposite.'

'I don't know anything any more, Highness, because you don't include me. Although I regret deeply missing breaking bread with you. I'm sure the Vizier kept you company, though.'

'Oh, you're not jealous are you, Pez?' Boaz's voice dripped sarcasm. He couldn't help himself.

'Of Tariq?' Pez asked, sounding incredulous. 'Now you jest, my Zar,' he said and the tone cut like a blade.

'I didn't think so. There's nothing to envy. He intrigues me, that's all.'

'Is it?'

'Well, surely his chameleon-like changes fascinate you?'

'In a different way to you perhaps, my Zar,' Pez said, and none of the pain in his expression had dissipated.

'How so?'

'You say you find him intriguing. Personally, I find him dangerous.'

Boaz gave a snort of disbelief. 'Dangerous? Tariq?'

Pez grew grave now. He did not say anything, simply stared hard at the Zar.

Boaz filled the awkward silence. 'But that's ridiculous. Dangerous to whom?'

'I'm not sure . . . not yet.'

'You're being paranoid. Who can Tariq endanger?'

'You, me, the Valide, your harem, do you want me to go on?'

Boaz shook his head as if needing to clear away the nonsense he was hearing. His voice was filled with sarcasm again. 'Pez, how is he dangerous to my mother, do explain?'

'Prior to your father's death, who would you say aligned himself most closely with Herezah the Absolute Favourite?'

Boaz looked away momentarily, as if mildly irritated to have led himself to this point.

'You asked me to explain, so I'm trying,' Pez said, his tone friendly as ever now.

Boaz sighed. 'All right, it was Tariq.'

'Indeed. I think now the Valide would have to all but make an appointment to meet him face to face.'

'She's in the harem. He can't—'

'Don't make excuses, my Zar, you know I'm right. And all the time that he's been curiously withdrawing from the Valide, he has invested that time ingratiating himself with you.'

'It is his task, his duty as Vizier.' Boaz was silently angered by the defensiveness of his tone.

Pez shrugged. 'I suppose so,' he said and began humming to himself.

'You're infuriating, Pez.'

'Oh, but that's my task, my duty as your royal buffoon, my Zar,' Pez replied, echoing the Zar's words, but there was no humour now.

Boaz sensed it and growled his displeasure. 'I won't have you treat me like a child.'

Pez rounded on him. 'Then don't act like one!'

It was the first time in his life that Boaz had been scolded in such stern fashion by his friend and it was obvious from his stormy gaze that he did not take it lightly. 'How dare you,' he said, a voice as wintry as though it were coming from the Shagaire icecaps.

Whether Pez had intended such provocation or not, it seemed he wasn't going to renege on his insult. 'I dare, my Zar, because I care about you.'

'Is this how you spoke to my father?' Boaz snarled, truly angry with Pez for the first time in their relationship.

'I had no need to.'

'And you will never have an opportunity to address me so again.'

Pez nodded, the realisation of the consequences of his firm attitude shown in his sad expression. 'Then Tariq has won, my Zar. Your father despised the Vizier . . . and for good reason.'

'Give me that reason!' Boaz bellowed at the dwarf. He sounded almost desperate.

Pez would not give him satisfaction. 'I shouldn't have to. You should feel it as I do,' Pez said and it felt like an accusation to Boaz.

The accusation hurt and Boaz reacted in a manner as if stung. 'Begone, dwarf. I'll choose to surround myself with whom I want.'

Casting caution out of the open window towards the Faranel, Pez gave his final warning. 'Yes, that's why I fear for you, my Zar. You should dismiss him as your father always wanted to. You can, you know, because your reign is still young. Mark my words, Zar Boaz, you will regret it if you don't. I am gone, Majesty,' he said and, despite his awkward gait, he managed a noble air as he walked towards the door.

Boaz spoke to his childhood friend's back. 'I shall summon you should I ever want to see you again, Pez. Don't visit me without invitation.'

Pez turned and nodded once. There was something achingly final in the way their gazes met, then locked, before Pez dipped his glance in required deference to the Zar and removed himself fully from the chamber.

Boaz sat down heavily as the door closed. His heart was racing and the painful sense of being cut away from something secure and familiar was his new companion. He had never felt as lonely as he did in this moment with the words of Pez echoing in his mind.

Pez felt hollow. That certainly didn't go according to plan. He had hoped to use the element of his surprise arrival to bluff his way through any question of his absence. But it seemed the Zar was already agitated about other events and Pez suspected his timing was ill-conceived. It was his own fault, though; he should never have ignored his duties to Boaz. His cheeks burned with the humiliation of what he had brought down upon himself. The frightening prospect that he no longer had the ear of the Zar — or his indulgence — took a strong hold over him. For the first time in over two decades, he was vulnerable.

Flying in had proved to be imprudent. What had begun as a jest to surprise the Zar had turned ugly and now down-right dangerous. Since the argument, he had travelled blindly, his legs moving as if on memory rather than direction, but found himself crossing the threshold of the harem and knew he would find comfort here.

She was sewing, a look of disgust on her face as she poked the tiny needle through her silk.

'Pez!' one of the other girls cried and it was obvious they were all looking for a distraction.

The tutor's pinched expression turned even more sour as Pez scratched at his own crotch and then belched. The class disintegrated into laughter and the helpless tutor, unable by palace law to banish the clown, took her leave but with a promise to return after the midday meal for more of the same.

'Let's swim with the fishes,' Pez suggested, pretending to glide through make-believe water.

'We're not allowed outside, Pez,' someone told him.

He looked to Ana, sucking at her finger she had pricked with the needle on seeing him. She smiled. 'We have to sew adequately first,' she sighed.

Already the class had broken up and girls were moving into groups, munching on the platters of fruit and confections being delivered by a host of servants. The garammala pipes would inevitably follow.

Pez glanced towards the food and back to Ana. It was an invitation she declined with a soft shake of her head. 'You're looking thin,' he whispered.

'And you're looking miserable. What's happened?'

He told her very briefly and watched as something akin to his own pain settled across her face. 'With Boaz in this mood he might permit anything,' he concluded.

'Are you sure he said that?' she asked, referring to the Zar's dismissal and warning.

'Quite. I could hardly mistake the finality of his words. Our friendship is done with.'

'I don't think so. Even the little I know of our Zar suggests he will think it through and regret the way the discussion went.'

'You may be right,' he whispered, moving to stand on his head and act out his part.

'Salmeo for sure will take every advantage of this new turn of events,' Ana said softly, frowning.

'And the Valide will relish any opportunity to return years of frustrating harassment with cruel interest,' he reminded, carefully watching that no-one was paying them any attention.

'Oh, Pez. What are we going to do to help you?'

'I must lie low for a while, not be seen around too much. Forgive me if I disappear.'

'Don't leave me.'

'I won't, I promise. I'd better go. I'll come tonight. Leave your window open.'

'My window?' she queried, watching him roll back to his feet and pull an ugly face at a girl passing by, who giggled. 'I'm on the top floor.'

'Just do as I ask,' he said and winked before skipping out of the room.

The Valide smiled as she took her seat in the Chamber of Silence. It had been so many years since she was in this area of the palace that she had forgotten it existed. This was the chamber where she had been first presented as a newly purchased slave to the Valide Zara of the day; a stern, seemingly permanently scowling woman, who fortunately lost her position soon after. Herezah recalled it all now. The scowling Valide's son, Zar Koriz, had died suddenly and his death had diminished his mother's long-sought and powerful position. He had fallen prey to the feared bloatfish, earning its name from the fact that it swelled as it died, gasping in the fishing nets. It was a delicacy in Percheron but needed very special handling by cooks to ensure that the liver of this fish was fully removed. It contained some of the most powerful toxins known at the time and eating even the tiniest morsel of the liver meant certain death. The Zar of the day was a fine cook, priding himself on being skilled in cleaning and gutting this favourite of fish with precision and did just that after one of his regular fishing expeditions. These were days when no-one dared even offer advice to the Zar unless asked, and although one of his newest aides found the courage to suggest that it would be best to take the fish back to the palace, the Zar scoffed. He wanted to cook the fish on the banks of the Daramo River, that flowed into the Faranel. It was on these same shores that the aide lost his tongue for his trouble and the Zar lost his life. The poison was swift but not fast enough to prevent immense suffering as the vicious toxin gradually claimed every inch of his body with paralysis. By the time his shocked party got the Zar back into the city, all of his major organs had burst and he was bleeding from his nostrils, ears, mouth, and was dead before he could even be laid in his chamber.

This story had always stayed with Herezah, not so much because of the colourful tale itself but because of this particular Zar. It amazed her that, despite this Zar's predisposition to punish his servants without mercy, for something so innocent as trying to offer him protection, he nonetheless had a deep soft spot for his stepbrothers and had refused his mother's pleas to execute them as each new Zar had done before him. Herezah felt fortunate that Boaz had still been immature enough that he could not prevent the actions she took on his behalf to ensure no heirs remained after Joreb's death. That said, Zar Koriz's compassion for his siblings had worked in her favour, for his favourite brother was Joreb and it was Joreb who took the throne, eyes still wet from weeping over his lost brother. It was Joreb who had chosen her from all in the harem for special consideration. Yes, she had plenty to thank the poisoned Zar for. Joreb's mother was more successful in insisting on traditional rights and the remaining stepbrothers were swiftly dealt with. Herezah was glad that her Joreb had found the courage to deal with his rivals, unlike his brother Koriz.

The new Valide, however, chose not to dismantle the harem, for the girls were still so young and new. Joreb inherited his brother's harem and with it came a precocious girl called Herezah.

She hadn't been in this chamber since that fateful day when the old Valide's stern gaze had fallen upon her and chosen her within seconds of that first glance. Her fate was sealed with that woman's glare, although her destiny – like any woman of the harem – was her own to carve.

And carve it I did, she thought now, pride catching in her throat as she saw her son enter the room. He looked taller, more imposing, and there was more colour in his cheeks. He was obviously getting out a lot more now than in his days as a prince. He also looked miserable. She wrongly presumed that his grim expression was all about fear of what he was about to witness. *He was always a squeamish one*, she thought, as he bent to take her hand.

'Mother,' he acknowledged, kissing her hand and placing it on his chest, in the formal way.

She felt a shiver of delight. He was certainly making a fuss with such a show of affection. Just being invited to this private event had been enough and she was going to put this morning's pointed discussion behind them. She had overreacted, she was sure. 'Darling, I'm sorry about my mood earlier. Forgive me. And thank you for sharing this with me,' she said smoothly.

To her surprise he waved away her apology as if it had not troubled him. 'I can't promise a fun afternoon, I'm afraid,' he said, falling heavily into his chair beside her. 'This is duty, not my idea of entertainment.'

Herezah was secretly pleased to know he continued to put duty ahead of his fears, but she knew she needed to say the right words to his admission. 'Then where is your clingy clown? Surely your court jester should be here alongside you to provide that entertainment,' she replied, and then, contriving still more concern, she looked to where the Grand Vizier stood patiently. 'Tariq, where is the dwarf?'

The Vizier glided towards the royal couple and bowed. She hadn't seen him in several weeks and, although this was a man in his senior years, he looked more dashing than she could have imagined. His beard was neatly groomed, not oiled, and shorter now – no longer demanding to be noticed. It was also no longer the rich glossy black that the Tariq of old had insisted on achieving through dye. He had allowed the peppery grey to emerge, and to Herezah's expert eye it looked far more distinguished. His neatly kempt hair was also now the same colour. She approved, although it still continued to fascinate her that this new person seemed to be emerging before their eyes.

He answered Boaz, not her. 'I was told he left your chambers not so long ago, my Zar. Perhaps you know better than I of his whereabouts,' he suggested, frowning.

Again Boaz waved away Tariq's concern as if it did not trouble him. 'I know not of his location, Vizier. Carry on,' he ordered.

Tariq bowed again and withdrew. A signal was given and, as a tray of refreshments was brought in for the royals, a small queue of young men was led in through another door.

'Is something wrong, son?' Herezah enquired, distracted from the Vizier and intrigued by her child's mood. And as only she could, Herezah moved straight to where her instincts beckoned. 'Are you upset about Pez?' He turned to her and by the surprise she could see in his eyes, she knew she was right with her wild stab in the dark. 'Has something happened to him?' She knew how much he cared for the dwarf. This would be the right initial question to pose — it showed the right balance of care.

'No, he is well. He has drawn my ire, that's all,' he said casually.

'Oh?'

'That's all,' he repeated and she could tell from his tone that he would not be giving her any more on this subject. That didn't mean she wouldn't make it her prime business to learn more but she had subtle methods for achieving that. And the notion that Pez had finally displeased a Zar was too delicious a prospect. This day was certainly turning out well. She patted his arm, smiling inwardly, but deliberately and deftly changed the subject as she reached for a glass of blood-red pomegranate juice. Quite fitting as a choice of beverage considering what was about to occur, she decided. 'I was just remembering how this chamber was when I was chosen for the Zar's harem.'

Boaz sipped the drink in his hand and she could see

it simply gave him something to do. He was clearly distracted, showing no interest in her comment. She tried again. 'So tell me more about the mute guard, Boaz.'

He sat up straighter, presumably understanding now that he must appear more interested. 'These men you see here,' he said, his goblet arcing across her line of vision, 'have been selected as my new private bodyguard.'

'Selected?'

'Volunteered first, then culled for suitability and finally interviewed by me as the final seal of approval.'

'And these fine young bloods are going to watch over you day and night. You explained that the Vizier was worried about some sort of attack.'

He nodded. 'These men are all trained in the fighting arts and can protect me. They have committed to memory a series of signals so we can communicate – they are all in perfect health.'

'I can see,' she said approvingly as the line of men stripped down to their plain white baggy pants, revealing hardened, sculpted bodies. She was reminded of the Spur in a similar stage of undress just a year ago and how that sight had brought a rush of blood to her cheeks.

Tariq cleared his throat and the royals gave him their attention. 'My Zar, Valide Zara,' he said, bowing graciously, 'these men will protect you with their lives. And in remaining close to you, my Zar, what they hear or see will never be revealed.'

Boaz nodded. 'Do you men all freely volunteer for this role?'

Each, except one, who had been kneeling now stood, bowed and said the words, 'I do, my Zar, I give all of me.'

Boaz frowned at the last man, who, at a signal from the Grand Vizier simply bowed and put his hand over his heart. Boaz glanced towards Tariq who gave a smug, almost imperceptible nod, as if to tell the Zar to remain patient, all would be revealed.

The Zar took a slow deep breath before he gave the next command. It frightened him to accept what these men were prepared to give for him. 'Let it be so,' he finally said. 'Proceed.'

Boaz and Herezah watched as each man's head was shaved in ritual fashion to the special chants of the Elim who were present. The song that the men in red recited was one of farewell, similar to the words expressed prior to being 'cut' as a eunuch.

Each of the volunteers was then given a tiny glass of a dark liquid to drink.

Tariq whispered nearby. 'We wait a short while for that to take effect.'

'What is it?' Boaz asked.

'The dulling potion,' Herezah answered for Tariq. 'It doesn't prevent pain but it puts the victim into an introverted mood, I'm told.'

Tariq nodded, impressed. 'The Valide is absolutely correct,' he said. 'It takes them within themselves. The physic who prepared this potion says it makes them feel safe, at peace. We could do anything to them.'

'That is considerate of you, Tariq,' Boaz commented, not used to any pity being shown in the more barbaric practices of Percheron.

Herezah's and Tariq's gazes met. Herezah looked at the Vizier, expecting to share a mutual understanding. They both knew that this was nothing to do with being considerate and although she anticipated that Tariq would pick up the cue and explain more to Boaz, she saw only amusement in the Vizier's eyes. She didn't understand but then there was little to understand about Tariq these days. Herezah explained the procedure herself.

'This is not done out of kindness, son,' she whispered, 'it is given to these men to keep them still. A struggling man is a difficult one to "cut" accurately. Putting your volunteers into the soft stupor we speak of will ensure an easier time of it for the administrators.' She had chosen her words with care.

'I see,' he said, showing none of the disappointment he felt surging through him. 'Mother, do you enjoy witnessing events such as this?'

'No,' came the reply. 'But I will never shirk my duty.'

'It was not your duty to witness this. I invited you to attend or not attend. The decision was yours.'

Herezah again risked laying her manicured hand lightly against his arm. It was done with affection and she was delighted that he did not pull away despite his grumpy mood. 'I understood the nature of your invitation. I do not feel compelled to be part of the grisly process of making a team of mutes. I do, however, see it as my duty to stand by the Zar, to support him in all of his endeavours, to help bear the burden of some of the less pleasant tasks and to share his pleasure at his successes. What you do today is unpleasant but important, Boaz. I know that you like beauty – in this you are your father all over again,' she said, smiling softly, 'and this is why I'm here, to be at your side through the uglier challenges of your role.' It was eloquently done.

Boaz was once again struck by his mother's strength. It wasn't a revelation – he had always known it but now she was using it to help him, seemingly, rather than to help herself. All of his life his mother had used him as her means of elevating herself. Perhaps now that she'd attained that role of Valide – something she had dreamed of since arriving at the palace, probably – she could give her attentions for selfless reasons. He didn't have Pez to talk this through with. The loss of his friend stabbed like a knife constantly in his back.

'Thank you, mother,' he said. And meant it.

They returned their attention to the approaching Grand Vizier. 'My Zar, Valide, we will now begin the Making of the Mutes. May I proceed? I must warn it is . . . messy.'

'Proceed,' Boaz said, knowing there was no way back now.

They watched as the physic in charge of proceedings, who was one of the Elim, blindfolded each of the men, except the last one again.

'Who is that fellow?' Boaz enquired of Tariq. 'I have not met him.'

'No, Majesty, you have not. But I will explain his presence shortly. The men are being blindfolded because it is believed that the Elim performing the maiming must not see the suffering in the eyes of each victim. It is considered bad luck.'

'Such a superstitious lot, the Elim,' Herezah said, 'they don't seem too worried by what is perpetrated on the women of the harem.'

Tariq left that comment well alone. He noted that the Elim caught his gaze and he nodded.

The first man was held, his arms pinned from behind.

'I can see now how the potion makes them compliant,' Boaz whispered to his mother.

He watched as the Elim physic encouraged the man to open his mouth and once that occurred it all happened very quickly, much to Herezah's satisfaction. Pincers pulled at the victim's tongue and within a heartbeat the bulk of the tongue was cut off in a single slice of a keen blade. To prevent fatal blood loss the stump was cauterised with a glowing brand. The man fainted, groaning, but to Boaz's relief there was no screaming or struggle.

'They will wait for him to recover before performing the deafening,' Tariq explained.

'Surely it would be more merciful to do it whilst he was unconscious?' Boaz enquired.

'But it would be considered cowardly,' Tariq followed up quickly. 'This is about bravery and duty, Majesty. I know you wish it to be easy on the men who give themselves so freely. But the maiming is all part of the test of their commitment. That's why they do not scream.'

The blindfold was removed and a cold linen was placed on the man's face to revive him. As soon as his eyes fluttered open, dazed by the pain, he was quickly restored to his knees and once again held securely, by two strong Elim this time. The physic reached for a vicious-looking needle and Boaz prayed to Zarab that he would not let himself down by looking away. He fixed his gaze somewhere slightly off the action whilst not giving away that he wasn't actually looking and then he made himself think of something beautiful.

Ana came to mind and this was no surprise. He saw the stabbing movement and resisted the urge to gag as a small, sharp spume of blood hit the physic's belly. Instead he thought only of Ana's face, Ana's hair, Ana's newly voluptuous body.

And as the other eardrum of the brave warrior was pierced, this time to the sound of a guttural growl of pain, Boaz decided he would not tarnish his joyous thoughts of Ana with this ghoulish activity. He turned his mind instead to the boating picnic he had planned and all the fun activities he had set up for the girls' enjoyment. Nobody from his harem would ever accuse their Zar of enforcing tedium in their lives. He imagined their squeals of delight at learning to fish and swimming carefree in the aquamarine waters. He was just wondering how he should organise to cook, on the riverbank, any fish that were caught, when his mother's voice disturbed him.

'My lion?'

It sounded to Boaz from the slightly strained query in her voice that this was not the first time she had said it.

'Yes,' he said, releasing himself from the spell of Ana. As he refocused he saw all the men bar one had ruined, bloodied mouths and running ears. Most were slumped on the floor against the helpful legs of an Elim to assist in retaining a modicum of dignity after their trauma.

'Where were you, my love?' Herezah asked, trying to lighten the tension swirling about him.

The smell of blood was thick in the room. He suspected she knew he had somehow vanished in spirit, if not in body, from the terrible maiming ritual. 'I was thinking,' he said and made it sound final. 'We are done, Grand Vizier?'

One fellow began to wail. The Vizier cleared his throat.

'That one might not turn out to be as suitable as we'd hoped. Yes, we have completed the maiming, Majesty.'

The maimed warriors were helped away, leaving one whole man in the room.

'And this last warrior?' Boaz asked.

'My great pride, Highness,' the Vizier replied and could not disguise the smug tone. He snapped his fingers and one of the Elim brought over the young warrior, whose gaze was fixed on the intricately patterned tiled floor. The slave knelt.

Maliz knew he must sell the notion of the mutes with precision. It was all about this one man, the reason for the whole campaign to install a ring of guardians around the Zar.

'This is Salazin, my Zar. He is the inspiration for this new personal protectorate you now have. I discovered him not so long ago. He is an orphan who has learned to tough things out the hardest possible way, Majesty, for Salazin was made deaf and dumb from an early age by an unfortunate illness.'

'Ah,' Boaz said, nodding with understanding. 'He needs no maiming.'

'He is perfect, Majesty, for Zarab made him this way.'

'And Zarab led you to him, Tariq?' Herezah asked, with a note of irony not missed by the Vizier.

'I like to think so, Valide,' he said and smiled privately at how close to the truth he spoke. Zarab had surely led him to Salazin and Salazin, he hoped, would lead him to Iridor.

'How did you come across him?' Boaz asked.

'I was giving alms to some of the orphanages, my Zar,

as you have requested. He was from one of the city establishments.'

'Not the one you aim to close?' Boaz replied. It was not really meant very seriously, more as something to say, but it obviously struck a harsh chord with the Vizier.

'As a matter of fact yes, Majesty. I paid the orphanage a visit to consider how we would dismantle it, find new housing for its . . .' he searched for the word, found it '. . . guests. I needed to consider what would happen to the sisterhood who care for these youngsters.'

'Where is this place we speak of?' Herezah enquired.

Boaz looked at his mother, his glare defying her to make a fuss. 'I have promised the Grand Vizier his own villa overlooking the Faranel. He has taken a liking to an orphanage and, although I'm yet to make a final decision, I have given him permission to consider how he will rehouse the present occupants.'

'Are you talking about the Widows' Enclave?' Herezah asked, frowning.

'I think it used to go by that name, yes, Valide,' the Vizier answered without hesitation.

'But that's for army families,' she said and it came out as an accusation.

'Originally, yes,' the Vizier said patiently. 'But we have not had war in living memory and so now only a few families of the unlucky injured or killed army members live there. It no longer serves its original purpose, Valide,' he said politely, adding, 'It's a huge place for so few people.'

'But not so huge for one, presumably,' Herezah replied tartly. 'My Zar, with your indulgence, I might return to my chambers now. Again my thanks for including me in this special ritual,' she said, inclining her head in thanks. She glanced somewhat angrily towards the Vizier and then turned back to her son. 'Perhaps you'll take supper with me some time soon.'

Boaz stood and helped the Valide to do the same. 'I shall look forward to it, mother,' he said.

Tariq signalled and two of the Elim were instantly at the side of Herezah to escort her back to the harem. She rehooked her veil across her face dutifully, as she was now leaving the company of the Zar, and elegantly glided out of the room between her burly companions.

Boaz sighed. 'The Valide does not approve of your plan, clearly.'

Maliz kept his counsel on that subject, schooling Tariq's features so the Zar could not gauge just how much Maliz wanted that villa and the luxurious surrounds it would provide for him. It was time to gild the truth. 'Salazin was one of the oldest in the orphanage. I gather from the sisterhood that he has no known living relatives. He makes no sound at all, my Zar. His deafness is profound.'

'No sound at all?' Boaz repeated, incredulous. 'So you have tested him?'

A sly smile crept across the Vizier's mouth. 'I had to, to be sure. I will not go into the detail of it, Majesty, but this young man cannot hear and he cannot talk. You can take my word for it,' he said, smiling fully now at the young man in question. 'He will see but he cannot listen into anything you say, nor can he repeat what his eyes show him.'

'So he cannot write what he sees, either?' Boaz enquired.

Time to reinforce the lie. 'The sisterhood confirm he is illiterate, which is understandable considering his afflictions.'

'The perfect mute, in other words,' Boaz commented, returning his attention to the bent head of his new protector.

Maliz nodded. 'Indeed, Highness. He is also the strongest of the warriors here. We tested them in this respect too and Salazin was by far the most adept with weapons and with fists.'

'His age?'

'From what I can tell he is around nineteen summers.'

'Let him stand,' Boaz commanded. The young man was raised to his feet. Boaz reached to lift the man's chin and saw that he possessed clear grey eyes. 'How will he know what is wanted of him?'

'The sisterhood have their own methods of communicating with him,' Maliz said. 'I have been taught its use.' He smiled. 'They had no choice but to teach me and now I have schooled all these young men. You, too, can learn it, Majesty. As for this one, he fully understands his role is to protect you with his life, my Zar.'

'If he has no family to give money to, what is his reward for offering his life to me?' Boaz queried. 'The others are presumably volunteering because they can offer their families security through the generous gold I presume you have offered.'

Tariq bowed his head gently. 'I did as instructed, my Zar. Each man has been so handsomely rewarded that each of their families is now well set up for the future,' he said and Boaz acknowledged this with a nod. 'As for Salazin, I cannot say what motivates this one,' he lied. 'Except to say that he wishes to serve the Zar. As you sit on your throne by Zarab's design, Highness,' Tariq said, warming to his tale, 'he sees you as our god's mortal incarnation.'

'Really? But he was raised by the priestesses – I would have thought—'

'No, Highness. He despises them, I gather. They are as glad to get him off their hands as he is to leave their care.'

'But without them surely he would have perished as a child?'

'I imagine so,' the Vizier said airily, as if this was trivial. 'It doesn't make him like them. He is a man of Zarab through and through. It is why he leapt at the opportunity to serve you.'

'That committed?'

'Oh yes,' Maliz replied, serious now. 'I must admit I believe Zarab's hand guided your father in his choice of heir. Most would feel the same.'

'I understand tradition, Tariq. I just find it hard to believe that in reality today's modern thinking still holds true to this belief.'

Tariq was astounded. He had not taken into account how protected and thus ignorant the royals had become. 'My Zar, with your indulgence, I might suggest that your life is too sheltered. We must rectify this.'

'Oh?'

'Yes, Majesty. We should let you meet some more of your people so that you may know how close to Zarab they truly believe you are. You are answerable only to our god – surely you know this?'

Boaz nodded. 'King of Kings, Mightiest of the Mighty,' he said wearily.

'Salazin has been raised in a cloistered environment, so his faith is strong. To him you are the embodiment of Zarab himself.'

'It strikes me as odd, Tariq, that the sisterhood would raise a child to believe so strongly in Zarab, when they themselves worship Lyana.'

Maliz, lurking inside Tariq, quickly stifled his inclination to react. The very mention of her name angered him but he reined in his disgust for fear of it showing in Tariq's expression.

'I mean,' Boaz continued, not noticing any change in his Grand Vizier's demeanour, 'the Goddess is everything to them, even though her time is long past.'

'Majesty,' Maliz began carefully. 'The sisterhood know that the orphanage and its very existence is at the indulgence of the Zar. Their time is long gone. They may not subscribe to it but they certainly understand that, outside of their few remaining numbers, Percheron worships Zarab. They would have no housing, no sustenance for themselves or the families they care for if not for the Zar's benevolence. They appreciate that these children need to be raised in the Percherese manner, despite what faith they privately hold close to.'

'You're saying this is their work, nothing to do with faith.'

Tariq nodded. 'That's a reasonable way of putting it, Majesty, although I might term it as their vocation. Their faith is sadly misplaced but it is also private. We tolerate their silent beliefs and they are allowed to pursue their vocation in caring for the sick, the lonely, the needy, the desperate, the orphaned and so on. The royal coffers make this possible.'

'And I am very happy to continue providing,' Boaz replied firmly. 'I gave a promise to a sister once that I would care for the temple and I have no intention of breaking my word.'

Maliz bristled beneath the calm exterior of Grand Vizier Tariq. It galled him that any Zar would offer any form of protection to the hateful sisters of the Goddess. 'Nor would any of us expect you to, Majesty,' he said, affecting a soft tone of injury. 'All I am saying is that their beliefs remain private. They are not in a position to convert disciples to their broken faith, Majesty. They serve Percheron by caring for those in need. It is separate from their faith.'

Boaz looked again at the still figure of Salazin. The man had not moved, not so much as blinked in the time they had talked over and around him, and about him. 'Your plan for Salazin?'

'He is the most complete of all the warriors we have chosen, Majesty. I would make him your most personal of all the servants. My desire is that he protect you every hour, every minute of the day. Whilst you go about your day, he will be your shadow. And at night, my Zar, whilst you sleep, he will watch over you.'

'When does he sleep?' Boaz asked, but it was a facetious question and he clearly required no response because he moved swiftly forward. 'And when I wish to have time alone?'

'I would not advise it, Highness.'

'Is that so?' Boaz asked, slightly amused now as he stepped down from his podium and stretched. 'Well, Tariq, I can assure you I will not be taking your advice in this regard. There will be occasions when I demand privacy that not even a deaf and dumb man can provide. As you've rightly pointed out, he still sees.'

Maliz caught on swiftly. 'Of course,' he said, bowing his tall frame in gentle apology. 'In which case, my Zar,

Salazin will be directed to search the chamber first before waiting just outside. Guards will always be present nearby.'

Boaz nodded. 'Let him rest, get acquainted with the palace. When does this begin?'

'Immediately, my Zar. The others will need to heal but Salazin will take up his duties from this evening, with your permission.'

'As you choose, Vizier,' Boaz said. 'And now I need to take some air . . . alone.'

The Vizier bowed, as did the mute warrior, until the Zar had departed.

Maliz beckoned Salazin, who followed him to a small room attached to the main chamber.

He signed: *I lied about your ability to read and write.*

The mute nodded.

Maliz continued: *The game has begun. You report to me on everything.* He emphasised the word 'everything' by signing it again before continuing. *His moods, who he sees, whatever he does, I want to know about it.*

Salazin smiled.

More importantly — far more important than the Zar, in fact — I want to know everything about the dwarf. His name is Pez.

Salazin answered: *It will be done, Master.*

The Vizier nodded slowly, the dark eyes of Tariq hiding the demon behind who knew now his secret weapon had been unleashed. The mute would, he was sure, deliver Iridor. Maliz was convinced that the messenger to the Goddess would align himself with the Zar and no matter how many times he dismissed it as fanciful, the feeling got stronger. Although he could no longer float free of the body he inhabited, he was convinced he could sense the aura of Iridor hovering nearby to the Zar. He had no idea who this was yet or even if his hunch was true but he could not dismiss it. His instincts demanded he listen to them. Iridor could be anyone but his cunning mind kept bringing him back to the dwarf. There was madness there. The strange-looking creature that resembled a man and yet such a cruelly twisted version rarely spoke a word of sense and even when there was momentary clarity it would dissipate into buffoonery almost immediately. He knew the Valide despised Pez, as did Salmeo, and Pez had been in the palace for decades . . . there was nothing novel about his presence. Everyone he had carefully probed had confirmed that the court clown was just that. He had been this way since his arrival and even Maliz had to accept that for the past year his observations had shown Pez to be an irritating, almost tragic innocent, trapped in his insane mind.

Iridor was far too wily to be this halfwit and yet something about Pez drew the Vizier back again. Just a vague feeling. Once, during his freedom – before he had cast out the soul of Tariq – he had felt Iridor's presence strongly and to his shock had felt the presence of the Lore. He had tried to find it again but it had disappeared in an instant and he had never traced it back to the person wielding it. His suspicions, for no good reason, fell on the dwarf when Pez had acted strangely in the presence of Boaz, whom Maliz and Tariq, when they were separate, had been watching. Yet he had no substance to this argument; only intuition.

Salazin would now spy constantly and if he could deliver Pez and the news Maliz longed to hear, then the demon could destroy him – and by turn the Goddess, whomever she was – before she had even the chance to rise again.

Tariq's smile turned nasty. He patted Salazin on the arm and signed: *Tonight you begin your life's most important task for Zarab.*

7

Ana now shared a sleeping chamber with only one other. History had shown that youngsters put into one main chamber tended to achieve nothing other than a lack of sleep. And although tradition had it that older women tended to prefer to congregate together for sleeping, many of the odalisques in this harem were still children. Even most of the older ones remained immature and giggly, with years of growing up to do before they could be considered sedate members of the harem.

Ana and her chamber companion and only friend, Sascha, were the most composed and Salmeo hoped they would lead the other odalisques by example. Sascha, a shy, intelligent young woman was not well this evening. Ana had guided Sascha, who was bent double with an ache in her belly, to find one of the Elim and have her taken to the harem's infirmary. The strong Elim carried the ailing girl and Ana found herself alone this night, which was convenient. The girls were no longer guarded outside their rooms — now that almost a year had passed, they were free to move around certain areas of the harem at night, without censure.

She toyed with the idea of going for a stroll but couldn't risk not being here when Pez came as promised, so she remained in her chamber, staring out of the open shutters at the bright moonlight, waiting for his curious arrival. Her lids grew heavy, though, and ultimately she drifted off.

Ana's peaceful slumber was disturbed by what sounded like flapping and when she rubbed some of the sleep from her eyes she realised she was staring at a magnificent snow owl, which was regarding her intently from her windowsill.

She was surprised into silence, awed by the majesty of the creature. Moving as slowly as she dared, Ana brought her feet to rest on the floor and then gradually stood, her gaze never leaving the owl, who was so still it could have been a statue.

It was that notion that startled her and made her whisper a single word. 'Iridor,' she breathed dreamily.

Before she could approach the owl, it changed before her sleepy eyes. She blinked, confused. Standing before her was Pez.

She laughed softly. 'I . . . I was dreaming, Pez. I thought you were an owl.' Ana rubbed her eyes again and yawned. 'You were so beautiful.'

'Was I? Good evening, Ana.'

'You were Iridor – do you know who he is?'

'He is the messenger of Lyana, the loyal companion of the Goddess.'

'That's right. You know your folklore.'

'It's not folklore.'

'That makes it truth,' she said jauntily, as though this were going to be one of their fun conversations.

Pez was in a more sombre frame of mind. 'That's right. It's why I'm here tonight. We have things to discuss, child.'

She grew more serious, sensing his mood and knowing his falling out with Boaz would be troubling him. She reached for a gown to throw over her bare shoulders. 'You left abruptly today. How are you feeling, Pez?'

He shook his head. 'I'm feeling said. I made an error today with the Zar and we can't afford to do that.'

'We?'

'Ana . . . what you saw just now . . .' He hesitated. This was not going to be easy.

'The owl?'

'Iridor,' he confirmed. 'That *was* me. I am him.'

She stared at the dwarf, eyes huge in the darkness illuminated softly by moonlight. Ana said nothing for what felt to Pez to be an interminable time. He knew she wasn't shocked speechless – although he could forgive her if she had been. No, Ana was thinking; he could see it from her frown and her vague expression. Ana was putting something together in her mind and so he waited anxiously for whatever her response would be.

It finally came. 'And Ellyana the crone?' It wasn't what he'd expected to hear but before he could answer she answered her own question: 'The crone forewarns the coming of the Goddess. But it begins with the rising of Iridor. The owl aligns himself with the woman who will be Lyana's incarnation for the next battle . . .' She trailed off, looking fearfully at Pez. It was as though the acceptance of him as Iridor was already complete in her mind. She had moved on to the greater problems.

'How do you know this, Ana?' he asked, feeling sure his instincts about this young woman were going to be right again, even though this time the reality frightened him.

'I don't know how,' she replied, gaze still far away. 'I just know things.'

'Such as?'

'Such as the names of the stone statues of Percheron. All of them.'

'They all originally served Lyana – do you know that?'

She nodded slowly. It struck Pez that she was scared now of what she knew. Perhaps like him she had tried to put it aside, deny it. He probed further. 'They were real once, Ana. Beloch and Ezram once roamed Percheron. Likewise the winged lions, Crendel and Darso, as well as the mightiest of them all, Shakar, the dragon. They all loved and served the Goddess.'

'They were turned to stone by Zarab. She had no magic to counter his spell. He used a special magic, not of the gods.'

Pez felt a thrill of excitement. 'That's right. Someone helped him. A mortal.'

'His name was Maliz,' she answered and instantly re-focused her stare on Pez. He felt the chill of it as she spoke the demon's name. 'He made a deal with the god. Give me immortality and I will deliver Lyana, was the promise from Maliz.'

'Go on,' he urged. He needed her to say it, to tell him everything, to confirm that his hunch was right.

'The bargain was struck,' she continued. 'Maliz, a sorcerer, was given everlasting life to rise each time the Goddess tried to reimpose herself on mortals. Maliz returns time and again and each time he has won . . . but this time it may be different.'

Pez could hardly speak, he was holding his breath so tight at hearing such a startling statement. 'Why is it different?' he asked gently, not wanting to disturb the momentum of her telling of the tale.

'The factors are the same. The crone identifies the new Iridor long before he rises. Maliz, who slumbers in any body he can claim, re-awakens and has the spiritual freedom to roam until he senses where Iridor will rise. He never knows who it will be – and everyone who is part of this eternal struggle is always different for each cycle. They have to find one another. Maliz chooses his next mortal body with care. It is the one he must live in and use to destroy Lyana.' She paused, but, at Pez's silent nodding, carried on with her story. 'When Iridor finally assumes his role, it triggers the rising of Lyana, whose spirit emerges through a mortal.'

'And so the principal players are complete,' Pez said in conclusion.

'Not this time,' she reminded. 'For this battle there is a newcomer.'

'Who?' he begged, aching for good news.

She shivered. 'I don't know. I have no sense of their name, whether it is a woman or a man, or even their purpose. Their role, however, will immeasurably change the very fabric of the struggle.'

Pez found himself holding his breath again but he knew it was his turn to give some explanation. 'And so we know that Ellyana is the crone who began all of this. She recognised me. She came into the harem, masquerading as a bundle woman some time ago, Ana. She told me to work out who I was. And at the temple I had a vision of who I was – Zafira saw my hair turn white. It was an omen of who I was to become.'

Ana nodded sadly. 'I should have guessed.'

Pez let her comment pass. She had already revealed much. 'There were many clues,' he began.

Ana interrupted him. 'Beginning with Ellyana seeking me out in the bazaar.' She smiled sadly. 'I thought I was noticing her but she already knew me. She was selling a gold chain. Lazar saw it too.' She faltered at mentioning his name; Pez heard it and felt assaulted by a fresh guilt. 'When we stepped in to save her from a poor bargain with one of the alley cats she gave me the piece in her hand. It had turned into a gold owl. I recognised Iridor.'

Pez sighed. He dug into his pocket and pulled out that same small gold statue. 'It found its way to me, Ana.'

She looked surprised. 'How? I gave that to—'

'Lazar, I know,' he said, to save her having to say the name again. 'He sent it to me.'

'Before he died? How could he?'

Pez was stuck. He didn't want to fabricate any more lies to this girl, especially if the truth spilled out under this pressure. He simply shook his head. 'I don't know. Another secret of the cycle of the war between gods, I suppose.'

She didn't pursue it. Ana suddenly sounded maudlin to Pez when she stood. 'Lazar was surprised that I knew the names of the statues.'

'He was surprised by everything about you, Ana.'

'Nothing surprised me about him. I loved that man.' Now she sounded wistful, only marginally easier on Pez's ears.

'I know.' And he hated that they were speaking of Lazar in the past tense. He wondered if Ana would ever . . . could ever, forgive him for such a terrible lie.

'Ana . . .' he began gravely and she interrupted him.

'I know what you're going to say next, Pez.' She looked terrified as she swung around to stare at him. 'But it can't be so.'

'What am I going to say?'

'You're going to name Lyana.'

'Then you do it,' he urged. 'You tell me her mortal incarnation.'

Ana held her face but she did not cry. She shook her head beneath her hands. 'It cannot be.'

'It is. You feel it. You know it. Ana, every time I have touched you I've felt the tingle of your magical being. I didn't understand it at first. And then I became familiar with it, noticed it less. But when I became Iridor and lived with this knowledge of myself for several moons I *did* comprehend the strange sensation when I touched you. I realised it was not a magic so much as a force and it was a bond between us. I guessed who you were becoming. And I was frightened for you – I still am but this is why we're together. This is why I will give my life as I always have before, to protect you. This time, Ana, my beloved Lyana . . . we will win.'

And now they both wept. Ana fled to Pez's arms and despite having to crouch and despite his limbs being too short to wrap her fully in an embrace, they comforted each other with the truth of who they were and the dangerous mission they now faced.

Ana finally pulled away. 'I don't know what I'm supposed to do.' And once again Pez was struck by how easily this young woman accepted the extraordinary. She had tried denying it, but in recognising the truth, Ana now acknowledged it.

'What we have always done,' Pez comforted. 'We go on instinct now.'

Ana wiped her eyes. 'Who else is on our side?'

'No-one in the palace,' he warned. 'I've cautioned you before and I hope you'll heed these words. No-one in the palace is your friend except me.'

'Not even Boaz?'

He grimaced. 'He certainly does not want my friendship any more. No, not even Boaz, because he is being influenced, and until the Zar begins to make all of his own decisions, I can't trust him . . . and you definitely must not trust anyone.'

'So we have no allies?'

'Zafira,' he said, wishing he could offer up the name he knew she still longed to hear. He hated Lazar in this moment for making him constantly face this situation, and promised himself the time was fast approaching for the truth to come out.

'Jumo,' she offered. 'Wherever that poor man is.'

'Ellyana, if she ever returns,' he concluded.

'Kett,' she added.

'Ah?' Pez said, as though enlightenment had occurred. 'What makes you say that?'

'I feel connected to him.'

'The Raven,' Pez said. 'That's what he called himself when he was barely conscious through his ordeal of being made a eunuch.'

'Bringer of bad tidings,' Ana added.

'Or simply a messenger. We must work out how to bring Kett closer to us.' Pez knew that the Raven always appeared after Iridor and before Lyana. Another servant of the Goddess, he was often referred to as the black bird of omen but he didn't want to frighten Ana. Kett was definitely someone that Pez would have to watch and somehow find a way to bring closer to Ana. If what he suspected was right and Ana was the re-emerging Goddess, then she would need to receive whatever message Lyana had passed on through the Raven for her.

'Well, without Boaz you have no pull in the palace any more. I must speak with the Zar. And perhaps I can help to mend this broken bond? It's not right, Pez. He knows your secret. It's dangerous.'

'I know this,' he said. 'But I have taken steps.'

'Steps?'

He found a smile. 'Ask me no more right now. Just trust me.'

'So what must I do?'

'Live. Be Ana. That's who you are. Continue life in the harem as it must be lived and the eternal struggle will take care of itself. I have no knowledge of how this unfolds, child. Each time we are reborn as different people with only a vague memory of the struggle taking place, not how each played out. Each cycle is different in complexity, even though the outcome has been the same for so many battles.'

'When was the last time?'

'Centuries ago. So many in fact that it is no more than myth in the minds of most.'

'So I go on our boating trip . . .'

'And you stay out of the eagle eye of Salmeo and the Valide as best you can.'

'That won't be easy. Everyone seems to think the Zar is going to choose me.'

'He will. It's why you are here, Ana, but that's irrelevant to your true reason for being.'

'I feel like I'm just a vessel, with various uses,' she said. Pez pursed his lips. She was right in this estimation of herself. 'I just want to be myself. To discover things, to learn, and not to be someone's slave.'

'I understand.'

'Do you?'

'You forget, I've been a slave to the palace for most of my life.'

'But, Pez, you have freedom. You can go out if you want. And now . . . now you can fly. Where do you fly to?'

He so wanted to tell her. He could even feel the words queuing up to spill out of his mouth and reveal his secret destination. He fought them down. 'I just fly,' he said instead.

She sighed as if she, too, wished she could fly. 'What about Maliz?' she asked, surprising him by the turn in conversation. 'If we know who we are, then surely he has known for some time that Iridor has risen.'

'Correct. And he's looking for us. He'll begin by focusing on Iridor,' Pez said. 'My magic is more obvious.'

'But why am I shielded?'

He shook his head. 'You are, it's how it is. I will reveal you,' he said sadly. 'I am the cause of our traditional demise. It is always me who is discovered first.'

'Are you frightened?' she asked, trepidation creeping into her expression.

He lifted his chin, folded his arms. 'Not at all.'

To his delight, Ana smiled and it was filled with warmth. 'Why?'

'Because you assure me that this time it's different . . . and I intend to find out why and because of whom.'

8

After leaving Ana, Pez had flown to Star Island. With the newfound freedom of his wings and the fact that he was clearly not required by the Zar, there was no need to remain at the palace this night. He knew he wouldn't be able to sleep anyway with his mind racing along so fast, and he found a ready companion in Lazar.

'Couldn't sleep?' Pez asked softly, approaching the hut and not surprised to see a familiar figure leaning up against the outside wall.

Lazar shook his head. 'And it's such a beautiful night anyway.'

'I forgot to mention last time that the beard is interesting,' Pez commented.

'It occurred to me I may need a new disguise,' Lazar said, scratching at it. 'Horrible things. I've been growing this for months and hate it.'

'How are you feeling?'

'Stronger. Much stronger in fact.'

'You look it – even in the moonlight.' Pez grinned at his friend's sneer. 'Truly. You appear almost your grumpy self again.'

'I feel like myself again,' Lazar admitted. 'The improvement is suddenly vigorous.'

'Weren't you warned it would be like this?'

Lazar nodded, pushed his large hand through his hair. 'Zafira was told as much. My strength would return rapidly once my body had learned how to manage alongside the poison. Presumably it has done that.'

'So what now?'

Lazar's voice hardened. 'Well, first you're going to tell me about Jumo. I demand to know his story and then I'll make a decision on what next.'

Pez felt a chill crawl up his spine. Lazar would not be in a good mood when he heard about Jumo. There was no point in avoiding it any longer, though.

'Where is Jumo, Pez?'

'By now I imagine he's roaming Galinsea,' he said, not giving himself any further time to think.

He expected a roar of anger, but it didn't come. Instead he had to stand beneath the simmering glare of Lazar, trying not to squirm amidst the thick, uncomfortable silence that now wrapped itself about him.

Finally Lazar spoke, all his good humour evaporated once again. 'Galinsea.' It wasn't a question. He knew the dwarf had spoken the truth. 'Who sent him?'

'He was determined to find your family, tell them of your demise.'

'I repeat, who sent him there? Only two of us know my background.'

'Then why are you asking?' Pez said, disgusted by his own sense of inadequacy beneath the burning stare of the former Spur, whose shaking anger was now visible.

'You told Jumo who I was?' There was threat in the tone.

Pez had never been scared by Lazar but for the first time he understood what it might be like to be this man's adversary. 'Yes, that was our agreement, remember? I tell Jumo should anything fatal occur. And because of Ellyana's bullheaded ways and your determination to follow them, you kept me in the dark about your survival for just long enough for me to make this error. It is your fault that Jumo knows.'

'Anyone else?'

'No.'

Lazar pushed away from the wall of the hut and strode towards the cliff edge. Pez had no choice but to follow like a shamed dog.

'Where's Zafira?' he asked, desperate for any conversation that might rescue the bad mood.

'At her temple,' Lazar growled. 'I'm well enough to care for myself now.'

'Lazar, I—'

'How long have I protected that secret, Pez?' he said, staring angrily at the twinkling lights of the city across the bay.

'I couldn't have Jumo rushing off blindly with no idea of who to look for regarding your kin and him in such a bereft state. I hope—'

'Sixteen years,' Lazar said with feeling, swinging back to glower at Pez. 'Painful, all of them.'

'Were you not ever happy amongst us in Percheron?'

Lazar waved away Pez's question as if it had no relevance. 'Do you have any idea what it takes to renounce one's heritage? Lineage? Realm? Crown?'

'No, Lazar, but that was your decision.'

'That's right. It was also my decision to keep it a secret.'

'You shared it with me.'

Lazar intensified his glare, exasperation flooding through

the fury he was barely controlling. 'I have learned a lesson this night. A secret is no longer a secret once shared.'

'How true!' Pez snapped, his own anger, fuelled by the frustrations of the day, also spilling over. 'Why tell anyone anything if you don't anticipate that you are empowering someone with that knowledge, Lazar? Jumo deserved to know the truth and we had an agreement. I followed it to the letter. You were dead as far as we knew. He was heartbroken – can you imagine how it felt to hear that the man he called his master and friend had died and his body had already been disposed of, and him not much more than a bystander to the suffering?'

'I have some idea,' Lazar replied, trying to sound reasonable but it came out like a growl. 'I'm allowed this anger. I was not privy to this decision to appear dead. It was made for me.'

'And I made another one for you. I told your closest and most loyal friend the truth. No-one deserved it more than Jumo, not even Ana.'

Lazar moved his head back at the mention of her name as though slapped. 'And you will tell her nothing!' he commanded.

'There is always danger in knowledge, Lazar, but be careful your precautions don't drift into cowardice. There's no threat in Jumo ever knowing the truth, no threat in Ana knowing either, and still you keep that knowledge of who you are a secret from your true friends.'

Pez's words were said so kindly it seemed to take the rage away. Lazar's head dropped, his chin almost touching his broad chest. 'When did Jumo leave?'

'The morning after the night of your purported death.'

'I am no coward, Pez. I have kept that secret to protect

those I care about. You were already well protected by your madness and Zar Joreb making you above almost all palace law. But Jumo is in danger.'

'From your family?'

'Possibly, I can't be sure, but now I know where I must go.'

'You're going back to Galinsea?' Pez stated his own shock so baldly that Lazar appeared to flinch. 'You're leaving her?'

When the former Spur turned his gaze on Pez this time there was only grief in his eyes. 'I am no good to her any more. She is a Zar's woman.'

Pez could not bear the disguised self-pity in that statement, nor could he tolerate for a moment longer Lazar's denial of Ana. It was time to tell the whole story. 'She is so much more. Ana masquerades as an odalisque. She was never a goatherd's daughter in anything more than accidental title. Ana is not who you imagine her to be.'

Genuine pain claimed Lazar's expression. Pez was privately stunned. He had known this man since his arrival in Percheron and watched his subsequent rise from prisoner to the city's top security position. This was a man who was so self-contained at the best of times that no-one, including Pez, could successfully second-guess what thoughts were going on behind those intelligent eyes. And Lazar was a master of control, his face rarely revealing his mood. Everyone knew Lazar to be incredibly talented at his job and well liked for his professionalism, fairness to others and loyalty to his Zar. However, they also knew him to be stubborn, difficult, arrogant and serious. To make the Spur of Percheron even break into a smile was something to be treasured and only very few, including Pez, could achieve that. Curiously, the very mention of Ana could shatter the invisible yet seemingly implacable fortress that Lazar had built around himself. Her very name seemed to have a magical quality, as if it were some sort of touchstone that opened the gates of the fortress, allowing the tightly imprisoned emotions to rush out.

Pez understood now. It wasn't the drezden that would be Lazar's weakness in life. It would be Ana. Since he had first laid his love-starved eyes on this young woman, she had become both his salvation and his potential destruction. Only time would tell which.

Lazar bridled at Pez's challenge. 'What do you mean, she is so much more? I know Ana as well as anyone. Better, in fact. I found her. I know who she is.'

'You know nothing, Lazar,' Pez said and watched a shiver pass through his friend as if he were cold. But Pez knew he wasn't trembling from a chill; Lazar was finding the courage to ask his next question and Pez was ready for it.

'Who is she?' the former Spur demanded.

'I believe she is Lyana, the Mother Goddess, incarnated in the flesh.'

A silence stretched between both men. Pez knew Lazar would neither ridicule nor try to counter such a claim, probably because he felt the truth of those words strike like a knife in his heart.

It was a long time before either spoke. Lazar broke the silence. 'How can you be sure?' he said finally. It came out as a choked whisper.

'Who can ever be sure about life, Lazar? But I feel it. I can't deny it any longer. I'm Iridor and she's Lyana.

That's why we're together in the palace. You know the old story, I presume?'

Lazar nodded, still choked. 'But that's all it's been to me. A story. The foundation of my faith, the tale passed down through centuries that was too seductive to ignore. Although the story tells us that Lyana was vanquished by Zarab, a few of us still believe she will rise again and prevail. I certainly felt a kinship when I saw her likeness in Zafira's temple. Galinsea now worships the land and the sea, the sky and its firmament . . .' Lazar shrugged, 'I feel I belong in Percheron where some still cling to the faith of the Goddess.'

'But Nature is what Lyana stands for, of course, so Galinsea is still true to her in its way. Lyana is about the land and the forces that impact on it — sea, sun, desert, storm. She does not put herself above the natural forces of our existence as Zarab does. He claims godliness over everything, power over the land and its forces, its—'

'But she is not real . . . not in the flesh anyway. She is part of a story.' Lazar's final words sounded like a plea.

Pez's passion evaporated as he turned grave. 'The story that founded your original faith is true. But you would also know the cyclical nature of that story — every few centuries, when Lyana feels strong enough she rises again to fight the demon who serves Zarab . . . to claim back her rightful place.'

'Yes, I know the tale. What has that to do with Ana?'

'She is part of the new cycle. I believe Ana is the mortal reincarnation of Lyana for the coming battle.'

'And what if you're wrong?' Lazar demanded. 'What if Ana really is just a young woman trying to survive in the Zar's harem?'

'No newborn, left alone in the desert, survives the much-feared Samazen windstorm, Lazar,' Pez reminded softly. 'No young woman can communicate the force of power that I am sensing unless she is truly enchanted by something of a greater imagination than any of us. Even you would have to be surprised at her knowledge of the Stones of Percheron – she knows every statue and its history . . . tell me how a goatherd's daughter can learn this? What about her ability with language? Perhaps you don't know how talented she is with tongues – why should you, you hardly know her? But it's extraordinary. And her composure, in one so young? Lazar, accept it, Ana is an ancient soul.'

'I won't,' he growled at the dwarf. 'You've given me nothing but conjecture.' Lazar ran both hands through his golden hair in a rare show of anxiety. 'I want facts, Pez. Give me something real that is unequivocal.'

'That's easy, Lazar,' Pez said, mindful of the pain he was inflicting. He wondered fleetingly whether this conversation might set Lazar back in his recovery. Or, he reasoned in the few seconds of silence he gave himself before answering his friend, this might be the catalyst for Lazar. It could galvanise him into action. Pez wasn't sure what that action might be but he'd had a quiet feeling of dread ever since Ana mentioned that this time the battle would be different. It had been gnawing at him that the difference might just be the prince of Galinsea. He couldn't be sure yet but his instincts had rarely let him down, and if it was true, then he needed Lazar strong. 'It is easy,' he repeated. 'Here's an undeniable fact: I can suddenly change at will into a white owl. Lyana's messenger of old has always been a white owl. The owl is called

Iridor. He rises before she does. He is the trigger that the demon senses to begin his grim work for his god. You speak with Iridor regularly; you have witnessed his transformation. You know who I am. You have heard of the black bird of omen?'

'The Raven. I knew him as the bird of sorrows.'

'That's right, he is known as this too. He gathers around her as well.'

'And he's shown himself, I suppose you're going to tell me.'

'Kett is the black bird. He said as much to me.'

Lazar looked as though he had been slapped. 'He named himself this way?'

'To my face he called himself the Raven. Do you still think this is all a coincidence? Or will you believe, as I suspect Ellyana and Zafira do, that Ana is the Goddess? Why else did she run to the statue of Lyana at the temple when she escaped the harem? Admit the facts, as I have had to. Ana is Lyana incarnate . . . even her name suggests as much.'

It was irrefutable. Lazar lifted his chin, his eyes raised to the heavens, and he let loose a groan of such torment it tore at Pez's heart. When the loosing of that emotion was done with, Lazar slumped to the ground, burying his golden-haired head in his knees that he encircled in long arms, and refused to look at Pez, which in itself was tacit acknowledgement of what the dwarf had claimed.

From between his knees Lazar croaked one word. 'Maliz?'

Pez sighed privately, pleased to move on and glad that Lazar knew his history. 'He, too, has . . . become. I know he is searching for me.'

Lazar uncrossed his arms and raised his head to turn

and face his friend. His expression was naked now. The fortress was ruined. Lazar was vulnerable and there was a mixture of fear and alarm spreading across his face. It was frightening to witness. 'You know that for sure?'

The dwarf shrugged mirthlessly. 'I feel it too. He is amongst us at the palace.'

Now the soldier looked horrified. 'That close! Ana's that close to danger?'

'He has no idea of her existence yet,' Pez assured but could see his words had little impact. 'What I mean is, he may have seen Ana but no connection has been made. We still have some time.'

Lazar ground his jaw. 'I can't fully recall all the nuances of the old tale.'

Pez thought it valuable to recount it now. He told it like a story and throughout his telling Lazar remained as still as a statue, absorbing all of the information as though listening to a battle strategy.

When he finished his tale, Pez sighed. 'Ana knows who she is. We talked about it this evening.'

Grief flickered across Lazar's already hurt expression. 'Had she any idea previous to this?'

Pez shook his head. 'I don't believe so. That said, Ana is very perceptive but if she did have any notion, she wasn't letting on. She accepted it more calmly than you have. She knew I spoke the truth . . . as do you.'

'How do I protect her?' Lazar said, standing now. Pez imagined this was the soldier's way of no longer allowing himself to feel helpless. He needed to move in order to feel in control again.

Pez didn't want to destroy what heart his friend had left. He needed him to remain courageous, so he chose the words of his response with care. 'You can't, Lazar. This is a much bigger game we now play. This is no longer palace politicking or even an enemy you can shake a sword at. This is now a battle to the death we enter and we have no control over it. We have no idea from where the fight will come, or in what form. It will be decided entirely by how cleverly we play the game. We are all somehow pieces in a game, as you described, and we need to work out our roles. We cannot protect one another – we must simply trust each other to do our duty as it unfolds and as our duties reveal themselves.'

'I'm involved?' Lazar asked, aghast.

Pez frowned, still unsure, yet somehow certain that he was on the right track. 'You must be. Or why would you be linked with us?'

'Chance, surely.'

'No, no, no,' Pez said, pacing now, warming to his own thoughts. 'Ellyana's interest in you was far too keen for you to be a chance or innocent bystander. She orchestrated the whole situation surrounding your apparent death. It's baffling.'

'She wants the palace to believe me dead, you mean?'

'Yes, except I don't understand why. I don't understand why Ana must be kept in the dark either, especially if she is Lyana.'

'There is only one reason for that kind of secrecy,' Lazar replied, 'and that's protection.'

Pez nodded, knowing he was hearing the truth. 'Who is she protecting Ana from, though, by keeping you secret, unless it's Maliz? But what does Maliz fear from you?'

'Death?'

'You can't kill him, Lazar. You'll need magic to do that

and even though you've all but risen from the dead, I know you possess no enchantments. My Lore skills tell me that much. You are merely mortal, my friend. No, Maliz does not fear you.'

'But Maliz does not know me either, presumably. Perhaps it's the secret of me being alive that is important.'

'Perhaps. I shall think on it further. But I would say this is all the more reason for you to remain in Percheron and that rushing off after Jumo into Galinsea is unwise. You cannot change anything. Whatever has happened, has happened.'

'More of your twisted dwarf logic?' Lazar asked, scowling.

Pez liked it when he scowled. He didn't want to ever see the vulnerable Lazar again. They couldn't afford for what might be their secret weapon to show his weaknesses. He needed Lazar angry, with all of his sarcasm and arrogance – and above all, courage – intact. 'Well, what I mean is that what's done is done. Jumo left almost a year ago to cross the ocean. If he has made it to the Galinsean royal family, then they already know of your death.'

'Pez, you're missing the point. I may have walked away from my crown, and my parents may well have considered me dead for all of these many years. Jumo's revelation will tell them I have been alive serving the Percherese Crown and that same crown has just put me to death. I'll give you one guess what comes next.'

'War,' Pez said in a whisper, horrible understanding dawning now.

Lazar nodded grimly. 'And swiftly. Beloved or not, my family will not sit by and allow the Percherese Zar to slay their son and heir. We know the Zar didn't have much involvement but that's not how they'll view it. Believe me, retribution will be sought. Revenge will be taken. It's a matter of national pride and I would suggest time is short. He left a year ago, near enough . . . two moons to sail, perhaps another moon or more to get an audience.'

'Weeks of arguing,' Pez said grimly.

'They'll need time to assemble their army.'

'And two moons to sail back.'

Lazar looked like a broken man. 'They are upon us within weeks at best calculations.'

'They will send diplomatic messengers, surely?' Pez's tone had a plea in it.

Lazar nodded. 'And if we follow that reasoning, then those people will be entering the city any moment.'

Pez agreed. Lazar's rationale was accurate. 'What can be done? We cannot fight both mortal and godly wars.'

He frowned. 'Against Ellyana's advice I think I must declare myself,' Lazar said, pacing again, and speaking aloud his thoughts. He strode along the cliff edge, thinking fast as he spoke. 'Galinsean invasion is a real threat and that changes everything. It is fortunate I am well enough to travel. I must show myself to Boaz – he must understand what we face now from Galinsea. I shall have to dream up an excuse for my long absence.'

'Stick with the truth of how sick you've been.'

'Yes, but Zafira claimed me dead, given to the seas. I need to counter that.'

'Zafira expects no quarter. Let her take the blame. You can say she said what she did of her own accord. You gave no such approval and you're only now well enough to present yourself. We shall give her warning for escape. I will go to the temple now.'

'Yes, but what reason for her deceit? Boaz is too bright to not ask for that reason.'

'Make one up. It doesn't matter any more. I leave to warn Zafira.'

Lazar nodded.

Pez felt obliged to ask the obvious. 'Ana?'

Now Lazar scowled. 'I can't help her finding out.'

'It will break her heart.'

'You can't have it both ways, Pez. Just moments ago you were arguing her case for knowledge. You can't protect her from the injury of that knowledge.' Pez nodded sadly as Lazar continued. 'More importantly, if Maliz has not recognised his nemesis yet, then I have time and you must see to it that you are not found out. That means I can make the journey to Galinsea the fastest way and prove that I am alive . . . hopefully avert war.'

'The fastest way?'

'Across the desert.'

'In early summer? Are you on a death wish?'

Lazar gave a derisive snort. 'I've stared at death's hungry eyes, Pez. It doesn't scare me.'

'Did it ever?' Pez asked but didn't expect a response; nor did he get one. He carried on his previous line of thought. 'Jumo could be back any day now.'

Lazar shook his head. 'I know Jumo. He has no reason to return to Percheron now. He will likely head north . . . home. I must prepare. I have to be present for when that inevitable war delegation arrives and I suspect that will occur sooner rather than later. Expect me in Percheron in two days. Warn Boaz.'

'I can't.'

'Why not?'

Pez looked anguished. 'We've had a falling out.' He briefly explained what had happened.

Lazar scratched his head. 'Then I shall be the gift you bring back to him to appease his anger. Boaz will listen to me.'

'You can't be sure that he will listen. He takes new counsel these days.'

Lazar understood. 'You mentioned once that Tariq had ingratiated himself.'

'Oh, it's much worse, Lazar. Grand Vizier Tariq now all but controls the Zar's waking thoughts – that's how it feels to me anyway.'

'You're overreacting, Pez. Like a jealous woman.' Lazar found a grin, much to the surprise of them both.

'I wish I was. Tariq is dangerous.'

'Tariq is a sop. I've known that man—'

'You don't know this one,' Pez cut across his friend. He gave a frown of pain. 'Tariq has changed, Lazar. He is so different you would hardly recognise him now.'

'No man changes that much.'

'This one has. It's remarkable. He even looks different. He certainly sounds different – not in his voice but how he voices his thoughts. They're intelligent, inspired, clever. There's new cunning in those eyes now, Lazar, that has nothing to do with the stupid self-importance and social climbing that the Tariq of old was known for. This Tariq is totally self-possessed. He requires no-one's sanction . . . nor does he look for it.'

Lazar shook his head with wonder. 'I can't imagine you're speaking about the same man.'

The dwarf threw up his hands in disgust. 'It is as though someone has possessed Tariq,' Pez claimed angrily and then at those words it felt as if his blood had turned to ice.

Lazar was feeling similar. Pez could see it reflected in his friend's ashen face, too mortified to speak as the truth of Pez's words sank in.

'Is it possible?' Lazar finally whispered, disbelief in his eyes.

Pez could hardly answer for the initial rush of fear and then the onslaught of a fury he had never felt in himself before. He covered his eyes with his deformed hands, as if to cover himself from the vision of Maliz smiling from behind the dark eyes of Tariq. 'Of course it's possible,' he croaked. 'More than possible. That's precisely what's occurred,' he said, fighting down the loathing so he could think clearly. 'Iridor rose. So did Maliz. And he chose Tariq as his vessel. It's so obvious now I can't believe I missed it.'

'How does that explain the miraculous changes in the Vizier?'

'Maliz the warlock was as vain as the summer day is long. He is using his magic to improve the body in which he is imprisoned now until his next death.'

'His destruction, you mean,' Lazar said and there was something cruel and hard in his tone.

It made Pez stare at his friend. 'I'll warn you again and you must pay this the attention it deserves, Lazar. Maliz cannot be killed by conventional means. You have to trust me on this. I can see where your thoughts are running to and if you think you can protect Ana by somehow trying to kill Tariq, then you are tragically mistaken. All you will do is declare yourself to the demon.'

'Then *what*?' Lazar demanded, frustrated and clearly shocked by the fear in the dwarf's voice.

'We move far more carefully. I think it's a good idea you return to the palace now. Yes, come back, Lazar, and let's see how the Vizier reacts to you. It will reveal much if he shows little interest other than the normal fascination we might expect for someone returning from apparent death. But if Maliz recognises something in you, we will know that, too, from his reaction. Are you prepared to risk it?'

'Risk it? I want his death, Pez. Of course I'll risk it. Somehow let Boaz know you have a special surprise being delivered. Heed my words. Two days. I'll be back in the city.'

It was already late and Pez decided to tell Zafira the new developments at daybreak. She could do nothing right now except spend a few sleepless hours before sunrise.

But he had one more errand to run this night. He alighted on one of the minarets that framed the palace as the first tentative lightening of dawn threatened.

Anyone looking up would have seen a large bird dropping silently through the air and disappearing beneath the rooftops.

The man waiting for him saw only the familiar shape of the dwarf, dangling awkwardly before clambering uneasily onto a balcony.

'Are we safe?' Pez whispered.

The man nodded.

'Anything?'

The man shook his head. 'Nothing out of the ordinary, I gather.'

'Tariq?'

'I have not seen him since the Zar retired and that was early.'

'Did the Zar say anything about me?'

'He asked his secretary where you were but the servant said he didn't know. The Zar said no more. He sent a note to the harem.'

'And?'

'He dictated that he was bringing the boating trip forward. He asked Salmeo to make preparations. They include you.'

'I see.' Pez didn't know if this was important or not but he liked having the information. 'Very good, Razeen. Be careful.'

'You must not worry about me.'

Pez nodded unhappily. The sense of confidence shown by Razeen terrified him. 'Focus on the Grand Vizier. I want everything you can tell me about him.'

'That will be easy.'

Pez found an uneasy yet soft smile for the person before him. 'Take no unnecessary risk.'

'I know, I understand. I will not threaten our task by stupidity – you can count on me.'

'I know, Razeen. Just absorb whatever you can but don't endanger yourself any more than you already have by being here.'

'I must go,' he replied. 'I might be missed.'

Pez nodded again. 'Lyana watch over you.'

The man, whose dangerous mission was to spy on the Zar, grinned in the cocksure way possessed by those with the sense of invincibility that only youth can provide. Pez felt the fragility of such delusion and shivered again, recalling Zafira's warning that this young man's life could be taken cruelly if any one of the palace sycophants suspected guile.

Pez promised himself to take even more precautions with these meetings as he watched Razeen step through the doors, which he knew led back into the suite of chambers that belonged to the Zar.

❧ 9 ❧

It was no good. Despite her best efforts, Ana could not contain the general excitement within the harem. And she could not blame a single one of her companions, for she, too, had felt her heart swell at the news this morning that their boat picnic had been brought forward – they were going out today.

For almost two weeks they had been trapped inside doing tedious needlework and tirelessly rehearsing court etiquette – how to behave when being addressed by the Valide, how to behave in front of the Zar, his guests, visiting dignitaries. There were endless lessons and although most of the young women took to these studies with enthusiasm – for they were keen to succeed in the harem – the bright days outside only served to make Ana feel listless and downright objectionable at times. It felt like punishment on these sparkling mornings to be cooped up inside. Even her pleasure at language studies had been sorely tested.

When Ana awoke this morning she didn't think she could bear another day like the previous one of stifling boredom, and even though some good sense prevailed and discouraged her from doing anything unwise, Ana couldn't help her mind wandering off to daydreams of how to escape this life. Physical freedom called to her softly like the breeze off the Faranel, but emotional freedom . . . perhaps that could never be attained, even in her daydreams. The pain of losing Lazar was her closest companion, a dull, soft ache; one she knew she would have to learn to live alongside for as long as she breathed.

The Valide's threat that the Zar would choose Ana in the near future had rattled her as well. She wasn't naive; she understood her role in the harem and she would have to have the brain of a bird to not realise that Boaz was already showing a hunger for her. She just didn't think it would happen so soon.

Thinking about the brains of a bird made her recall the chilling conversation with Pez from the previous night. Fear wasn't what she was feeling as a result, though. The morning had certainly brought trepidation as she replayed in her mind Pez's careful discussion and how he had somehow made her speak the knowledge that she found lying deep within her. But no, the realisation did not frighten her – if anything it made her feel empowered, as if suddenly everything around her felt trite and point-less. That wasn't a hard leap for Ana, for she had never wanted to be part of this life, but it had given her Spur Lazar and for that she felt a modicum of gratitude. If the old Zar had not died, if the palace had not needed to assemble a new harem, if Herezah had not wanted to punish Lazar by sending him on his girl-hunting task that he found so distasteful, if the step-mother had not been so ready to sell her into slavery and rid herself of the orphaned child she detested, then she might never have known such love in her life as she felt for the Spur.

They had taken him from her but they would never

be able to take away her feelings for him or her brief but vivid memory of touching him, looking into those eyes of his and recognising the sorrow deep within, sensing his secrets and, yes, his startled desire for her. She had seen it all and understood how he struggled against the tide of his emotions, knowing how wrong it would be. There was nothing wrong in loving one another; their love was pure and would always remain that way, for it had never moved beyond the unspoken pain of forbidden yearning.

So certainly no fear this morning. A sense of danger, perhaps even a feeling of recklessness now that she knew they were finally breaking out of the harem and could have a day of freedom on the water.

The subsequent squeals of anticipation and unrestrained joy from the general harem population at the news even brought a smile to the thick lips of Grand Master Eunuch Salmeo.

'We do our best,' he said to Ana, his tongue darting out to moisten those fat lips of his.

She had apologised several times for the girls' lack of composure, struggling to contain her own pleasure.

His huge hand waved away another of her softly spoken requests for forgiveness. 'They are still children, Ana, I understand.'

She knew this to be a lie – Salmeo would never understand childhood needs – but schooled her expression to remain contrite. 'I promised the Valide that I would assist, Grand Master Eunuch,' she tried to explain but again he stopped her.

He smiled indulgently, confusing Ana. 'Fret not. The Valide places much faith in you, Odalisque Ana, and I'm sure your skills in leadership will be a great help in preparing the girls for this outing.' He paused momentarily. The smell of violets had assaulted her as he spoke and, combined with Salmeo's cloying sweetness, it set her nerves jangling. The Grand Master Eunuch continued. 'Which is why it is a little sad that you cannot join the rest of the harem on this trip.'

Ana thought she had heard wrong. She stared at him, frowning in confusion.

'Oh dear,' and he sighed softly, 'perhaps the Valide has not already mentioned this, but she requires your company today and has asked that you remain, that you do not go out on the water.' He gave a *moue* of sympathy. 'She should be here any moment and will no doubt explain.'

'Remain behind?' Ana asked, unable to hide her distress. 'But I've been looking forward to this outing as much as the others,' she gabbled, and was going to say more but with force of willpower stopped herself.

'I appreciate the timing is not ideal,' Salmeo replied, his light voice all the more irritating for its contrived tone of sorrow on her behalf, 'but I am led to believe that you and the Valide have a special understanding. Is this right?' Ana stared at him baffled so Salmeo filled the awkward silence. 'Apparently you are to assist the Valide in all her needs. You've agreed to be reliable and trustworthy . . . no rebelliousness.'

Ana shook her head, clearing the cobwebs of disbelief that this could be happening. 'I have agreed to that but—'

'Ah,' he interrupted and smiled as if all was confirmed then.

'But I never—'

'Hush, Ana. No rebellion, remember?' Salmeo said

lightly and giggled behind the chubby, bejewelled finger he held to his lips to silence her.

Anger took over but short of scratching his enormous face with frustration, Ana steeled herself to remain composed. 'As the Valide chooses,' she managed to grind out politely, even bowing with some semblance of courtesy, but as she straightened she could see in the eunuch's eyes his delight at spoiling her day. They had planned this then. This was deliberately done to build her hopes and then dash them. She began to wonder whether Boaz was in on the plot to destroy her best intentions to behave. She didn't think so but she also couldn't understand why the Valide would provoke her. When they had met, Herezah had appeared – to all intents – to be making a huge effort for the two of them to be more companionable.

Ana's perceptiveness had told her that Herezah had long ago worked out that in order to remain close to her son she would also need to approve of his women, especially his wives. While she had chosen all the girls herself, it was up to Boaz to select which of them would fill the premium positions.

She and the Valide had got off to a very poor start, Ana understood that. Her escape had humiliated the harem but Ana was sharp enough to work out that Herezah's cares were not really centred on the harem. The harem was her seat of power, the realm over which she presided with her fat partner in cunning, but it was not where her heart was. Her heart was with power and ensuring her ties with the Zar were never fractured. Ana's desires were with neither. They were all clearly given over to a helpless love for the former Spur. And Ana took some silent pleasure now in the thought that Lazar had desired her in return – a goatherd's daughter – over the elegant, sophisticated and undeniably beautiful Valide. Was this Herezah exacting her revenge at Lazar's support for a slave girl? Ana wondered. Or was this all about preventing Boaz from spending time with the odalisque he seemed to be favouring?

The Valide swept into the room, gorgeously attired in tightly bound dark silks today. She was certainly not going on any boat outing judging by such sumptuous attire. Ana's heart sank – it was definitely true then. She watched the Valide glide effortlessly towards her, not even glancing at Salmeo, who was giving orders to his small army of eunuchs as they prepared to escort the troupe of young women into the world outside.

Ana bowed as graciously as she could. 'Valide,' was all she would trust herself to say.

'I see there's an air of hysteria in the harem this morning.'

Ana nodded. She would have to continue the charade. 'The girls have just found out that the Zar's boating trip is taking place today. They've been looking forward to this since joining the harem.'

'I don't doubt it,' Herezah answered in her smoky voice. 'And you, Ana, you don't echo their joy.' Her smile was bright.

'Not since hearing that I will not be joining them on this outing, Valide. I understand that you need my services.'

'I do.'

Ana nodded. She dared not say more as she was busy fighting back the tears that the Valide and her chief eunuch had some keen ability to win from her.

'Why so sad, Ana? Does a day with me sound so disappointing?'

'Forgive me, Valide,' Ana replied, bobbing a small curtsey. 'I allowed myself to anticipate a day out on the water. I am struggling a little, I'll admit, to resign myself to the idea that I will not be enjoying this freedom.'

'Ah, freedom,' Herezah echoed. 'A powerful notion, eh?' Ana nodded, desperately trying to hide the misery. 'But what makes you think that freedom has been denied?'

Ana watched the now fully veiled girls being herded out of the chamber where they had gathered. She could see beyond to where Salmeo's army had trunks of provisions to take with them, no doubt from fresh clothes to drying linens if the girls decided to swim. And from the kitchens Ana could imagine another army was steadily marching with an endless array of baskets carrying sumptuous food worthy of the Zar's special picnic for his women.

She sighed. 'I imagine you have some work for me to do, Valide,' she replied.

Herezah's eyebrow lifted in sardonic style as she appraised this wilful young woman. 'If you call a shopping expedition into the city work, then so be it,' the Valide said in return.

Ana couldn't help her display of surprise. One hand covered her mouth to stop the shriek before it was loosed.

Herezah smiled. 'I can't imagine what Salmeo led you to believe, my girl, but we are not working on a fine day like this. I promised you an escorted trip into the city, did I not?'

Ana nodded dumbly.

'Well, hurry up and get ready.'

'We're going together?'

'Who else did you think would have the right taste and experience to choose fabrics and jewellery for a Zar's wife?' Herezah commented archly. Then laughed at Ana's still disbelieving expression.

'I shall give you until the next bell or I leave without you. Fully veiled, remember.'

'I'll be ready in moments,' Ana said to the Valide and wanted to hug herself. Perhaps it would be a day of freedom after all, and with the reckless mood this had rekindled in her, who knew what could happen?

Boaz was not sharing the same pleasure. He had welcomed the girls of his harem theatrically and with a certain dashing charm that had them giggling beneath their veils but, although it was hard to pick who each might be when they were attired in this manner, his first hungry stare had not picked her out.

He watched them now excitedly clambering aboard the royal barges that had not felt the water for years, according to the Vizier.

'Are you sure you won't be coming with us today, Grand Vizier?' he offered again, not really interested but needing something to say as he searched for Ana.

'No, my Zar. There is plenty of dull paperwork for me to plough through and as boring as it is in comparison to a day out on the river in your fine company and amongst these bright young things, I do think I must remain dutiful.'

'Your self-sacrifice is impressive, Tariq,' Boaz quipped.

His high-ranking servant grinned back and shrugged. 'I shall take much pleasure in hearing about it tonight.'

'You will take supper with me, Tariq.'

'Very good, Highness. An opportune time to run through some important items. I shall take my leave, my Zar, and wish you a wonderfully uplifting day enjoying the natural wonders of Percheron.' His dark gaze slid over the boats filled with young women and both of them knew he wasn't referring to the river or the scenery.

Boaz nodded and then shook his head ruefully. Tariq had now taken to making clever jests, smacking of a wit that the Zar had never once witnessed in the Vizier during his time as heir. Tariq had always seemed so self-obsessed and sexless that it had not once occurred to Boaz to imagine the Vizier was interested in women, and yet Boaz had regularly seen the appreciation in a new roving glance that the Grand Vizier paid the female servants in the palace.

He beckoned to Salmeo, who lightly hurried towards his Zar. 'Majesty?'

'Where is Pez?'

Salmeo looked at him blankly. 'I have not seen him, my Zar.'

'I specifically asked Bin to ensure he was here today to entertain the girls.'

The Vizier seemed to overhear this conversation and stepped back close to the Zar. 'If I may, Majesty?' Salmeo scowled but Boaz nodded. 'Bin did mention that he hadn't been able to locate the dwarf.'

'I see. So he will not be with us today.'

Both his senior servants remained silent.

'This is not good enough! The Zar's clown, who enjoys significant indulgence, should at least be present when the Zar wants him.'

'I couldn't agree more, my Zar,' Salmeo replied, privately

revelling in such a public rebuke for the despised buffoon. He never thought he'd see the day when the Zar criticised Pez.

Tariq nodded. 'Highness. Let me see if we can find him now. You will still be a little while loading the boats. May I try for you?'

Salmeo's scowl darkened. Both of them knew who had impressed the Zar the most with this exchange. He tried to ingratiate himself. 'Zar Boaz, perhaps if the Vizier cannot locate your jester, I can have him hunted down in your absence?'

'He's not an animal, Grand Master Eunuch. You make it sound as if you'd enjoy the chase. Would you beat him with a stick when you catch him?'

Salmeo sensibly remained quiet although it was obvious he seethed at the amusement sparking in the Vizier's eyes at the Zar's comment.

Boaz turned back to his Vizier. 'Thank you, Tariq. If you can locate him easily, then I think the young ladies would benefit from his sense of fun today.'

'And if not, my Zar?'

'Inform him of my displeasure,' came the curt reply.

The Grand Vizier bowed and took his leave. Salmeo remained, his bulk overwhelming the trim figure of the Zar. 'I did not mean any insult, Highness,' Salmeo said humbly.

Boaz turned to stare up into the eunuch's hooded gaze, buried deeply amongst the folds of flesh. The man never failed to revolt him. 'You have never found Pez amusing.'

'But I know you do, Highness, and your father before you. I would not let anything bad happen to someone so important to our Crown.'

Boaz smelled the violets on the man's breath and was again reminded of his slippery ways. His mother had warned him often enough and he knew Salmeo was saying what he imagined the Zar wanted to hear. This didn't stop him feeling a sense of anger drop like stone within him at the eunuch's honeyed words, at odds with how he was feeling about Pez right now.

'The dwarf is not my favourite person just at present, Salmeo. It is true he has displeased me but please don't imagine that gives anyone the right to treat Pez in any way other than has always been demanded in this palace. That said, you would all do well to know that I will not tolerate any form of insubordination, not even from him.'

Salmeo blinked slowly, his tongue flicking out to lick his lips. He looked like a reptile when he went through this ritual. 'Of course, Highness. I will remember this. Are you sure there is nothing I can do to help with the dwarf?'

'Just find him,' Boaz ordered, frustrated further now that he'd revealed to this cunning man his displeasure at Pez. He had not intended to but not sighting Ana and the disappointment of his run-in with Pez was ensuring he was feeling hollow on a day that was meant to be all about fun. New feelings were coursing through him as well. It's not that he didn't understand them – he accepted that he was maturing and new urges were shaping – but he felt as though he was no longer in control of his moods. The smallest things seemed to darken his humour. He needed Pez to talk to and now had banished him in anger for the dwarf's seeming secretiveness . . . and jealousy of Tariq, of all people. Boaz smirked inwardly at the irony – how odd that the Vizier seemed to suddenly be his closest companion and most useful servant. He noticed Salmeo was still regarding him intently and pulled himself sharply from his thoughts. 'Where is Odalisque Ana, by the way?' he demanded, hoping to throw the eunuch off the scent of his falling out with the dwarf.

He watched the eunuch's expression rearrange itself from intrigue to a carefully contrived impression of sympathy. 'Odalisque Ana will not be joining us today, Highness.'

Even though discontent was knifing through him at not spotting her easily, it had not yet occurred that she wouldn't be present. The shock of the news showed how it wounded by his crestfallen face. Where Ana was concerned it seemed Boaz could not hide his feelings as easily as he did about everyone else. 'Why ever not? Is she unwell?'

'She is in fine health, Majesty.'

'Then where is she?' His tone was indignant now.

'She is with the Valide today, Highness.'

Boaz frowned, totally confused. 'My mother? What is this about, Salmeo?'

The huge man shrugged but kept it courteous. 'She did not share this with me, Your Highness,' he lied. 'I was simply told that the Valide wished Odalisque Ana to accompany her today on a trip into the city.'

'To do what?'

'I don't know, Majesty. Womanly things, presumably.' Now Salmeo smiled, showing the gap between his teeth. 'The Valide is looking for new fabrics and she prefers to choose them herself. I imagine she sees taking Ana along with her as a special honour to confer on an odalisque.'

Boaz thought differently but this time he resisted sharing what was on his mind. 'Are they still in the palace?'

'Sadly, not,' Salmeo lied again. 'They left early.'

A new swell of fury was driving Boaz now and he voiced a snap decision he wasn't sure he wanted to make just at this time. But his thinking was clouded by the sense that he was being manipulated. This would put everyone back on notice about who was in charge in the palace. 'I see. Have Odalisque Ana fully prepared for me this evening.'

The word 'prepared' had special meaning to the keeper of the harem and its effect was immediate and dramatic. 'Prepared, Highness? Do I understand you correctly?' Salmeo blustered, clearly caught off guard.

Fortunately one of the new mutes, Salazin, rescued him by arriving and bowing low before the Zar.

When the man was at eye level, Boaz fixed an angry enquiry on his face, irritated hugely to be interrupted.

One of the Elim spoke up. 'He needs to run back to your chambers, Majesty. We have forgotten—'

'Yes, yes, don't trouble me with these trivialities!' Boaz admonished. The Elim and the mute retreated, Salazin running at full speed to retrieve whatever had been left behind.

'Apologies,' Salmeo said, 'I believe the Grand Vizier has instructed the mutes never to leave your side without royal sanction.'

More irritation flickered in the Zar's darkening eyes. He ignored the man's explanation and returned to their original conversation. 'You asked whether you understand me. We both speak Percherese perfectly well, Grand Master Eunuch. I think my plain wording should make it precisely clear for you. Tell me what you understand by my order,' he demanded, deliberately keeping his voice low but the threat was still there.

Salmeo actually took a step back. Boaz liked that he'd shocked the fat eunuch.

'My understanding, Highness, is that you wish Odalisque Ana to be readied for bedding by her Zar. That you choose to claim her virginity this night.'

The Zar beamed, not prepared to show even a slight clue of how much that statement petrified him. 'Good, I'm glad I made myself perfectly plain,' Boaz replied as condescendingly as one could when staring up at someone. 'Don't make any excuses for disappointing my wishes, this time, Grand Master Eunuch. I shall expect to see her.' He added as a vicious parting shot: 'After my supper, which I'm taking with the Grand Vizier.'

He turned and stalked away to the boats, leaving the keeper of the harem to think on his Zar's unspoken threat.

☙ 10 ❧

Salmeo knew he had to catch the Valide before she left the palace for her private outing with the odalisque. It appeared as though their crafty plan was to be outwitted by the Zar and his helpless infatuation for the girl Ana. Herezah needed to learn of this sudden and unexpected turn in events. He found her draping herself with the dark veil that would cover her tight silks from head to toe for her excursion.

She looked at him, surprised. 'I permitted you only because my servants said you were breathless. So presumably this is important?' she sneered at him.

'Highly,' he said, sucking in air.

'Zarab save us! That run has cost you, eunuch. More than important then . . . dangerous even?'

'Very,' he managed to say in between bending over slightly to help himself breathe.

'Well, get on with it, Salmeo. I'm about to depart the palace. The karaks have arrived and I don't want to linger long enough for the sun to warm them too much.'

'Valide,' he began, wondering how best to deliver this news. She regarded him, her irritation evident in her glower as she fought to remain still long enough to hear whatever this news was. 'It's about Odalisque Ana.'

'What of her?' she demanded, irritated.

'The Zar has chosen her. Just now,' he said, not sure how to read the mask that was her expression.

Silence seemed to have engulfed Herezah and he watched her complexion blanch as she struggled to absorb his words.

He decided it was easier for him to fill the dread silence. He couldn't even enjoy her shock because Ana being chosen had implications for him as much as the Valide. 'I have just been ordered by the Zar to prepare her for tonight.'

'Already? Are you absolutely sure?' she croaked, her full attention given to him now.

He nodded grimly. 'There is no mistake. Your son made it embarrassingly clear what he intends for the girl. We are too late, Valide.'

'Nonsense!' Herezah admonished, rapidly gathering up her wits and regaining her composure. 'We just have to put our plan into action faster.'

'It's impossible,' Salmeo said, shaking his head in surprise. 'The Zar means this night.'

'And she will be gone by tonight!' Herezah snarled at him in a low, angry voice. 'See to it. Make all the preparations that we've discussed. The girls will return tired but happy, presumably – we might as well keep that mood going with a little surprise of our own. Not only Boaz can offer them treats.'

Salmeo looked thoughtful now. 'Perhaps it can be achieved,' he said, nodding, thinking it through.

'It will be, Grand Master Eunuch. Make it happen. I am going out now with Ana. We will not be long. Her taste of freedom will be brief and I'm sure will put her into the right frame of mind . . . especially after I allude to what's in store for her sooner than she could have ever imagined.'

The slyness of Salmeo's grin spread across his face until it danced in his dark eyes. 'Clever, my Valide. Oh, and I have more news that will please.'

'Oh yes?'

'The dwarf has done something to displease your son. In fact he is so deep into his displeasure that I did not have to find this out by clandestine means. Zar Boaz actually admitted it to me in a state of high temper.'

She had suspected as much from Boaz's behaviour but couldn't imagine he would admit it to Salmeo. 'You jest.'

The huge black man shook his head. 'Told me himself that the dwarf had displeased and that he would not tolerate such insubordination from his servants. He tried to steer it into more general terms but he was clearly referring to Pez.'

'Was Pez present?' she asked enthusiastically, hungry for the details.

'He's gone missing,' Salmeo replied, fuelling her hunger more. 'But no-one knows where or why.'

Herezah clapped her hands. 'Excellent,' she purred. 'This could be a special day for us. Where is the Vizier?'

'He is remaining at the palace, says he is very busy with work.'

Herezah made a disparaging sound at this. 'Busy spying perhaps. I will go now and you will put into action all that is necessary. Keep an eye on the Vizier; I'm interested to know what he does when he is not answerable to the Zar.'

Salmeo nodded that it would be done. 'Enjoy your shopping expedition.'

She smiled cruelly. 'You know I will.'

Ana was veiled, flanked by two Elim and patiently awaiting her high-ranking companion for the day. She smiled from beneath the veil at Herezah when she appeared, also escorted by her own Elim and trailed by the Grand Master Eunuch. Ana hoped the Valide would see the smile touch her eyes so that Herezah would know how much this meant to her.

She bowed. 'Valide,' then turned to the eunuch, 'Grand Master Salmeo.'

'Valide, I shall see to your instructions,' Salmeo said, bowing to Herezah. 'Enjoy your morning, sisters,' he added as he straightened. He gave some whispered orders to his senior Elim and watched the women as they were guided out of the shadows of the cool palace's interior and into the sharp sunlight of the day.

Ana squinted. 'This is very exciting for me, Valide,' she gushed helplessly, allowing one of the Elim to assist her into a karak.

Herezah was being given similar assistance into her karak. 'I hope you have a wonderful time, Ana. This freedom is my gift to you,' she said, smirking beneath her veil.

Herezah gave the signal and the bearers lifted the two karaks and easily bore them down the palace pathways towards the main gates. Ana had been told it took some time to clear the palace grounds; she remembered how long it took just to get to the main gate on that terrible day a year ago when she had had to witness her Uncle

Horz being impaled. He died so bravely. She hoped she could show the same courage with all that was ahead. But right now all she could think about was a day's freedom; she settled back and savoured the reckless sense of being on a grand adventure.

In her own karak, Herezah plotted precisely what she was going to say to her naive companion that would provoke her into making the biggest mistake of her short life.

Pez arrived back at his small chamber to find a note. He recognised instantly that it was from Razeen and its hastily scribbled scrawl clearly reflected the urgency of the contents.

Pez gathered he was in further trouble with the Zar. Apparently he hadn't presented himself for the boating trip, and cursed himself for it – he'd forgotten in his rush to warn Zafira. Razeen had told him he was to be included during their recent clandestine meeting and although he gathered it had been brought forward, no-one had told him it was leaving this morning. He shook away his irritation. There was nothing to be done until the Zar returned and summoned him. More frightening was the news that Boaz had chosen Ana and instructed the Grand Master Eunuch to prepare her for tonight.

Unsure of what to do but knowing he had to do something, Pez changed into more formal dress for the court and waddled out of his room, only to be assailed by two massive Elim.

He began to dance and gabbled a stream of gibberish. They guided him, gently but equally firmly, beyond the halls of the harem and into the palace proper.

'Where go we?' he sang.

This made sense so one answered. 'Pez, we have orders to bring you to the Grand Vizier.'

Pez felt as though his throat was being clamped and he knew it was fear.

'Vizier, Vizier,' he sang, thinking fast.

'The Zar asked him to find you,' the other Elim said, knowing it was hopeless but trying to get some sense into the dwarf.

The Elim found Pez strange, irritating at times, but also held him in high affection. The loyalty of their two Zars to this curious individual meant plenty to the Elim who held loyalty as the single most important quality in anyone. And so they were loyal to Pez, no matter how much he frustrated them on occasion.

'I don't want to see a snake,' Pez whinged, childlike.

'But you must,' the first said softly, smiling. Pez's madness was making odd sense. 'It is what Zar Boaz wishes,' he added, hoping that would soothe the dwarf.

It had the opposite effect. Pez was disturbed that Boaz might have given the Vizier permission to do more than simply find the court jester — perhaps police him, or even punish him? Of course Boaz could not know who lurked beneath that surface. It was a terrifying prospect that he would have to face this man, knowing now who he truly was.

He took the last remaining moments he had, no longer struggling, but bringing all of his Lore skills to the fore. He forced all that was Iridor deep within himself. It must be hidden from Maliz, buried so far away that the demon could not find it even if he looked for magic. He wondered if Maliz already suspected him to be Iridor and he knew he would be lying to himself if he didn't accept that Maliz was not just suspicious but now searching for evidence. He prayed to Lyana to guide him in this confrontation.

Make my madness my armour, oh Mother. Encase me in your love, protect me from evil, let my Lore confuse him and keep me safe, he whispered, his lips barely moving.

He would need to give his best performance and somehow throw the Vizier off his scent.

There was still so much to achieve before Maliz killed him.

Ana sighed with a sense of restless wonder as the karak moved beyond the Moon Courtyard and through the palace gates. With the Stone Palace perched on a hill, she knew she must hold on for safety now as the Elim adjusted their grip and began the descent. The sense of freedom was so tangible she was sure the air smelled sweeter, the colours were brighter, and all the darkness that lived within dissipated to leave her lighthearted. She burst out laughing and then she wept. Her emotions were clashing into one another and Ana really didn't know how to feel other than elated, and yet she felt teary. She considered her situation and knew that her tears were because she understood this was only temporary, and that sadness made the joy of being out amongst the people even more poignant.

The karak was no longer travelling at an angle; the road had begun to straighten out and Ana risked a peep through the curtains and wrapped her arms around herself with pleasure to see a mass of people going about their mid-morning business.

Women chatted to each other, children clasped tightly

on their hips or holding their hands. Men rolled carts laden with goods and she even spotted a few of the soldiers mingling with the general population. They reminded her of Lazar and a fresh gust of grief swept through her mind. It was always there, always ready to poison her day, but she must not let Lazar's shadow fall too fully across this day. This was one day she was keeping as shiny and free from darkness as she could, no matter how hard returning to the palace would be.

Voices intensified and Ana again peeped between the silks to see that they were entering narrow streets and she knew this led down to the bazaar. She heard the Elim giving orders, clearing the crowd from around the karaks, and she imagined the fascinated stares of people, curious to know who from the palace had come into their midst.

Suddenly Herezah was leaning into Ana's karak. 'Come, Ana,' she said conversationally, and then the Elim were helping Ana to alight. She noticed more servants from the palace had trailed them – Elim – and they would remain with the transport until the women returned.

Flanked once again by her red-robed guards, but this time her arm encircled affectionately by Herezah's, Ana stepped into the slow-moving stream of people and felt the lightness that had imbued her heart instantly turn to a weightlessness. She felt as though her sandals were no longer touching the ground.

'I can hardly breathe for excitement,' she whispered to her companion. 'It's been so long since I was amongst real people.'

Herezah gurgled with seductive laughter. She didn't seem to take offence at Ana's innocent jibe. 'It always feels like that the first time,' she replied. 'Enjoy yourself. I cannot promise when we might do this again so make the very best of the short time we have.'

'Oh, I will, Valide . . . and thank you. Thank you for spoiling me. I'm not sure I deserve your faith.'

'I trust you, Ana,' Herezah soothed. 'Just don't get too seduced by freedom,' she cautioned and laughed again as they were swallowed up into the first dome of the great bazaar.

'Ah, Pez,' the Grand Vizier said, smiling, but Pez noted not even a tiny flicker of warmth touched those cold, dark eyes.

'I was promised flowers,' he stated angrily.

'Oh, and you shall have them, Pez,' the Vizier said, the smile not faltering.

'And cherry juice.'

'Of course.'

Pez burped and shook himself free from the hold of the Elim.

'You may leave us,' Maliz said to the men in red. Both hesitated. 'Fret not, I shall not harm him.'

They had not forgotten Tariq's behaviour at the flogging of Spur Lazar, when he had dared to kick at the dwarf who had, to all intents, accidentally rolled across the foot of the Vizier during one of his usual acrobatic manoeuvres. But the Elim offered Pez absolute protection by royal proclamation and they took this task very seriously. One bowed and stepped forward. 'Grand Vizier, we are never permitted to leave the dwarf unattended in the palace in the company of someone outside of the harem.'

'Is that so?' Maliz replied, remembering now the frustration that Tariq experienced over the detestable dwarf.

He had made an error, for the Vizier would know the palace etiquette, and so he deliberately pulled Tariq's mouth into a sneer to let the Elim know he was being sarcastic. It made no difference. They were always grave in their duty, and either missed the nuance or treated it with disdain.

The man nodded solemnly. 'He has the full protection of the harem and the Zar, as you know. Forgive us, but we are not allowed to let him out of our sight.'

Pez began to sing, covering the smile he felt tugging at his mouth. Perhaps he would be safe. He wanted to kiss the Elim for being so rigid in adhering to their rules.

'But he comes and goes as he chooses – or so I understand,' Maliz replied, working to hide his irritation, Pez noted.

The man nodded again. 'This is true, Grand Vizier. Pez is permitted complete freedom within the harem. Beyond its boundaries he is always escorted – as is anyone from the harem.'

'I'm assured the Zar's clown travels way beyond the boundaries of the palace and into the city!' Maliz grumbled, no longer able to disguise his discontent.

Now the man shrugged. 'He is disobedient,' was the only reply he gave, much to the Grand Vizier's irritation.

Pez began to dance, singing loudly at the top of his voice. It was his intention to frustrate the Grand Vizier as fast as possible.

'Can you quieten him?' Tariq asked of the guards over the racket.

The Elim leant forward and touched Pez gently on the shoulder. He didn't fall silent but he stopped dancing and murmured softly to himself, picking his nose and wiping whatever he could find in it on the furniture. He stole a glance at the Grand Vizier and took pride in the disgust he now saw in the man's expression. He farted for good measure just as the official opened his mouth to speak. It closed again.

'Is this the best we can do with him?' Maliz enquired of the Elim.

The more senior one gave a soft shrug of helplessness. 'He is contrary, Grand Vizier. No-one controls him.'

'Pez.' Maliz finally addressed him directly.

Pez stopped all activity and gave the man a beatific smile.

'Good. The Zar is very unhappy with you, Pez.'

Pez gave a sulky look and then bent down to grab the turned-up toes of his ridiculous court shoes. Both Zars loved them for their comical effect and had many pairs made up in various fabrics. They were deliberately too large for his feet and Pez had even attached bells to this pair for added humour. He shook them now.

'Look at me, please.'

He did so and felt the first tentative grope of magic pull at the protective shield of the Lore and saw recognition burn in the formerly dead-looking eyes of the Vizier. He had anticipated as much. But finding a shield meant nothing. It could be interpreted many ways. His insanity could be seen as that shield and he used his disguise to full effect now, screaming and screaming straight into the man's horrified stare.

Pez's screams were legendary and to be avoided at all cost. The Elim grabbed for him and covered his mouth. He continued to struggle despite their strength as it disguised the shudder he felt at the insistent probing.

Suddenly he stopped and became peaceful and then he began to count – in Derranese – backwards and loudly, each number interspersed by spitting gobs of whatever he could muster directly at the Grand Vizier's beautifully crafted darkwood table. He hadn't been in the Vizier's chambers before but Lazar had told him how vulgar and ostentatious the whole set-up was under Tariq. Well, there was no sign of Tariq here, Pez thought, spitting forcefully at the exquisite table, just one of several simple, priceless and supremely elegant pieces that sparsely furnished the huge chamber.

'Stop that!' Maliz yelled and Pez now sensed that the probing magic's link had been broken. He silently sighed his relief as he continued to count and spit.

'Grand Vizier. Pez must not be shouted at.'

'Can you not stop him behaving so?' Maliz demanded, impotent fury only barely repressed.

'We could remove him.'

The counting suddenly stopped and a soft sound of remorse issued from Pez, dragging everyone's glances helplessly to where he sat and stared at the widening puddle around his satin trousers.

'Oh, Zarab save me!' Maliz exclaimed, both astonished and angered. 'Get him out of here and have that filthy mess cleaned up.'

'Yes, Grand Vizier,' both Elim murmured, stifling their amusement.

'I want to stay here!' Pez screamed as the men bent to lift him. 'I haven't finished yet.'

'Get him out!' the Grand Vizier roared, determined that nothing further was going to be released from the dwarf's body into his chamber.

The men rushed Pez from the scene of his crime, dangling between them in their haste to get him clear of the Grand Vizier's wrath. After closing the door they put him back onto his own short legs and gave rueful glances at the damp trousers he stood in.

'I'm uncomfortable,' he complained, seemingly sane again.

'That wasn't wise, Pez,' one said, taking advantage of the moment of clarity within the dwarf.

'I had plans to leave something bigger behind,' he said before gently shaking himself clear of his escorts' hands and fleeing down the corridor. There was no time even to think on what had just occurred or the hideously precarious situation he now found himself in with no allies at the palace, save the loyal Elim – and they would never disobey their Zar. It was Ana who was in danger now and he'd already lost so much time with the Vizier.

There was only one person he could turn to. He needed to warn Lazar.

'Look how it sparkles, Ana,' Herezah breathed into her ear. 'Imagine yourself naked and wearing only that emerald.' Ana's eyes widened in shock at the suggestion and Herezah laughed softly. 'Don't be coy, Ana. I know a beautiful body hides beneath all of these robes. You've just got to be taught how to show it off to its best glory. Nothing works better than a precious jewel.'

Even veiled, Ana looked baffled. 'Valide, I . . .'

Herezah was firm. 'You must accept. And you must learn to use your body in ways you've never dreamed, to excite, entice and above all, keep the Zar enamoured of you.'

Ana shook her head softly, returning her gaze to the emerald. 'It's beautiful but gems have never fascinated me the way they do other women.'

Now Herezah clicked her tongue with exasperation. 'It matters not whether you appreciate them, Ana. This is about pleasing your Zar! Boaz loves emeralds, it is the stone of his birth. But I think tonight you should be dressed in blue. It will set off your golden hair beautifully, so perhaps a sapphire?'

The jeweller nodded and disappeared to the back of his store, returning almost immediately to reverently polish and place an exquisite jewel pendant into the waiting hands of Herezah.

'This is perfect! You must please him by wearing it . . . perhaps dangling between your bare breasts, or across your naked hips . . . wherever he thinks it suits you best.' She laughed again but kept it light, almost conveying a fondness.

'I shall consider it,' Ana replied, trying to be diplomatic.

Herezah rounded on her, shooing the jeweller away so she could speak privately to Ana. 'You don't understand anything, do you?'

Ana shook her head, confused, frowning. 'I don't know what you mean.'

'I think you're being deliberately vague, Ana,' Herezah accused but was, again, careful to keep her voice friendly, as if they were familiar companions, used to this sort of banter. 'I have already warned you of what my son will require from you.' A murmur of a laugh came from behind the veil. 'After all, you are from the harem.'

'Yes, you did, Valide. I'm not being evasive, just getting myself prepared—'

'But there is no more time, Ana,' Herezah said, reaching for her arm and squeezing it as a friend might for emphasis. 'He has decided.'

'Decided?' Ana repeated, feeling dull suddenly, not at all in tune with the Valide's comments.

Herezah voiced her amusement, her eyes sparkling at Ana's innocence. 'We'll take this,' Herezah called to the jeweller, who nodded and reached to take the large light-coloured sapphire pendant. 'Match up a gold chain with it and have it delivered to the palace for tonight. The Grand Master Eunuch will settle with you.'

He bowed and disappeared behind the silk curtain that divided the shop from his back rooms.

Herezah watched the shock deepen in the girl's eyes. She elegantly sipped from the raspberry-coloured glass of apple cinnamon tea that had been served prior to being shown any of the jewels.

Ana thought it should have cooled beyond the Valide's liking but she watched Herezah go through the motions and it gave her time to think too. Except her thoughts were too fractured and painful to be of much help to her at present. One moment they had been looking at the light glistening through a seemingly perfect sapphire and the next Herezah had her in bed with Boaz. The day was already ruined, and it had hardly begun.

'What are you thinking, Ana?' Herezah enquired finally. 'I don't understand your hesitation.'

'Valide, I just didn't imagine this would happen so soon.' Ana's eyes were full of pleading now, somehow hoping her new mentor would help her.

'I was barely thirteen when Joreb chose me.'

Ana covered her mouth with her hand to stop the cry she felt sure might escape otherwise.

'He was gentle the first time – I was but a child.' She saw Ana begin to say something but stopped her by continuing. 'He took me five times that night. My virginity was well and truly paid to my master by the following morning.' Now she watched horror stare blankly back at her. 'He called for me six nights in a row and only left me on the seventh because he was tired from his hunting that day. Not a part of me didn't ache. Not an inch of my body wasn't bruised, bitten, scratched, pinched – all out of affection, of course. Not a single bit of me minded. I was the winner.'

'Thirteen,' Ana repeated, not daring to disbelieve the Valide, knowing in her heart she heard the truth of what had perhaps shaped this hard woman.

Herezah shrugged. 'I learned fast – as you will. And you are past fifteen, Ana. A woman by anyone's standards.'

'When, Valide?' Ana begged.

Both knew what she meant.

There was no point in lying. 'Tonight.'

Ana gasped.

Herezah became matter of fact. 'He announced it this morning to Salmeo. You have been chosen. You are to be . . .' she hesitated, trying not to let the cruel grin behind the veil touch her eyes which were showing only sympathy '. . . prepared,' she finished.

'Prepared?'

'Bathed, oiled, smoothed. Every hair from your body must be waxed and plucked. Every hair on your head must be polished until it reflects the light of the moon. Your teeth must gleam, your breath must be sweetened, your nipples must be painted to excite the Zar. You will be given the varada leaf to chew to stimulate your own desires – it works faster than the smoke. It also widens your pupils to make you more alluring. You will be powdered and perfumed and finally you will be draped in a silken gauze and then you will crawl to his bedside on your knees before opening yourself up to the Zar and doing whatever he asks of you.'

'How long have you known?' Ana asked, too stunned to respond to the images Herezah's words had prompted.

'I was told just moments before we left. All the more reason to ensure you had a wonderful time in the bazaar – your last chance at freedom. I never had this chance that you have. But as I said earlier, this is my gift to you. So come on, let us go now and look for fabrics and a beautiful present that you might bring to your Zar this evening.' Then she gave her tinkling laugh. 'Actually, he needs no gift beyond your body, Ana. It will be enough, I'm sure.'

She led a silent odalisque from the jeweller's. Over the next couple of hours Ana was ushered from shop to shop. Herezah made all the purchases. Ana was barely more than an observer now, unaware of the Valide's insistence that all these items must reflect Ana's new status as First Chosen, incapable of responding to her queries on this fabric or that, as the Valide chattered on, seemingly oblivious to the dread quiet at her side.

'Perhaps you may be Favourite by tomorrow morning,' Herezah whispered conspiratorially to her silent companion. 'Joreb made me Favourite on that first night.'

Ana was past tearfulness. Now she was simply fearful, and fright was turning to something hard and obstinate.

As Herezah spoke by her side about glassware and beautiful silver, magnificent rich fabrics and even ideas for the design of her own porcelain, Ana stared at the wondrous roof of the bazaar. There in its beautiful blue and white painted tiles she found calm. The intricate pattern of flowers and birds became abstract from this distance and in taking her gaze on a journey around the ceiling it permitted her to escape.

She didn't even notice the icy sensation coursing through her body or the fact that in giving herself over to the art that brought her peace and beauty she was actually reaching over into another side of herself; a side she had never known existed.

And then she heard the voice in her mind. *Who is this?* It sounded both hesitant to speak and yet terrified not to. She recognised it instantly.

It's me, was all she could say in her shock at being able to communicate in this way and her despair at what was babbling on beside her.

Ana?

She could feel his relief washing through her own mind. *How are we doing this*? she asked.

No idea. Simply confirms you are who I assumed.

I know I accepted it quietly when we spoke – probably because you make me feel safe, but it suddenly frightens me. Are you so sure this goatherd's daughter is who you think she is?

Yes. Why else are we linked? How come we can now talk to each other without hearing but simply using our minds?

I don't know.

I am Iridor and you are Lyana. I have learned to accept it – now you must. When she didn't reply, he filled the silence. *Where are you? I hear a lot of noise.*

*In the bazaar with the Valide. I know where you are – you're
flying.*

How do you know that?

I can hear the wind rushing by, she said wistfully.

Have you heard about Boaz and what he did this morning?

A moment ago. I can't think straight.

Don't be scared.

Why not? I can't escape this time.

I'm working on it.

What do you mean?

He suddenly sounded evasive. *Now that we can do this
– we'll talk again in the same manner soon.*

Don't go, Pez!

I have to . . . er, Ana, forgive me, I am just joining someone—

Pez cut the link but not before she heard someone's
voice. It was a voice she had not thought she would ever
hear again. It weakened her still further and yet it lifted
the weight from her heart and her spirits began to soar.
Surely it couldn't be? Was she imagining it because she
was so distraught?

No. She heard a man say 'Hello, Pez' as clearly as if
he was standing by her side.

'Well,' a new voice interrupted her reverie, 'I think
we're done, Ana. You're going to look stunning tonight,
I promise.'

Ana tried to refocus her gaze on the eyes of the Valide,
who was regarding her intently from behind the dark veil.

'Are you feeling unwell?' Herezah enquired, staring
hard at the glazed confusion of her companion.

Ana felt the Valide touch her arm, she was shaking her
shoulder, and at that her thoughts swiftly snapped back
to where they needed to be if she was going to survive.

'What's wrong?' Herezah persisted.

'I think a ghost just passed by me.'

It was an old saying in Percheron. 'Ooh,' Herezah shivered, 'you know a ghost walking by signifies that death is beckoning?'

Ana shook her head. 'This one meant life.'

Herezah frowned to show that Ana wasn't making sense. 'We leave now. I hope you've enjoyed your excursion, Ana. It is your last as a virgin but need not be your last time of roaming from the palace. If you stick to your bargain, you can do this again some time.'

'Thank you, Valide,' Ana replied politely, hardly listening to the woman, her thoughts already teasing at the problem of where Lazar was. The thrill of imagining him alive had already passed and was rapidly being replaced by shaking anger that she had been tricked. The man she loved had duped her in the worst possible manner . . . and just as devastating, her only true friend was in on the duplicity. Pez was involved – he was visiting Lazar now. She felt the sharp sting of betrayal for being so innocent and easily persuaded that Lazar had died. She began to lose herself in a swirl of thoughts. Her naivety had permitted her to believe Lazar could love her back and this had thwarted her ability to see through the ruse – for surely this is what it was. He couldn't possibly have deliberately set out to hurt her. And not Pez, not after this morning's conversation. But why? Why would Lazar fake his own death? Why would her uncle admit to the crime? There had to be explanations but Ana could find none, returning with sorrow to the original notion that this was a treachery against her.

Her shaking became visible.

'Zarab save us! What's come over you, girl?' Herezah exclaimed, watching her charge disintegrate before her.

And then Ana knew nothing more. She was not aware of slumping to the floor, her fall only barely broken by Herezah's quick action. She was heedless of people rushing around her, a strong Elim guard lifting her easily and carrying her all the way back to the palace.

She only knew who she was again when she woke to find herself draped on her own bed, pungent smelling salts erupting through the cloudy fog to bring her back from the darkness.

And she returned to her full senses, enraged.

∽ 11 ∽

Eyes normally light in colour, although never a window into his thoughts, were now darkened by news that hurt him to his soul. He worked hard to keep his expression even as the fresh information was delivered but his brow creased and then dipped, hooding his haunted face still further. His lips, rarely smiling, were pressed together as though determined to deny any words escape to thus betray their owner.

Finally Lazar let go of the breath he hadn't realised he'd held so tightly in his chest it ached. 'Boaz said it this morning?' he repeated, demanding confirmation, although not needing it.

'This is what I have discovered.'

'From whom? You were not there, I take it?'

'From a reliable witness.'

'Why are you being evasive?'

'To protect you.'

'From what?' he sneered, slamming his hand down on the scrubbed table in the cottage.

Pez remained patient. He'd had longer to accept this news. 'From information that can incriminate. Trust me, Lazar, you do not want to hear this.'

Lazar did but he didn't have time to fret over Pez's

secrets right now. Ana's life was about to change once again. 'And she's with Herezah, you say?'

'Apparently. The Valide has taken her shopping.'

Lazar shook his head. 'In all my years at the palace Herezah has never gone shopping. She has the sellers drag their goods up to the palace for a private showing.'

Pez nodded. 'And if she doesn't like anything, she makes them keep repeating the process until she does.'

'That's right, she enjoys their frustration. She can't have changed her ways.'

'Well, perhaps because she's getting Ana ready for her son . . .' Pez watched Lazar's scowl intensify '. . . and Ana did say that Herezah had made a bargain and this was the first part of their deal.'

Lazar snorted. 'And you believe it?'

'No,' Pez had to admit.

'She's up to something.'

'Lazar, whatever the Valide's intentions might be with this trip into the city, they are negated by what Ana faces later.'

The former Spur stomped out of the cottage, his unintelligible grumbling suggesting he didn't need to be reminded. Pez noted that Lazar walked freely now. His large, determined stride had returned fully. The stoop had gone, as had the sallow look of a man so sick it seemed kinder to help him to an easy death.

At least this day had brought something positive with it. He caught up with Lazar.

'Anger is not helpful,' he counselled.

'It is to me, Pez. Don't lecture me.'

The dwarf pulled a contrite expression. 'I have to tell you something else. Something extraordinary.' Lazar turned his angry glare on his friend. It was clear he wanted no further surprises. Pez told him anyway. 'Ana spoke to me even though I was flying and she was in the bazaar. That's how I know she was shopping.'

'What do you mean?' It was a reflex more than a genuine question but still Pez looked exasperated.

'Don't be dim, Lazar. She spoke to me. We can talk across distance, using our minds . . . and our magics.' This clearly didn't please Lazar from the grimace on his face now. If anything it seemed to bring more grief, and Pez realised that Lazar learning more about Ana's potential as something far more than an innocent trapped by circumstances only made it harder for him.

'I'm sorry,' he said. 'I thought it might enlighten you.'

'Oh, it enlightens me all right, Pez. According to you she's Lyana, Mother Goddess!' Lazar roared, no longer able to contain his fury. 'But it still doesn't save her a rutting at the end of Boaz's newfound manhood, does it?'

Pez stared at Lazar, shocked. He had never seen this man so worked up. In fact he didn't know Lazar was capable of showing even a tenth of this much emotion. Ana certainly touched a buried nerve in the former Spur. He couldn't help himself. 'And can you blame him?'

'What?' Fresh fury etched itself even deeper across his face.

'Can you honestly deny that you harbour similar desires?'

Pez didn't see it coming. Not even the Lore could save him the frightening effect that a strong backhander has when it connects perfectly with a jaw.

He blinked slowly, dully, realising he was lying on his back, staring up at the bright sky over Star Island. His whole head hurt with a splitting pain. Lazar's concerned expression suddenly hove into view and Pez felt his face being rather tenderly bathed with a cool, damp linen.

'What happened?' he mumbled and then groaned at the pain from his jaw that sent lights sparkling through his mind.

'I hit you,' Lazar confessed, a deep sense of shame in his tone. 'I had no right to,' he groaned, his anger gone as fast as it had arrived.

'I deserved it,' Pez said, holding his jaw and not speaking very clearly. 'Help me up.'

Lazar gave an anguished moan. 'No, Pez, don't forgive me so easily. I deserved your criticism. My saintly attitude is flawed and you've seen through it, as did Herezah within moments of meeting Ana.'

Pez tried to shrug but couldn't. 'As I say, can you blame him?' he managed to grind out.

'No.'

'Envy is a terrible thing,' Pez added. 'I think my jaw's broken.'

'I don't know how to say sorry.'

'I can fix it. The Lore has many skills and I think healing cracked bones is not beyond it, although your sickness was.'

'I'm so ashamed, Pez, and yet I pride myself on always being in control of myself and my actions.'

'The heart is a law unto itself, Lazar. You have no control over it.'

'Nevertheless, I—'

'Stop, please. I know you're sorry – I can see it on your face, hear it in your voice. I too am sorry for goading you in such a ruthless manner. So we're both sorry and I can fix my jaw, although I refuse to mend your aching hand. Let it hurt for a while,' he said, his tone kindly now and infused with gentle jest. 'Let's get on with the important matter at hand.'

Lazar nodded, contrite. He rubbed the back of his hand that had connected with Pez's large jaw. 'What do you suggest?'

Pez spoke awkwardly. 'Get to the temple. I need you in the city faster than we planned. Perhaps with Zafira we can think this through.'

'But Ana?'

It hurt Pez to talk but he ignored the screaming pain from his jaw momentarily to say what needed to be said to Lazar. 'Ana is not yours, Lazar. She belongs to the Zar. She is only a vessel for something far more important to all of us. Ana is nearing sixteen. She is a woman and ready to face the hurdles of her sex. Harem women pleasure the Zar. It is his right and we must not try anything stupid to unsettle the balance of the palace, Lazar. We have far higher things at stake.'

'What about what Ana wants?'

Cruelty was needed then, Pez decided. 'It doesn't matter what Ana wants. You bought her as a slave. She is expendable in all of this. This is about destroying Maliz – that's what we're here for.' He coughed, the pain too great to go on.

Lazar's expression grew stormy again. 'That might be what you're here for, Pez or Iridor, whatever you prefer to be called these days – but I am not a slave of Lyana. I will not be manipulated. I accept that Ana has a role – one I purchased her for . . . something I have to live with – but I don't have to forget who I am and what I feel simply because some age-old crone demands it. You dance to Ellyana's tune too readily, dwarf.'

Pez shook his head sadly. 'You are fooling yourself, Lazar. You're in this struggle up to your neck, as I am. We may not know why but your role will become clearer.'

'So be it,' Lazar said with resignation and then his tone softened. 'Again, forgive my assault. I will find a way to repay the debt I now feel I owe you.'

Pez sighed. 'As you wish.'

'I shall see you in the city,' Lazar said as farewell.

He watched the snow-white owl take off gingerly from the cliff edge. Then he returned to the hut to pack a small sack of items, none of which, save a small bottle of liquid and a tiny gold owl, were important to him. His mind was filled with how to get himself off the island quickly and back onto the mainland, as well as a disguise and devising a method for achieving entry into the palace. It felt empowering – after such a long sense of impotence – to be making plans and taking positive action. More than anything, the activity kept his thoughts occupied and did not permit him to dwell on the final imprisonment – being Chosen – of the woman who owned his heart.

Salmeo had been summoned to Herezah's salon and, now seated, he was delighted at being served the bright red pomegranate tea by her own hand.

'Did your excursion go well, Valide?' he lisped as she settled herself back into a divan plumped with thickly feathered cushions.

'Oh, very well,' she answered, amusement in her voice. 'Ana fainted.'

'At the news?'

Herezah smiled. 'It was a slow build-up. She thought she had her emotions under control but it was rather fascinating to watch her gradually disintegrating over our shopping expedition. Rather naive of her to think Boaz at almost seventeen isn't going to want to bed her or indeed a dozen women.'

'She's a strange one. Sometimes when I observe Ana it's as though she is beyond the other girls.'

'What do you mean, Salmeo?' Herezah queried, interested but baffled.

'Oh, it's fanciful, Valide, I know, but it's as if she knows something important the rest of us don't. And that gives her this immense aloofness and the courage she has demonstrated.'

'Not so courageous today,' Herezah remarked with a sneer. 'But I take your point. She certainly doesn't lack for spine. In fact she doesn't stop surprising me with her insight and forthright attitude.'

'Presumably that will be her undoing, Valide,' Salmeo said, daintily replacing his teacup on the table between them. 'It's that sense of herself that will push her over the edge into taking risks.'

Herezah nodded. 'Precisely, and I'll walk naked through the bazaar if I'm wrong that she doesn't take that risk tonight.'

'She'll take the bait, you think?'

'I have no doubt in my mind. You're ready?'

'Completely. We'll let her think she's got away with it for a while.'

'Which will make the hunting down and ultimate capture all the more sweet.'

'Actually, my Valide, I think the Zar's decision does work in our favour.'

'It's not like you to take so long,' Herezah teased. 'Boaz did us a favour. His announcement forces her hand but it makes her now answerable to him, rather than the harem.'

'Yes, his punishment rather than ours.'

'And he will be worked up, I'm sure. I know Boaz and how high his passions can run. He is such an intense boy, really. Ana's actions will provoke a violent response for his disappointment, I imagine.'

'I think we can count on it, Valide.'

Ana was led to the magnificent domed building, attached to the harem through a tiled walkway, that housed the bathing chambers.

As all members of the harem were currently enjoying their boating picnic, Ana was the only odalisque present. Everyone else was a servant or attendant and each charged with the information that this girl had been formally chosen by the Zar.

Each new young woman to be called to the Zar's bedroom to relinquish her maidenhood held special significance. But the First Chosen for a new Zar, also to present him with her virginity, was symbolic for the success of this man's rule and for his harem.

In this instance it was even more dramatic for all involved. This was a virginal Zar choosing his first virgin. Ana's head attendant, Elza, was impressing upon the silent Ana the enormous responsibility she now carried.

'Everyone will be looking to you to make this go

smoothly. You must please the Zar more than any other who might follow in your footsteps. And you must remember, this is also his first time. You will be guiding each other. His pleasure is paramount. Yours is a gift from him if he so chooses.'

'And if he chooses to hurt me?'

Elza did not hesitate. 'That's his wish,' she replied firmly as she slipped the robe off Ana's naked shoulders.

Kett was kneeling, gently helping her to pull her feet from the tall wooden pattens that the girls wore into the bathing chamber to lift them away from the constant water that flowed across the marble.

'A soak first,' Elza said, guiding Ana into the vast pool. 'Then we begin,' she added ominously.

Ana had not yet experienced the full bathing process. It hadn't been necessary until now for any of the girls to do much more than mere bathing, although they had been learning about the long and tedious hours that they would spend in preparation each day for the Zar once he became sexually active with the members of his harem.

Kett walked her into the pool and she noticed that, undressed, his body and face had lost the pudginess of childhood. His cheeks were lean and his big dark eyes regarded her with concern. He was naked save a linen around his waist that protected his modesty.

'Relax, Miss Ana, the warmth will soothe,' he comforted.

Ana slid into the pool, allowing the water to cover her head. When she emerged, Kett was still standing chest-deep watching her.

She decided to be candid. 'I feel very awkward about you seeing me naked.'

'I've seen you before in this state and it was my undoing,' he said gravely. 'Please don't be embarrassed on my behalf. All that makes me a man has gone, Miss Ana.'

She didn't believe him. 'No . . . um?' she struggled to find the right words.

He understood. Shook his shaved head. 'No feelings at all,' he lied. 'I'm told they got me early enough to take away the manly urges.'

She swam over and touched his hand beneath the fizzing waters. Both knew his longing to be a normal man would never dissipate but Ana had no idea of where that longing directed itself.

He shrugged gently to cover the thrill of her touch. 'I have been rewarded by being made your servant.'

'My servant?'

'You have not been told? The Grand Master Eunuch Salmeo himself has appointed me to you.'

Ana was instantly suspicious. 'But why?'

'A special gift for today, I gather, although it sounds as though it may be more permanent.'

Elza bustled back with pots of various description. 'No more time wasting now, Kett,' but it was an empty request. She knew that talking whilst bathing was all part of the relaxation ritual. It was good for the girl to be conversing; took her mind off the fear. She was pleased that Kett had been sent to them today. He would be very good for young Ana.

'May I wash your hair for you?' he asked Ana.

'Thank you, Kett,' she murmured. 'You look so strong,' she remarked, noticing his sculpted body as he helped her up and led her to a separate pool.

He gave a soft sigh. 'I always wanted to be a warrior

and the Elim have taught me that I am one, even though . . .' his voice trailed off.

Ana felt his pain and filled the awkward moment with light conversation. 'So you've been training hard?'

He nodded, although she couldn't see this as he stood behind her lathering up her hair. 'Yes, I have almost completed my Elim training. I will be given my full-time role soon. I hope it's to protect you.'

She found a smile. 'What do I need protection from?'

He shrugged. 'Who knows? I shall do whatever is asked – I belong to the harem.'

'Just as I do,' she reassured, hoping to alleviate the wistfulness he clearly couldn't shake. 'We are kindred spirits, Kett.'

Kett worked in silence for several minutes, carefully soaping up Ana's hair with a mix of suds and egg yolk to make it shine, before rinsing it, then beginning again, each time massaging her scalp until it tingled.

'It's a shame to waste all those egg whites,' she commented sarcastically.

He giggled, whispering, 'When you're older we use them to smear around your eyes to help with wrinkles but for now I'm sure we can send them off to the Valide.'

They both shared a conspiratorial laugh.

'Are you scared, Miss Ana?' he dared.

'Yes,' she replied candidly. 'But, like you, others decide my fate for me.'

She heard him pause before he replied. 'It need not be that way,' he said, tipping a bucket of clean, cooler water over her head.

'What do you mean?'

He came around to face her, looking abashed, as if angry

with himself for saying what he did. 'Now we must wash your body,' Kett said, his eyes glancing away from hers.

Ana turned to see Elza approaching.

'Come, Odalisque Ana, Kett will now soap your body.'

Ana felt instantly coy. 'Can I not do it, Elza?'

The senior attendant laughed, her bare breasts over the top of her loose pants wobbling with the mirth. 'You have to get used to the touch of a man, although Kett here is hardly that.' She laughed again but not unkindly. 'You must also get used to this routine. If not him, then another of the youngest eunuchs will attend to your bathing.'

'Why not you?' Ana persisted.

'I am senior, Miss Ana,' Elza said archly, 'I have more important roles.'

Ana felt sorry for the woman. They were both slaves, both prisoners of the harem. The only thing that separated them was age and desirability in terms of the Zar's needs, and yet here was Elza trying to take solace from the fact that her slaving duties were considered more important than Kett's, but not as important as Ana's perhaps. She sighed to herself. Status existed everywhere, even amongst the downtrodden.

They sat Ana down on a stool near a fountain of running water.

'Just let him do what he must,' Elza said. 'Get used to it. He's been practising. He knows what to do for you.'

Ana didn't want to make trouble for Kett. She looked towards his downcast gaze and knew he felt as awkward about this as she did. Neither had a choice once again. Elza had already left them, although she was not far away and would supervise, presumably.

'It's not your fault, Kett,' Ana assured. 'I suppose we'd

better get over the discomfort of our situation and get on with it.'

He looked up and she knew he fought his treacherous eyes and their gaze that moved unhappily towards her breasts. It was not his fault. He could not help it, no matter how much he protested that they had taken everything from him that made him a man. And she liked Kett – had always somehow felt responsible for his sorrowful situation, even though she knew in her heart that her circumstances that night had been equally helpless.

Ana reassured herself that Kett would get used to the sight of her body and she would get used to his ministrations. They just had to overcome this initial delicate beginning.

'Right,' she said brightly. 'Do I need to do anything?'

'No, Miss Ana,' Kett said, snapping his attention back to his duty.

He reached for a soft sea sponge and dipped it into some perfumed suds in a bucket and then gently lifted Ana's slim, long arm, proceeding to soap it from fingertip to shoulder. She had to admit it felt good and before long she relieved Kett's embarrassment and her own by closing her eyes and losing herself as best she could in her own thoughts. It was the invigorating surprise of being doused with cool water that brought her out of her musings on reaching Pez through some form of magical link.

A voice cut through her thoughts. 'Come, Odalisque Ana, now for the massage.'

Ana had never experienced the massage, apparently unique to the Percherese, but she had heard plenty about it this past year in her training.

'You must lie on the marble floor over here,' Elza said,

pointing to a large raised area. Ana noticed holes in the marble through which fizzed warm water. She couldn't imagine how that happened and she wasn't given time to consider the ingenuity of the men who had designed this system.

Ana dutifully lay down, no longer bothered by her nakedness in front of Kett, his black skin gleaming from his exertions and a contrast to the bright red loincloth of the Elim that hooked around his waist and saved her the sight of his wound.

'Kett has strong fingers,' Elza said. 'He will make your body feel loose and pliant.'

The water bubbling through the holes made the marble slippery and Kett was able to spin Ana into any position he needed. At first she laughed when he took her leg and pulled her around so he could work on her shoulders first.

'Behave,' Elza warned, frightened that Salmeo or worse, the Valide, might choose this moment to enter the pavilion and take umbrage that everyone was having too much fun over a serious process.

'I was told the women use this time to entertain one another, Elza.'

'This is different, Odalisque Ana. There is no-one here but ourselves and this is no ordinary day of bathing,' she reminded, her expression stern, hiding her fear.

Ana fell silent, knowing it wasn't worth the breath arguing the point with Elza who had no power, no matter how hard she tried to convince herself that her role had real status in the harem. She watched the slave walk away as Kett dragged her into the middle of the marble where it was hotter. She sighed as the heat melted through her body and his fingers busily worked down her back now.

'What did you mean earlier?' she said softly.

'Pardon, Miss Ana?'

'You suggested that others need not decide my fate.'

Kett didn't answer immediately, although she felt his tell-tale pause from his massaging, then he resumed, harder now. 'I spoke out of turn, Miss Ana,' he finally said.

'She's not here, Kett. Tell me what you meant.' Ana could sense him checking for Elza's whereabouts. 'Please.'

He spun her around again and this time knelt close to her head as he pretended to work on her neck and shoulders. He whispered, 'I overheard Salmeo organising for the bundle women to come up tonight. It's a treat for the girls.'

'Another one. We are spoilt,' Ana commented tartly.

'I think he said the Valide wanted to add something to their day so she can share in their fun.'

'Doesn't sound like the Valide.'

He hissed softly to stop her saying anything too harsh. 'Be careful, Miss Ana.'

'Why? The Zar wants my body, they can hardly hurt me.'

'They can afterwards,' he counselled and Ana knew he was right to caution her.

'Go on,' she urged.

'It's just that I know one of the women. She can be bribed.'

Both fell silent as the implications of this hung between them.

Ana broke the tension, her breathing suddenly shallow. 'How well do you know her?'

'Not well. I've got to know her through my work for the harem. Salmeo uses me for errands and I come across her from time to time. I know she is corrupt. I know she can be bought.'

'What's her name?'

'Sheffa. She usually brings the cheap shawls.'

'Can word be got to her?'

'Possibly, I don't know.'

Ana could hear the pain in his voice and she spun herself around now. They both looked for Elza before she said more. 'You did the right thing in telling me, Kett,' she assured. 'Can you get word to her? Please, I'm begging you. Tell her I will give her something of immense value tonight if she will carry me out.'

Kett looked forlorn, terrified. 'I wish I'd never mentioned—'

'But you did. And I haven't forgotten it since that day on the terraces when you first shared the tale of the odalisque who escaped in the bundle woman's wares, and I know you told me because you want me to escape.'

'I can't bear the thought of you going to the Zar unwillingly,' he said, skirting the whole truth.

'Neither can I. But escape is my risk alone. I'm prepared to take it. How can we contact her?'

'I can probably do it myself. I'm frightened though, Miss Ana. I wish I had not put this idea into your mind. It is wrong of me but no-one understands better how it feels to be trapped. I can't escape but perhaps you can.' He was babbling, torn between her safety and his desire to free her from the Zar's claim.

'Do it, Kett. But keep yourself safe. The danger must be mine alone.'

Elza was back and they both quietened. 'I take over from here now, Miss Ana.'

'What's next?' Ana asked too brightly, covering their sudden hush in conversation.

Her new enthusiasm was noticed by the slave. 'You seem very alert.'

'That's not a bad thing, is it? I found the waters refreshing,' Ana replied, feeling the excitement and tension of her embryonic escape plan shaping.

'No, but the waters are meant to relax, not make you too jumpy.'

'I'm not jumpy, Elza.'

'Well, don't try and convince me you're excited,' she said, a hint of sarcasm icing her words.

Elza knew her too well. 'I just want to get it all over and done with, to be honest.'

'That's fair enough too, Miss Ana. I understand. Next we have to remove your body hair.'

Ana stared at her. She had heard that high-born females and those who married above themselves strived to keep their bodies free of all hair, save what flowed from their head. Her stepmother had scoffed at the notion, claiming it was an idle pastime for idle women. No-one Ana had ever met had the time or inclination to follow this practice.

'Now don't look at me like that, Miss Ana. This is the way of the harem.'

'How is it done?'

'A paste,' the woman replied simply. 'Come and lie here on these warmed towels.'

Ana did as she was told, watching somewhat fascinated as Elza lifted the lid on one of her many pots before beginning to smear the pungent paste onto Ana's shins first.

'Quicklime and orpiment – crystals of arsenic,' the

woman explained as she worked deftly with her spatula. As she finished attending to the second leg with the paste, she reached for a small grey implement.

'What's that?' Ana said, sitting up.

'A mussel shell that's been sharpened. Watch,' Elza said, as she used the fine edge of the shell like a razor to lift away the paste and with it the soft golden hair on Ana's legs. She repeated the process on Ana's arms and underarms, and then removed the modesty sheet covering her middle. 'Now for the important bit,' she said, grinning and slapping Ana's thigh, 'so our young stallion can see you in all your glory.'

Ana groaned, couldn't bear to watch any longer and laid back as she felt the paste stinging between her legs.

'We cannot leave this on for too long or the arsenic will corrode your flesh.'

'It's burning me now.'

'It will,' Elza said matter-of-factly. 'I must use it on all the orifices, Miss Ana, nose, ears . . .'

'Say no more,' Ana warned, cutting off wherever next Elza was going to list and feeling sickened as she felt the slave turn her over and push her legs apart once again.

'On your knees, girl, make it easier for me.'

Ana felt her eyes water with the humiliation of this activity. She thought of her father and his simple life, simple needs. She thought of her brother and sisters and how she would give anything to be living with them again, and she thought of the statue of Lyana, whom Pez believed Ana now represented. And then she considered this pampered prisoner life she was now being committed to and her mind snapped itself into the stony decision. Escape, be it out of Percheron or by death, was her only option. She would take her chance tonight, no matter what happened.

When Elza was satisfied, after an embarrassingly long and close scrutiny, that Ana was free of all superfluous hair, she pulled on a small rough hessian bag over each hand.

'Now what?' Ana asked testily.

'I must polish your body. Turn over and be quiet, child.'

Elza began to rub every inch of her charge with the rough bags whilst Kett scrubbed the soles of Ana's feet with rasps. Ana no longer found any of it diverting. The humiliation she still felt fired her imagination further, revelling in the notion that she could cheat Salmeo and Herezah. She didn't enjoy the idea of snubbing Boaz, who had in all truth been nothing but a friend to her, but even that relationship had this dark side to it, where she was expected to give her body for his use.

She remembered Lazar's voice, coming through Pez, and it made her feel hot where she shouldn't and this angered her even more. She would show them all. Ana had no proof that Lazar was alive and she had not yet seen Pez to confront him, but her ears had surely not deceived her. That was the voice with which she had comforted herself this past year, by playing over and again in her head memories of conversation with Lazar. But she had not imagined it. It was Lazar who spoke, and it would explain Pez's hasty closing of their link.

She flicked her hair angrily. 'Are we finished?'

Elza had finished, apparently, because she told Kett to bathe Ana again before she was to be oiled.

Ana grimaced but said nothing, dutifully obeying the woman who was in charge of her preparation. After another dip in the heated waters, Kett smoothed warmed perfumed oil from her neck to the tips of her toes, rubbing it in gently.

It was a marvellous sensation and Ana genuinely did feel every inch of herself relax beneath the strong-fingered ministrations of Kett, for perhaps the first time since entering the palace.

Warmed pouches of wheat were placed on her eyelids whilst Kett finished smoothing the oil into the front of her body and Ana felt herself drifting into a light doze, until she heard a voice that she recognised, and it instantly chilled her to the marrow.

'Almost ready?' the voice lisped.

'Just her hair to be dried, brushed and dressed,' Elza said softly.

'Kett, you've done well,' said the voice, 'she looks calm – just how we need her.'

Kett said nothing and Ana felt frozen to the marble-surfaced table on which she lay, naked and vulnerable.

'Ana,' Salmeo said firmly. 'You are almost ready in your preparations.' He removed the wheat bags and she managed to muster a small amount of defiance to load into her stare. 'Just hair and clothes to go,' he continued, hardly noticing her glower but looking up and down her body making soft noises of appreciation.

'I don't need your help to get dressed, Grand Master Salmeo,' she replied but carefully tempered her voice.

He stroked her belly, and his gap-toothed smile was prompted at her flinch. 'No, but I am required to perform one final act upon you before I hand you over to our Zar for his pleasure.'

She sat up, fearful, and Elza made a hushing sound.

'Now, Miss Ana, this is the usual practice, the way of the harem.'

'Don't touch me,' she warned Salmeo.

He sighed theatrically. 'Pity, I thought we could make this easy on you, Ana.' He clapped his soft hands and four grave-looking Elim arrived. 'Do I need to ask these men to assist?' He held his sharp-pointed fingernail in the air, freshly painted red for the occasion. 'Make a decision, Ana. It can be a crowd or it can be intimate – just the two of us . . . again.'

She knew she had lost her small fight and nodded, holding back the tears at her hopeless rebellion.

A signal from Salmeo dismissed the Elim. Ana stole a desperate glance at a frightened-looking Kett and nodded, begging him to understand the intent of her message. He nodded back. He had understood.

Salmeo missed neither gesture, although he pretended he noticed nothing. 'Go about your other business, Kett. I've left a list of errands – they require you to go to the bazaar.'

Kett bowed and hurried away, hardly daring to believe that he had all but been given permission to go precisely where he had planned to.

'Can Elza stay?' she begged.

'Leave us, woman,' Salmeo said cruelly in answer. 'She cannot save you this, Ana. Where is the emollient?' He directed his question at the slave who dutifully held out a pot of the paste Ana recognised from her first night in the palace. Then she patted Ana on the leg and left her to Salmeo.

They were alone and so she closed her eyes to shut him out.

'As I told you once before, Ana, you can make this go easy or if you fight me you can make it hurt.'

'Just do it!' she growled, tears flowing freely now through her tightly clenched eyelids.

She missed his lascivious smile as he first caressed her between her legs before he plunged his fingers into her body once again, taking his time, massaging her so she would open more willingly. He moved his fingers into and out of her, lingering, knowing just where to touch her to win a gasp.

'Feels nice, doesn't it,' he said, knowing she was holding her breath at the sensation. 'Don't clench against my fingers, Ana. Relax yourself. It's good practice for Zar Boaz.'

She refused to say anything, hating herself for responding physically, even though his touch made the bile rise to her throat. Sadly the effect it had on her traitorous body was the opposite, although she fought against rising in tandem with the soft throb he had won from her beneath his pudgy fingers.

'Now, Ana,' he said, voice thick with his own lust, 'I can see you'll be very responsive to our Zar. Right here,' he said, pushing and rubbing harder, 'is where he needs to touch you to make you slippery and ready for him. If he doesn't do it, do it to yourself, girl, or what he does do will hurt badly. He will have little idea, I'm guessing. All clumsy thrusts and eagerness, I'm sure, not precise and soft . . . and knowledgeable like Salmeo,' he lisped in a lover's voice, tantalising her further with his oiled fingers until she groaned. She tried to push his hand away but he slapped her hard.

'Don't, Ana. This is my time with you and I'm giving you a very good lesson. Without this advice it could go badly tonight. Remember what I've said, what I've shown you today.' Ana felt her whole body trembling, privately begging him to finish what he'd begun, but still somehow resisting the call of his insistent fingers.

Suddenly he stopped and she all but shrieked, not sure whether it was from disappointment or relief.

'No finishing for you, Ana. We want you swollen and eager like this. You must remember this feeling. This is the point you must reach tonight before he enters you and then you will be ready and it won't hurt and you will satisfy him because your own urges will be in concert with his. Do not try and take your own pleasures either, my girl.' He ignored her soft panting. 'The Valide will give you strict counsel before you are led into the Zar's chambers, but heed my own warning – you are there purely to satisfy Zar Boaz, not the other way around. You will do everything he requests, perform any act he requires. Do you understand?'

She nodded bleakly, hating the unsated feeling that her body was experiencing as it slid from the delicate ecstasy that the eunuch had so cunningly achieved. Salmeo's little finger slipped back into her and she gasped again.

'Relax, Ana,' he said and she saw his smile this time as his tongue flicked out to moisten his lips. 'Now to the true purpose of my visit. I must break your hymen so you don't give our Zar any trouble entering you.'

And Salmeo put his stained red nail to its ugly purpose as Ana arched her back and cried out her pain and her resentment.

She bled, proving once again that Lazar had delivered the perfect prize to the harem.

∽ 12 ∾

Pez's plans to see Zafira had unravelled. He had not been able to find her in the morning as he'd intended and things were getting rather late in the day now after his run-in with Lazar. He had tried to find Ana but had learned through one of the Elim that she was being prepared for the Zar. He made use of the quiet to wield the Lore to help mend the crack that Lazar's fist had inflicted on his jaw but it didn't do much to lessen the pain. That would be with him for a while until it fully healed.

He decided that flying to the temple was just too risky – he had been flying too much lately. Instead he slipped away from the palace in the late afternoon and took a stroll down to the temple. As always when passing through the grand bazaar Pez got lost in his own thoughts. He loved it in this bustling, thriving city within the city, but because there were so many people around him, and Pez had allowed his concentration to lapse, he did not notice the figure that followed him down the hill from the palace and blended into the moving mass of humanity.

He was instantly recognisable to most but unless he was actually performing for them they tended to leave him to himself as many were frankly scared of the contrary dwarf. Pez did nothing to alleviate this vague sense of disquiet for passers-by and kept up a mindless stream of gibberish interspersed with humming. It took little effort on his part and allowed him to drift in his thoughts until he arrived at the temple, where he did find Zafira, laying out some sea daisies before the statue of Lyana.

He cartwheeled around the temple, inwardly begging the Goddess to forgive him his silly antics in her place of quiet worship, knowing in his heart she would likely find it amusing.

'Ah, Pez, I wondered when I'd see you.'

'I want some fruit,' he called aggressively, rubbing his jaw gingerly from the pain of talking. He grabbed her arm, listing all the names of the fruits he loved, and dragged her into the far corner, checking surreptitiously that there were no other people in the temple.

'I came earlier,' he whispered.

Zafira was surprised by his behaviour but then again took it in her stride. She had long ago given up second-guessing why Pez did anything. 'I had things to do.'

'Well, I have more important things for you to do. I told you, I need some fruit!' Pez respected her privacy but couldn't hide his own worry.

'Oh?'

'Take me to your kitchen, flitchen, gitchen, ditchen.'

Zafira beckoned. 'Come, Pez, I have some fruit upstairs,' she said, openly playing along. Then whispered: 'Let us take a final cup of quishtar together before our lives change irrevocably.'

'Mine already has,' he mumbled.

But she had turned away and Pez was not forced to see

the pain fleet across her wrinkled face at his words. He followed her now in silence, dragging his knuckles on the ground as he had seen the monkeys in the zoo move, slowly ascending the stairs.

Once upstairs he moved to the window, staring out wistfully.

'We are alone,' she confirmed, sensing his anxiety, needing to assure him that he could drop his act.

He didn't turn from the window but spoke softly. 'You must leave Percheron today . . . now.'

She smiled gently. 'Leave?'

'It's time,' he said, more kindly. He glanced around, ensuring no-one could possibly eavesdrop, and as an extra measure reached out with the Lore, felt nothing. He said what was on his mind. 'I know who Maliz is.'

Zafira took her time answering. Pez assumed it was so she could wipe the alarm from her expression at his words but he was wrong. Fear was etched clearly on her face and had no intention of leaving. 'Already?'

He nodded, shouted out the names of more fruit in a demanding voice this time before dropping almost to a whisper again. 'It can be no-one else. He sensed my presence at the palace and knows Lyana will be close, but then you already know who she is.' He didn't mean it to sound quite like the accusation it did. 'I want pomegranates!' he yelled and then fell quiet, staring out from her window at Beloch, as Zafira maintained her own dread silence whilst she brewed quishtar.

He tested his surrounds once again with the Lore and finally permitted himself to feel safe. 'Is it my imagination or does Beloch have cracks in his stone that were not there before?'

Zafira joined him at the small window, handing him a steaming bowl of quishtar. 'I've never seen that before and I look at Beloch every day. How odd.'

'His brother's too far away for me to note if he's cracking too,' Pez said, wincing at the hot liquid around his aching mouth.

'They are crumbling like us,' she said sadly.

'We've never been stronger, Zafira, we have to believe this.'

'Who is it?' she said, an edge in her voice.

'Can you not guess?' It wasn't meant to be mischievous. He wanted to see if the clues were strong enough for Zafira to work out.

She frowned and sipped her brew. 'I obviously know him for you to suggest I guess.'

He nodded gravely and she held his stare.

She puzzled at it for a few moments before saying, 'The Vizier?'

Pez closed his eyes momentarily in silent despair. Maliz had been under their noses for perhaps a year and they hadn't noticed. Yet the clues had been there – Zafira's guess confirmed it.

'Am I right?' She sounded incredulous.

He nodded sombrely. 'I believe Maliz has taken over Tariq, yes.'

She turned away from the window, distracted but not disbelieving of him. 'How can it be? How did we miss it?' she hissed.

'It is the way of how he works, Zafira. We are not meant to know. That's his disguise but it works in our favour too. He doesn't know who we are either.'

'But the changes – they're so obvious,' she countered,

frustrated as she put her bowl down. 'We should have been more focused. We should have been looking for him.'

'And we would not have arrived at this conclusion any earlier, I'm sure of it.'

'What makes you sure of his identity?'

'Something Lazar said triggered the thought and then it was so obvious I've hated myself since,' he said, touching his jaw.

'What's wrong with you?'

He waved away her enquiry to let her know it wasn't important.

His discomfort was instantly forgotten when Zafira exclaimed 'Ana!' clutching a hand to her chest.

Pez nodded. 'You could have told me what you suspected and not let me have to work it out for myself,' he admonished softly.

'Ellyana insisted we say nothing to anyone about Ana.'

He disliked Ellyana all the more for hearing that comment. She had known from the start about all of them but continued to deliberately keep them in the dark, blundering around, not trusting anyone but themselves. He forced himself to move on, rather than dwell on Ellyana. 'Well, Lazar and I agree that Ana is safer at the palace than anywhere else. She has certain protections that the harem gives her. Tariq has little access to her physically.'

Zafira sneered. 'Protection of sorts. If Maliz suspected who Ana is he would already be making his moves to destroy her.'

'Well, he doesn't suspect yet, but we have to be very careful. That's why I think you should leave the temple, leave Percheron.'

'What prompted this? Tariq?'

'Everything! Tariq, Lazar returning to the city, which will reveal you as a liar. And I discovered that Ana's been formally chosen by Boaz. She will be presented tonight. There's so much to discuss but no time.'

The priestess did not seem perturbed by any of this news and returned to Ana's true role, the one that mattered to Zafira. 'Have you spoken to Ana about . . .'

'Yes. She accepts . . . as Ana always accepts.'

'She has known all along. She just had to find it deep within. She was drawn to Lyana's statue, the temple, she knew.'

'I wish I knew what happens next.'

'None of us do, Pez. That's how it always is. We fight when required.'

'Fight? How?' He aired his thoughts aloud only through frustration. Pez knew Zafira had no answers.

She shook her head helplessly. 'I really don't know. That's why I won't leave.'

'You have to leave,' he insisted. 'You are in danger here.'

'More danger than you or Ana?' Pez hadn't expected her to debate the point and had no ready answer, so she continued. 'Don't be naive, Pez. I felt the danger before you did. You may recall our conversation here thirteen or so moons ago when I mentioned that I felt I was part of something but didn't know what. I was frightened, you may also remember.'

'I do.'

'Well, I'm still frightened but now I know what I'm part of and I won't run from it. Lazar's return is the least of my worries. This is my calling. This is why I'm here. I just wish I wasn't so old and useless to her cause, but still Lyana has chosen me as she has chosen you and Ana.'

'For what?'

'I don't know. Perhaps I've already played my part. Perhaps in having conversations with you and Lazar on the evening of the Choosing and then Ana through that same night, my role is already done. The temple is where we have all met. It might be that I bind us through the temple which is the focus of Lyana in Percheron – all that is left of her.'

Pez followed her line of argument. 'Not all. The stone creatures echo her rule.'

'What use are they to her now?' she asked, and there was a tone of hopelessness in her voice.

'Who knows? When we were moving Lazar from the temple on the day of his flogging to Star Island for secrecy, Ellyana made us row her up to Beloch so she could touch him – perhaps we should read something into that gesture?'

'Bah, that was out of respect.'

'No, Zafira. I paid attention. She spoke to him. It was a chant or a prayer or just words of encouragement. I couldn't hear what she said but I understood their intent. She was communicating with the giant.'

The priestess appeared sceptical. 'What's your point?'

'I feel like I'm ploughing through a swamp in my thoughts. I have no point. I have only seemingly meaningless observations to offer.'

'You think the stone creatures of Percheron are somehow involved in our struggle?' she asked incredulously.

He shook his head, knew it sounded ridiculous. 'As you say, none of us know much at all. We fight when required.'

The thought of the giant being somehow alive lingered

between them, though, and they both glanced again at the impressive crack down his near side.

'You don't think he's crumbling, do you?' she said flatly. 'You have a different idea of what's occurring here.' It felt like an accusation now.

Pez looked at her and his dark eyes gleamed. He shrugged. 'He could be emerging.'

More surprise for Zafira. 'Well, for all the fear you've brought with you today, Pez, I'm pleased you haven't lost your whimsical style. A giant emerging from stone?'

'He was entrapped in stone. He was real once.'

'We're talking centuries and centuries ago. You think he lives?'

Pez grinned and there was mischief in it. His expression heartened the priestess on a day when her heart should feel dark and heavy, aching with grief at the knowledge that Maliz had already risen.

The dwarf continued. 'I don't know, I'm simply airing random thoughts.'

'There's nothing random about you, Pez. You are the messenger, we should heed your words.' She looked again at Beloch. 'Why now?'

Pez became serious again. 'Ana said something intriguing. She mentioned that this time, this battle, it would be different. I don't know what she means by that – I don't even know if *she* does but she seemed determined that the struggle would be different.'

'And you think it could be Beloch and Ezram?'

'Zafira, my mind is wandering everywhere,' he admitted wearily. 'Yesterday I was convinced it was something else, today I'm thinking it's the stone creatures.'

'All of them? Crendel, Darso?'

He nodded. 'If the giants, why not the others?'

The priestess shook her head in attempt to ward off his incredible ideas. 'Who did you imagine it was yesterday?'

'I don't know if I should share my thoughts, Zafira. You don't share what you know.'

The accusation hurt. She grimaced. 'No more secrets between us, Pez, I promise.'

He regarded her for a long time, decided she meant it. 'I thought it was Lazar.'

'Why?'

'Because I know he's not random either. He is involved for a reason. Ellyana's loyalty to him suggests that. She wanted him to live but she wanted no-one to know. She has been waiting for something . . . something to occur or some secret signal to be given.' He shook his head. 'I hate all this guessing.'

'Well, if it's any consolation, I can't confirm if he's the difference but I do know Lazar is involved.'

He swung around and faced her expectantly, a sense of anger behind that expression.

She explained, her palms up to suggest it was not much to go on. 'Ellyana admits she doesn't know what his part in this cycle is but that he is involved and will play a critical role. She said, as we were fighting for his life, that never before had the Lazar aspect been involved. He was a new player in the game of gods. This time it was to be different.'

'That's how Ana feels but she didn't pinpoint Lazar. How could she? She thinks he's dead!'

'I promise that's as much as I know,' Zafira concluded. 'I can't tell you if he makes the difference but he is certainly an innovation and perhaps Ellyana was suggesting that he could be the element that tips the scales.'

'How? Why?'

She shrugged in answer. 'Ellyana was determined to save his life, although I think there were moments there when she, too, felt we had lost him.'

'Why the secrecy, though? Why so much pain for those who care for Lazar?'

'As always, secrets can protect. I have to presume that she is deliberately keeping Ana and Lazar apart, deliberately keeping him away from the palace. Jumo's pain cannot be helped. But she probably gave herself time to see how Lazar fits into the whole battle. And now that you've discovered the Vizier for who he truly is, I can only say she was right in doing so. If all of Lyana's warriors were in one spot, it would give Ana away immediately.'

'Well, it won't last, Zafira. As I said, Lazar's returning to the city.'

'What use is that anyway?'

'Anything's better than wasting away on Star Island. How long did you think you could keep that man trapped there?'

She pursed her lips, knowing he was right. 'Not much longer. It's why I wasn't here when you came.'

He understood. 'Ellyana?'

'She needs to know his condition. Perhaps she suspected he was ready to make his move.'

'And you went to meet her.'

'No,' she said, sitting down heavily. 'I go to a particular spot and tie a message to a homing pigeon. I don't know where it goes but this morning's message was that I didn't think Lazar could be contained for much longer.'

Pez grimaced at the secrecy, the whole manipulative way of Ellyana. 'He'll be back tonight.'

'What is he going to do?'

'Present himself to Boaz, as far as I know. Lazar has nothing to hide. But blame will be accorded to you, when they realise you lied. That's why I want you to go.'

She began to shake her head but Pez persisted. 'You are more use to Lyana alive, Zafira. The Zar will not spare you once he knows it was all a ruse – an out-and-out lie to his face as well – and that's how Lazar will have to tell it. Let's be truthful here, he had no hand in the decisions and terrible manipulations anyway.'

Zafira considered what Pez was saying.

He pressed further. 'Live, help us.'

She nodded. 'Where shall I go?'

'Anywhere but here. Go to Z'alotny – to the burial ground of the priestesses.'

She looked at him ruefully. 'Appropriate – at least when the Zar executes me I'll be in the right spot.'

He ignored her comment. 'It's safe, private, no-one goes there. Give me two days and then I shall either come to you or get word to you and we'll work out what to do from there. But you have to leave here now.'

She nodded. 'I shall go.'

'Make haste, Zafira. I don't trust anyone at the palace.'

'I shall be gone within an hour or so.'

He reached around her tiny figure and hugged her. 'Go sooner if you can.'

Maliz twirled the stem of a goblet of pale wine between Tariq's thumb and forefinger as he considered what he'd just heard. 'You're quite sure?'

The man nodded.

'And he didn't stay very long, you say.'

Now the man shook his head.

'Did he bow in the temple to Lyana?'

'No, Grand Vizier. I watched carefully. He did no such thing. As I told you, he arrived doing acrobatics through the temple. There was no respect for the place he was in. He spoke briefly to the priestess – well, screamed to tell the truth – about wanting some fruit and she seemed familiar and rather kindly towards him. He dragged her to the back of the temple and I could hear him still yelling about fruit and listing all of their names. Finally, she took him upstairs to give him some. I could hear him demanding a pomegranate. That's when I left for fear of being seen. I waited and he came out not long afterwards clutching an orange. He kept smelling the orange—'

'Yes, yes, I understand. He didn't touch the sculpture of Lyana?' the Grand Vizier persisted, determined to connect Pez with the Goddess.

'He paid her no heed whatsoever,' the man confirmed, bowing for good measure. 'He was as annoying and silly as he usually is.'

'Keep shadowing the dwarf whenever he leaves the palace. I will pay you well.' He tossed a small pouch that landed at the man's feet with a solid thump.

'Thank you, Grand Vizier.'

'I pay for your secrecy too, Elaz. Don't speak out of turn to anyone or I shall close your lips forever.'

The man nodded, eager to be dismissed. Maliz waved him away and replayed in his thoughts what he had discovered. There was no proof, then. The dwarf behaved true to form. Perhaps the priestess was simply a friend or someone who took pity on the idiot. But why go to the temple? The coincidence of it being the sacred place of Lyana was irresistible to Maliz. He would have to learn more.

He would begin with the priestess.

13

Ana had never looked more stunning than she did at this moment. Even she was surprised by the solemn yet dazzling person staring back at her from the glass.

'He will adore you,' Elza whispered, praying to Zarab that the girl would put behind her the episode with the Grand Master Eunuch that had left her trembling, bleeding and puffy-eyed from weeping. She remembered how, when she had tried to comfort the young woman. Ana had exclaimed that she was not crying from grief, but from anger.

'I don't care,' Ana replied stiffly, her rouged lips making her scowl seem alluring rather than how she intended it.

'Miss Ana, please. Let this go well for you. To be First Chosen is one of the highest prizes. Look how the harem honours you with its finest jewels. I hear the Valide herself chose and bought them for you. The Grand Master Eunuch put them around your neck himself to honour you.'

Ana's voice was waspish when it came. 'For your sake alone, Elza, I am not ripping these jewels from my neck and wrists and ankles.'

The slave gasped. 'They are worth more than ten of me, child.'

'And I hate them. I don't want them.'

'What do you want, Miss Ana?'

'Freedom. Leave me, Elza.'

'No, I cannot. I have promised to escort you into the divan suite. Grand Master Salmeo says the other girls must see you in all your finery before you are taken to the Zar's chambers.'

'So he can make the other girls jealous, so they will hate me?'

Elza shrugged, embarrassed. 'I must do as I'm told, Miss Ana.'

'Let us go now then, for I cannot stand the sight of myself a moment longer. I am like the jewels – pretty but dead.'

Elza shook her head, worried whether they would ever tame this girl.

The Grand Vizier arrived at the Sea Temple as the sun was dipping low behind the statue of Ezram. The giant looked to be framed by a halo of fire whilst the sky had blistered to a burning orange as if in final salutation to the day. Its farewell cast a bright glow onto the waters to make the bay appear like a cauldron of molten gold, but the Vizier did not appreciate Percheron's theatre of natural beauty. Maliz was entirely distracted, grimacing at being so close to the worshipping place of Lyana, and his revulsion only intensified when he stepped into its cool shadows and saw the sculpture of the woman he reviled.

Lyana watched him too, her expression as hard and as unyielding as the stone she was formed from. Maliz felt his bile rise at being in her presence and as he approached Lyana he could no longer control his revulsion and he spat at her. His spittle slid down her chin to land on her left breast and whether it was a trick of the eye or simply the way the slit of dying golden sunlight made a last effort to light her, the liquid seemed to stain the pale stone from which she was crafted.

Maliz sneered. 'I will destroy you again and again, Lyana,' he said softly, cruelly. 'The faithful will never worship a woman.'

He was disturbed by the arrival of a tiny person, an old priestess who had descended the stairs with a small sack. At first she covered her surprise at his presence with a quick smile – the sort she kept for someone come to pay quiet homage, he guessed, but Maliz noticed how the smile died fast on her wrinkled face. She tried to disguise the alarm but he saw it all clearly. It was his first clue.

'Grand Vizier Tariq?' she asked, over-brightly he thought. 'What a surprise. How can I help you?'

'Perhaps you can,' he replied smoothly. 'I am looking for Pez.'

She frowned. 'The Zar's buffoon?'

'The only Pez I know of in Percheron,' Maliz said dryly.

The priestess shook her head. 'Pez is not here, Grand Vizier. I'm sorry your journey has been wasted.'

'He has been, though, hasn't he, priestess?'

To her credit, Zafira didn't so much as blink at his trap. 'Earlier today, yes. Silly fellow was looking for fruit, of all things. He can be quite contrary – as I'm sure you must know – but I feel sorry for him most of the time,' she said and he noticed how she wrung the corners of the sack ends in her hands. Another clue. The priestess was nervous.

'I'm sorry, you know me but I don't have your name?'

'I am Zafira.' She put the sack down and pushed her hands into the pockets of her aquamarine robes to appear relaxed. He thought it was more likely an attempt to steady them.

He pressed on, keeping his voice friendly. 'So Pez visits regularly, Zafira?'

'I wouldn't say regularly,' she replied, trying to find a breezy smile. 'He finds kindness here, Grand Vizier. He calls whenever his odd mood swings bring him and I have no warning. If I can help him to calm I usually do. Sometimes all the troubled soul needs is some time.'

'Does he communicate with you?'

Now she gave an expression of disdain. 'As well as he communicates with anyone. He speaks gibberish most of the time.' Now she looked quizzical. 'I'm sure I'm not telling you anything you don't already know, Grand Vizier, as you are around him in the palace and see him so much more than I.'

'I have very little to do with him.'

'I find myself in the same position. Pez is welcome here as anyone is welcome. No-one is turned away. But his trips are rare and, although he did stop by today in a fractious mood that was apparently solved by an orange, he's not here at present. Now if you've finished with your questions, I'm actually in a hurry,' she said, bending to pick up the sack again.

'Are you going somewhere, Zafira?' As Maliz stepped forward, the priestess shrank back. It was his best clue yet. She had no reason to be fearful of him and yet it was obvious she was entirely disturbed by his presence. 'Do not be scared of me.'

'I'm not,' she said too quickly.

'Your voice shakes, is something wrong?' He took another step towards her.

She retreated again and now he was sure. 'No. You just surprised me and I have to be somewhere.'

'Where?'

Zafira mustered some indignance. 'Somewhere private, sir.'

'Away from here.'

'Yes.'

'Why the hurry?'

'Because I'm late.'

'Can I escort you there?'

'No, Grand Vizier. I'm capable of finding my own way. Frankly, I'm surprised that you can be bothered with one of Lyana's servants.'

It was a mistake. It gave Maliz the opening he needed.

'What makes you think I would make such a distinction?' He could see the fear taking full hold of her now, see it taking flight in her startled eyes that displayed her understanding that she had made an error in even mentioning Lyana. As far as Maliz was concerned, there was only one reason that anyone would be terrified of the Grand Vizier. They would have knowledge that inside the body walked a demon.

He laughed aloud, deep and menacing, as it all clicked into place in his mind. He had found one of Lyana's disciples. It was a start.

The battle had begun.

Ana entered the divan suite to the sounds of rapturous welcome as the other odalisques rushed to touch her gown, her precious jewels, her polished skin and shining golden hair. She was dressed in a shimmering pale blue outfit that was little more than gauze, just as Herezah had envisaged. Edged with silver and dusted with diamond glitter, Ana's every movement, however slight, made her entire body sparkle. Her hair was worked up in a delicately wrought silver clasp, studded with diamonds, and to add insult to injury, after Salmeo had finished with her, he had ordered her ears have further piercings and these were now hung with diamond drops and sapphires. Her nose had also been pierced and the curiously slight injuries – for all that pain – were now covered by diamond studs. Ana took grim amusement in believing that had this been the middle of the day and not early evening no-one would have been able to look at her for fear of being blinded by her dazzling presence.

After a few moments that she considered fair to allow them to express their wonder, the sounds of appreciation continued to escalate rather than lessen and so Ana begged the girls to stop. She did not enjoy the celebrity and her mind was filled with the notion of escape again. Ana knew the risk was huge; knew it was going against the promises she had made to Lazar, to Pez, even to the Valide. To fail in her bid this time would mean death but the prize for success would be freedom and after her meeting with Salmeo earlier, death did not frighten her. If she made it out she had already decided that she wouldn't go home. There would be no point. The palace would hunt her down and Salmeo would likely have her family killed out of spite. No, she had no home any more. Instead, she would head west – perhaps to Merlinea where others told her Lazar came from. The west still respected Lyana and perhaps she could find a convent or temple that might take her in for a while. Her thoughts extended to even living the life of a priestess if they would have her.

She came out of her musings at the insistent touch of a youngster called Prem.

'The bundle women are coming tonight as a special treat for us,' she gushed.

'I know, I'm looking forward to it too,' Ana said, trying not to show just how earnestly she meant it. 'Did you all have a wonderful day on the water?'

That set off a chorus of conversation that Ana was pleased to lose herself in whilst she nervously awaited the arrival of the bundle women. One of the Elim sidled up. A man called Olam, whom she liked.

'Miss Ana.'

'Yes?'

'We are to escort you to the Zar's chambers at nightfall.'

'I will see the bundle women with the rest of the girls, won't I?' she asked anxiously. 'It's just I missed out on the river barging with them.'

He nodded reassuringly. 'Yes, Miss Ana. I will collect you as soon as the bundle women have departed. They are due any minute. You will miss your evening meal but the Grand Master Eunuch felt it was best you go to the Zar empty rather than full.'

She smiled wanly and nodded, using her folded hands in her lap as the only modesty she could provide for herself, although Olam's eyes were fixed upon her own.

'Can I organise something light for you before the bundle women come, Miss Ana?'

'I'm not hungry, Olam.'

'I understand,' he said, backing away after a short bow.

'Not hungry? I'm starving,' Prem groaned.

Sascha, sitting nearby, laughed. 'You've been eating all day, Prem. You'd better watch yourself or you'll get fat and the Zar will never want to lie with you like he does with Ana and then you'll never have a chance at being a wife, or to give him an heir.'

Prem looked mortified at the threat and Ana felt equally mortified but for other reasons. The girls were taking this all so lightly. Was she the only one who feared the Zar's touch? No, she knew that wasn't true. They would all be as frightened as her on their first time with a man but this went deeper; Ana did not want to be bedded by Boaz, whereas they all apparently did. She had listened to them talk about his handsome looks and what it would be like to be alone with him. They were all accepting of their roles as odalisques and already planning ahead in their minds to their own special first night with the Zar. As Sascha's comment attested, some of the older ones were already thinking about children – about trying to give him an heir quickly.

But she was revolted by the thought. And it was not because she was too young, too frigid, too uninterested by sexual liaison. None of that was relevant. There was only one obstacle, and its name was Lazar. Lazar was the only man whom she wanted to touch her – the only man she wanted to touch tenderly in return. Although if it were true that Lazar was alive she felt sure any chance she had to touch him might be squandered in the form of a punch. She had put that simmering thought of him lying about his death to the back of her mind for the past few hours but now it had erupted to wound her again. And Pez was in on the lie, and that meant so was Zafira . . . and Jumo? Had Jumo rushed off to Merlinea to find Lazar's kin, as Boaz had explained, or was that all part of the elaborate ruse? She blinked back a tear of self-pity and forced a bright smile onto her face.

'Well, at least you'll have the benefit of my experience with the Zar,' she said amiably to the now-small crowd that had gathered around the conversation. 'I can tell you what he likes.'

They all laughed and then someone noted the Elim arriving — several of them — which meant the bundle women were here. Squeals of childish joy exploded and the older girls, more demure, stood, gathering close to Ana, their unheralded leader, to await at a polite distance. All the girls had veiled without having to be asked. It was not necessary, of course, but the Valide had insisted they get into the habit so that it became an instant reaction to any stranger.

Right enough, behind the first four Elim came a motley assortment of brightly dressed women, all veiled, and carrying the enormous bundles they were famous for.

'The Grand Master Eunuch said we can have whatever we want. The palace will settle the bill,' Sascha whispered.

'Very generous,' Ana replied tartly and then sighed at how easily Salmeo manipulated the harem. But her only concern now was wondering which of the women might be the one she was looking for. She bit her lip in consternation at the worrying thought that she and Kett had not even planned how the woman would recognise her. Ana had to presume that Kett would have given such a detailed description that the woman would pick her out in an instant, and for the first time that evening Ana was grateful for the sheerness of the garments she was draped in. Her face, along with the rest of her body, was clearly visible.

She watched the girls peeling off from the main group to look at the various trinkets, fabrics, scarves, even some wooden toys for the youngest in the harem. The Elim had departed but would wait just outside the divan suite, leaving the various eunuch servants to watch from a discreet distance.

Ana saw a woman dressed in darker robes approach, her face fully veiled save a tiny slit for her eyes. She held her breath. This was it. She had no idea how they were going to do this or even if it could be pulled off but she cast a prayer to Lyana to guide her in this daring move and nodded carefully at the woman.

The woman nodded back and surreptitiously pointed to an area in the suite that had a number of marble pillars. Ana understood. She beckoned to the woman to lay out her wares in and around the pillars, saying that it was less crowded over there.

The stranger hefted the huge bundle from her back to the floor and Ana noticed her black hands, her fingers shaking as she untied the knot that held all the goods within. Finally they spilled out.

'Ribbons,' Ana commented nervously, for want of anything better to say.

The woman looked up, regarded her from behind the veil. 'No-one else but you wants them,' said a voice she recognised.

She stared into the dark eyes she could just see behind the veil. 'Kett?'

The figure nodded. 'I'll explain later. Just do as I tell you.'

Ana was too flustered to think straight, but hope surged upon realising that Kett was easily strong enough to lift her; whether the woman would be able to carry her had been worrying her since they had first hatched the plan.

She watched Kett spreading out his hundreds of ribbons and stole a glance around the room. Everyone was occupied. Even the servants were distracted. She wondered why the Elim had so curiously left the room but could only thank Lyana that they had. No-one was paying any attention to her any longer. She whispered this to Kett.

'Yes, we are fortunate but there's going to be a distraction as we draw close to the end of the session to help. I suggest you go and look at the other wares – be noticed.'

She did so, strolling around behind the other girls who were fingering the trinkets. She took her time, finally arriving behind Sascha, who was intrigued by a tiny red bean that one of the sellers was showing her. Ana moved closer to watch. The bean was no larger than her own small fingernail and a tiny part of its top had been cut away and replaced by a beautifully shaped lid of ivory that fitted snugly into the gap. She couldn't imagine anyone carving anything so small. The woman now expertly removed the lid and tipped the contents from the bean into Sascha's palm. Both girls gasped with pleasure to see a dozen fragile, exquisitely carved elephants that Ana had to squint at to make out.

Sascha was kneeling and now turned to look at Ana. 'Aren't they breathtaking?'

'How does one work on anything that small? They must carve looking through a magnifying glass.'

The woman nodded and Ana could see her grinning through her soft veil. She didn't have many teeth.

'Very good price for you,' she said, holding one of the beans out to Ana.

'Take one,' Sascha urged. 'We both will.'

'Yes, why don't you have one of those lovely items,' Salmeo suddenly said from behind her, the waft of violets sickening as it enveloped her.

Ana froze. How could she have not heard him arriving behind her? Why was he here? Surely it was not time yet! She forced herself not to look towards Kett for fear of giving him away. The Grand Master Eunuch was far too sharp not to notice a fearful glance. Instead she took a steadying breath and turned to face her nemesis.

'I have nowhere to put it, Grand Master Salmeo, as you can see,' she said, defying him to stare at her painted nipples which showed somewhat grotesquely through her gauzy gown.

He accepted her challenge and didn't look the slightest bit coy about enjoying the sight of her body. 'My dear, fret not. If you prefer not to use the tiny pocket of your gown I shall have it sent to your chamber immediately. Does anything else take your fancy?' His lisp was worst when in his flirtatious mood.

'I have not finished looking yet, Grand Master Eunuch. I shall hang on to the bean, I like it.'

'Carry on, then,' he replied sweetly, his tongue flicking out between the gap in his teeth as he smiled fondly at her. 'Take all you want, Ana. Tonight is yours but be ready, for Olam will come for you shortly.' He made to leave and then turned back for a parting shot. 'I hope you're not too sore from our intimate time together this afternoon,' and gave her no chance to respond.

Seething, wanting to scream or throw something at him, hurt him, she watched the huge man lightly glide away, and a nagging thought begged her to pay attention to it, but she was distracted by a beckoning sign from Kett and the reminder that the best way to hurt Salmeo was to beat him at his own game of cunning.

She held up her bean at the bundle woman. 'May I?'

The woman nodded enthusiastically and was then diverted by Sascha and several other girls wanting some of the bright red beans. Ana took her chance and the added precaution of saying to Sascha that she needed to relieve herself.

'Hurry,' Sascha replied. 'There isn't much longer before they leave, you'll miss everything,' and turned back to the trinkets.

Ana returned to Kett.

'I'm not sure we can risk you in this,' she warned. Her voice shook. 'Not now Salmeo—'

'Forget about me, Miss Ana,' he cut across her words. 'I am here now and no-one suspects. If you wish to go, let us do it. If you have second thoughts, or are scared, I can leave with the other women and no-one will be any the wiser.'

'I'm not scared for me,' she admonished in a whisper. 'I'm worried for you.'

'Don't be. This is my path. The path of sorrows.'

She had no idea what he meant by that comment and no time to consider it because a loud squeal went up behind them.

Ana swung around to see that a bundle woman had obviously brought in a basketload of kittens. There were surely three litters involved as a veritable army of tiny cats was scattering in all directions and the girls as well as bundle women and servants were giving chase.

'Now!' Kett demanded, pushing her and pointing at the huge square of cloth. 'Curl up tight!'

Ana had no time to reconsider. She leapt into the middle of Kett's bundle and within moments found herself encased in the gloom of his musty-smelling wares. She was careful to ensure no elbow or toes pointed anywhere and held herself as small and as round as she could. Ana was very supple and it used to be a game she'd play with her father – she never thought of him as a step-father, even though he had found her as an orphan – that he could roll her around their hut just like a ball. She used that talent now to make herself invisible in the bundle.

She could hear the commotion around her as cats were noisily rounded up. Above her she could sense Kett fiddling with the bundle and securing the knot that would keep her from falling out. It also made him look less conspicuous to be busying himself with preparing to leave, she guessed.

A gong sounded and signalled the end of the bundle women's visit. Soft sighs of disappointment greeted the gong and then she could hear men's voices as the Elim began to hurry the bundle women out of the divan suite.

'Where is Odalisque Ana?' she heard one ask. It was Olam.

Ana held her breath. This was it, both she and Kett would be impaled or something equally hideous for another of her reckless, selfish acts.

It was Sascha she heard responding. 'She went to relieve herself. She came and told me just a few moments ago, so she shouldn't be long.'

'I shall be back to fetch her. There are some traditional rituals we must adhere to for the First Virgin before we take her to the Zar. Please tell her . . .'

Ana never heard what she was supposed to be told by

Sascha, for Olam's voice faded into the distance as Kett hurried away and she settled as best she could to the bumpy ride.

She presumed they hadn't brought the bundle women through the entire palace to the harem. There were many entrances and exits that could be used as short cuts. The servants used them all the time to come and go, and she prayed now that the Elim would be keen to move the sellers as fast as they could from the harem.

Zafira fled from the advancing Vizier, tried her best to escape up the stairs, but at her age and with her knees, no longer capable of such punishment, she predictably gave way after about six steps and she all but collapsed under her own weight. Maliz was in no hurry.

As he strolled up the stairs to where she lay he made a tut-tutting sound of exasperation that he had had to go through this theatre. There was no longer any need for pretence. He had guessed correctly; there was no doubt that she knew who he was, and now what he needed from her was information.

'Where did you think you might run to, old woman?' He grabbed her bony ankle and ruthlessly pulled her backwards down the stairs, her chin, ribs, elbows smashing savagely against the stone. He smiled at her shrieks of pain.

At the bottom he flipped her over, took a fistful of her robe and pulled her up to face him, deriving pleasure in her ragged breathing as she tried to cope with the pain.

Zafira found the courage to open her eyes to look upon evil, and Maliz was surprised to see nothing but defiance in those rheumy eyes now. Gone was the fear, and definitely gone was the pretence. His prisoner moved her head to stare at the statue of the Goddess behind him and she began murmuring a prayer to Lyana.

He shook her as a hunting dog might shake its quarry once caught but she ignored him, continued with her prayer, finally finishing with a beatific smile.

'I am done, Maliz. Do what you will.' Her voice was as cold as the pillar he had her shoved up against.

Maliz snarled and pushed her harder against the pale stone. 'You name me, priestess. I'm impressed. I thought your lips might burn to say it.'

She snarled back through her agony. 'Enjoy your small victory, demon. It is pathetic and it is your last.'

He laughed, threw her down to the floor and heard a brittle bone somewhere in her body protest with a snap. He kicked her viciously, that same shard of bone now puncturing a lung. She shrieked and then wept, her mouth open in a silent scream as spittle puddled on the floor beneath her, mottled with blood.

'Your end is close, priestess. Just listen to your breathing. Why don't you make it easy on yourself?'

'How?'

'Tell me who she is.'

'And then what?' she sneered through the pain.

'I shall snap your neck in an instant and there will be no further suffering.'

'And if I keep my secret?'

'You will die in agony.'

'And you think that scares me?'

'It should.'

'She has spoken to me, comforted me that she will prevail this time. You are as good as dead, Maliz, so enjoy your last conquest. My death is meaningless, for my work is already done. You are too late.'

Maliz knew he was being baited but still he couldn't ignore her derision or the suggestion that Lyana would prove more powerful on this occasion. He kicked her as hard as he could, relishing it as more ribs gave way beneath his foot.

'How does that feel, priestess?'

Unbelievably to his ears, she laughed, although blood flew from her mouth. 'Each blow speeds me closer to my Goddess. Lyana is mocking you, Maliz.'

'Who are your companions?'

Her scorn came out as a gurgle of blood that rattled in her throat and spilled from her nose and mouth. 'All of Percheron.'

This time Maliz picked her up and threw her against a pillar with a sickening crunch, knowing it was idiotic to kill the only link he had to Iridor and Lyana. But his need for bloodletting and venting his anger had to be answered. She looked to be dead – was certainly almost gone to her god.

'Is the dwarf Iridor?' he demanded close to her bloodied face.

'No,' she croaked, her tone filled with derision. 'The dwarf is an idiot, as you well know. I will never tell you who Iridor is but he is hunting you as we speak, Maliz, and more's the pity I won't live long enough to tell him who you are.'

A new thought struck Maliz and as distasteful as it was, the destruction of Lyana overrode everything. 'Zafira, before you leave this plane, I'm thinking I should send you to the bitch goddess with the seed of the demon,

Maliz, running down your thighs. It has an intriguing irony, don't you think?'

At this her eyes flew open and he knew he had hit on the right threat. How strange, if he'd struck on the idea first he could have saved them both a lot of effort. He reached for her robes and began lifting them. 'No-one comes here, priestess, no-one will rescue you from this. No-one but me, that is.'

Her robes were already pulled above her knees, revealing her withered thighs. Maliz fancied nothing less than performing a sexual act with this old crone but he knew now it was the one thing that might loosen her tongue.

'I know you wanted to go to your goddess as the virgin you gave yourself to her as. But I'm afraid I've got a rush of blood at having roughed you up, Zafira. I feel a strong desire to release that pent-up lust . . . and sadly for both of us, you're the closest thing.'

He pressed his point by climbing on top of her and her weak attempts to push him off were laughable. He ripped open her robes now to reveal her wrinkled and naked body.

'Not very attractive, Zafira, but it will have to do,' he said, reaching to loosen the top of his trousers.

'No,' she begged. 'Do not desecrate me or her temple.'

'One word will do it, priestess.'

'I do not know who she is,' she pleaded now, all defiance gone, replaced by terror. 'I promise you, I know not who is Lyana's vessel.'

He believed her. From his experience it was too early for Lyana to have fully come into her new incarnation. 'One word, Zafira,' he repeated.

'What word?'

'Who is Iridor? Speak his name and I will finish you off quickly.'

'No rape?'

He shook his head. 'A single word.'

She nodded, closed her eyes and he watched her breathe a short prayer that begged forgiveness. Then she opened her eyes and said the name he had been waiting to hear.

It did not surprise him. But it did enrage him.

∞ 14 ∞

Ana had lost sense of time and geography. She had heard some voices – men's voices – and presumed it was the guards moving them through the various gates, although she had no idea which.

All she knew was the swaying rhythm of Kett's hurried movements and just moments ago she'd felt herself tip dangerously forward but her heart leapt at this new position. Surely this meant they were free of the palace and already moving downhill towards the bazaar. But she didn't dare make any sound . . . not yet.

Kett had broken into another jog. She must be feeling unbearably heavy and he must see his destination, she thought, for him to risk breaking into a run. Within moments she felt herself dropping and then hitting the ground with force but the fabrics in the bundle around her cushioned her fall.

Ana could hear Kett's laboured breathing but waited until he opened the bundle before she said anything, for she couldn't be sure he hadn't simply dropped her from exhaustion.

'Miss Ana!' he hissed. 'Are you hurt?' The familiar eyes behind the dark veils were filled with concern.

'Are we safe?'

He nodded. 'For a short while. Did I hurt you?'

'No, Kett. You've saved my life.' She sprang to her feet and hugged him, ripping off his veil so she could look upon his sweet, trusting face. 'Such a risk you took.' She shook her head and began kissing his cheeks now.

He was still breathing hard but managed to laugh. 'Hush, Miss Ana. We're not that safe!'

'I've got to get out of these clothes, Kett. Have you got anything? Where are we?'

'I have everything already arranged. Behind those big olive jars are some ordinary street clothes. Make sure you are fully veiled or that hair will give you away, Miss Ana.'

They had shared too much nakedness already for her to fret about her lack of modesty and she was quickly ripping off her silken blue robes. She undid the jewellery about her neck.

'You take these.'

'I don't want—'

She ignored his protests. 'Don't sell them here. They're too recognisable. I can't have them about me. Give them away if you want, but not here.' He nodded. She piled the rest of the jewellery into his cupped hands. 'Use the gold to pay off whomever you have to.'

'I don't have to pay anyone.'

She frowned as she pulled the street clothes on. 'What do you mean?'

'I couldn't tell you in the palace. But when I came to the bazaar looking for that friend I told you about, I was stopped by a woman. She was very young and beautiful. She asked me not to use the corrupt bundle woman but to go in disguise myself.'

'And you did, just like that?'

Kett smiled. 'She was very persuasive. She named me – knew who I was, and who I represent.'

'Who you represent?'

'I am the Raven, Miss Ana. The black bird of sorrows.'

'What does that mean?' she said, confused, as she smoothed down her clothes. She reached for the veil but didn't put it on yet.

He shrugged, began pulling off his skirts. He stood naked, save his loin cloth. 'I don't know, to be honest. All I know is that I serve her. Lyana will guide me.'

She looked sharply up at Kett. 'Lyana?'

'You, Miss Ana, I serve Lyana through serving you,' and he smiled.

'Kett, I—'

'No. Let's not talk about it. We both serve Lyana, we both have our roles to play. I don't know what being the black bird means, although the lady seemed to look sad for me as we spoke. Perhaps that's why I'm the bird of sorrows.'

She looked baffled by Kett's words. 'What was this woman's name? Did she tell you?'

'Ellyana. And I could refuse her nothing. We must hide all the clothes,' he warned and they busied themselves tidying up all clues that might give away that Ana had been here.

She nodded, understanding now. 'I'm frightened by the risk you took,' Ana persisted. 'Promise me you will leave the city tonight, Kett, as I must.'

'It's a pity we can't leave together.'

'Too dangerous. And if I get caught I don't want you caught with me.'

'You won't get caught, Miss Ana. Where are you going?'

'Get dressed, Kett. I'm going west. I have no idea how but I shall do it somehow. I am getting as far away from Percheron as I can. What about you? Any ideas?'

He was pulling his trousers on. 'No plan. Like you, as far away from here as possible. My mother has people in the desert caravans – perhaps I can join them.'

She shook her head. 'No, Kett! No-one who knows you or your family. Do you hear me? Salmeo will find you and he will kill everyone you love or even know. Go in the opposite direction. Go east. Get on a ship and sail away from here. You have a fortune in jewellery you can sell. Do it wisely and you will be a made man.' She looked embarrassed by her clumsy choice of words.

He graciously let it pass. 'And so we shall never see one another again.'

She shook her head with a sad smile. Before she donned her veil and before he could pull his shirt on she reached up to take his face and put her lips against his. She kissed him long and softly. There was no desire in it, only sincere friendship and gratitude.

They pulled apart instantly at a noise behind them. Ana felt as though her insides had turned instantly to water. Standing in the space where a curtain had only moments ago kept their secret, stood Salmeo, surrounded by his Elim, and a horrified-looking Valide.

'Get them,' was all Salmeo said. Herezah said nothing but her look of pure hatred towards the friends spoke droves to Ana.

Pez was arguing with Bin.

'Must see my Zar!' he said, stamping his foot. 'He has my butterflies.'

'Pez,' Bin said calmly. 'I've explained he does not want to see you. He will call you when he does. He is preparing to meet with Odalisque—'

Bin was unable to say any more because Pez had begun one of his famous screaming sessions.

Bin backed away, unsure of what to do. Pez began to writhe on the ground, the intensity of his shrieks getting more piercing. One of the mutes happened to look outside the door to summon Bin and frowned when he saw the dwarf on the ground.

'I wish I were deaf like you,' Bin murmured. He nodded expectantly. The mute gave the signal that the Zar wished to see him.

'Thank you, Salazin.' Then shrugged his shoulders towards Pez suggesting he was lost as to what to do with the dwarf.

Salazin came into the vestibule where the Zar's secretary worked and walked towards the writhing creature on the floor. He pinned the dwarf's short arms behind him and lifted him easily, shaking him like a doll to be quiet.

Pez stopped his noise and a look of relief swept across Bin's face. 'Thank you again, Salazin,' and he used the practised sign language to say he didn't know how he was going to stop Pez.

Salazin pointed to the Zar's chambers.

Bin shook his head quickly. 'No.'

The mute put the dwarf down, and Pez remained mercifully silent as the mute signed with his fingers that it would be a good thing for the Zar and his pet to be friends again.

Bin sighed. Gave a look of resignation. He signed: *It's your throat. I'll deny I had anything to do with this.*

Salazin grinned and he was the only one of the mutes who did not have a gaping wound in his mouth.

He picked Pez up again as if he weighed nothing and strode into the room, Bin running behind and making merry protest for the Zar's benefit that Salazin was forbidden to take the dwarf in to see the royal.

Boaz was in his dressing chamber. One other mute was in attendance whilst the Zar's dresser fussed over the outfit that had been chosen for the Zar to greet his first virgin in.

The Zar glared at Bin and then at Pez who again stayed silent. Bin bowed, as did Salazin.

'I couldn't stop him, Majesty. Pez arrived and was making a dreadful noise outside – only Salazin didn't suffer the blood-curdling shrieks of the dwarf – and although I said you did not wish to see Pez, Salazin believed you might.'

'It's important,' Pez whined, picking his nose. He was also tapping his foot and this was a sign to Boaz that it was more than important. It was urgent. Pez had information that couldn't wait and was of a dangerous nature. Long ago the two of them had worked out a code using physical signals to communicate simple messages. They'd employed it throughout Boaz's childhood and, although it hadn't been used in over a year, Boaz felt the sentimental pull at his heartstrings – no matter how angry he still was at Pez – at that tapping of his foot. Pez obviously needed to talk to him and had had to swallow his pride and risk the almost certain rebuke coming his way by being here.

Boaz maintained his stony silence that ensured everyone other than the two mutes felt the discomfort. Finally he slapped away the dresser's hand. 'I'm ready,' he said. The man bowed, knowing he had just been dismissed.

Bin continued his lament. 'Forgive me, Zar Boaz. Salazin just picked up the dwarf and brought him in.'

Boaz signed a query to Salazin. He, Bin and the Vizier were the only people permitted to know the secret signing language and each was proficient in it now, although Boaz was by far the most talented using this challenging form of communication. Sometimes the mutes themselves didn't know what he was asking when the speed of his hands became too intense for them to follow. All but one, that is.

Salazin answered his Zar's query. *Because, Majesty, this is your great friend, as I understand it, and I think he will die of heartbreak soon if he can't be with you.*

I said not until I summoned him. Do you defy me, Salazin?

No, High One. I care deeply for your happiness and I know Pez makes you smile. Even a dog could be forgiven an indiscretion by its master, Majesty. This is a special night for you. Let it be a happy one.

Salazin is a clever one, Boaz thought wryly to himself. Tariq picked wisely. The truth was, Boaz really liked having Salazin around. The young man's presence was always comforting and indeed calming. He never communicated unless asked to and had the knack of disappearing into the room they were in. There were times when Boaz could forget the warrior was nearby and yet the mute was always alert, always ready to leap to the Zar's needs. Yes, he liked Salazin immensely and this was why he forgave the mute this interruption.

'Leave us,' he finally said. 'I will speak with Pez.'

Salazin nodded, didn't have to hear anything to see that the Zar had agreed. Bin bowed, relieved.

The Zar spoke directly to his mutes now through sign language. *I want privacy with Pez. You can wait outside.*

All three men left.

'Thank you,' Pez said tentatively into the silence after the door closed.

'I suppose you put on one of your shows out there?' Boaz said absently, looking at himself in the tall glass.

'The best,' Pez agreed.

'I told you to wait until I wished to see you.'

'That might have been never, my Zar.'

'And so what if it was?' the Zar replied, determined not to let Pez have his clever way.

'I would not be able to give you the important news I have discovered.'

'Which is?' Boaz said, feigning boredom — he even yawned.

'Lazar is alive,' Pez said flatly.

Boaz was instantly focused. He swung around to face the dwarf, his expression fluctuating between disbelief and anger that Pez might dare taunt him in this way.

Pez quickly explained. 'It has all been a ruse, Highness . . . but not of Lazar's doing and not of mine. Lazar nearly died, it's true. But I've found him. I've been looking for him on your behalf since I first heard the unbelievable news of his death.'

'You've been looking for him?' Boaz's voice was soft, uncertain, almost apologetic.

'It's why I kept leaving the palace, my Zar. I never trusted the information we were told, even though delivered by a friend. Lazar might well have perished but he would not have had his body committed to the sea. He was a man of the desert. That's where he would wish to lie, not on the bottom of the Faranel.'

Boaz looked shaken now. 'Why didn't you share your mistrust?'

'You've never really given me a chance. We rarely get time alone any more, Highness. It is not something I could just drop into casual conversation. I needed to be sure.'

'What about Jumo?'

Pez shrugged. 'Another victim of the lie.'

'Where have you found Lazar?'

'He has been recuperating on Star Island.'

Boaz's eyes widened in shock. 'How did you know?'

'It was a wild guess, Zar Boaz. None of us truly believed he might be there but, yes, perhaps we should have checked. In the end I did, on your behalf.'

'Well . . .' Boaz spluttered, unsure of what to say. He had a hundred questions, Pez could see.

The dwarf held his gnarled hand up. 'He has been very sick. Deathly sick. Unable to fend for himself. That's why it's taken so long for us to learn the truth. It took weeks for him to find full consciousness again, move without help. A year before he could walk unaided. That's how the priestess was able to spin her terrible tale. Lazar was unable to defend himself.'

Naturally, he held back that he had helped get Lazar to Star Island in the first instance.

'But why did Zafira lie?' Boaz asked, aghast. He had trusted the old priestess; liked her, too.

'You will have to ask her that, my Zar. I am as injured as you by her lies. She and I were friends.'

Boaz looked utterly confused. 'But with all her efforts she saved his life, didn't she?'

'This is true. Why she would tell you he was dead when she alone nursed him back to health, I cannot say, although I have my suspicions.'

'Which are?'

'Well, there is no doubt someone wanted Lazar dead by the presence of the poison. I'm guessing Zafira went down this extraordinarily mysterious path in order to protect him. She let whomever the murderer was believe that he had succeeded, and this gave her time to nurse him back to full health.'

'But if she'd come to me—'

'Ah, but there was, to all intents, a murderer on the loose, Majesty – he was in the palace and she wasn't prepared to risk that he would not try again once he discovered he had not fully succeeded in killing the Spur. I suspect she simply didn't believe you could protect him.'

'Let's get the priestess here. I have to talk to her directly.'

'We cannot, Majesty.'

'Why?'

'She has disappeared.'

'Disappeared?'

Pez nodded gravely. 'I went to see her at the Sea Temple today and she has gone.'

'Suspicious?'

'I can't say. Possibly not,' he said carefully.

'And Lazar?'

'Is coming to you tonight. He wishes to present himself. I thought it only fair to warn you, High One. It was a shock for me when I found him and I didn't want you to be placed in an awkward position.'

Boaz looked gently at his friend. 'I have wronged you,

Pez. I was angry at your accusations but you are the true friend in my life.'

'I would never do anything to hurt you, my Zar, and I'm sorry I made you so angry. I have been . . . shall we say, preoccupied.'

'It is forgotten,' Boaz said, waving their differences aside. 'My concern is how this is going to look.'

'What does it matter how it looks? You have your Spur back. You had no part in the ruse. Let's be honest, my Zar, the city folk of Percheron will care only that he lives and will celebrate his return.'

'That's right,' Boaz agreed, thinking it through. 'We are innocent in this. We believed what we were told by someone we thought we could trust. And a crime was still perpetrated against him, and someone took responsibility for it.'

'Whether he was guilty or not,' Pez finished the unspoken words that Boaz could not.

The Zar continued, ignoring the interruption and the pain its words provoked. 'The Crown has nothing to feel guilty about.'

'Nothing at all, Majesty. Just welcome your Spur back with open arms.'

Boaz nodded. 'How can I ensure this is kept secret for now?'

'Why would you want it to be kept quiet?'

'Just for now. I would like to speak with Lazar before it all becomes public knowledge.'

'I can't wait to see Salmeo's face when he claps eyes on Lazar,' Pez said knowingly.

'My mother's face is going to be a picture too,' Boaz offered sourly.

'I shall go, Highness,' Pez said.

'To Lazar?'

He nodded.

'Tell him to come in the early hours, and hooded. Tell him to bring this.' He bent over a piece of parchment to quickly dribble some green wax on it from a special candle that burned only in the Zar's rooms. Then, using the great seal he wore around his neck on a beautifully wrought chain, he imprinted his personal mark into the soft wax. 'This will gain him instant access to the palace. I will send one of my mutes to escort him. He is not to be recognised.'

'Why the early hour?'

'I have a meeting with Ana.'

Pez nodded knowingly and then muttered a phrase in a language the Zar did not recognise. Pez smiled sadly. 'Roughly translated it means "take a wife tonight".'

The Zar looked suddenly coy. 'It is my intention.'

'That is good. I go now,' Pez said hurriedly. 'I'm glad we're friends again, Boaz.'

Boaz grinned wryly at him. 'Of course, no-one but you and I will celebrate.'

'I don't doubt it,' Pez replied. 'I shall return,' he added, leaving the Zar's chambers in a series of somersaults, before cavorting down the hallway.

'Ah, and so the world rights itself,' Bin said wearily, more to himself than anyone else, for he had only mutes for company.

Pez raced back to his chamber. It was time to become Iridor.

He flew silently through the warm air, his spirits feeling marginally lighter for restoring the balance of friendship between himself and Boaz. He had begun to worry about being alienated in the palace. It had occurred to him that Boaz, in his anger – if it persisted . . . and Boaz could always be so single-minded – might even ban Pez from being able to roam everywhere he wanted.

He scanned the bay from his vantage, hoping to see Lazar being rowed back to the mainland – although he suspected Lazar would doggedly row himself back. There was little movement on the water this night, though – it seemed the twins would have a quiet evening, he decided. He alighted on Beloch and scrutinised the giant. It was not Pez's imagination; distinct cracks had appeared up and down the stone of the giant's body. From afar, as most people viewed them, they were noticeable but perhaps not intensely eye-catching unless one stared at them each day with interest, as he or Zafira might. But close up the cracks looked serious – it was as if Beloch was simply falling apart, crumbling to the floor. Although this saddened Pez, he still couldn't shake the notion that the giant was not dying as such but being reborn – getting ready to emerge from the stone casing which had imprisoned him.

'Are you, Beloch? Are you rising, as I have and Lyana must, to fight the coming battle?'

If he expected an answer, he didn't get one. The only sound was the distant rumble of the city and the lapping of the water around Beloch's feet. Not even the lonely cry of any seabirds broke the silence, and the ships were still, anchored for the night. Lazar was not here, not yet anyway.

Pez sighed and in his owl guise turned to face Star Island where he felt he should go and hopefully catch the former Spur before he left. His gaze was distracted momentarily from the dark mound in the distance where a few torches burned to guide any night travellers, to an unfamiliar shadow on the Sea Temple. It instantly struck him as odd that the new spire, which Boaz's donation had paid for, looked misshapen. He concentrated, and as his sharp owl eyesight focused carefully, any lightness of heart, however vague, fled in that instant of anguish. Pez felt dizzy from fear at what he thought he might be seeing. And with a heart growing heavier by the second, he found the courage to lift from Beloch's head and fly straight towards certain despair.

Ana and Kett stood in Salmeo's salon, trembling with fear in the warm night air. They hadn't allowed Kett to finish dressing so he remained half naked, whilst thrown at Ana's feet was her pale blue First Virgin outfit, stained and torn. Her jewellery was laid at Kett's feet, a chilling glimpse of what the Grand Master Eunuch planned to accuse him of.

Ana was in a state of deep shock. That she was destined to die was obvious and in her mind almost not worth fretting over, but Kett was a different matter altogether. Kett, her friend who had risked so much – he would die too and she was sure that Salmeo and Herezah would show no mercy and not permit it to be anything but truly ghoulish.

She was ashamed of herself for being so gullible. From the moment she had seen Salmeo licking his lips in that doorway of the bazaar, she understood with a vicious clarity that she had not escaped at all. For all her ingenuity and daring, she had been permitted to leave the harem; it was another of Salmeo's and no doubt Herezah's cunning manipulations. They had wanted her to try another escape and so they had done everything they possibly could to encourage her in this attempt.

She went over it in her mind now. Herezah's supposedly surprise trip to the bazaar gave her the perfect opportunity for the carefully and beautifully crafted conversation that would ultimately push Ana into making a rash decision. And then, of course, Salmeo's revolting touch. She felt sure when it came to Sascha's turn – as beautiful as the girl was – Salmeo would break her hymen and it would be a process over and done with relatively swiftly. He had lingered with Ana and he had aroused her and driven her into such a state of revulsion towards herself at responding to his touch that she would do anything to distance herself from his repulsive being . . . even attempt escape. She let out a laugh, although it came out as a dry sob, that Salmeo had even urged Kett on his errand to the market – it was all so deliberately and exquisitely constructed. They had known everything the pair of them would do before Ana or Kett could even attempt it. How naive had they been to think they could fool the palace's most cruelly manipulative pair with their pathetic escapade.

Even the Elim had been specifically ordered to stand outside the divan suite so Ana could make her escape attempt and feel safe that no guards had been in the room. How stupid had she been not to listen to the nagging voice inside. It had been trying to tell her that the Elim *never* left the girls entirely alone or unsupervised. That ruse alone should have set off every alarm in her head.

Ana now realised that the whole business of the bundle

women and the treat for the girls was a sham too. Salmeo had set it up to make it as easy as possible for Ana to make this audacious attempt – just so that he could entrap her. How low would the Valide and Grand Master Eunuch stoop to ensure she never got close to Boaz? She grimaced inwardly – they wanted nothing less than her execution and she had blindly walked down the pathway as purposefully as if they had put a ring through her nose and led her by a rope as one would a dull beast. Salmeo had probably planted the idea in Kett's head. She felt ill inside thinking how excited he had been to tell her of the brave odalisque who had risked everything to escape the prison of the harem and had succeeded by hiding herself in one of the bundles. She had believed it because she wanted to, because she was so desperate to get away from Salmeo and the threat of Boaz's bed. And she had acted as only a fool would.

The only aspect of this sorry tale that Ana couldn't attach to Salmeo's and Herezah's careful planning was the woman who prevented Kett from using a genuine bundle woman. He had called her Ellyana and admitted he did not possess the power to deny her anything. She recalled how he referred to himself as the black bird of sorrow. She understood now. He was a pitiful individual indeed and in his short life had known so much sorrow.

'Kneel in the presence of your Zar, slut!' Herezah commanded and Ana was dragged from her miserable thoughts to realise that Boaz had entered, his face a mask of misery at what he saw. Nearby stood one from the Zar's new corps of bodyguards, a mute she knew was called Salazin.

Elim pushed her to her knees, although she needed no

help. She was ready to collapse from shame and despair at her own stupidity.

A terrible silence descended and Ana felt as if they'd all become statues. It made her think of Beloch and Ezram, curiously enough — she had never had the opportunity to talk to them, although she had promised herself she would. And Crendel and Darso . . . all the other beautiful sculptures she had made a pact with herself to visit with the new freedom that the Valide had granted. She had planned to talk with each — she wasn't sure why . . . she felt compelled, as she felt compelled to visit Lyana's sculpture at the temple. Her bid to escape had eclipsed all other plans, however, and now she would not see another day and she would never look upon them again.

'Tell me,' she heard the Zar say.

She heard the rustle of silk as Grand Master Salmeo bowed and began constructing his sordid story.

'Odalisque Ana had been prepared for you, my Zar, as you requested this morning. We had seen to it that she enjoyed a special day that marked her new status as First Chosen Virgin. In fact the Valide took her alone, save a few Elim, into the grand bazaar to personally select her jewellery and other accoutrements for the occasion. It was a high honour given to one so young.'

Ana heard Boaz sigh. Perhaps he, too, already accepted that truth would be spun with dark threads of lies before Salmeo offered up his damning scenario.

The Zar spoke to them now. 'Ana, Kett, you may remain kneeling but I would prefer you faced your accusers.'

They both reluctantly lifted their heads, although Ana could not meet the Zar's pained gaze.

Salmeo continued. 'Odalisque Ana was told that you

had made your choice and had given your command concerning her. She was prepared in the ritual fashion, Majesty—'

'Which you no doubt played your critical part in, Grand Master Salmeo?'

'Of course, Highness. That is one of my duties,' the eunuch said with no aggression. His voice was gentle, his lisp pronounced. He felt entirely in control. And now, as he began to wave his arms, warming to the tale, the fragrance of violets assaulted Ana. 'The Valide granted the odalisques a special treat in the shape of a visit from the bundle women. In fact—'

'Why?' Boaz asked, turning to his mother. 'The girls had already enjoyed a long day on the water. Why was more of a treat necessary?'

'My Zar, I did not realise one could ever have too many treats,' Herezah replied, lacing her tone with hurt indignation. 'I grew up in the harem, I know how few and far between the moments of fun can be. I was hoping as Valide to change that for your odalisques. They are still so young and I may be old but not so old that I can't recall the dullness forced on youth in this place. Perhaps wrongly, I thought if I personally gave them a special treat it might encourage the younger ones to feel less daunted by me.'

Ana watched Herezah finish her explanation with a plaintive shrug and considered the Valide a true master of role-playing. She was to be admired for her chameleon-like ability to be anything to anyone that she chose to be. Ana despised her.

'I see,' Boaz said noncommittally, although Ana sensed he saw straight through the veneer of his mother's tale. 'Continue,' he said to Salmeo.

'Well, Majesty, we allowed Ana to enjoy some time with the other odalisques. She had, after all, missed out on the boating trip with her Zar and we decided to let her share the treat of the bundle women.'

'That's very generous of you, Grand Master Eunuch,' Boaz said. 'Ana, did you select anything from all the wares on offer?'

Ana was forced to confront Boaz's pain and was about to shake her head when she remembered the bean and felt the damnation of it and how it incriminated her still further. Truth was best. 'Yes, Zar Boaz. At Grand Master Salmeo's insistence I felt obliged to accept this.' She dug into her pocket and pulled out the tiny bean of elephants. She uncapped it and tipped the contents into her palm. 'They are ivory, Majesty.'

'How intriguing,' Boaz said, leaning down to stare at them with fascination. She could smell his freshly bathed hair. Bathed for her. 'And you say the chief eunuch encouraged you?'

She nodded. 'There is nothing I want for, Majesty—'

'Except your freedom, obviously,' he replied sharply.

Ana looked aggrieved but he was right – she could hardly deny it. 'Yes, Highness. I have made a habit of proving that, haven't I?' She caught the look of anger from her accusers at her familiarity with him but ignored it and decided that, although Boaz was slowly building a case to help her, she hoped her next words might bring this charade to a close. 'I have no defence, Highness. An opportunity presented itself and I took it.'

'May I?' Salmeo cut in.

Boaz nodded unhappily.

'My Zar, this is not a simple case of Odalisque Ana

seizing a rare chance in a bid for freedom. I think a year ago we were able to make this argument on her behalf because of her age, newness to the palace and, through my fault, genuine opportunity that was taken on the whim of the moment.'

'And this time?' the Zar queried, knowing he would be dealt a crushing case against Ana.

'Well, this time it was premeditated, my Zar,' he exclaimed, filled with well-practised indignation. 'Odalisque Ana could not have escaped the palace without carefully setting up her plan first. She and the eunuch, Kett, were in this together from the start. They had ample chance during the whole of today in each other's almost-exclusive company to hatch and test their plan. Forgive me my directness, Highness, but there was absolutely nothing spontaneous about Odalisque Ana's decision.'

'And why would Kett aid Odalisque Ana? Do you see it as revenge for the justice meted for his error more than a year ago?'

And Boaz could see the mistake he'd made in asking such a question. He took it all in during the few moments he had between asking it and wishing he never had. He saw the way his mother's shoulders relaxed as she knew he had walked into the trap, saw the way Salmeo's eyelids narrowed a fraction as his Zar took the bait, saw Ana fully close her eyes in resignation at what was surely coming and in the way Kett slumped still further knowing his fate.

'Kett is an enigma, my Zar,' Salmeo began, his voice soft, almost tender now. 'He has loved Odalisque Ana since the day he saw her naked and frightened in the Choosing Room. They shared a deeply emotional experience when he was cut, Majesty, and from then on I think in Kett's disturbed, fevered mind he and she were meant to be together. I think he now believes, in his twisted logic, that he's in love with one of your prized women, my Zar.'

'That's a lie!' Ana yelled, hating the inflammatory words and how well Salmeo could play the situation to provoke the Zar.

Herezah gasped and Salmeo pursed his fat lips and both looked to Boaz to censure her.

Boaz did not like what he was hearing, as was clear from his darkened expression at the news of Kett's adoration of one of his women. 'Ana, let the Grand Master Eunuch finish. You will have your chance to speak, for this is the most serious of accusations. Continue,' he ordered.

'I was going to say, my Zar, that no man would risk so much for a woman unless he had a special devotion to her, although I grant you we found all of Ana's precious jewels with his belongings. I still don't believe Kett did it for wealth. He could hardly sell any of these jewels locally. No, Highness, Kett had more spiritual reasons, you could say, for aiding Odalisque Ana in her misguided plan.'

Ana opened her mouth to protest and shut it again at Boaz's glare.

'Finish your sorry tale, Grand Master Eunuch, I find it distressing to drag it out any longer.'

Salmeo bowed his head. 'Of course, Highness. We found the pair of them in a grubby backstreet of the bazaar in what could only be called a regrettable position.'

'Be specific, Salmeo. I want all the facts, not innuendo.'

'Very good, Highness. As you wish. Odalisque Ana was

discovered unveiled, all her palace clothes thrown behind an olive jar, whilst her companion was all but naked. This in itself is a damning set of circumstances that demand the most stringent of punishments, Majesty. However, that is not the full extent of your odalisque's treachery. She was also found in the arms of her eunuch companion, their lips in warm embrace.'

Now Boaz shot Ana a glare of such rage, she had no doubt that he was ready to pronounce the death sentence.

'I'm sorry, son,' Herezah said softly from the background. 'She is a vixen and a user of men.'

Boaz did not reply to his mother. Instead his blistering gaze was fixed on Ana. 'It is your turn, Ana. Can you refute any of what is levelled against you? And if so, you must provide proof of your innocence.'

Ana knew it was hopeless. Boaz's eyes looked glazed with jealousy and it was doubtful he would see much reason now that Salmeo had primed him so skilfully. Furthermore, Boaz could not, would not, overturn such fundamental harem rules. She was caught with another man – she had to all intents and purposes cuckolded the Zar.

Her next decision was made to deliberately inflame her accusers still further.

She had nothing to lose and only pleasure to gain from watching Herezah's gathering fury as she swapped into the Galinsean language. 'I prefer not to debase myself further with trying to justify my actions, which Grand Master Salmeo has related with such creative embellishments, Zar Boaz. May I suggest you do the honourable thing by your crown, Majesty, although I beg you to spare Kett. He is such an innocent and was driven by a desire to serve,

Highness, which I would imagine you might consider an attribute in any slave.'

Herezah's expression of deep hatred seared Ana as effectively as if she had thrown a lamp of burning oil at her. Salmeo simply looked amused by her eloquent soliloquy, even though he understood not a word, while the Zar blinked several times as he first struggled to translate and then digest her cutting words.

'You wish to die?' he asked, aghast, but privately distraught. Did she not know that he loved her?

Again she replied in Galinsean. 'It is where this is all headed, Zar Boaz. It would be naive for us to think otherwise. Let us make it easier for everyone and prevent a late night of recriminations and tears.' She swapped agilely back to Percherese. 'I am guilty, yes. I have made my second attempt at escape from the harem and I fully understood the consequences when I made that decision. Sadly, I roped an innocent into my plan. May I add that I did not kiss Kett out of lust as suggested but purely in thanks for his unselfish risk-taking.'

'Zar Boaz, this is all very noble,' Herezah cut in, exasperated. 'The fact of the matter is, an odalisque has been found unveiled in the presence of a man – a half-naked man at that. In this there is no argument.'

'If you can call Kett a man, Highness,' Ana said calmly. 'The harem took that status away from him in all but title.'

'We had no choice, Highness,' Salmeo lisped. 'Kett broke a sacred rule. And now he has done it again. I cannot see why any mercy should or indeed can be shown to a person who has already been given a second chance for redemption. He has snubbed that opportunity.'

'I agree,' Boaz said, noticing the shock register on Ana's face. 'Kett, I have no choice in this but to get my palace in order. I will not brook this sort of disobedience. I demand loyalty. You understood the consequences, I'm sure, of your actions should you have failed.'

'I did, Highness, and the truth is I would do it again for Miss Ana,' Kett replied more bravely than he felt.

Boaz nodded, determined not to show his despair at now having to pronounce sentence not just on the woman he loved but on a childhood friend also, someone he could tell was at the mercy of love too but unable to hide his feelings as well as the Zar had learned to. 'I admire your courage, Kett. You will be ganched tomorrow at noon, your body tossed onto the death hooks to squirm and die. May the hooks find their mark and kill you swiftly.'

'No, Boaz!' Ana begged.

He ignored her, needed to exert his authority and ensure control over his own emotions; if he looked at her now, her expression could undo him. 'Take him away,' he commanded the Elim standing nearby.

Without further ceremony the young eunuch was pulled to his feet and hurried from the room without so much as a chance to say farewell to Ana.

Ana wept. 'You brute! You are callous like your mother, Zar Boaz. I can only pity you and the people of Percheron.'

Without warning Herezah stepped up and slapped the kneeling odalisque with such force she toppled sideways. 'Don't you dare take his or my name in vain. You are nothing!' she spat, a rare emotional outburst from the woman always in control. 'You are not worthy to so much as look upon him again. Slut!'

'Mother,' Boaz warned. 'Step back or return to your chambers.'

'My son, I will no longer listen to these filthy words from this girl. You have heard what she has done this day and let me add that I, too, witnessed her kissing the half-naked black eunuch. She might as well have been naked herself in a public place in the presence of another man. All our sacred rules have been flouted by this one girl since her arrival. You have no choice but to take punitive measures, as your father before you would have. I shall take my leave,' she finished, breathing hard, eyes glittering furiously as she took a lingering look at her son before formally dropping a low curtsey. She straightened, took a final scathing glance at Ana and left without another word.

Into the silence Ana pushed Boaz further still. She would not live again under the harem rules and, true to herself, would rather die than be returned to Salmeo's and Herezah's care. 'You should listen to your mother, Boaz, you probably always will.'

Salmeo looked set to explode into laughter and applaud her pluck. It was obvious he had never heard anyone speak to a Zar with the disdain that this slip of a girl was this evening.

Seething beneath the huge eunuch's not very well disguised mirth, Boaz could no longer protect Ana from herself. He had reached his own limit of tolerance. His position as Zar demanded he punish her, and fully.

'It seems you have a death wish, Odalisque Ana, that you would provoke me so.'

'Pronounce sentence, Zar Boaz, I tire of this audience.'

He shook his head with wonder; imagined what his

father might have visited on a woman who talked to him in this way. Although he had many of his father's characteristics, he would not reduce himself to strike this woman, even if she deserved another blow for her insolence. But as he thought this, he had to quell the equally strong feeling of sickness he felt at losing her. Through it all he admired her. Admired her dauntless attitude and her ability to trust the spirit of her own convictions. She was a match for him all right, but perhaps too much of one? He would never know. He had taken it for granted that Ana would be his wife, his Favourite; he had envisaged many nights of pleasure as well as stimulating conversation stretching before him. He could never have foreseen that he would be required to sentence her to death.

Boaz swallowed — he had absolutely no choice, and Salmeo's delight in his Zar's discomfort was all too plain to read on the eunuch's face. No, he must exert his status; the future security of the royals was doomed if a mere odalisque could influence a Zar to back down. He took a steadying breath, hating her in that moment for forcing him into this position, and found his voice: 'Odalisque Ana, it is my painful task to advise that you will be escorted from here to the palace pits. Tomorrow at dawn you will be taken from there, secured in a weighted velvet bag, rowed out on one of the barges to a private spot on the river and drowned.' It was the least painful death he could contrive . . . but it was still the execution that he was obliged to deliver. She said nothing in response during his pause. 'And there at the bottom of the royal river I hope you find peace and the people you have lost.'

She nodded. These were the first meaningful words she

had heard during this meeting. 'Thank you, Zar Boaz. I shall be reunited with my Uncle Horz and Kett, all of us executed on your order. I shall be candid with you. I am not afraid to die. I am more afraid to live.'

Boaz turned to the eunuch. 'Salmeo, leave us. I wish to say something to Ana in private. Make arrangements to have her taken to the pits in a few moments.'

Salmeo's tongue flicked out between the gap in his teeth to wet his lips to say something and then obviously changed his mind. 'At once, Highness,' he lisped.

When the huge man had departed, Boaz offered Ana his hand to help her to her feet.

She took his gracious offer silently. 'I want you to know that I am deeply sorry, Zar Boaz, for all the displeasure I have caused you personally. I meant you no insult. You have been nothing but generous to me.'

He regarded her through angry, wounded eyes. 'Odalisque Ana, I cannot accept that apology,' and he couldn't help but derive a measure of satisfaction, albeit sad, that he had managed to penetrate her defences and injure her with his comment. 'And I must tell you this before you go. No-one else knows of this yet, and I suspect you could say it is my parting gift to you on a night when I aimed to make you my wife.' She bit her lip, unsure of what was coming. 'You may well be reunited with Horz of the Elim, as you say. I hope so. Kett will join you later, of course. But in case you were hoping, you will not find Lazar anywhere near your watery grave, Ana, no matter how hard you search.'

'What do you mean?' she asked, the hairs on the back of her neck lifting with dread anticipation, the confirmation of what she believed to be true.

'I mean that he is alive. I am seeing him in a few hours.'

'Alive?' She whispered. It was a shock to have her suspicions authenticated.

He nodded. 'Pez found him.' She looked dumbfounded as the truth of her fears of betrayal by two of her few allies settled like lead weights around her. 'I'm sure Lazar will be devastated to learn that his efforts to preserve your life with his own were always in vain. Guard!'

'No, wait!'

'Too late, Ana. I have adored you since I first saw you and I would have treated you with kindness and tenderness all of your life. Your disdain for me and my position is a wound I must learn how to heal now.'

The door opened and the Elim moved in to escort Ana to the palace pits.

Boaz did not move, remained as still as a statue long after Ana had been taken away. Finally Salazin stepped forward, melting out of the shadows. He signed: *My Zar, can I escort you back to your chambers?*

Boaz nodded. He had never felt this empty and he knew now he would never love another woman, as he had this one, nor permit himself to.

Pez alighted on the spire above the grisly scene. It made no difference that he was in his Iridor shape. He still wept. He wept for his friend, he wept for her suffering and he wept for all the supporters of Lyana.

Zafira's life was the first lost in the battle. He knew it would not be the last but that was cold comfort as he looked down upon the tiny figure, broken, bloodied and impaled upon her own temple's new spire.

As if in respect for his grief, a cloud scudded across the sky and blocked the moonlight, casting the owl and the body into darkness. He took the opportunity to change into his dwarf shape and wiping his wet cheeks, gingerly moved down beside Zafira. He kissed her cool cheek and was alarmed when she gasped.

'Zafira!'

'Ah, Pez,' she whispered. 'He came for me.'

'Don't talk, I'll—'

'Listen!' she croaked, coughing blood in her struggle. He held her head as she no longer had the strength to do anything but slump and die. It was a wonder she could survive as long as she had. 'He asked a lot of questions about you.' Her breath was ragged. 'I put him off your scent as best I could.'

'How?'

'By letting him hurt me and then making him think I was begging to tell him who Iridor is.'

Pez wept harder as she somehow unbelievably gave a pained burst of a laugh. 'Who did you accuse?'

'Salmeo,' she whispered, and died with a smile on her face.

'Lyana speed you to her,' Pez said reverently and then set about his ghoulish task of lifting Zafira's near weightless body off the sharp spire.

Pez gave Zafira's body to the sea, near to the temple that she had given her life's work to. When it was done he climbed back up the stairs to sit out on the roof where he said another prayer for her soul and her sacrifice before once again returning to his owl shape.

Perched on the spire that finally took his friend's life, he could see a small boat being rowed across by a single man. There was no mistaking this man, either. It was the one he sought.

Ana sat on the cold ground of the area of the palace known as the pits and trembled. What an abominable mess her once happy, uncomplicated existence had turned into. She groaned, wished Lazar had never come to their home in the foothills. Wished he had never come into her life.

He was alive. She hugged her knees tighter and allowed herself the luxury of pity. With only this night left in her life, what did it matter if she filled the hours with tears. She had no reason to be strong, no-one to be strong for any more. Death was very welcome, for everyone she had trusted since leaving her home had betrayed her. The man she loved had been the greatest liar of all but Pez was a close second. She hated them both in that moment, even more than Herezah or Salmeo. At least with the latter two she had always known their propensity for treachery. But Lazar and Pez! She wept harder and prayed that dawn would come fast and finish the misery.

Lyana indeed! If she was Lyana, where was the magic that might take her away from all this?

'Dead?'

Pez nodded. He was back in his dwarf form, having flown down to the boat. Lazar had not been surprised to see him but Pez's news had stopped his friend from rowing any further. They drifted for the moment as the former Spur digested the tidings. 'I've just given her corpse to the sea. I thought it was fitting.'

'So he's declaring himself,' Lazar mused, his voice morose.

'Not really. Maliz believes no-one will ever know about Zafira and presumably he took steps to hide his actions. Certainly the temple's the loneliest of places — no-one would have disturbed them.'

'But we have the truth.'

'Yes, he doesn't know this, of course. He thinks Salmeo is Iridor.'

At which they both shared the same bitter thought that he would make an incredibly big owl.

'Cunning Zafira,' Lazar said. 'Courageous to the last.'

'True. If you saw what a mess her body was in you'd understand just how brave she was.'

'So this is the beginning?'

'Yes. First blood to the demon. Not the last, I'm sure.'

Lazar didn't respond to that comment. 'You've spoken to Boaz?'

'We've put our differences behind us, or so he believes. You see, the difference I have with him is Tariq – or Maliz, I should say. He thinks I'm suffering jealousy. Poor Boaz, if only he knew.'

'Would it make any difference?'

Pez frowned. 'You're right, probably not. He is dealing with Tariq the Grand Vizier and obviously responding well to the man's counsel, whilst we now see him only for the snake he is . . . the demon in disguise.'

'Except we have to be careful that this counsel he gives is not detrimental to you or Ana.'

'Or you.'

Lazar looked up from the oar he had been gently manoeuvring to prevent them turning circles as they drifted.

'I've told you, you are as much a target as I am.'

'I don't think so, Pez.'

'Still believe you're a coincidence, eh?'

Lazar nodded, although he didn't look completely confident.

'We'll see. In the meantime, your Zar is shocked at my news of you being very alive, of course, but also thrilled. He wants to see you in secret. No-one is to know of your presence, so we shall have to wait a few hours and you must arrive hooded.'

Lazar wasn't surprised. 'Ana?'

'I have not seen her,' Pez said and offered no more. 'Are you all right to keep rowing?'

'I'm not an invalid!'

Pez bristled at Lazar's angry mood. 'Good, because once Herezah learns the truth, she'll start warming her bed for you,' he replied.

Lazar growled softly, returned his attention to rowing and allowed his thoughts to finally drift to Ana and how she was going to react to learning that he was alive, perhaps even being permitted to see him. As much as his heart leapt at the thought, he did not look forward to it.

The Grand Vizier sipped the sweetened wine and eyed his Zar who seemed restless, distracted. 'Yes, as I was saying, I had some business to attend to in the city. And I gather there's been some excitement in my absence.'

Boaz turned from the window he was staring absently out of towards the Sea Temple, little knowing his friend, Pez, was about to launch himself from its roof and alight on a small craft in the bay to share some grievous news with its infamous occupant.

'Excitement? I suppose you could call sentencing two people I like to hideous deaths exciting.'

'I'm sorry, my Zar, that was tactless of me. This task seems to be a habit for you.'

Boaz couldn't take offence at his Grand Vizier. Unlike his former cringing self, the man seemed to be able to blend just the right amount of sardonic attitude into his otherwise direct manner. And Boaz far preferred that hard-edged bluntness to the soft and slippery cunning of Salmeo. Neither had it stopped gnawing at him that his mother was involved this time in the latest intrigue that would have palace tongues wagging. He would be speaking to her about it.

'Odalisque Ana is my First Chosen. I had hoped to make her a Favourite, more perhaps.'

'You are that fond of her? Already?'

'She is my equal,' he replied softly. And when the Vizier raised his eyebrows at the comment, Boaz explained. 'Not in status, obviously. But her mind is sharp and agile. She is mysterious. Her peers are like open books that are read without much interest, whilst Ana is closed, fascinating. The others are also vain, already scheming for my attention. Ana, however – easily the most beautiful – is hardly aware of the effect she has on me. I could never be bored around her.'

'My, my, that sounds like a woman to hang on to.'

'Except she's determined to shun this role in the harem. I simply can't save her from herself.'

Maliz realised which woman he was talking about. He hadn't met her but Tariq's memories gave him the knowledge he needed, which he was grateful for or he could have walked straight into an error. He remembered now talking to Tariq during the preparations for the flogging of the Spur that all surrounded this same woman. An intensely exquisite-looking woman, he recalled.

'What happened?'

'She attempted another escape.' He smiled in spite of his mood, sounded almost proud to the Vizier. 'Truly audacious this time. She could have got away with it if not . . .'

'If not for?'

'Salmeo. My mother too, I suspect.'

Maliz's inward sneer at the mention of the fat eunuch nearly showed itself but he reined in his reaction. 'Why would the Valide have any interest in the girl?'

'She has every interest in who I might take for a wife. I think she might have feared this was happening too early.'

'Zars have taken wives far younger than you, Majesty.'

'But they didn't have Herezah for a mother, Tariq. I could be wrong but I imagine my mother sees every potential lover of mine as a wife and thus a threat to her own power. It has only been a year since I took the throne. I would hazard she had hoped for a little longer to build her own empire.'

'You choosing Favourites, wives, even siring heirs is not something your mother can avoid for long.'

Boaz looked awkward at the thought of children so soon. 'No, but with Ana it was probably happening too fast. It's true I would have elevated her quickly.'

'And death is unavoidable?'

'You know the rules, Tariq.'

'Not of the harem necessarily.'

'Attempted escape is one of the worst sins but the worst — in the eyes of the harem down the ages — is if one of its women commits adultery and cuckolds the Zar.'

'She didn't!' Maliz exclaimed, hugely enjoying the tale, yet trying to sound sympathetic.

'No, I don't believe she did but she refuses to defend herself against the claim, and both Salmeo and the Valide unfortunately discovered her in a very compromising position. What they saw can't be argued unless Ana herself can prove otherwise.'

'A very twisted web. And so she and the person who helped her escape must die, I'm presuming.'

Boaz's expression melted from suppressed to open pain. 'Correct. I have no choice, much in the same way as I had little choice with Horz. Ana has broken ancient, sacred rules not once but twice . . . and indeed so has Kett.'

'Kett?'

'The black eunuch. We grew up together, can you believe. We were playmates until my position in my father's reckoning became all too obvious and my mother did not want us remaining close. It's strange, you know, when we were little I had this whimsical notion that Kett reminded me of a bird. He used to flit around, always busy, always industrious . . . usually dreaming up games for us to play.' Boaz smiled sadly. 'My sorrowful little black bird.'

Something erupted in Maliz's mind but he was exhausted from his exertions at the temple, as well as mellowed from the wine coursing through his veins. He was already pouring a third cup, and he was having such fun with this tale of woe that he paid scant attention to a nudge of familiarity. 'So, deaths at dawn, I'm guessing?' When his Zar gave him another look of exasperation at the heavy wit, he put a hand up to ward off the reprimand. 'Forgive me, Highness, I don't mean to be insensitive but if I can help you look at this objectively, then please permit me to say that this woman could have made a mockery of you. This just cannot be tolerated. Your father ruled with a tough fist, my Zar, and you could do a lot worse than follow in those footsteps. Too much leeway in a place like the harem – that I can only presume exists because of a very rigid structure, an adherence to ritual and ancient rules – can bring a dynasty down if unchecked.' He saw Boaz's rueful look and shook his head.

'No, hear me out. It doesn't take much to topple a Zar or his control. If the people sense that he can't control his own women, then what respect do you think they'll give the Crown? Your manner of ruling must begin with the harem. In truth, I like the way you're creating your own traditions but it would be dangerous, my Zar, to allow anyone – and I include Salmeo and the Valide in this respectfully – too much familiarity with you. The harem is the true seat of your power. It's the secretiveness of it all that adds the lustre to the Zars of Percheron down the ages. The traditions, the structure, they must be protected at all costs, otherwise I feel you could be toppled from within.' He could tell Boaz was paying attention now. 'At least no real harm has been done and you have an entire harem of no doubt unbelievably beautiful girls to work your way through. I saw them as youngsters but the older ones would have matured this past year. Truly, such incredible choice. Far better to spread your seed amongst them than become too devoted to one so early, especially one so headstrong, my Zar.'

Boaz looked crestfallen. 'My father once said something quite similar to that. He said a wise Zar lay with as many in his harem as he could, and should have many, many sons so he could choose the perfect apprentice and the most suitable heir that erupts from his furrows . . . is how he put it.'

'The advice is sound. Lots of sons, Majesty. It not only keeps the women on their toes but the obvious advantage is that you can select the ideal candidate to hand your precious crown to.'

Boaz sighed. There was nothing new in what he was hearing but Tariq justified the approach with a fresh passion that Boaz needed to hear. 'Ana's execution is at dawn – private drowning – the harem way. I refuse to be present. Kett at noon – a public ganching.'

'That should bring a crowd running – we haven't had one of those in a while.'

Boaz looked aggrieved. 'Forgive me, Tariq, I have an appointment to keep,' the Zar said, putting his own goblet down to end their meeting.

Maliz was surprised. 'So late?'

'Er, yes, I need to prepare, you understand.'

'Must be someone important to keep a Zar from his bed.'

'I won't be doing much sleeping tonight, Tariq. I might as well keep working.'

'Of course, of course. I did have a few things to discuss with you, my Zar, but all can wait for the morning.'

'Good. Until then. Salazin will see you out.' He gave the signal.

Outside the door Maliz signed to his spy: *I must know who he is seeing.*

Salazin nodded, signed back: *The priestess?*

Will trouble me no more.

And Salazin smiled tightly.

Salazin was sent to escort the hooded figure from the main gate – this was a sign that the Zar gave permission for this man not only to enter the palace compound but also to be given access to the Zar himself. Nevertheless, four of the Elim searched the man before escorting him to the Zar's wing of the palace. Outside his suite, the Elim broke away and left Lazar with the four fearsome-looking mutes.

Pez came skipping down the corridor to meet him.

'These are interesting fellows,' Lazar murmured.

'Vizier's orders,' Pez muttered back before breaking into song about crocodiles eating the royal barges.

Bin met them. He bowed as he did to all visitors. 'The

Zar has asked me to admit you upon presentation of his seal,' he eyed the hooded figure with unabashed curiosity, 'although this is most unusual.'

Lazar said nothing, held out the small piece of thick parchment that carried the Zar's seal, the unique wax indisputable. Salazin had given it to him.

'Thank you. Please wait a moment.' Bin knocked before disappearing into the room with Salazin hot on his heels. Pez was flapping his arms as if trying to fly and spouting a new rhyme about elephant droppings.

Bin emerged and gestured to Lazar to come forward. 'You may enter.' At Pez's movement to also join the visitor, Bin objected. 'Er, Pez, don't you think . . .'

'No, no, don't touch me,' Pez shrieked. 'The Zar is my friend. I need pomegranates, and he's got them all!'

Bin stepped back. He didn't want to provoke a repeat of Pez's last screaming performance. He looked at the visitor, embarrassed. Lazar shrugged as if to say it mattered not to him and so Pez, clutching the stranger's robes, danced into the Zar's chambers, sticking out his tongue to the astonished secretary.

Inside, Bin apologised to his Zar as Pez hopped around the room, apparently sniffing out hidden pomegranates.

'He can stay,' Boaz said, his eyes on the bowing visitor, who was hidden from top to toe by the jamoosh.

'Can I serve refreshments, Majesty?'

'No. I want privacy now. We require nothing further.' The servant looked disappointed.

'Thank you, Highness,' Bin said, bowing and backing out of the chamber.

There was a moment's awkward pause after the door closed and Pez damped down his noise to a soft humming purely for appearances in case anyone was listening at the door, although his Lore told him no-one eavesdropped.

Lazar inclined his head towards Salazin. 'A new friend, my Zar?'

Boaz smiled slightly. It felt like a comforting warmth to hear that familiar, albeit sarcastic, voice again. 'This is Salazin; he's a mute. One of the new retinue of body-guards the Grand Vizier insists upon. He can neither speak nor hear. We three are alone, in other words.'

Lazar pulled off the jamoosh and Boaz, preparing to embrace the man, stepped back, shocked. 'Your hair!' was all he could stammer.

'After all that's happened, my Zar, I thought there should be complete honesty.'

'What does this mean?'

'This is my true colouring.'

'And the beard?'

Lazar shrugged. 'In case I needed a disguise.'

'Anything else?' Boaz asked, still stunned that it was Lazar before him but not the Lazar he remembered.

'The other truth I should share is that I am not from Merlinea. I am a Galinsean.'

Another shock. 'Galinsean! But—'

Lazar, ever impatient, opted to move on quickly past the confusion. 'Everything I apparently stand against, yes, Majesty. Forgive. It is a long story and the lie I told so many years ago was all about protection. I was young, cautious. And then after your father's generosity, I didn't want to let him down, and because I gave my heart to Percheron, the lie never felt dangerous. I was never a threat to this realm and never once since stepping foot into your city have I given anything but profound loyalty to the

Percherese Crown. Nothing has changed since the attempt on my life . . . other than my hair colour.'

Boaz stared at the proud golden-haired man who stood before him – Lazar, yes, but not Lazar. This man looked older, leaner, less angry perhaps because his eyebrows were lighter and because of the soft beard he had finally allowed to grow; and the hair colour, before so at odds with his eyes, now fitted perfectly.

'I am no enemy, Highness.' Lazar bent to one knee to press his point.

Boaz was moved. 'I will hear that long story from you one day, Lazar, but right now let us drop the formality. You have been returned from the dead and I am grateful to Zarab for granting such a gift.'

He didn't notice Pez wince. Lazar stood and, reluctant to make the first move, allowed Boaz to move forward and grip him at the top of each arm. 'I can't believe it's you, Lazar,' he said, beaming, 'welcome back.' And then the Zar of Percheron hugged his old friend briefly before adding, 'My mother will be delighted.'

Lazar shot him a look before all three men in the room, bar the mute, laughed. 'Amazing what a year does,' Lazar said, admiring the composed young man before him. Boyhood had certainly left him. 'You have your father's wit.'

'Thank you, I'll accept that as a compliment. You will, of course, accept back your old position as Spur? I never filled it, you know . . . something beyond grief prevented me from doing so.'

Lazar glanced towards Pez, sharing the same vague notion that Boaz might be one of Lyana's supporters, still to be discovered. 'I wouldn't presume—' he began.

Boaz waved away Lazar's humility. 'Nonsense! Galinsean or not, I have no doubt of your loyalty, although perhaps you should dye your hair again, especially as you're the one who has helped put the fear of the Galinseans amongst us.'

Again they shared a moment of amusement.

'I accept.'

'You had no choice,' Boaz said lightly but none in the room disbelieved him.

'I think Galinsea and possible invasion is something we must now really fear, Boaz,' Lazar said, dropping all formality and amusement. There was a new edge to his tone and the Zar paid attention.

Boaz looked quizzical momentarily and then he understood, his quick mind grasping what had upset the balance. 'Jumo?'

Lazar nodded.

'But surely your family, however distressed or enraged by the news, cannot move the whole of Galinsea to war?' There was a thick silence as Boaz looked from Lazar and then to Pez but received no answer. 'I take it they can,' he finally said, unable to hide his surprise.

'I'm afraid so,' Lazar replied sheepishly. 'You could say they are influential.'

Pez cleared his throat. He and Lazar had promised each other honesty and this extended to their Zar.

Lazar ignored the gesture. 'The point is, we need to be very cautious. We have to step up training for the Shield and I believe we need to put it on alert. All the plans we've had in place are no longer hypothetical. This is serious. The Shield needs to understand that war could be imminent.'

Boaz looked astounded at this warning. 'Lazar, who in Zarab's name are your parents?'

Lazar hesitated. 'I am of noble birth, Highness. Suffice to say they have the ear of the king.'

'And he's looking for an excuse,' Boaz muttered, deflected from his path. He sighed. 'All the more reason for you to take up your role as Spur again as quickly as possible.'

'Can we keep my re-emergence quiet for the time being?'

'Hardly,' Boaz said and meant it. His expression suggested that Lazar was deluding himself suggesting such a thing.

'A few hours perhaps?' Pez offered, sensing Lazar's reluctance.

The Zar nodded. 'At most. Let's use that time to hear about everything that's happened since the last moment I saw you.' He saw the pain flit across Lazar's face and added softly, earnestly, 'Lazar, if I'd known the trouble you were in I would have put the whole medical fraternity at your feet. You were hidden very effectively from us and then I was informed − reliably, I thought − that you were dead and already given to the sea. Even Pez was taken in by this.' Neither man listening glanced at the other for fear of revealing the full truth. Thankfully Boaz was speaking passionately now and missed their momentary awkwardness. 'It was all so convincing, so hopeless. I wouldn't wish the torture you endured on anyone, although you understand Ana's punishment could not be escaped.'

'You know I do.' Lazar's eyes narrowed. 'I am informed you have formally chosen Ana.' He said it flatly. It was not a question, simply a statement and it held no censure or approval.

Boaz gave a wry shrug. 'For whatever good that has done me,' he answered and there was a note of injury in his voice. 'Yes, I have formally chosen her. She is not just the most exquisite woman in the harem but also the most engaging to me personally. The other girls are too giggly, too excitable for my taste – they are still young, I suppose, and nervous. Ana is different. She has the ability to make me feel every inch the Zar whilst somehow never being subservient . . . not even when she's prostrate giving her obeisance.' He shook his head in bewilderment and then grinned sadly as he made an attempt to lighten his speech. 'A skill no doubt she has learned from you, Lazar.' It did not win the amusement he'd hoped. 'I want to be in her company all the time but it seems I am to be denied.'

During Boaz's response, Pez watched Lazar's attitude shift from deliberately aloof – and he knew how hard that was for Lazar to achieve whenever Ana was being discussed – to intensely attentive. He saw the lips of the Spur thin as an expression of anger, or was it fear, took hold. Pez felt a similar tingle of anxiety creep through him. Boaz was building up to something and Pez had no inkling what was coming at them, other than more bad news.

'Why are you to be denied, my Zar?' Lazar managed to ask evenly enough.

'I'm sorry for both of you that you have to hear this now when we should be celebrating your return to the palace,' he said. He eyed them both before continuing – it came almost as a warning that he was not to be questioned. 'Odalisque Ana is to be executed in a few hours.'

∽ 16 ∽

The ship had glided near to the twin giants, announcing itself with torches, rather than horns. Had Lazar and Pez been rowing from Star Island just a little later, they would have seen her. She was now anchored at the mouth of the Bay of Percheron, her timbers creaking as they gently rocked on the calm waters lapping at Ezram's feet. The night itself was no longer calm, however, with soldiers of the Percherese Guard now lining the shore and more arriving as each minute passed.

A flotilla of smaller craft carrying armed men bobbed silently in the bay itself as they watched one of their senior officers board the foreign vessel, all no doubt silently wishing that they had their Spur to lead them in what felt like a prelude to something infinitely more dangerous to their city.

The senior officer, also wishing Spur Lazar was handling this meeting rather than him, cleared his throat and announced himself to two sombrely dressed but nonetheless elegant men who received him.

'I am Captain Veria of the Shield.' He gave a clipped bow of courtesy but said no more, his mind racing as to why a Galinsean ship – obvious by its flags and the crests of the Crown of Galinsea all over it – was in the Faranel and how many ships of war were arriving behind it. He knew that not far away his men were going through the motions of the drills they had practised over and over under Lazar's command, none of them truly believing it might ever come to this. Attack had been promised for so long – for centuries – that the threat seemed no longer real and yet here it was standing before him. He swallowed hard and hoped the two men – who in all truth did not look like soldiers, more like dignitaries – did not notice his nervous gesture.

The elder of the two had white hair clipped back behind his head. He was clean-shaven with a flinty gaze. His companion was still golden-haired but that, too, was whitening at the temples. They both looked to be in their sixth decade.

The elder spoke in a halting version of Percherese, his pronunciation squashing the light, almost musical language into something hard, guttural. 'Captain Veria, we wish not to startle. I he Marius D'Argenny and he be Lorto Belsher.' The sentence was so badly constructed it was almost comical but Veria found nothing amusing about their presence as they bowed deeply.

'Galinseans?' the captain asked, still incredulous enough to offer the obvious, but glad his voice was steady.

They nodded. 'We cannot speak no more language, need interpreter,' Marius explained with great care. Then he gestured with his arms to suggest they were not an immediate threat. 'Sailors,' he added, pointing to the men. 'No fighting man.' Then he waved the Percherese soldiers to come aboard. Captain Veria understood it meant that they were free to inspect the ship.

'Forgive my bluntness, brothers, but why are you here?'

Marius frowned. 'Messengers. Interpreter, I beg. Zar must speak.'

It didn't matter that they could no more understand his language than he could theirs. Veria reacted as if they would grasp his words with the greatest of ease. 'Are you mad? Do you really believe I'm going to let you anywhere near the palace?'

Marius and Lorto put their hands up in submission. They did not understand. 'Interpreter,' Marius implored once again, whilst his companion encouraged Veria's men to search everyone and the ship.

The captain looked around, exasperated. They could keep this up all night and still be no further by dawn. He considered the two men. It was obvious they were not in a position to be of any threat with just a handful of sailors. He thought about how Spur Lazar might have handled this. Lazar always impressed upon his senior men to trust their instincts. *Your gut will tell you more than the naked eye*, he used to say. *Listen to it*. Captain Veria listened to what his instincts told him. And he decided he could not risk the Crown's wrath should he send these messengers on their way without at least informing the Grand Vizier. They could, after all, be making a visit that might benefit both realms. He was a soldier not a diplomat and could not make political decisions. Tariq could make the final choice on whether or not to involve the Zar – let the blame rest with the Vizier. His option chosen, the captain signalled for his men to board the ship.

'You will not mind if we take up your offer to search the vessel?'

It was obvious what he was saying; even though they

did not understand the words, they grasped their meaning. Both men shook their heads.

'And you won't mind if we put your crew under guard and shackled.' Veria gestured that he would be tying up the men.

Marius shrugged as if to say it mattered not.

'Good.'

'Us?' It was the first time that Lorto had spoken as he pointed to himself and Marius.

Veria held up a hand. 'You wait here,' he said, pointing to the deck of the ship.

They understood and nodded their thanks.

He sent a runner to summon Grand Vizier Tariq in the hope that he might know someone who understood Galinsean.

A storm was gathering within Lazar. The shock of the Zar's news had sunk in and he now felt numb physically but emotionally he knew he was losing control and that was too dangerous in present company. A whole year's worth of rage was coalescing into something white-hot in its burning intensity. He knew he had to get out of the Zar's chambers before he either self-destructed from the fury he was barely repressing, or it simply exploded, taking the Zar with it.

He had hardly heard a word either Pez or Boaz was saying; he knew they were talking to him, at him, but he had turned inward, trying to wrest back control of the angry creature within. With a mighty effort he focused on the Zar who was actually shaking him by the shoulders now. Boaz let go of him as if seared. One look into that enraged gaze was frightening enough to force anyone back at least a step or two.

'Lazar, please, say something.'

The Spur shook his head to clear the flashes of light, the visions of Ana, the sensation of his back being stripped open and poison surging through his body, the memory of endless nights of fevered delirium and days of only near-consciousness and yet they brought extreme pain whereby he longed for the fever to roar in again and drag him away. Lies, treachery, betrayal. He thought of poor Jumo and then remembered Pez's sickening story of how Zafira died impaled on her own temple's spire. And he thought of Ana and her death.

And amongst the images and the terror, he heard a stranger's voice, then two voices, then a dozen voices all calling to him, all saying the same thing in synchrony. They whispered but he could hear them above the roar of his blood and the crowding noise, like thunder, that came with his memories.

'Lazar!' It was Pez stepping into view, slapping his face.

Release us, the voices whispered.

And then they were gone. Everything was silent, save the thum of his heart beating in his chest.

He looked about him. He was seated, must have stumbled to a chair at some point, and Pez was at eye level.

'Are you all right?' the dwarf asked tentatively.

He could only nod. Lazar rubbed his face, gathered his wits. This was not an auspicious beginning for his role as reinstated Spur.

'Can I get you something, Lazar?' Boaz asked, his voice heavy with concern. 'I know you're upset, perhaps a wine or even something stronger, a shot of terimla?'

'No. I shall be fine. Forgive me my behaviour. The news is a true shock. I—'

Whatever he was going to say was interrupted by frantic knocking at the door.

They both turned to Boaz who had given clear instructions he was not to be disturbed. Pez reached for the jamoosh that had been cast aside earlier and handed it to Lazar, who moved swiftly to cover himself.

'Wait,' Boaz said, moving to the door. He opened it slightly and Pez and Lazar listened to him take a very brief message before he held up his hand to Bin at the door. 'Give me a moment, Bin.' He closed the door and turned back to them. 'There's something going on at the harbour and the Grand Vizier is apparently on his way to speak to me. It sounds urgent.'

'I shall leave, Highness,' Lazar said, 'and go to my house, but I shall return in an hour or so, if you'll permit. I need to see Ana.'

Boaz sighed. 'She can see no-one, my friend. However, please, return in a couple of hours. Salazin will take you through my private chambers so you can leave without being seen.'

He signalled to the mute. Nothing further was said. Lazar and Pez removed themselves hurriedly behind Salazin.

Grand Vizier Tariq was shown into the Zar's salon and, considering the buzz that Boaz could feel emanating even from his servants, the Vizier looked surprisingly unfazed.

'What is this all about, Tariq?'

'Majesty, please forgive us this interruption at such a late hour.'

'I presume it is of vital importance to disturb me?'

'It is, Highness. Quite vital indeed. A Galinsean ship

is presently anchored in the shallow waters just outside our harbour. On board a Marius D'Argenny and his companion, Lorto Belsher, await your approval for an audience. Neither speaks Percherese beyond a few words and absolutely no-one speaks Galinsean, other than you, Highness. I think we have no choice but to bring them to the palace.'

Shock upon shock. 'Just one ship, two men? What do they want?'

'Your guess is as good as mine, my Zar. Apparently they are messengers, or so Captain Veria seems to believe. The ship has been thoroughly searched and the only oddity we turned up was a strange fellow who claims to be your former Spur's friend and once manservant.'

'Jumo?' Boaz asked, hardly believing the coincidence in timing.

'Yes, I believe that's what he called himself.'

'Bring them before me.'

As the Vizier departed to make arrangements, Boaz turned to Salazin and signed that he was to personally fetch the man who had been here earlier. And to return him quickly to the palace but through the back entrances, using the same seal of authority for any guards who questioned him.

Boaz met the Galinsean representatives in his Throne Room, a vast and magnificent chamber with an impressively tiled ceiling of crimson and deepest blue. As this room was one of the highest points of the palace, soaring windows on either side provided a near-panoramic view of the city below and onto the harbour where the torches, still burning on the foreign vessel, outlined its presence just outside the harbour.

A gentle lightening in the sky from ink to charcoal and a bright pink slash visible through the eastern bank of windows told Boaz morning was almost upon them and his belly twisted in the knowledge that Ana would already have been woken for her dawn death. He imagined, as he waited for the Galinseans to be shown in, that she would probably be saying some prayers. She would refuse food or water. She would wear something simple, neutral and she would no doubt look stunning all the same as she prepared to be consumed by the waters that ran into the Faranel.

He had cast aside sorrow over her death. It was a useless emotion for this particular person who appeared determined to go to that dark place. And having listened to the Vizier's wise words, Boaz had realised that no matter how many times she might be saved, Ana would probably find a new way to bring the wrath of the harem upon her shoulders. She did not fit here. There was almost a sense of relief as this thought slotted itself firmly into place in this mind and Boaz began to appreciate that perhaps the drowning was a kindness to her so that she would no longer suffer, no longer have to struggle with her life or find new ways to cope with her frustrations. He still could not witness her death but he began to wish the news would come that she was drowned. Then he, too, could get on with finding new mates, siring heirs, and forgetting about the woman who surprised and delighted him so much. She had his heart but he knew he didn't have hers. So for this, too, he could let her go. Boaz wanted some affection now — even if it was contrived and given from women too scared not to or too cunning not to appreciate what it could earn them.

Real love was too painful, he decided. Better to be like his parents – making a great match in mind, in bodies, in what they could both achieve. Love was immaterial. Respect, pleasure in each other and friendship were more enjoyable, surely, than the heartache of loving someone.

A gong was sounded, bringing him out of his moody thoughts and back to the Throne Room where the Galinseans were about to be presented. Despite its size the room felt crowded. Soldiers, Elim and the mute bodyguard were in maximum attendance. There was no question that the Zar of Percheron was well protected from the strangers who were brought in between a small company of Shield men, led by the Grand Vizier.

Boaz weighed the two men up. As the Vizier had explained, they certainly did not look dangerous and, having recovered from the shock of seeing Lazar with his true light colouring, he could now see the likeness that apparently existed between all Galinseans, not that anyone would know for sure. Apart from Lazar, these were the first men of the western realm he had seen.

Both men knelt without needing to be asked or told. They touched hand to forehead, lips and heart in the region's way of welcome and salutation. They spoke together in their halting Percherese, their thanks.

Boaz responded stiffly with a welcome in Galinsean, glad to note he got his tongue around the hard accent. He reached for the words and asked them to raise themselves. As they did he noticed quickly stifled amusement on the younger of the two's expression.

He set his jaw firm and, again forming the words as accurately as he could, he asked them their business, except in Galinsean it obviously wasn't making much sense. They did not smile but they looked puzzled.

In Percherese, the man known as Marius shrugged gently, 'Forgive. No understand.'

Boaz seethed. His Galinsean was hardly fluent but he thought he was capable of conversation and certainly of making himself understood. He would not leave himself open to ridicule, especially with such a large audience.

'Fetch my tutor!' he told Tariq.

Everyone waited for an uncomfortable and protracted period whilst the sleepy man was dragged from his bed and summoned to the Throne Room. Soldiers brought him bowing and cringing into the room, dishevelled and terrified.

'Don't be frightened, Rustaf. I want you to ask these men, please, in Galinsean, what their business is in our city.'

Rustaf looked even more terrified, his eyes darting between Zar and foreigners.

Boaz nodded for him to proceed. He did so.

Again Marius answered, but this time in Galinsean, explaining something that Rustaf now looked baffled by.

'Well?' Boaz demanded.

'Majesty,' Rustaf quailed, 'I do not understand their Galinsean. I can get odd words but no real meaning. From what he said I think we're both speaking a foreign version of the language to each other.'

'You mean I've been learning Galinsean for all these years and can't make myself understood?'

Rustaf bowed. 'Highness. I have taught you only what I myself was taught. I fear perhaps our library has only the Old Galinsean. We do not speak the colloquial form, not even the high court form, perhaps. Please forgive me but we have no experience of conversing with Galinseans.'

Boaz growled his displeasure and stood angrily. 'Grand Vizier, did you not tell me that Jumo was on that ship?'

'Yes, my Zar. He is waiting outside.'

'Bring him.'

Salazin knocked at the door of Lazar's house and should not have been surprised to have it answered by the owner himself. After all, the man had been dead for a year, so why would he have servants at the ready?

Lazar frowned. 'What are you doing back here?' Then he shook his head as if to berate himself for asking a deaf and dumb person a question. He opened the door further and called to Pez. 'Salazin has returned.'

Salazin's eyebrows lifted to see the dwarf waddling out to greet him – as far as he knew, Pez had been left at the palace when he had escorted Lazar back to his house earlier. It wasn't necessary to walk with the Spur all the way but Salazin had wanted to see where he lived in case he needed to return one day.

Pez looked equally quizzically at him. 'Razeen? What are you doing here?'

The man looked startled to be spoken to. His dark eyes darting towards the Spur.

'Razeen. Spur Lazar is one of us. He is one of Lyana's followers and he is, to put it graphically, up to his very arse in the same pursuit as us.' Pez's expression softened at seeing the flicker of a grin in the mute's face. 'I promise, you may speak freely before him.'

Lazar looked all but offended. 'Speak? This is a mute!

And why are you calling him Razeen? The Zar introduced him as Salazin.'

Pez sighed. 'Long story, Lazar. Just listen, this must be important.'

Razeen, known as Salazin in the palace, bowed to the Spur. 'I have come to fetch you again for the Zar.' His voice sounded scratchy from lack of use. He cleared his throat. 'Two Galinsean dignitaries have arrived aboard a vessel that is anchored off our harbour. No-one can understand them and their Percherese is sorely limited. The Vizier has organised to bring them to the palace in the hope that our Zar will be able to converse with them.' He stopped abruptly.

'Galinseans? Is it a war vessel?' Lazar looked stunned, the surprise of the mute speaking already forgotten in the wake of this alarming news.

'No, Spur, I don't believe so, or I think everyone would be more flustered. I'm gathering it is a ship of peace.'

Lazar grunted. 'No such thing in the Galinsean fleet. You can tell me your long story on the way back Pez. Let's go. There isn't much time before dawn.'

'I've told you, you cannot interfere.'

'And you think that will stop me, dwarf?'

The odd trio, one short, one masquerading as a mute and the other fully covered in a jamoosh ran out of the house bound for the palace.

～ 17 ～

Elza showed Ana how she looked in a small hand-held mirror. Ana didn't even bother to glance into it.

'What does it matter,' she said softly, 'how I am clothed or my hair is dressed? All will be ruined shortly.'

'Even in death you will be beautiful.'

'Leave me, Elza,' she said abruptly. 'I am ready. I await my summons.'

Left alone she said a prayer to Lyana to watch over her father and siblings, to protect Pez in his secrecy and to give Kett strength to face his death as she now faced hers. She begged forgiveness of her Goddess for Kett's suffering once again and also for not fulfilling what she was perhaps born to do. She felt baffled that she was Lyana's incarnation – surely there would be internal clues. Pez had more than enough indication that he was a disciple of Lyana. But she? All the early doubts came into sharp focus for her in this quiet hour as she faced her death. If she was Lyana, then she was failing her followers before she'd even had a chance to do anything positive towards answering their faith. What good was she as an embodiment of the Goddess? Yes, the curiosity with Ellyana in the bazaar over the statue of Iridor and then being able to communicate with Pez through a mind-link, even his claim of transformation were oddities she could not explain but there had to be a mistake. If she was Lyana, she would not be in this position. No. As much as Pez urged her to believe, Ana secretly held that it was Pez's desire rather than truth. He wanted her to be something special. Wanted her to be part of this strange battle he was part of. She, unfortunately for him, knew in her heart that she was nothing more than a goatherd's daughter who had consistently let down those who trusted and loved her. Death she now welcomed as a release from the responsibility of having to try again.

She spared a thought for Boaz, who must still be struggling with the decision, but Ana knew her fate was best for him. He wanted something from her she could never give. Love was beyond them. Her heart was no longer hers to present to any but the man who had owned it for more than a year. And now finally her thoughts turned to Lazar and her mood found the darkness she needed where he was concerned. Ana, convinced that Lazar lived, allowed the betrayal that the knowledge brought to give her the courage to face this death with gladness.

He must hate her very much for causing the whipping to have pursued this terrible lie, feigning his death, tricking all who relied upon him, and through his actions ridiculing the love she held for him. Again she reminded herself that it was a one-sided love. He had never behaved in any manner but formally and correctly towards her; he had never sought such a heartfelt commitment from her and he had deliberately kept her at arm's length. The fault was hers, she berated herself. She wanted his love and so she had convinced herself that he felt the same way. It was delusion to have ever thought that he had taken such a punishment because he loved her. He was noble and honourable – that's why he took her flogging. A Stone of Percheron – isn't that what everyone said of him? Cold, remote, incapable of love?

She tried to blot him from her mind as the tears came. But her thoughts were treacherous. One minute they assured her he had no feelings for her, other than those of duty, and the next they were giving her the memory of him calling out her name as he suffered at the end of the Viper.

Try as she might she could not deny that he had spoken it in agony but there was such passion too, such yearning. And she also could not forget the way he looked at her just before the suffering had begun – his gaze searing through the veils that hid her eyes as if searching for her lips to see her speak his name in response and in love.

Ana wept. She didn't need to be drowned to be killed. She was well and truly destroying herself on the harem's behalf. Now she no longer knew what to believe. Finally, as she steadied herself with the notion that death was within her reach – and thus escape from everything she despised – it mattered not how she viewed Lazar. In the end she allowed herself the small comfort that she had not misread the Spur. He had called out her name on the day of the flogging; that was how he had bade her farewell and he had done so with love. She would take that to the bottom of the river as her dying thought.

She heard a sound behind her and turned. Shadowed in the doorway was the unmistakable shape of the Grand Master Eunuch.

'Ah, sweet child, and so you finally shed those tears,'

he lisped. His swathes of ruffled silks made a rich sound as he stepped into the pit, light of toe and bringing with him the fragrance of violets. 'It is near dawn, child, and time to go to your gods . . . or goddess, if you please.' He giggled like one of the young girls in the harem at his supposed jest.

'Who will be in attendance?' she asked, drying her face hurriedly with her hands, not wanting Salmeo to see any further grief from her.

He tutted. 'Surely you don't want an audience?'

'No. That's why I ask. I am hoping no-one is there.'

'We need witnesses, Ana, to sign your death statement.'

'Who? Not the Zar?'

He smiled cruelly. 'You flatter yourself, child. No, the Valide and I will be doing the honours — if that makes any difference to you?'

'That is suitable,' she said and then said no more, leaving him to work out precisely what she meant by it.

'You look very beautiful, almost ethereal and very fitting on this ghostly dawn. Wait until you see it, child.'

'Why do you say that?'

'Oh, you'll see soon enough. The boatman and executioner await you, Ana, my dear. Do you need another moment to say a final prayer?'

'No. I'm ready.'

'Good.' He signalled to someone outside. A member of the Elim entered. 'Bind her.'

'Salmeo.'

'Yes?'

'Tell me how Kett is?'

'Oh, not nearly as brave as you, child. But I do have some good news for him. He will not be ganched as originally commanded by the Zar. He is to be drowned also.'

'How come?' she asked, secretly pleased.

'Something to do with dignitaries arriving unannounced. The Zar does not want the palace gates to be crowded by eager onlookers of an execution. I have no further details, only an order from our Zar that Kett's sentence is to be changed to drowning.'

'Why not drown us both together?' she asked fiercely.

'Perhaps,' he said. 'It's certainly a warm morning and I'm not sure I could face the discomfort of standing in the hot sun later and listening to Kett's dread wails.' And he laughed. 'Now come, child. I know those shackles are tricky to manoeuvre but I'm sure you'd rather walk to your place of death than be carried.'

Jumo bowed solemnly to Boaz. As with Lazar, the man looked as if he'd aged since Boaz last saw him. He found a sad smile for the loyal servant.

'Jumo, welcome back. I have some news to share later,' he said cryptically, unable to announce it so publicly yet. 'But for now I must ask if you can help us at all with our Galinsean visitors that we cannot communicate ably with.'

'They are here, Majesty, because of what I had tried very hard to share. That Lazar had died.'

Boaz assumed as much. 'I see. And did they understand you?'

Marius and Lorto watched the exchange with studied interest, frowning as they tried to grasp one word in five or six as the Percherese spoke their fast, fluid and elegant language.

'I'm afraid they did. There were a lot of gestures and hand waving, pointing and frustration. It took me a whole day of difficult explanation to get some semblance of the news across to them.'

'Thank you. Can you explain then why they are here?'

Jumo looked at his Zar with an expression of disbelief. 'To hear it from your own mouth, Majesty, that you did execute the favourite son of Galinsea.' He said this in innocence, unaware that the Zar did not already know the truth of Lazar's heritage.

A murmur went up around the room and the Zar glared, his eyes roving past soldiers and Elim alike. He couldn't blame them, however. This news that Lazar was a favourite of Galinsea was a shock. All but he still assumed the man was of Merlinea.

'And then what?'

Jumo looked appropriately embarrassed that he had to answer this. 'The obvious, Majesty,' he began but his eyes shifted as he spoke – a mute had entered from behind.

Boaz noticed him too and signalled him to come forward. 'Carry on, Jumo,' he urged, as the mute signed a well-disguised message to him.

Maliz, also watching these proceedings with great interest – albeit detached, as though he were participating in a piece of high theatre – felt a spike of frustration that he couldn't make out what was being exchanged between the Zar and the mute. Salazin was being deliberately careful, which was odd – he'd have expected the mute to be deliberately careless so that he, the Vizier, could easily make out the conversation. He did not let that frustration show on his calm expression, however, as everyone heard Jumo finish what he'd begun.

'. . . considering the weight of offence, Majesty, I would hazard they will declare war.'

Now a fresh murmuring erupted.

'They've come here masquerading as peacemakers but in truth to declare war?' Boaz asked, incredulous at such audacity. He noticed neither of the visitors looked in the least bit fearful for their own lives, which could so easily be taken from them at a single command from the Zar. He gave a final signal to Salazin, who moved towards the door behind the Zar. 'Silence,' he called to those still reacting to the mention of war.

Jumo cleared his throat, realising he could no longer fully protect the secret from the audience. It mattered not anyway, he now decided, with Lazar probably long picked clean by the creatures of the sea. 'Highness, I cannot know for sure because I, too, am at the same disadvantage with language. But in light of who Lazar was,' he said carefully, 'I can appreciate their need to seek the truth. This is not a declaration of war yet. From what I can tell, these men from the Galinsean palace hierarchy have been sent on a mission to establish the facts.'

'But how did they think they would do that with the language barrier?'

'That is my fault, Majesty. I conveyed somehow that you were fluent in Galinsean.' Jumo looked suddenly mortified that he'd insulted the Zar.

Boaz rescued him. 'Fret not, I have been taught a more ancient tongue of the Galinseans,' he said generously. 'It seems their language has long since evolved.'

The Grand Vizier stepped forward, clearly tired of the talk and keen for some action. 'Your Highness, how may we solve this issue? Frankly, if these men are here to declare war, I say we execute them now and send their ship back from where it came, all crew dead and the vessel torched. Let that be our message to the Galinsean pigs who covet our realm.'

'Nothing too inflammatory then, Tariq? Diplomacy at its most subtle.'

Maliz was unfazed by the sarcasm at his expense. None of this mattered to him personally, although war between the realms could aid him in his own mission. With Percheron engaged in battle, no-one would pay any attention to his more sinister business. 'A declaration of war needs to be met head-on, Zar Boaz.'

The Zar's eyes narrowed. It was the first time in a year he had felt himself out of step with his chief counsellor. The man seemed eager for the realms to clash and he also appeared too casual about something so critical, almost enjoying everyone's angst as though it mattered not to him. How could this be? Surely the Vizier would do anything alongside his Zar to prevent war coming to peaceful Percheron? He didn't have time to ponder it now but he was not going to allow his realm to go to war simply because it felt threatened or needed to save face. Thank Zarab Grand Vizier Tariq was not running this realm or they'd probably already be engaging Galinsea in battle. Of course, no-one but Pez could know he had the ultimate answer to their problem and he thanked his god again that Lazar had been returned from the dead. 'I am not a warmonger, Grand Vizier. Let me show you how I will resolve this issue — without it escalating into bloodshed.'

Boaz raised a hand and silence fell heavily across the room as a door behind him opened and a tall, golden-haired man strode into the Throne Room. Boaz did not turn to greet the man or accept his low bow.

'Your Highness,' the man said and Boaz watched Jumo first, taking secret delight in watching the former servant's eyes widen in shock and his mouth gape. There was no fooling the man from the north. He knew who this was instantly, just from the way the newcomer walked, and in spite of the beard, although it seemed no-one else reacted quite as fast.

The Vizier looked quizzical, the soldiers hesitant, unsure of what this stranger's arrival meant. Pez danced in from another entrance but even his antics could not sustain a lengthy distraction from Lazar, who had everyone's attention but looked uncomfortable with it as he approached the visitors at a nod from the Zar.

Jumo was now trembling in disbelief but no-one except the Zar could see this. Boaz smiled as the teary man reached for Lazar as he passed, as though Jumo needed to reassure himself through touch that this man was real and not a vision. A look from Lazar obviously communicated that their reunion must wait.

'Marius,' Lazar said, holding out his hand. He looked and nodded at Lorto. 'We have not met,' he said to the younger man, 'but welcome to Percheron, my home for the last sixteen years or so, and to its Stone Palace.'

The familiar sound of that voice was resonating within the minds of the uncertain soldiers. Even the senior members of the Elim were shaking their heads with disbelief now. But more shocking to everyone in the room was that the old man, Marius D'Argenny, fell to his knees before Lazar.

'Lucien, Majesty.' He kissed Lazar's feet in the Galinsean way of greeting royalty.

'Majesty?' Boaz repeated, on his feet now, perturbed.

Lazar bowed to Boaz and quickly spoke a few guttural words to the two men now kneeling, their heads touching the ground at his feet. 'Zar Boaz, please forgive this untimely show.' His voice was now clearly recognised by his soldiers, whose once solemn expressions were replaced with a combined look of relief mixed with disbelief.

'Shield!' Lazar spoke into the increasing noise. 'This is your Spur commanding you to return to your barracks and posts. I shall speak with the men as one soon. Go now.' His voice softened in acknowledgement of their obvious joy. 'Please,' he added. 'All will be explained.'

They hushed instantly at the command of their Spur, quietly filing out of the Throne Room, obviously no longer required to protect the Zar. Spur Lazar could single-handedly protect their ruler.

'Elim. You may return to your quarters too,' Boaz echoed, keen to clear the room and have a more private discussion. Something complex was happening here and he didn't think it should be publicly exposed just yet.

The men in red followed the soldiers, leaving behind the bowed visitors, a shaken Jumo, the Grand Vizier, clearly baffled, silent Salazin, and Pez, who was walking around the rim of the room on his hands, making noises like a duck.

Boaz took charge. 'Tariq, in case you haven't guessed, may I reintroduce you to Lazar, who has returned to us from the dead and was reinstated an hour or so ago as our Spur.'

Maliz knew how much Tariq detested this man and yet he felt nothing towards him. It was a surprise to see him but it had no impact on his task. Still, it made for interesting times. 'Ah, the late-night visitor. Spur Lazar, welcome back. That was something of a theatrical entrance, I must say, and my, how you have changed.'

Lazar looked at the shrouded eyes of the Grand Vizier, searching for the demon that lurked behind them, knowing this man, or whatever he was, wanted to destroy Ana and Pez, had already murdered Zafira and was capable of anything. Despite this knowledge he knew he must show nothing in his attitude towards the Vizier. 'I could accuse you of similar change, Tariq, you look very well, very rejuvenated,' he replied, understanding now all of Pez's warnings about the Vizier's 'improvements'.

Boaz interrupted whatever his Vizier was going to say in response. 'Lazar, will you explain why these men are paying such homage, why they called you Majesty?'

Lazar glanced towards Jumo, heard Pez stop his duck noises, felt his heart hammering in his chest as his long-held secret was about to be revealed.

'Your Highness, may these man stand, please?'

Boaz nodded and Lazar spoke quickly in Galinsean. Both men moved slowly to their feet, looking at Lazar with quiet awe that was not missed by the Zar and simply served to further frustrate him.

'Well?' he prompted.

'Zar Boaz, this is very difficult for me to reveal to you. It is something I kept from your father . . . rightly at the time we met perhaps, but maybe wrong of me to perpetuate the secret for so many years.'

Boaz frowned. 'Secret? What secret?'

'My true identity, Highness.'

Boaz was catching on that this was no longer something

personal. Lazar's secret, as he termed it, obviously had far-reaching effect for it to create such tension. 'Is Percheron in genuine danger?'

'It was.'

'Your parents are not Merlinean, not even just straight-forward Galinsean aristocracy, are they?' Boaz held his breath, his quick mind had guessed but could hardly believe what it was anticipating being confirmed.

'No, my Zar. In this I have beguiled you and your father before you.'

'Marius D'Argenny called you Lucien. Is this your true name?'

Lazar nodded. 'I took on my new persona many years ago. I was once Lucien. I am Lazar.'

Boaz felt soft flutters of panic within his belly but refused to let them take hold and fly. He was the Chosen Son of Joreb and would not let his father down. 'And Lucien, I'm presuming, is one and the same son of the King of Galinsea.'

'He is.'

Boaz shook his head with shock; suspecting something and having it confirmed provoked two different gut reactions. 'How can this be?'

'It is a long story, Highness, as I warned earlier. But it is nothing to do with Percheron. Coming here was an accident – as you know, I was captured by Slaver Varen – not that I have regretted it. Well, perhaps recently . . .' He trailed off, sounding unsure.

Boaz was hardly listening, his mind now racing. 'How bad is it, Lazar? I know my history but Galinsean contemporary politics is not my specialty. There are several sons in the royal family, am I right?'

Lazar nodded grimly. 'I am one of three sons. I have a sister too.'

'But which son are you, Lazar?'

Now the Spur looked deeply abashed. 'First-born, Highness.'

Boaz closed his eyes momentarily to stem his rising alarm. 'Galinsea believes we executed the heir to its throne?'

'It seems so by the presence of these dignitaries.'

'Jumo, what in Zarab's name possessed you? Had I known where you were headed I would not have permitted it.'

Jumo hung his head. 'Having lost my master, Highness, and in the manner we lost him – through betrayal and treachery from within the palace – I no longer cared about anything. It seemed the right thing to do. I admit I wasn't thinking too clearly in my grief. I had to get away from Percheron and I needed to somehow do more for my friend than I had.' He stopped, embarrassed at such a long speech.

Boaz knew there was little point in arguing what might have been. He returned his attention to his Spur. 'Well, perhaps you could explain to them what actually occurred.'

'Yes, Highness. Excuse me a moment.'

The Zar and Vizier waited patiently as the Spur flipped from Percherese into the guttural language of their traditional enemies. Questions were asked by the messengers and answers given. Boaz could tell from their faces what they were learning as their expressions moved from interest to disdain, despair to dawning understanding and finally puzzlement.

'What are they frowning at?' Boaz enquired.

Lazar looked uncomfortable again, flicking a glance

towards Pez who was miraculously quiet in the corner, smelling his shoes. 'They wonder why my survival was kept a secret from you.'

'Indeed.'

'I have told them that it is as baffling to us as to them.'

'You did tell them about Zafira and that she has disappeared so we cannot even ask her immediately?'

Pez watched and so did Lazar as the Vizier's attention moved from vague interest to riveted intrigue at the mention of the priestess. Lazar tried to disguise his anxiety at Boaz even mentioning Zafira in front of the Vizier. It was not the Zar's fault, of course, but now it gave the demon a new line of pursuit.

'Not yet.'

'You knew the priestess?' Maliz asked predictably.

Lazar looked nonplussed, deliberately gave the impression that the question seemed irrelevant. 'I ran across her from time to time. In my line of work you get to know most people in the city.' He turned away.

Maliz persisted. 'But how is she connected to you?'

'Yes, I'm sorry, Tariq, I'm only just realising that you know none of this,' the Zar said. 'After the flogging Zafira cared for Lazar but she told us – that is, Jumo and myself – that Lazar had died and that she had given him to the sea at his request.'

'Why the priestess?' Maliz asked, his voice husky with keen interest.

Lazar shrugged. He didn't have a ready answer for the demon's interrogation and had to move very carefully now for fear of pointing in any way to Pez and thus Ana.

'I took him to the temple,' Jumo said into the silence. Jumo's eyes flicked from Lazar to the Vizier. He could hear Pez humming softly, but carefully avoided looking at him, having picked up quickly on Lazar's reluctance to explain more to Tariq. 'Does it matter why now?' he asked, loading his question with disgust. 'Lazar was dying. We needed somewhere peaceful, private. We went there in our misery. Is that wrong, Grand Vizier Tariq?'

Maliz seethed within – he had missed something but was not yet sure what it was. There were links here but he couldn't connect them. He needed time to think. 'No, not at all. I just can't imagine why a man of Zarab would be taken to the place of the fallen goddess.'

Again something gnawed at Boaz in this curious answer from his counsellor and the vehemence behind it. Jumo was right; why did it matter where Lazar had been taken? What mattered were the lies that followed. He said as much before adding: 'Tariq, I want you to put your ear to the ground with all your networks and see if you can find out more about Zafira's disappearance.' He noticed Lazar quickly hide a smirk that emerged. 'You too, Spur Lazar – use all the resources required to track her down. We cannot understand your situation fully until we have her explanation. The Galinseans deserve that.'

Lazar translated for the visitors.

'And if we cannot locate her?' the Vizier asked.

'Well, we must find a new way to appease our aggressors.'

'Zar Boaz?'

'Yes, Spur? Incidentally, is that how I should address you, or is there a formal title I should now accord you? Are you still our Spur or—'

'I am your Spur,' Lazar said, cutting across the Zar's words.

Boaz paused, watching Lazar intently for any guile before he nodded. 'All right, go on.'

'This small delegation is not simply on a fact-finding tour.'

'Oh?'

'No, Highness. They require a representative from the Percherese Crown to travel to the Galinsean capital and explain formally what has occurred . . .'

'Why?'

Lazar continued as if the Zar had not spoken. 'With your assurance that I am alive.'

'Can we not just send you in person, Lazar? I hate to lose you so soon after having you returned to us but we are still under the threat of war, presumably until this is done, am I right?'

'Yes, my Zar.'

'However, your countrymen don't seem at all intimidated by being here. They obviously don't fear for their lives, so perhaps war is expected to be averted,' Boaz noted.

'My father will carry out his threat if Marius and Lorto are not returned whole to Galinsea, together with your emissary.'

'You are my emissary. Are you not proof enough?'

Lazar looked pained. 'That's part of the long story, Highness. I cannot return to Galinsea with ease.'

'But Jumo told us long ago you had talked about it only—'

'Talk is talk, Highness. I was considering taking a journey from Percheron – an extended one, yes – but whether I would ever go back to Galinsea is questionable.'

'Why? Is it dangerous for you to return there?'

'You could describe it that way. I have been formally banished.'

'But you're the heir! They've sent a delegation to learn of your fate. Zarab curse me, they're prepared to declare war over you.'

'All true,' Lazar replied, frowning in his discomfort. 'But that doesn't mean they forgive, Highness.'

'Zarab save me, Lazar. What could you do to your family that would have them pull in two such passionate directions? They would slaughter a nation for you but not forgive you?'

'I'm afraid the King of Galinsea can be capricious, Highness. His Queen more so.'

'By dangerous I take it you mean potentially fatal?'

'Potentially, or thrown into the dungeons for the rest of my days. I am more useful here and my loyalties are to this Crown.'

'Why, Lazar?'

'I renounced the throne, Highness. The why of it seems irrelevant after so long.'

Boaz shook his head. He thought of the possibility of sending Ana but she had no status and was in fact a condemned woman, about to die. Her Galinsean was pidgin anyway, of little use to the court. 'I can't send you and yet I have no-one, not even myself, who speaks Galinsean adequately enough to make themselves understood in that capricious court!'

It was only then that Boaz became aware of Pez dancing nearby, mimicking a woman's voice. He was talking nonsense, of course, and that was Pez, although Boaz knew the dwarf's antics well enough to understand when his friend was conveying a message.

Pez leapt onto the Zar's back and although this startled everyone, the Percherese in the room all knew better than to react to anything the dwarf did, including this clownish behaviour involving the royal.

'Go away, Pez, this is not the time,' Boaz said, struggling to loosen the dwarf's grip.

'Trust me, she speaks contemporary courtly Galinsean fluently,' Pez whispered before leaping down and moving away, breaking wind in time with each step.

The Vizier snarled his disgust and the two visitors looked at each other, unsure how to react.

'Forgive our palace clown,' Boaz muttered, trying not to show that he was shaken by Pez's secret. Time was too short to dwell on it; Ana could already be dead. He composed himself. 'Lazar, what about Ana? I understand that Ana can talk courtly Galinsean like she belongs in your palace.'

Lazar didn't wait for permission. 'Where?' he growled over the back of his shoulder.

'The River Gate. Hurry! Second Bell marks the moment.'

⟢ 18 ⟣

Salmeo was right. It was a curious morning, filled with foreboding. The Elim prayed to Zarab as they had escorted her behind the enormous eunuch to the region of the palace known as the River Gate. Ana, too, was entranced by the strange, eerie light this morning had brought.

She had never witnessed such a phenomenon and yet somewhere deep in her memories it was yielded up to her what this was, in the same strange way that she knew the names of the Stones of Percheron or that volcanoes existed in the world. This was a rare eclipse when the moon shielded the sun, bringing an odd twilight to the day when it should be brightening to full morning.

The dark side of the moon seemed to mourn the proceedings and this interpretation was not lost on those gathered – Salmeo had to urge his Elim forward, to fight their fear of this sign from the heavens.

Ana smiled, convinced now that Lyana was talking to her in a subtle manner; soothing her, showing Ana her command of all things natural. It was a genuine comfort and Ana took it to mean that Lyana would prevail in this battle – it helped her to believe this, even if it didn't come to pass. Zarab and his followers like Salmeo would not keep winning, keep destroying people's lives. A new era was dawning in Percheron and it began with Boaz but would finish with Lyana's triumph. He would bring about the revolution in the palace that would filter through society and perhaps change Percherese life forever, whilst Lyana would restore the age of the priestess and harmony. She hoped so. Salmeo, Herezah, even Tariq, and their kind were primitive. Their time and traditions had passed. Boaz would usher in the new era as he introduced new laws, new rights, new lives. These thoughts gave her courage and the sight of Kett gave her intense relief. He was here. They would die together, and quickly, Lyana in their hearts and peace in their minds.

Lazar had never run so hard in his life. He saw none of the people around the palace he encountered, didn't feel the stone walls he careered off or the toe he broke as he tripped. Speed was his only focus and he ignored the burning in his lungs and the protest from his legs and the harsh breathing at his throat. Speed was all that mattered because speed alone would save Ana's life.

Coming behind him were Pez, whooping and screeching – a madman picking up on the lunacy around him – as well as the Zar, also moving swiftly but understanding it would be unseemly for Percheron's ruler to hurtle through his palace. It was true he had never strode this fast before. Jumo, too, was at his side, not permitted freedom through the palace and needing the authority of the Zar. The Galinsean visitors had been left in the care of the Grand Vizier; they would be served refreshments as they waited, confused, in the Throne Room for the next update from the heir to their throne. They had no idea why he had suddenly run out of the chamber but suspected it was connected with them. Lucien was a serious sort and not prone to flights of fancy.

Lazar kept running. Damn the River Gate – the furthest point in the palace. He knew once the Second Bell was sounded, Ana was as good as dead. He had to beat it, no matter if it cost him his last breath.

Ana stood, composed and demure, in the gently rocking boat. Alongside her boat was a second and in it, shaking with fear, was Kett and another Elim. Kett looked ghostly in the eerie light cast by the eclipse. Nearby, at the river bank, was the Valide and her lisping henchman, the Grand Master Eunuch. And standing further away were the two Elim who had escorted her with Salmeo to her place of death. Not far from them sat a scribe who served the harem for any matters that needed recording on paper for the library or for other formal reasons. Witnesses aplenty, in other words.

Before her stood an enormous man. He was Elim, and one she had never seen before. Ana realised that the top of her head barely reached the middle of his chest; he had to stand inches higher than even Spur Lazar who was the tallest man she knew. His solemnity was tinged by dread, and Ana knew it was not only the executioner who was feeling disturbed by the strange twilight.

Fringing the black disc of the moon was a gossamer halo of sunlight. Again Ana was struck by the notion that this was Lyana talking to her, talking to them all, mocking the killers and uplifting Ana's spirits. Soon her and Kett's bodies would be safe within their watery graves, whilst their spirits would rise to the bosom of Lyana, where she would welcome them. There would be no such welcome for Salmeo or Herezah and this gave Ana more comfort as the Grand Master Eunuch began speaking.

'Odalisque Ana, this is Faraz. He is the Elim responsible for executions within the harem,' Salmeo explained lightly as if introducing a guest for dinner.

She nodded at the huge man and he responded in kind, nervously glancing up towards the sun and moon, suddenly a single, glowing sinister body in the heavens. Everyone but Ana was unnerved by its presence.

'Ana, you understand why you give your life today?' It was the Valide, as usual drawing out the agony for as long as possible, but even her voice sounded strained and she, too, uncharacteristically lost her nerve and looked up to the skies.

Ana fixed the Valide with a long look. 'I've worked it out, Valide, thank you.'

'Perhaps you could explain it to us so we can bear witness that you did most certainly understand the charges brought against you. It is tradition.' Again it was all so polite they could have been having a conversation just prior to heading out on a barging excursion.

'My naivety led me to make some rash decisions, Valide,' Ana said cryptically. 'I trusted people I should never have thought capable of honesty. I broke the law of the harem . . . again. Is that clear enough?'

'Be careful, Ana,' Salmeo cautioned.

'Or what? You'll kill me?' She actually laughed at him and it felt wonderful to see all his visible flesh quivering.

Her triumph was short-lived. It was Herezah's cold voice that cut through her amusement. 'No, but I'm sure you would like to go to your death knowing the family in the foothills that you care about so much is not punished for your misdemeanours. Your uncle's death should have been sufficient for your selfish pursuits. I'm certain the other two deaths on your hands – those of Lazar and Kett – are more than enough.'

Ana's resolve crumpled. She looked visibly shaken at the threat. 'Can we just get this done with, I beg you? I have nothing further to add. Forgive my offence, Grand Master Salmeo, you may appreciate that I am trying to find courage to die bravely.'

Salmeo's scar lifted as he smiled, the gap in his teeth looking cavernous, now and then filled with the plump pink tongue that seemed to taste the air like a snake. 'I accept your apology, Odalisque Ana,' he lisped, 'and agree we should get "this" – as you put it – underway, for this strangely dull morning is already warm and these dark silks are not breathing as well as they should.'

Herezah made a tutting sound in sympathy. 'You should have changed into the summery lightweight silks already, Salmeo,' she admonished. 'Odalisque Ana, you gave me your promise, your absolute word, that you would never attempt escape again from the harem. Do you remember that warning?'

Ana hesitated, realising now how brilliantly this pair had cornered their prey, then played with it before releasing it into that well-constructed false sense of freedom before pouncing again, this time fatally. She had to admit it, they were superb crafters of the darkest deeds. She recalled the conversation well and how innocently Herezah had led her through the discussion, extracting that promise for this very moment when she would hurl it back against her. Ana really did want to die now. She wished Pez might have come along so she could hug someone goodbye at least. But he was probably with Lazar, and that bleak thought hit her as she answered the Valide. 'Yes, I remember giving you that promise.'

'Which you promptly broke that very evening.'

'Yes, Valide.'

'No-one helped or encouraged you? This was your own decision?'

The scribe was busily recording the facts on his tablet of paper, trying not to look above at the halo of ethereal light surrounding the moon.

'All of my own doing,' Ana echoed. 'I coerced Kett into aiding me. He felt obliged.'

'That won't save him, I'm afraid, Ana, but we appreciate your candour.'

Salmeo looked to the scribe, who nodded. 'We are ready, then. Step into the bags, please.'

The Elim helped the bound Kett into the black velvet sack. To his credit, Kett was stoic, his eyes firmly on Ana, and whilst she was sorely reminded of a similar scene of despair not so long ago, during his emasculation, where they drew strength from each other, Ana was thinking how much like a frightened bird Kett appeared. Trembling, silent, helpless.

'It will be quick, Odalisque Ana, fear not,' Herezah said.

'The stones at the bottom of your sacks make it so,' Salmeo added.

'I don't fear death, Valide,' Ana said. 'The thought of remaining a slave to the harem is far more daunting and a worse sentence than drowning – I'm sure you of all people understand.'

Herezah held on to the gasp of indignation that

threatened to explode. Instead she fell back on her usual expression, a sardonic smile. 'Well, I suppose you'll never know the difference between Valide and odalisque, young Ana, although I do, and the worlds are markedly apart. Sleep well in your watery grave.'

To prevent Ana saying anything further to infuriate his mistress, Salmeo spoke and his tone brooked no interruption. 'We await the toll of the Second Bell. You may tie them in.'

The two men in the boats got busy pulling the bags up around their victims, at which point Kett began to fill the tense silence with a stream of gibberish. Ana caught a glimpse of him before she herself was pushed deeper into the darkness of her death bag and it seemed as though her friend had fallen into a trance. And it was in that same moment that the solar eclipse passed. The moon shifted, and blinding, golden sunlight hit them all so ferociously that everyone shielded their eyes. It bought her just a fraction of a moment more and it was as if Kett alone was bathed in his own tunnel of glorious light and he appeared to be fully a bird — a proud raven . . . the black bird of omen.

And then she was plunged into the velvet void as Faraz secured her bag with ties. She could hear Kett's muffled voice. He was jabbering in ancient Percherese, she realised with alarm, the likes of which no-one around her would probably know existed once, for it was so different to the Percherese spoken today. It shocked her to hear him speak it. It possessed a harsher quality to it, more like Galinsean, and delivered with none of the elegant intonation of the contemporary language. Kett spoke in a monotone that seemed to match the trance he had succumbed to. She could not explain how but she understood every word:

'I am Lyana's Raven, bird of omen, and bird of sorrows,' he said over and again until Ana thought that's all he was going to say before they drowned him. To hear him quote Lyana frightened her more than she wanted to admit. Pez's warning that Kett might be a messenger rang in her ears.

She heard muffled complaining from Herezah and the chilling words from Salmeo: 'Stick that knife of yours into him, executioner, we cannot bear the noise.'

To her relief the Elim executioner refused. 'Forgive me, Grand Master Salmeo, but tradition allows a prisoner to say prayers at any stage during his execution.'

'That doesn't sound like prayers to me,' Herezah moaned. 'It's another language.'

'Nevertheless,' the executioner replied in a stunning show of stubbornness that Ana could have kissed him for.

'Kett!' she shouted, and then in the same ancient Percherese that was so annoying Herezah and Salmeo she bade him farewell. 'We shall meet again in Lyana's arms,' she comforted and felt hot tears stinging her face that Kett should die so lost and so confused.

'I am the Raven and you are the Mother,' he suddenly said, frightening Ana to her marrow. 'This is my omen. You must live, you must let the Goddess live and you must help the creatures and the giants to live. Maliz has killed the priestess. Now you must find the Rebel . . . you must find the Rebel.' He kept repeating the final five words and over his chant she heard the Second Bell sound and the words 'Drop them' from Salmeo.

Ana felt herself picked up by the Elim executioner as though she was no weight at all and she heard him whisper a plea for forgiveness through the velvet before he grunted softly and dropped her over the side of the boat.

Cold hit her like a slap and then she was gasping as the river flooded into the bag and surrounded her as she sank to the depths. She meant to gulp down the water and aid the drowning but the shock of it finally happening prompted a primeval desire to hold her breath and live for just a few brief moments longer, Kett's ominous warning resounding in her mind as the stones dragged her deeper still and her lungs screamed for air.

❦ 19 ❦

Lazar heard the Second Bell and its tolling stopped him in his tracks. He bent down, hands on thighs as he sucked in air and then he straightened with rage and shouted a mournful howl of despair. He could see the River Gate, could see where an Elim executioner peered down into the depths and where Salmeo and Herezah were turning towards his keening with expressions that were triumphant, replaced with confusion.

He was too late. Ana was gone.

He yelled his anger again but something akin to pain passed through his head and then the voices came again. *Save her!* they urged through his yelling, familiar yet belonging to people he didn't know; had no idea how they could enter his mind or speak to him in this way. There were the same whispering voices.

Who are you?

You must save her, they persisted and then with fury driving their tone: *Go!*

Fear, he decided, was the final factor that gave him the impetus once again to hurl himself forward, even though he felt spent. Salmeo approaching, his face frowning in confusion as to who this stranger running at them was, raised a hand but Lazar ignored him, launching himself headfirst into the river.

He knew it was deep enough to dive into and he prayed to Lyana to guide him through the waters. Fortunately this river came down directly from the mountains and was stunningly clear until it blended with the Faranel. Then it joined sea water and took on the cloudy aquamarine of its bigger cousin, but for now, with the sunlight penetrating and the day bright again, he could make out the position of the boats. Lazar swam deeper and deeper, knowing he had moments, if any.

He found one sack, struggled with the ties before he opened it and was horrified to see the body of Kett float up, the young man's dead eyes staring sadly back at him. Lazar could not waste another second on Kett and looked around wildly, his body beginning to beg for breath as he spied the other sack crumpled on the riverbed. He reached for it, his fingers not working as fast at the ties as he needed them to. Panic was not an emotion Lazar understood or had experienced more than once in his life. When it had occurred and he realised how one loses control of thought, deed, action in that useless energy, he had promised himself all those years ago never to panic again.

He had stayed true to his oath but could not keep it now: he felt his whole body give in and lose control, although somehow, miraculously, the ties came free on the bag, as did the breath from his mouth in his urgency. He was almost certainly going to die himself in the next few moments if he did not inflate his own lungs. His beautiful girl floated up into his arms, lifeless, her eyes closed, ethereal in death.

He would not accept. Closing his mouth over hers, he

gave her whatever little was left of his own air before he pushed up and away from the darkness towards Lyana's sunlight.

Lazar burst through the surface, gulping for sweet life; his lungs felt like twin furnaces but he sucked in air and, treading water, blew it into Ana's mouth again and again, weeping as he did so. He could remember the last time he cried – it was a dozen or more years ago, when as a young man something special had been taken from him. He would not permit it again. He gave a silent prayer to Lyana that if she gave this girl life, then he would never ask any more of the Goddess or her disciple. He would not follow through on his year's worth of suffering or his promise, made on the island when he was still battling to live, that if he ever saw Ana again he would find a way to show her his love.

Arms reached for them both but he had no sense of being hauled from the water, or being dragged onto the riverbank by the impossibly strong arms of Faraz. The executioner pushed the gasping Spur aside and pumped Ana's chest several times before he, too, went through the motions of breathing life from his own lungs into hers.

In his dazed state, watching the huge black man tenderly kiss Ana with life, Lazar became aware of Salmeo talking at him and Herezah from afar giving orders. But he ignored both. He watched the Zar's party arrive, Jumo hesitating at the gate, whilst Pez showed no such fear, cartwheeling until he arrived at Ana's side.

'Let me,' he whispered to the Elim, who sat aside, stunned by the urgency and authority in the dwarf's voice, shaken that the mad jester had spoken sense at all.

Lazar watched as Pez closed his eyes and laid his hands

on Ana. He sang a song about goat's udders as he did so and it had a sufficiently vulgar quality that anyone who didn't know better might assume the clown was making fun of touching Ana's breasts rather than using the Lore to search for the tiniest echo of a pulse.

Herezah pointed at Lazar. 'And who is this stranger?' she demanded of her son as he arrived, all protocol ignored in these unusual circumstances.

Boaz was not given a chance to answer, for Salmeo now joined in the fray with his own frustrations: 'My Zar, Ana is dead. She has been executed as you sanctioned and as required by the harem. I—'

The Zar held a hand up to stop them both as he watched Lazar take over once again, pushing air into seemingly dead lungs and pumping her chest to expel water, get the heart responding.

'Well?' he asked the men fighting for her life, holding his breath. His own feelings aside, Ana was their hope now and with her death went Percheron's safety.

'Who is this madman who leaps into the river and brings out an executed odalisque with not so much as a by-your-leave?' the Valide demanded, looking at the dripping stranger who continued to ignore them all. It both appalled and disgusted her to see them trying to create life from death, although she would be lying if she didn't privately admit to being fascinated to gaze finally on her enemy's corpse. Still, she hated how protocol was being flouted. This was her show, the harem's business, and nothing to do with the Zar or his visitors. Disgruntled that her son was more interested in Ana's body, she addressed the golden-haired stranger. 'You! Who—'

Ana gave a small cough. Everyone around her became suddenly still and silent. In fact no-one who wanted her to live dared so much as breathe until she did. She suddenly spasmed and drew in a huge gasp of air before exploding into a violent cough, vomiting water, struggling to get that first easy breath. Lazar, who held her, became conscious of the pair of disbelieving and enraged stares focused on Ana and did not want to be seen to be too intimate. He wanted to hold her, feel her warmth, her life returning as her body warmed again close to his skin. He wanted to kiss those lips, not just connect with them and breathe life through them. But he must deny himself, keep his promise, for it seemed that Lyana had answered his plea.

He knew now, for the second time, what it was to panic from the heart because you love someone and can't bear for them to suffer for even a moment. He had had every intention of interrupting proceedings but he didn't know how he was going to do it. For once he was grateful to Galinsea and her aggressive attitude, and he felt in debt to his parents for taking offence at his presumed death, even though they had probably wished it a hundred times over when he had been living at the Galinsean palace.

Ana was breathing steadily again now, looking around, dazed, confused.

'Ana?' Her Zar took charge.

She took a long time to focus, unaware of who sat behind her, his head hung with relief. 'Zar Boaz? Where—'

'Ana,' he began, then cleared his throat. 'This is a terrible thing we have done to you.'

'Is Kett alive?'

'It doesn't appear so, Ana. I imagine he committed himself to the river as courageously as you did,' he replied, trying to lessen the blow of the news.

'Then why am I here, Highness?' Her voice was filled with despair. 'Surely this is not your idea of a jest?'

He put his hands up in a warding gesture. 'No! I would never be involved in such a thing. Ana, you were rescued because Percheron needs you.'

Pez had sidled up and in a childish manner stroked her hair, humming a lullaby. It was his quiet way of consoling her for the loss of a friend and comforting her during this traumatic moment. It also reminded her to be careful. Then he skipped away, glancing once at Lazar, who now silently pulled himself to his feet behind Ana.

His movement attracted the attention of the Valide. Their eyes met and in that few moments of numbing stupor she recognised who was standing before her, even though her mind was telling her that her eyes were lying. Suddenly Ana's revival was no longer of immediate concern. The Spur was back from the dead!

'Lazar?' Herezah announced, not really a question but that's how it sounded to everyone, her utter bewilderment. In fact, so complete was her astonishment that her hand covered her open mouth behind her veil.

Ana, still weak, turned, dizzy and unsure of what she'd heard from the Valide, to look into the eyes of the man she had been told was dead. Her lips formed the word, she even thought she'd spoken it, but no voice came when she repeated Herezah's exclamation. This silent communication between them completely consumed him.

'Mother,' Boaz began but he stopped talking when the

Valide began to laugh, although no-one could see the tears in her eyes, and they were not from amusement.

Her intensely agile mind must have crashed through a dozen scenarios as she tried to piece it together and yet what she said surprised even her. 'Every bit the Galinsean you tried to pretend you were not,' she said, her tone cynical and cutting. 'Hair dye. How simple, Lazar, and how truly cunning.'

'Mother, we shall discuss this shortly. You require an explanation regarding the revival of a supposedly executed criminal from the harem and will have it, but right now I need the physicians to look at Odalisque Ana. Elim, if you please . . .'

Ana had not moved. Her body was rigid, her eyes filled with dread that her suspicions were confirmed. Lazar had held her gaze, even though each moment it lingered it pierced his heart deeper until the wound seemed so great he felt sickened. There would be no speedy recovery from this injury. He knew exactly what she was thinking, understood her sense of betrayal, and whilst the Valide hurled her taunts, he barely heard them. He felt dead inside but at least Ana was alive. Lyana had granted him the living death he didn't think he would have to face and try to survive again.

The Elim helped Ana to her feet and it was Faraz who offered to carry her; gently insisted, in fact. When she was gone, Boaz didn't even give his mother a chance to reignite her burning enquiry.

'Mother, you should know that in the Throne Room there impatiently await two Galinsean dignitaries, who can essentially begin a war on Percheron if I provide the correct ammunition.' He let that notion sink in before he continued, watching her angry eyes become wary now behind her veil. Not even at her most imaginative could Herezah have guessed that this was the reason for the Zar interrupting an execution. 'I have no intention of giving them even a spark for their tinder and right now appeasing the enemy is far more important to me than appeasing your anger.' As he paused she opened her mouth to speak but Boaz refused her. 'Lazar's presence has been explained and that explanation was due me alone. He is the Spur of *my* Shield and, as you know, he is answerable to no-one but the Zar. When we have solved our immediate dilemma, and at my convenience, I will sit down and take you through this strange set of circumstances that have brought about today's excitement. Until then, Lazar and Ana are all I have between Percheron's peace or Galinsean war. Please excuse us.'

It was a stunning censure and both the palace dwarf, doodling in the sand on the riverbank, and the Spur felt this speech was Boaz's coming of age. They had borne witness to a new Zar – an all-too-young Zar – finally accepting the full responsibility of his Crown and not cringing away from one ounce of its weight. There was no doubting who sat on the throne of Percheron now and, more importantly, that that person did not have strings attached to him that led back into the harem where a Valide and a Grand Master Eunuch felt they had the ability to manipulate him.

In another situation, Lazar might have applauded loudly. On this occasion he simply bowed his head in courtesy to the Valide and followed his Zar who had already turned to leave. Pez hurried behind, taking careful aim before accidentally treading on the Valide's gown and her long veil, momentarily dragging back her head. Being mad, he didn't even have to apologise, not even acknowledge it, so he didn't and completely ignored her exclamation of outrage.

Salmeo remained sensibly silent.

✑ 20 ✑

Maliz, disguised as Grand Vizier Tariq, had played his role as dignitary to perfection, even though his own mind was churning. It was fortunate that the Galinseans did not require conversation but he had arranged for a table to be dressed in an anteroom connected to the Throne Room and servants had set up an enticing feast for the visitors. Seated on exquisite embroidered cushions, arranged on the floor, the two men had capitulated to the Vizier's urgings to refresh themselves with some food whilst they waited.

It had actually not been long. Marius and Lorto had just begun nibbling on the decadent array of brightly presented food when the Zar returned. They struggled to their feet to bow, and Boaz, not prone to cynicism, was nevertheless uncertain whether the two visitors were bowing to the Zar of Percheron or the Crown Prince of Galinsea who was directly behind. He made a promise to himself not to let this be an obstacle to the diplomacy he must now engage in.

'Ask them to make themselves comfortable again, Lazar,' he urged and listened as, in three briefly uttered words, the Spur had them both seated again.

He joined them. As a show of goodwill he allowed a

servant to wash his hands in a bowl scented with orange blossom before he dismissed all servants and reached for a small flatbread. Boaz was not hungry, not after what had just gone on, but he knew that the breaking of bread together was one of the fastest ways to make all strangers feel at ease. His history lessons had taught him that both Galinsea and Percheron followed the same tradition that generosity at the table – even to an enemy – was the highest form of hospitality and diplomacy. He dipped his bread into a thickly oil-slicked bowl of chickpea paste and ate.

Lazar, at the Zar's encouragement, followed suit. He too thought it wise that Jumo and Pez opt to remain in the Throne Room, next door.

'Make some small talk, Lazar – I don't care what you say but put them at their ease.'

'They are at ease, Highness,' he assured, before beginning a conversation that the Zar had no hope of following.

Whilst this occurred he looked to Tariq and said softly, 'We might yet save this situation, and our secret weapon is Odalisque Ana, can you believe.'

The man shook his head. 'I thought she was being executed, Highness.'

Boaz sighed. 'So did I, Tariq, so did I.'

Lazar was already talking to him again so he stopped his chat to the Vizier. '. . . about where we've been.'

Boaz frowned.

'Excuse me, Highness, I've explained where we've been, because we left so suddenly.'

'Are they shocked?'

'A little.'

'Barbaric Galinseans surprised by an execution?'

Lazar did not show that he bristled at the criticism of

his countrymen. In fact he was surprised himself that after so many years of considering himself a Percherese he could be affected in this way. 'No, my Zar, more intrigued that we would kill a girl for her ingenuity instead of perhaps reprimanding but making use of that bright mind.' He shrugged with mild apology. 'Galinseans are pragmatists. They do not hold to tradition as closely as the Percherese.'

'Have you explained anything further?'

'Not without your permission, Highness. Shall I do so now?'

'Go ahead. Let them know what we're planning in terms of the emissary. I presume they understand your reluctance?' he asked, and Lazar nodded. 'Proceed. Tariq, come with me,' he said, motioning towards the door. 'Excuse me to them, Lazar, for just a moment. I need to brief Ana.'

Lazar acknowledged his Zar but did not break from his discussion with their visitors.

Tariq followed Boaz outside. 'You'd better brief me too, Highness. I think I'm rather confused.'

'Yes, I intend to. What I need right now is for you to organise for Ana to be brought before the visitors as soon as possible. She is being checked over by the physicians at present and I don't doubt she's in shock and not in a position to pay us the attention we require but you need to impress upon her the importance of what I need her to do.'

'Which is?'

'To travel to Galinsea as my emissary.'

Maliz arrived at the harem where he was met by the Elim.

'I'm here to escort Odalisque Ana, at His Majesty's request, to the Throne Room,' he said to the eldest.

'I must fetch Grand Master Salmeo to speak with you.'

Oh lovely, Maliz thought, *just what I need*. 'Thank you.'

The eunuch arrived shortly and paid the Vizier no salutation. 'She is not ready.'

'I shall wait.'

'I can send her with an Elim escort, Tariq, you need not linger for such lowly duties.'

'Nothing on behalf of my Zar is lowly. He expressly asked me to bring her.'

'She is still with the physicians, unless you want her coughing up river water all over the esteemed dignitaries.'

'I'm sure that won't help our cause but apparently she is all we have.'

'What is meant by this insult to the harem?' Salmeo spat, no longer able to maintain his calm facade. 'This girl was to be executed. The harem deals with its own. What is the Zar thinking by interrupting our private and traditional proceedings?'

'Well, Salmeo, I'd suggest he's thinking of you and I. Should it come to war, we'll be amongst the first to be put to the sword. The Galinseans hate our traditions, you know, and the harem would be one of its major targets.'

'I do not understand.'

'No, I can see that. The harem has different meanings to different people, Salmeo. To you it is home, it is life, it is tradition – you know nothing else. To the Zar it is his most treasured investment, from where he will choose his heir. To the Valide it is her seat of power. To the people of Percheron it represents their heritage and an extension of all that is beautiful in their realm. It stands them apart from other kingdoms that do not follow suit.'

'And to those other kingdoms, something else no doubt,' Salmeo interrupted.

Maliz didn't mind, he had nothing better to do just now until he could get some peace to ponder all that he had learned. 'Ah, and now we come to it, you catch on fast, brother. To other kingdoms it is the symbol of Percherese wealth and decadence. It is, I don't doubt, envied, coveted and thus a target of hate. It makes our Zar different to all the other kings who follow a more monogamous marriage system, even though I imagine they lie with whomever they wish behind the palace walls. To destroy the harem is to destroy one of the key aspects of what makes Percheron so covetable, so exotic, so different.'

'And tell me, Tariq, how does Ana fit into this campaign to save the harem, to save Percheron, as the Zar suggested?'

'I'm afraid I'm not at liberty to discuss matters of state so openly, Salmeo, I'm sure you understand, but suffice to say that Ana will be taking on a new official capacity for the Zar.'

'This is outrageous!'

'I suggest you take it up with Zar Boaz, Grand Master Eunuch, I am merely the escort today. How long before she is ready, do you think?'

'Wait here,' Salmeo said, and turned on his heel.

Maliz did as asked and took the time to replay in his head the conversation about Zafira. It was intriguing that the Spur, back from the dead, had been nursed to health by Zafira. Coincidence perhaps? Unlikely, though. Centuries of battling the Goddess had taught him to suspect everyone. Was the Spur involved? Is that why his death was contrived, his survival from the poison and his wounds kept a secret . . . but why? And then why come back? He pondered this for some time before the silent answer echoed in his mind. He came back to be close to Lyana perhaps, but who is she? he mused for the umpteenth time. She's close, possibly not arisen yet, but Iridor was and his only suspect was the dwarf, who was proving himself to be every bit as mad as everyone assured the Vizier he was. The priestess's claim that Salmeo was Iridor was a ruse, he was sure, or he would have known from being around him so much. He hadn't yet had a chance to meet up with Salazin, who might yield some fresh information.

So far he had Pez, Lazar, and this odalisque as potentially being involved but none were showing any of the usual signs of being close to the Goddess – the nervousness of her disciples was usually his first inkling that he was getting closer to Lyana but Pez was impossible to read in his insanity, Lazar so remote it seemed he was passionate about nothing, and he hardly knew this girl. Tariq had met her on a couple of occasions but paid little attention. That she was beautiful and a troublemaker was as much as Tariq's memories could offer.

But Lyana was clever, he admitted to himself. She had tried many guises over many cyclical battles. She had been an old woman once, other times she had given herself the most ordinary of looks and roles – one year a merchant's wife, another a harlot, even a simple bread-seller once. He smiled remembering her most audacious attempt to confuse, when she had rebirthed herself as a young lad. That had not worked very well – the female form was best.

As he was thinking this, Salmeo emerged once again, this time with the girl fully covered in the simplest of dark gowns and matching veils. The sea-green eyes appeared dulled, uninterested.

The Grand Vizier stood. 'Odalisque Ana?'

She didn't respond until Salmeo murmured something to her.

'I am,' she finally said, not looking at anyone or anything in particular.

'Is she all right?' Maliz asked testily.

'Well, she's drowned once today, if that helps clarify things a little, Grand Vizier. Then she was revived, pulled back from the brink of death. The physicians say there is no outward sign of damage but, as you can see, she is vague, to say the least.'

'And this is who shall save Percheron. My, my . . .' Maliz said, deciding he was going to enjoy this episode, especially now that he'd established that this young woman was not the reincarnation of Lyana. He hadn't expected her to be, but as she seemed to be attracting so much attention from the day she arrived, it had crossed his mind to somehow contrive to meet this woman and the Zar had given him the perfect excuse. Had she been the woman he hunted, he would have felt it; would have felt every inch of his body respond to her magical presence. And her magic would have triggered his and released him from being entirely the prisoner of Tariq. Although he would die again as the Vizier when this battle was done, her arrival gave him his full powers – as it had always done before – fed his fury, nourished his desire to destroy her once again. He needed her to cross his path soon, for until such time he was vulnerable. Oh yes, none of his enemies realised that until Lyana's presence made itself physically felt, he was entrapped by the mortal man and could die as any mortal. It was his darkest secret and once again he thanked Zarab that Lyana had never known this. Her supporters always assumed he possessed his demon skills permanently. Maliz shuddered: it would be so easy for Iridor – whoever he was this time – to stick a knife into him or contrive a death by any number of means, and the Vizier would die, taking with him the demon.

Maliz grinned, smug that they had never discovered this . . . and never would. Whoever Iridor might be, he was no doubt treading very carefully, wary, believing that the demon could not be murdered in his sleep, poisoned during dinner or simply meet some seeming accident. He would warn her other disciples too, no doubt, that Maliz could not be killed by conventional means. In fact . . .

'Vizier Tariq, what are you smiling about?' Salmeo's lisping words cut through his thoughts.

'Ah, forgive me, Grand Master Eunuch. I was just thinking how sad it is that we hide our most treasured possession – great beauty – behind the veil. I have seen this girl, I know her magnificence. She will take our visitors' breath away.'

'How little you understand the harem, Vizier Tariq, and how obvious that you have no wives of your own. Our women are never to be paraded, their beauty is protected and enjoyed only by their husbands.'

Maliz did not want to debate with the eunuch now. He was vexed that he'd been caught off guard momentarily anyway and if he continued this conversation that irritation might show itself.

'Our Zar awaits, Salmeo. And no doubt he'll decide whether or not to allow the glow of this young woman to fall upon others. Odalisque Ana, if you please?'

'Elim will accompany,' Salmeo warned.

'As you see fit.' He turned once again to Ana. 'Come with me, my dear, it seems you're suddenly the most important person in the whole palace, next to the Zar,' Maliz said, just loud enough for Salmeo to hear as he guided Ana away from the harem.

'Grand Vizier, forgive me, but I don't understand,' Ana pleaded.

And he believed her. Her eyes were so large and filled with confusion that he felt a strange thrill of sympathy for this young woman. This was not an emotion he was used to experiencing. He recalled her outstanding beauty, remembered the sweetly innocent body that didn't seem to match her oddly confident, direct manner that so upset Tariq and Salmeo at the time. 'I can tell you some more – as much as I have been told. I know they're waiting for you, Odalisque Ana, but let us take the slower way to the Throne Room so I have a little time to explain.'

'That's generous of you, Grand Vizier.'

Maliz smiled. No-one had ever accused him of that trait before. 'How does it feel to return from the dead?' he asked conversationally.

She didn't pause before replying, as he had anticipated. 'I feel angry.'

'Why?' This was not the answer he had expected and she intrigued him.

'Because I hate this place and everyone in it. Death was my ultimate escape.'

There was true venom driving this statement and he loved to hear the passion in her tone. He could begin to appreciate what Boaz saw in this particular girl and he almost regretted telling the Zar that she was inconsequential. Far from it – this woman was exciting. 'That's a very sweeping statement, Odalisque Ana. Do you not crave life? How about everlasting life?'

She stared at him as they walked, conscious of the Elim trailing silently behind. 'No, Grand Vizier. Life has not treated me kindly and there is nothing to look forward to in age. Dying young is appropriate.'

The girl could be Lyana with that sentiment, he mused, but none of his senses were on alert. This was no goddess walking in disguise at his side. 'Do you really hate everyone here?'

'I wouldn't have said it if I didn't mean it, Grand Vizier Tariq.'

'I thought you were friendly with the dwarf,' he probed, just for good measure.

'Pez has no sane process of thought. No-one is friends with him because it's impossible to understand him.' He could tell she was being careful with this question and his ears pricked up. 'I do, however, feel constantly sorry for him. Pez is trapped in his mind as I am trapped in the harem.'

'That's a clever analogy, Odalisque Ana. Do you notice any moments of clarity with him, though? Could he be pretending, do you think?'

'Grand Vizier, why are you asking me this odd question?'

'Oh, nothing,' he shrugged, intrigued now by her fluster. Was she hiding something? 'Simply baffled by him.'

'But you've known him for many years, surely? Why would I throw any more light on his sanity?'

She was certainly direct and very composed for someone of such a tender age. Definitely a match for the Zar. 'Yes

I have, but Pez, amongst his swirl of insanity, very clearly detests me.'

She laughed. 'Yes, he can be contrary to certain people.'

'Who else, would you say?'

'I can't imagine,' she replied but there was again the careful tone.

'Well, myself, the Valide certainly, and without doubt, Salmeo. His hostility, that seems to be couched in humour, is carefully directed. But never at the Zar, never at you presumably, Ana, never at the Spur.'

He watched her bristle at the mention of Lazar. He smiled inwardly. How delicious this was – secrets upon secrets. He'd definitely hit a nerve there. 'Of course you know the Spur has also returned to us from the dead,' he continued, happy to leave the other thread of conversation for it was leading nowhere anyway.

'Yes,' she replied, brisk and to the point.

'Ah, is he one of the people you hate?'

'I told you, I hate everyone.'

'Including me?'

'Yes.'

'How sad. I thought we were getting on rather well.'

'That's not the same as liking someone, Grand Vizier.'

'No, indeed. You have a good grip on diplomacy, Odalisque Ana, and that's why you'll make a fine emissary for our Zar.'

'Grand Vizier,' she said and could not hide the fractiousness in her tone, 'you promised me an explanation.'

'I did. Here it is, for what it's worth.' He explained about the Galinseans.

'Here in the palace, threatening war?' she asked, incredulous.

'Not openly. But the suggestion is clearly there unless we can convince the Galinsean royalty that Spur Lazar is alive and well. Perhaps we can say the execution was a jest and apologise profusely that the Galinseans don't share our sense of humour?'

She sneered at his sarcasm. He couldn't see her mouth but her eyes were incredibly expressive. He rather adored her and loved goading her to watch the spark of anger flare in them.

'But why is Spur Lazar so important?'

'Ah, and now you have hit the crux of the matter. I cannot explain this but, from what I gather, if he is dead so are we and thus we must convince them that blood flows strongly in his veins.'

'How does this involve me?'

'My dear Ana, have you not realised that you are the only person who speaks Galinsean with such fluency?'

'The Zar does,' she countered.

'And you know full well that it is not the same language that he speaks.'

She nodded, abashed. 'He speaks an ancient form of it.'

'Which makes absolutely no sense to our Galinsean dignitaries.'

Her frustration got the better of her. 'Spur Lazar is alive! Lyana save me,' she cursed, 'why can't he just go and present himself?'

Maliz stopped, entranced. 'Now why would you call down the help of the Goddess?'

'I . . . I . . .' she faltered, 'a slip, Grand Vizier. I admit I support the role of the priestess but I have never openly practised,' she assured.

'That's right,' he mused, 'when you escaped the first time they found you in the Sea Temple, didn't they?' He nodded for her. 'Lyana's temple.'

'Is that so wrong?'

'It's unusual.'

'Are you a hater of the Goddess too, Grand Vizier?'

He liked the way she attacked when cornered. 'I'm afraid so. I follow Zarab, child.' He stored her 'slip' away. Perhaps he shouldn't take his eye off Ana, or Pez for that matter. She was far too careful when discussing the dwarf and her love for Lyana was rather damning. Still, she wasn't Lyana – that he was utterly certain of, and was pleased in a strange way because killing this feisty and beautiful woman would be a shame. He would enjoy watching her lead him to Lyana, though, as he was now gaining in confidence that this girl was somehow involved.

'My spiritual leanings are irrelevant, Grand Vizier – you were explaining to me why Spur Lazar could not sort out the situation by presenting himself.'

'I can't explain that because I am not privy to the details but the Zar seems to understand that this is not the best strategy. Presumably the Spur's life is in danger if he goes to Galinsea.' He had decided that Ana should learn the truth from the lips of others. It would make for some entertainment, he was sure.

'And that leaves me – that's why I was plucked from the death waters,' she finished.

'Correct. You speak fluent, current and courtly Galinsean, as we all understand it. As I said earlier, you are now the single most important person in the whole of Percheron, save the Zar himself.'

'No wonder Salmeo and the Valide are so disgusted.' He laughed with genuine mirth at her comment and again she stared at him, trying to work him out. 'Forgive my indiscretion, Grand Vizier.'

'Nothing to forgive, my dear, I find them both slippery and conniving, to say the least.' Now she looked shocked and he laughed again. 'I suppose I shouldn't be admitting that to an odalisque.' She shook her head, her eyes telling him she was puzzled by him, a little frightened. 'Then we have both shared a secret that the other must protect. You have told me of your love for Lyana and I have told you of my hate for two very important people in the palace. Are we conspirators?'

The eyes behind the veil narrowed.

'You have nothing to fear from me, Odalisque Ana. Whatever you've heard about me may have been true once but no longer. It was all a ruse. I am loyal to Zar Boaz and, as you may have noticed, have become very close to him. I don't care for what his mother might advise him, or for where the fat black eunuch might lead him.' He watched his words take effect – a fragile bond suddenly linking them, he could see it reflected in those green eyes. 'I will do whatever's necessary to protect the Zar and his personal interests rather than follow any of the agendas of the grasping mother. We are fellow haters, Ana. Your secret is safe with me.'

She was taken aback and momentarily forgot the warnings that had been impressed upon her. She reasoned that both Pez and Lazar trusted Boaz and he had obviously taken the time to learn about Tariq and trust him. She didn't need to be told by the Vizier, she had watched how they had become close, had heard Boaz speak only praise of his counsellor. She made her decision. 'Then so is yours, Grand Vizier,' she replied.

'Good. What happened to the black eunuch boy, by the way?'

Her eyes misted and took on a faraway look. 'The bird of sorrows is dead,' she said sadly. 'They managed to drown Kett.'

Maliz was speechless. The whole of Tariq's body was stiff with tension. He finally found his voice. 'Kett, that's right. Why did you call him the bird of sorrows?' he asked, trying to cover the choked feeling in his throat.

Ana was still talking in a dreamy voice. 'Oh, he called himself the Raven. It's funny, I always thought of him as a little black bird, scared by his own dark shadow sometimes and yet always courageous when he needed to be.'

Maliz could feel his body trembling now. He was close, very close. He had won a small amount of Ana's trust and she had delivered something exquisitely important to him through a moment of carelessness. Ana may not be Lyana but she *was* involved in the struggle for the Goddess's supremacy. Perhaps her involvement was inadvertent or only minor but this girl was his first real clue to his prey. He could not keep her any longer from her duty – especially as they had arrived – much as he would like to have seized this chance to interrogate her further. 'We are here, Ana. Zar Boaz is counting on you – in fact all of Percheron is counting on you – to use your eloquence and diplomacy.'

Ana thought of her father, of her young brother and sisters and for them alone agreed to do whatever was required to save Percheron from war.

She nodded, pulling herself from her dreamy thoughts. 'I am ready, Grand Vizier.'

He smiled warmly. 'When we are not in formal situations, you must call me Tariq. Thank you for your discretion and trust. I will help you in your endeavours all I can.' He had sensed where her loyalties now lay. 'Perhaps I can get a message to your family, send them something? Money?'

Her eyes shone. 'Why would you do this?'

'Because I have no-one to spoil and I'm glad you were rescued and we had this opportunity to get to know one another a little. You hold my secrets now. For keeping them between us let me reward you for that friendship in the way I know will count.'

'We are not friends, Grand Vizier . . . not yet. Not money but a message, yes, or even news that they are well would mean everything to me.'

'Consider it done, child. Now, here we go . . . impress.'

Ana nodded her silent thanks. Behind the shrouded eyes of Tariq, the demon Maliz smiled.

21

Ana's shock at seeing Lazar again — blond, bearded — almost unnerved her as she entered the chamber and she stumbled slightly, but she took the few moments as she knelt to her Zar to compose herself. In the fleeting second that their eyes met she saw that Lazar looked as full of dread and discomfort as she felt. She took in the toll that his fight to survive had obviously taken on him.

'Ah, gentlemen,' Boaz began. 'This is Odalisque Ana. Rise, Ana.'

She did so but kept her eyes lowered. The Grand Vizier stood protectively alongside but there was no sign of Pez. Perhaps that was a good thing but she could feel the weight of Lazar's stare, feel the heat of it sear past her veil once again, and onto her skin, where it rested like a lingering kiss.

'Ana, you may remove your veil,' Boaz said gently. 'I want you to meet some esteemed guests of Percheron.' It was also a command to raise her eyes. She did as her Zar bade her and ignored the flare of pleasure in the strangers' eyes as they looked upon her fully. 'This is Marius D'Argenny,' Boaz said, his hand gesturing towards an older, silver-haired man with a stern face but lively eyes. 'And this is Lorto Belsher. Neither speak Percherese but

I have told them you can speak Galinsean that they will understand.' She looked at the Zar and he gave her an embarrassed but encouraging smile. 'You and I will talk privately shortly. Please go ahead, Ana.'

She could feel Lazar's presence to her left as if he were a glowing brazier, radiating heat, and despite her anger and desire to be ice to him, she nevertheless felt the pull of that warmth and the comfort it could offer. The thought of feeling his arms wrap around her, hearing him tell her he loved her and that he never meant for her to suffer by his actions . . . the pull of him was so seductive, she felt herself sway slightly.

'Ana?' It was Boaz again, gentle but firm.

She rallied, forced herself to ignore the familiar, yet strange man nearby, and she smiled for the visitors, before, in flawless, courtly Galinsean, she welcomed them to the city of Percheron. A lengthy conversation with the dignitaries ensued that only Ana and Lazar could follow. Boaz and his Vizier could do little more than settle sympathetic expressions on their faces and hope that Ana's words hit the right chord.

At some point Ana realised that Lazar had joined the discussion, offering her helpful insights into the Galinsean royalty. She had paused, nodded, but still not looked at him, and only now turned fully to gaze upon the man at length – the man who dominated her thoughts, had been her reason for living, and indeed for dying. His golden hair suited him and suddenly no longer looked strange but right. The beard, however, hid the sculpture of his face and she longed to see it removed, imagined herself smoothing her hand across that firm jaw he ground so hard.

There was such sorrow reflected in his pale eyes that it nearly undid her. She felt a dry sob catch in her throat but the occasion demanded she carry herself with dignity this day. Boaz needed it from her and it was the least she could do for the Zar, considering the way she had abused his trust. As well, her own family's safety burned in her mind. She did not want war to visit Percheron.

'Spur Lazar, pardon my ignorance, and gentlemen, perhaps you'll forgive me for not appreciating the subtleties of the background to this situation, but I have to wonder why you three cannot simply return to the court of Galinsea. Lazar's presence would surely negate the need for war.'

Marius gave her a soft smile but deferred to the Spur.

Lazar cleared his throat. 'Yes, Odalisque Ana, that is the obvious path to follow . . . except I cannot.'

Just to hear him speak her name again made her feel weak. She clenched her nails against the palm of one hand to steady herself. 'May I ask why? I need to understand what undercurrent passes beneath us here.'

'It is because I have been excommunicated from that court,' Lazar answered, his tone direct but his words not so; she sensed the discomfort he had in answering.

'I see.' She hesitated but then persisted: 'Again, forgive my dullness here, gentlemen, but is it normal for Galinsea to go to war over someone they don't care about?'

'It is Lucien's status that is the problem, my dear,' Marius replied.

'Lucien?' She looked at the old man quizzically.

'I am Lucien,' Lazar cut in. She saw him take a slow breath as if working hard to keep his emotions controlled.

She stared at him for a long time. She did not need to

say anything for Lazar to appreciate what her look meant and what sort of pain he was further inflicting upon her.

When Ana spoke again her voice was colder now. 'And, sirs, if you'll permit my question, what is Lucien to the Galinsean court?'

This time Lazar chose not to answer. Marius flicked a glance his way and then replied for him. 'Odalisque Ana, I realise people here are only just learning the truth of your Spur's background. I know how difficult this must be for him and for the Percherese Crown. But these are dire times and I have to placate an angry King. Before you, Odalisque Ana, is Crown Prince Lucien, heir to the throne of Galinsea.'

Ana's already unbalanced world rocked on a new axis. She felt dizzy at the revelation but through the confusion everything about Lazar suddenly made sense to her. She understood him even more deeply now for this admission, but none of that realisation helped relieve her sense of betrayal. He had deceived her, deceived everyone.

'Royalty,' she said, as if testing the word, then she gathered up her pain in the way she was becoming used to and put it aside. 'Thank you. Now I understand why you need a third party involved.'

'You speak our language beautifully, Odalisque Ana,' Lorto said, his first words to her.

She smiled, liking both the Galinseans for their sincerity. 'Thank you, sir.'

'In any other situation, you would be most acceptable,' Marius was quick to add.

Lazar frowned and Boaz instantly picked up that there was a problem. 'What is it?' the Zar interrupted. 'Ana seems to be discoursing well with them.'

'She is flawless, they like her very much,' Lazar reassured. 'We have hit a snag, it seems. I'm about to find out what, my Zar. Please indulge us a few moments longer.'

Boaz nodded, concentrating hard on the foreign words flying about him as the four people who spoke and understood Galinsean conversed once again. Finally he watched Ana bow in what looked to be resignation. They all turned to the Zar.

'Explain, Ana,' he said.

'My Zar, forgive me. I can certainly act as your emissary but my status is such that it will not make a strong enough impression on the royal family of Galinsea.'

'I don't understand.'

'I gather they need someone high-ranking from Percheron. The Valide, the Grand Vizier . . . perhaps—'

'None of whom speak Galinsean!' Boaz cut across her, his exasperation spilling over. 'How am I expected to keep both Percheron and Lazar safe? If I send him, they'll likely kill him. If I don't, they'll destroy us.'

Silence descended on the room and rested on everyone heavily. It was Lazar who broke it.

'I will go, Highness. My life has been forfeit for some time with my family and until not so long ago you accepted my death. Let me take my chances.'

'Your death was never accepted, Lazar, never! I will not risk you, not again. Percheron needs you now more than ever. There has to be another way.'

'There is,' Lazar replied evenly, although none could know what it would cost him.

All eyes shifted to the Spur, except Ana's, which remained studiously lowered, unable to look upon him without suffering. She could hear in his voice, however, that his idea did not sit comfortably with him.

'Share it!' Boaz commanded.

'May I see if it is acceptable with the Galinseans, Highness? I fear they're wondering what we're discussing and they sense your frustration. It does not look good that we alienate them at this delicate stage.'

'Go ahead,' Boaz urged. He wanted resolution and allowing the Galinseans to hear this new plan first was the least of his troubles.

As Lazar spoke to the two men, Ana's eyes widened and then her mouth opened slightly. The Zar and his Vizier could tell she was shocked by whatever Lazar was suggesting.

'Spur Lazar, no!' She surprised everyone with her outburst. It didn't take an interpreter to understand her exclamation.

After the momentary pause in which Lazar glared at Ana, he returned to explaining to the intrigued guests.

The Zar spoke in a soft voice for Ana's hearing. 'Ana, you and I must speak alone later, there is much to clear between us, now that you – er, will be amongst us again.'

She said nothing, inclining her head slightly in politeness to his wishes.

Marius nodded, said something to Lazar, who now turned back to his ruler and bowed. 'They agree, Highness. The idea is acceptable to them.'

Salmeo felt unprepared for this storm. For once this was none of his making and it was rare for him to feel quite so helpless. The shock of Ana's revival had already sunk in and been dealt with by him but the Valide had held on to her rage, was unable to let it go yet.

'Emissary! To the court of Galinsea, no less.'

'It's baffling, Valide, I agree.'

She clenched her fists and groaned. 'The sight of Lazar diving into that water and then coming up with her makes me sick to my stomach! How can he be back?'

'More to the point, Valide, how could she have not drowned?'

She ignored him. 'They usurped my authority, Salmeo. It is not right that harem business is interrupted by outsiders.'

'I know, but this was the Zar's wish. We are not in a position to contradict your son openly, Valide.'

'I don't need the obvious stated, eunuch,' she spat.

Salmeo disagreed but kept his counsel. Even though she was not raising her voice this was the first time in adulthood he had seen her so flustered. She *did* need the obvious stated so she didn't make a ghastly error in her passion. Ana's survival, once again, combined with Lazar's re-emergence on the scene, had reduced the Valide to a shaking wreck. He had ordered her pomegranate tea infused with vinko to restore calm to her. It was taking its time working, he noticed, another indication that the Valide's emotions were spinning well beyond her usual icy control.

'Forgive me, Valide. I meant not to offend. I simply wanted to convey that the Zar had taken full charge of proceedings – he even had the Vizier fetching Ana! What next? He was obviously not taking any chances.'

'Why not send the Grand Vizier to Galinsea? They are

as close as brothers these days,' she said, disgust lacing her tone.

'He does not speak Galinsean.'

'Then Lazar, for Zarab's sake! The man's alive – isn't that what this is all about?'

He nodded, determined not to fuel her anger himself and thus get burned. 'I am as confused as you are, Valide. Please sip your tea, we can't have your voice hoarse for when you are presented to the Galinsean dignitaries.'

'If I'm presented, Salmeo. It seems Odalisque Ana is all that my son needs these days. Now she's his diplomatic representative at foreign courts!'

He could see her pulse pounding at her temple.

'I suspect only because she can speak the language fluently, Valide, no other reason.'

She was about to hurl more abuse his way, for want of a better target, when the bell sounded outside.

'Come!' Herezah ordered. Her personal attendant stepped inside. 'Yes?'

'Valide, forgive my disturbance, but it is the Zar's secretary, Bin, with a message he must deliver personally.'

'Well, he can wait, I'm busy,' she growled back.

The young man looked terrified. 'My sincerest apologies, Valide, but it is urgent, of the highest importance and direct from the Zar's mouth, I am told to inform.'

Herezah scowled. How much worse could this day get? 'Send him in,' she said, her hand waving in disdain.

Bin entered and bowed. 'Valide, Grand Master Salmeo, please forgive my interruption.'

'What is it?' Herezah said, her tone biting. 'If you've come to invite me to supper with the Galinseans, they'll be waiting a while. I need several hours for my toilet.'

Bin bowed low again. 'I do bring an invitation, Valide, but not for supper with the Zar.'

'What then?' she sneered.

'He would like you to attend and witness his wedding.'

∽ 22 ∽

Against her wishes and without an option, Ana was hurriedly whisked from the Throne Room to be prepared for her marriage in the finest garments that could be assembled in such a short time. The Galinseans were shown to some accommodation where they could rest and freshen themselves.

Boaz asked Lazar to join himself and the Vizier in a private courtyard. Pez was nowhere to be seen but it was probably best he made himself scarce under these trying circumstances, the Zar thought.

Lazar had barely moments to spend with Jumo, who still wore an expression of incredulity as they walked along the palace corridors towards the Moon Courtyard.

'I can't believe it,' the faithful servant said again. 'And you look so different.'

Lazar shook his head. 'None of this need have happened if only I'd been asked.'

'But they said you were unconscious, incapable of speech and then you died. What else could we believe? Even Pez was duped initially, I gather.'

'He was. I owe you some explanation of what really happened, my friend, but right now we must make arrangements.'

'Yes, I understand the urgency, but I feel so responsible. This war threat is because of my hasty actions.'

'Don't, Jumo! You are the last person to be blamed for this mess. Ellyana is the villain. She and Zafira deliberately kept all information of my survival from you . . . and worse, perpetrated the lie of my death. I'm so sorry.'

Jumo grimaced. 'I knew I was being manipulated at the time but I couldn't work it out. I still can't. Why? What is there to gain through Ellyana's actions except chaos?'

'I think that's precisely what she was after. Or more accurately, unpredictability. Be patient. There are some things to tell you but we must prepare to leave for Galinsea. The Zar awaits me.'

'You're going?'

'I'm not letting Ana go alone.'

'But she's not, she's—'

'She might as well be. No, I will be escorting her as far as the capital, if Boaz will permit it, and I can't see him refusing me. After she is delivered I can melt into the city crowds but at least I'll be there.'

Jumo nodded. 'All right. What do you want me to do?'

'Horses through the foothills, camels to take over from the edge of the Waste. Get fat old Belzo off his backside and doing what he does best: securing the Shield's supplies. We need to be self-sufficient – you know what a long journey it is.'

'How many are going?'

'Marius and Lorto can return on their ship and hopefully allay any eager Galinsean warships. Our party will be three, and no more if I can help it.'

Jumo pulled an expression of uncertainty and Lazar

knew what was going through his mind. He wanted to take some more men but he held his tongue on this, deferring to the Spur's knowledge of what may or may not incite the Galinseans further. He moved to the next most obvious question. 'Why the desert, Lazar? Surely ship is the best way?'

'It's too slow. We have to stop any invasion before it leaves Galinsea. The desert is our only hope. Marius and Lorto will take their ship and hasten to the main flotilla. There they will prevent the Galinsean warships from moving any closer to Percheron and instead get word to my father via birds. By then, hopefully, we'll already be there and royal decree will go back to the warships ordering them to return to Romea.'

'But you can't even enter the city of Romea apparently.'

Lazar grimaced. 'I know. I'm hoping to have a plan before we get there.'

Jumo could do nothing but smile. 'Typical. Leave it with me.'

Lazar gripped the man's shoulder. 'Thank you, Jumo . . . especially for your patience.'

The little man shrugged. 'You're alive, that's all that matters to me. I must go, I have a lot to organise in a short time.'

'Tell Belzo quality camels or I'll . . .'

'I know, I know . . . you'll kick his fat backside.'

The two men grinned. Even though the trip already smelled so dangerous, it felt good to be preparing to travel again together.

'Ah, Lazar,' Boaz said, welcoming the Spur into his private courtyard. 'Come, come.'

'Apologies, Highness, arrangements needed to be made.'

'My mind's a whirl – yours must be too.'

The Grand Vizier handed Lazar a cup of strong wine.

'I think we all need this,' Boaz reflected. 'Heartfelt thanks to you for coming up with an acceptable solution all round.' He raised his glass to his Spur.

'It's radical, Highness,' the Vizier said.

'Not really, Tariq. Quite normal, I would have thought, for me to choose a wife from my harem.'

'I'm just imagining how it will reflect, Highness, that you've chosen a condemned prisoner who was actually in the process of being executed.'

Lazar bristled. 'The Galinseans know none of that, Vizier, and we can keep it that way. As far as they're concerned, this is a woman who speaks their language with grace and fluency and who is married to the Zar . . . that's a Queen in their eyes.' He looked at the Zar. 'You will make her Absolute Favourite, of course. Her status must be the highest there is.'

'Of course,' Boaz said, his heart pumping with anticipation and nervousness. It was obvious to his companions that he was thinking upon how life could swing from one extreme to another in a blink. This morning he was counting the bells, the very minutes to Ana's death . . . now he was counting more minutes until he took her as his wife. 'I can only imagine the fury in the harem at how events have turned out,' he said, smiling ruefully and then added, 'I only wish I could have saved Kett in the chaos as well.'

The Vizier looked thoughtful. 'You misinterpret me, Spur. I think Ana – the little I've seen of her – is magnificent. We took some time together before she came to the

Throne Room . . .' He watched Lazar's eyes narrow, saw the body tense. So, the Spur felt the same way towards Ana as she did him. Very interesting. Another relationship to watch. He smiled. 'The Zar asked me to explain to her what was happening. I found her to be exquisite yet feisty, a good listener and yet sharp, quick to assimilate information. She is precisely what is required for this role. I was actually referring not to the Galinseans but to those who stood to benefit by her death . . . those a little closer to home.'

'You mean my mother and Salmeo,' Boaz said it for him.

Maliz didn't flinch. He had nothing to lose but oddly enough he rather cared for Boaz and now Ana. Their lives were infinitesimal on the scale of his own, both of them merely vehicles for a greater agenda. But still they had both managed to get under his skin somewhat, make him care, just a fraction, for their earthly pursuits. And so he preferred to be frank with Boaz, guide him properly, knew the Zar could handle constructive criticism if offered genuinely and at the right time. The Zar was no fool when it came to either the Valide or the eunuch. 'Yes, of course I do. I'm not suggesting the Valide created the situation but we'd all be lying to ourselves if we didn't see how she stands to gain by Odalisque Ana being out of the way.'

Defence came from an unexpected quarter. 'Whether it's Ana or some other wife, it has to happen. The Valide understands the fragility of her own existence. She always has,' Lazar replied.

'That's generous of you, Lazar,' Boaz said. 'My mother's mind works in fantastic ways sometimes. To be honest, there are moments when I could despise her but there are many more when I can only feel the highest admiration. She has survived and prevailed in an atmosphere of fear and suspicion. I've lived in the harem, neither of you have and neither of you can begin to imagine what my mother has had to do to raise herself to the position she now has.'

Both men nodded thoughtfully. He continued. 'I agree, Vizier, my mother can protect her position as long as I don't take a wife. Ana was always a threat – as are all the women, as Lazar rightly argues – but then the ironic part is that the Valide herself chose Ana as the perfect wife. She always intended that Ana be Favourite.'

'Just not so soon,' Lazar added.

'That's right, not so soon. My mother's waited a long time to achieve her position and I for one can't blame her for wanting to hang on to it for a little longer.'

'She doesn't lose her status, Majesty,' Lazar began.

'No, but the beginning of the slide is there, isn't it? A wife is taken, an heir is born . . . it's only a matter of time.'

'But, my Zar, you are still so young, you have many years before you hand over to a son,' the Vizier commented.

'On the face of it, yes,' Boaz said and he frowned, 'but things happen in life, Vizier, that none of us can foresee. If I'd said to you a couple of days ago that we would be trying to avert a genuine threat of war with Galinsea, you most likely would have laughed at me, called me paranoid. And yet here we are taking extreme measures – prepared to send a very young woman into incredible danger to protect ourselves from that very invasion.'

'What are you saying, Highness?' Lazar asked, not sure

where this was leading and whether Boaz was having second thoughts about the wedding.

Boaz shrugged. 'Nothing profound, simply pointing out the strangeness of fate. That my father took a harmless fall from his horse — of a sort he had taken many times before — but on that last occasion he was killed by it. The previous Zar died from accidental poisoning because he enjoyed bloatfish. None of us have such a firm grip on life that Zarab can't take it whenever he wishes. All I'm saying is that my mother has every right to feel angry at how things are turning out. Yes, she probably silently cheered Ana's demise because I had already announced my intention to choose her . . . it has taken her so long to attain this status and now it's being whittled away barely a year into her son's reign. If I died by accident tomorrow, my mother would be finished and chaos would abound in the palace.' He stopped abruptly, having not meant to give such a lengthy speech.

'Hurry up and sire a son on Ana then, Highness, that's my advice to you.' Maliz laced his tone with humour and Boaz grinned but the demon had deliberately chosen his words to watch the reaction from the Spur. He got precisely what he expected.

Lazar cleared his throat. 'Zar Boaz, we must leave immediately the nuptials are done with. I'm not sure there will be time after the ceremony for . . .'

'Oh come now, Spur,' Maliz drawled sardonically, 'are you going to deny a man his wedding rights?'

'I . . .' Lazar looked flustered. 'Zar Boaz, I—'

Maliz laughed inwardly. So secret lovers within the palace. Forbidden, dangerous love . . . the best kind. 'Well, if not a wedding night, at least a chance to consummate the marriage, make it real. Surely this will sit more easily with our Galinsean dignitaries if they know this marriage is genuine.'

Boaz was nodding, much to Lazar's dismay. Maliz wanted to clap, he was enjoying himself so much.

'You're right, Tariq. If nothing else it will give appearance of authenticity,' Boaz agreed. 'Good, that's settled,' he said, unable to disguise a distinct flush at his cheeks, 'Ana will join me for a few hours after the ceremony. It is fitting, I do need to talk with her after all that has occurred.'

Now the Vizier did grin openly. 'Talk? Yes, indeed Highness. I'm sure you will enjoy your conversation but just let it be known that the marriage is consummated. All in the pursuit of diplomacy, Highness.' He could feel Lazar seething.

Boaz nodded again. 'You may prepare to leave in the cool of the evening, Lazar.'

He tried not to show that he was gritting his teeth. 'As you wish, my Zar.'

Maliz really had to stop himself from laughing out loud now. It seemed the Zar, for all his intelligence, was dull when it came to women, or so one-eyed that he couldn't even sense what was obvious . . . to him anyway. Maliz returned his focus to Lazar, enjoying playing the Spur as much as laughing secretly at Boaz. 'Are we not led to believe that it is dangerous for you to enter Romea, Spur?'

'It is,' Lazar answered and wasn't doing a terribly good job of disguising his anger. 'But I am the only one who can lead Ana there safely, successfully.'

'Ah, so you get her to the city and then turn her loose

alone? Surely she needs an entourage? We can't go to the Galinsean court like peasants, Zar Boaz.'

'Again, you're right, Tariq. Lazar, we need to think this through better. There should be more in the party for the reason our Vizier points out. This is a royal visit. Granted it's also a diplomatic visit but my wife needs more than you're offering. As it is you won't be able to go into Romea, so that leaves who? Jumo?'

Lazar was already shaking his head. 'Zar Boaz, I must counsel you otherwise. Going across the desert is fraught with dangers. I cannot protect a large party.'

'You cannot protect us anyway, Spur,' Maliz chimed in, suddenly including himself in the party. It was not missed by Lazar, who grimaced. 'Surely this is such an important diplomatic mission it requires at least some of the usual pomp accorded such an event? We need to appear strong, confident, even if we are terrified out of our wits.'

Lazar's eyes blazed their anger. Boaz was having none of it, though. 'Lazar, I know this does not please you. Believe me, it does not please me either to have to send anyone to Galinsea, but Tariq is right. This mission is far too important for Ana to be cast into the enemy's den alone.'

He knew he was beaten. And if good sense hadn't prevailed, he might have reached his fingers around the throat of the all-too-helpful Vizier who seemed to be deliberately baiting him. This was not Tariq — not by any stretch of the imagination. Someone else lurked behind those dark, mischievous eyes. He had no doubt now that Tariq was gone, replaced by the demon that Pez had warned about. And Maliz had been with Ana — it was this fact that was driving his fury. She had been in such danger without realising it. He had to speak with Pez.

'Who exactly would you suggest might make this party more acceptable, Majesty?' Lazar asked.

'That's a good question, I'll admit it. Time is so short we don't have many options.'

The Vizier piped up again. 'I shall go, Highness, if you deem that suitable.' Maliz didn't look at Lazar but could feel his dislike all but reaching out towards his throat.

Lazar reacted as if stung. 'As head of security in Percheron I would recommend that we need our head counsel – the Grand Vizier – close to the Zar.'

'Well, I agree with both of you,' Boaz said, shrugging. 'Lazar's right, I feel you should always be close to the palace, Tariq. That said, you do have very high status and are closest counsellor to the Crown. It would be a good-will gesture to send you.'

The Vizier nodded sagely, then frowned as if thinking through a new idea. 'It occurs to me to suggest that you should also send Pez, as a gift, Highness. Laughter is a great way to leap cultures, bridge our differences and so on.'

'Zar Boaz, I must protest,' Lazar interrupted. 'Really, this is not a circus I'm taking across the desert. I'm trying to stop a war!'

'So am I, Lazar,' Boaz said, a fraction coldly, and the Spur knew he was no longer talking to a young man slightly in awe of him. This was a Zar and he was demanding respect from his Spur.

'Forgive me, Zar Boaz.'

'Nothing to forgive,' Boaz said, sensibly waving the moment aside. 'We are all worried, and it may not appear so but I am fully sympathetic to your task of guiding people safely across the desert. It's frightening just to think of you taking that route. It's absolutely necessary, of course?'

'For speed, yes, Highness. By sea it would take two moons. Not fast enough to avert warriors hungry for booty. Marius and Lorto will stay the warships in open sea and send messages back to Romea. I'm hoping that by the time the birds arrive, Ana will have already argued her case with the King.'

Boaz sighed, drained his cup. 'Right, here is my decision. Lazar, you will escort Absolute Favourite Ana, together with Grand Vizier Tariq, and the Valide will go as Ana's escort . . .' He held up his hand to prevent the furious outburst threatening to erupt from Lazar. He glared to stop the man making a mistake. 'Ana needs the guidance of an older woman and whatever my mother is, she can be relied upon to be courtly and incredibly perceptive when it comes to people. I want her there at that palace, especially as I realise you can hardly risk discovery. You will also take Pez – he will make good entertainment for our royal neighbours.' He looked at Lazar in a way to suggest that he was sending the palace clown for help rather than hindrance. 'You will take a dozen of the Elim and four of my elite guard, the mutes, who will have the express task of guarding my wife, alongside yourself. Lazar, you can take as many or few of your men as you wish, although I would prefer that you left the city fully secured by the Shield in your absence. Zarab knows what might come at us in the meantime, especially if Marius and Lorto cannot head off all or some of those warships.'

There was nothing Lazar could risk saying. Instead he maintained a stony silence. It was the Vizier who did all the talking in response.

'Very good, my Zar. Please excuse me so I can make arrangements for gifts for our counterparts in Galinsea. Er, Spur Lazar, perhaps you can guide us in this?' He smiled and received a scowl in return. It mattered not. He continued: 'The exchange of wedding presents will take place in three hours, Highness. I'm sorry it won't be the lavish affair it should be for your first wife but I know you understand. We will do our best to impress with a wedding feast. May I suggest you rest until then. Spur Lazar, when do we leave?'

'At nightfall, as the Zar wishes,' the tall man growled. 'We can reach the foothills by midnight. Sleep until an hour before dawn and set out on the camels then.'

'Camels? Lovely,' Maliz replied.

Lazar needed to escape. 'Excuse me, Highness. I need to brief Jumo on the extra supplies we shall have to organise.'

'Yes, go by all means and ensure you take the royal tents. And Lazar . . . ?'

The man looked back, the obvious war inside only barely sheathed.

'As unhappy as you are, I want you back here to witness my marriage to Odalisque Ana.'

'I wouldn't miss it, Highness,' Lazar said and Maliz chuckled silently to himself.

23

The entire palace had swung into action, and to his credit, Maliz, drawing on Tariq's fastidious eye for detail, was orchestrating most of the arrangements. The kitchen had never worked more ferociously, although a feast for such a modest number of people was easy for the cooks to achieve. No Percherese wedding, rich or poor, peasant or royal, was complete without rice, tinted yellow with saffron. And in this instance, because it was the Zar and it was also his First Chosen, the golden rice was scattered with precious jewels, supplied by Salmeo.

Salmeo had quickly moved himself past the disappointment of the failed execution. He was an opportunist at the best of times and from a young age had never lingered too long over any situation gone awry – there was always something to salvage from any circumstance, if you approached it positively. Already he was thinking ahead to the new court within the harem that would now have to be established to cater to an Absolute Favourite. Ana would need to be separated geographically from the Valide, as well as the other girls, as tradition demanded. She would now have her own retinue of slaves to serve her as well as a personal assistant. As much as he found Ana a thorn in the soft belly of the harem, Salmeo found her spirit challenging as well. Secretly he thought she was good for this closeted, spoiled community, and her headstrong way would also ensure some balance might be kept. As much as he placed his lot in with Herezah, too much power to the Valide might see himself undone. Ana's presence would keep that potential power controlled. The way things had turned out was not altogether bad for him. He was still in charge of the harem, and Ana, no matter what her role was on behalf of Percheron in Galinsea, was still a member of that harem and thus under his jurisdiction, as was Herezah. If he played them off against each other with his well-honed skills, then he could be on top of things again. He would have to impose his own authority, of course, as soon as Ana came back to them from her diplomatic travels.

He had returned from personally delivering the cache of exquisite gems to the kitchens, leaving behind a trustworthy Elim to watch over their use, so that they didn't find their way into dishonest pockets. Now he made his way to a suite of rooms in the harem where he knew they were preparing Ana. She would have already been through the rigorous bathing ritual, and as he walked in, Elza and her helpers had Ana naked in their circle. They lofted soft-scented powder at her, dusting her entire body with a light mist-like covering of fine talcum that clung to the already applied oil of frankincense. The room was filled with the fragrance of the spice gently overlayed by honeysuckle, jasmine, gardenia – there was more but he was so overwhelmed by the smell that he could no longer pick out the individual flowers that contributed to it.

'Are your hands readied, Ana?' he lisped and she turned, her face a mask. He had anticipated anger – a scowl at least — but there was nothing. She was blank but hate emanated from her.

Ana lifted her hands, palms downward, and showed him the intricate pattern of painted henna that stretched from her fingertips to halfway down the length of her hand like short gloves. Her feet were stained with the henna bark also and dusted with gold so she glittered.

In a velvet pad he carried the jewels she would wear this day as well as the grit of diamonds that would be the final layer of dusting so her body sparkled for the Zar. The jewels themselves were the same ones Herezah had worn when she had married Joreb. It seemed fitting. These belonged to the harem rather than Herezah, who possessed more than enough precious stones to look after a small harem of women herself. Joreb had always been so generous and especially to his Absolute Favourite.

Salmeo knew all of it was meaningless to Ana but he enjoyed the slaves' exclamations at the beauty of the pieces when he unrolled the velvet.

'Emeralds only for this special day,' he said, allowing the sun passing through the shutters to spark a fire within the magnificent jewels he held aloft. 'To match your sad eyes, Ana,' he said.

'Perhaps because I'm not dead.'

Elza's face twisted in embarrassment at Ana's directness but she remained silent, shooing away her helpers now that the Grand Master Eunuch had arrived.

Ana suffered Salmeo's appraising gaze over her body.

'Very, very nice. The drowning seems to have caused no longterm damage.'

'None that you can see.'

'Manners,' Elza hissed as she hurried by Ana to pick

up the baskets of dried, crushed petals that formed the talcum along with chalk.

'I have no reason to be polite to him,' Ana said louder and Elza trembled. 'He has tried his hardest to destroy me but like a bad smell I keep returning to spoil his days.'

'Indeed you do, child,' Salmeo said, his thick lips pulled into a pert grin, 'however, it is not altogether as unpleasant as you think. But try not to goad me, Ana, remember when you return—'

'If I return.'

He ignored her interruption. 'When you return you will be all mine again, and while you may well be First Chosen and Absolute Favourite of the Zar, you will also be simply Ana, a member of this harem.'

'You can no longer hurt or threaten me, Salmeo. I despise you but you are nothing, the mere slime that gathers around any powerful person.'

'Is that so? I imagine you've suddenly given up caring for your family, then.'

He noticed she didn't flinch, wondered what had changed that she was so resilient.

'You cannot threaten me with my family's welfare any more. They have protection now.'

'From the Zar?' He laughed. 'He wouldn't even know who they are.'

'But the Grand Vizier does and should anything happen to my family that seems accidental or unusual it will find you, Salmeo, because I have already warned Tariq of your threats.'

'Tariq now, is it?' He covered his anger well.

She nodded. 'You share the same status, I gather. May I suggest you don't attract his ire – he has the Zar's respect, unlike you, and I imagine he's every bit as cunning as you or the Valide.'

Salmeo inwardly fumed but to her he smiled softly, put a fat finger against his lips. 'Shh, be careful, Ana.'

'I'm not scared of you or her any more. I think I died today – a few more seconds and no-one could have revived me. Nothing scares me any more.'

'You feel strong now, Ana, but I assure you, once you're back it will be different. I can make others suffer and all the time you'll know it's because of you. Young Sascha, for instance—'

'You leave her alone!'

'Then there's the shy, pretty Lesan.'

'I swear—'

'What do you swear, child?'

Frustration engulfed her. 'Nothing,' she said, sensibly holding her tongue against revealing anything further.

'Good. Treat me with respect, Ana, and perhaps we can start again with a nod towards your new status.'

She stared angrily at him but said nothing.

'And be careful with Tariq. There is something rotten there, something I can't fathom. He will not exchange his favours lightly.'

'You worry about your own relationship with him.'

'Don't say I didn't warn you. Now turn, Ana, let me place these jewels around you. Elza, bring your silks, it is time to dress Ana for her marriage.'

Boaz rose, looking as elegant and eligible as his mother had ever seen him in dark, glimmering emerald robes over white silks. He stepped down from the dais and took her hand. She bowed, fluid and magnificent in her own multi-layered silks of various colours. She had never got herself ready this fast before. When he raised her he kissed her hand. 'Welcome, mother.'

'You honour me, Zar.'

'As you should be,' he replied.

Her eyes glittered with the anger she had had to bury over Ana's startling change in fortune. It was unbeliev-able — one moment a prisoner in the process of being executed, the next she was marrying into the Imperial Court of Percheron. It was not lost on Herezah that Ana now had equal ranking with herself within the harem. That it shattered her did not show, but inwardly Herezah was in turmoil. 'This is a surprise for us all.'

'As much to me as well. As you're aware, I had formally chosen Ana but it was Lazar's idea to make her my wife, and a very good one that might just save our city from being sacked.'

The Valide turned to where she sensed the Spur stood. He, too, looked dazzling in all white, his face tanned and more chiselled than she could ever remember. Despite her fury, she felt the familiar thrill through her body at the sight of him. As usual, his expression was unread-able. From behind her veil she smirked. 'Is that so, Spur?' she purred, expertly hiding her own alarm at what was occurring this day.

'It's what we all wanted, isn't it, Valide? From that very first day we all saw Ana we knew she was perfect.'

'Not so perfect perhaps, now that we know how head-strong she is and how much she hates everyone here, to what lengths she'll go to impress that upon us.'

'Still,' Boaz said, hating the way these two people close to him crossed swords at every opportunity. 'It's the right thing to do and Ana can be the difference between blood-shed – our blood, that is – and peace. I think we all have to remember this and forget what has gone before.'

'Fret not, my Lion, I shall be a dutiful mother and treat her as I would my own daughter.'

'Thank you. I am grateful you say this, because I need you to act as her guardian.' His mother frowned. 'What I mean is you will be going to Galinsea as Ana's escort.'

The perfect composure slipped. It wasn't often Boaz witnessed such a thing. 'What?'

'She needs a woman by her side, someone of your calibre to assist. Take a couple of the slaves to see to both your needs. Ana is representing us in the Galinsean palace – she needs you to ensure she is groomed appropriately, and it is fitting that someone of your stature is alongside her to offer counsel should she need it.'

'Boaz, really, I—'

'My mind is made up. Believe me, I've already had this fight with Lazar. But he is resigned to my decision and I trust you will not argue the point.'

Herezah looked incredulous. He had honoured her with honeyed words and now, with that same sweetened tongue, he was wielding them as a weapon, lowering her to the status of nurserymaid.

'It seems we are underway,' he said, distracted by the signal from Bin that the very brief ceremony, purely an exchange of gifts, was about to begin and would seal the marriage.

Pez scampered in ahead of everyone, cartwheeling and whooping for joy. He was dressed head to toe in emerald and white to honour his Zar. Boaz laughed. It was good to have his friend back. Behind Pez came the Galinsean party

— Marius and Lorto looked refreshed, as well as bemused by the frivolity of the dwarf. They were accompanied by the Grand Vizier together with a host of Percherese dignitaries, all hastily assembled. Herezah grimaced behind her veil. It was not traditional for the Zar's marriages to be displayed publicly. It seemed vulgar to her that something so steeped in tradition and mystery was being paraded almost as a piece of entertainment. Joreb would turn in his tomb, but then, although Joreb enjoyed tradition, he had always encouraged his elder sons to think as daringly as their imaginations permitted. *We must move Percheron forward*, he used to tell the older boys on the rare occasions he gathered them together. *It's valid to keep an eye on the past, respect what's gone before, but don't be left behind by not keeping your other eye on the future.*

It seemed to Herezah that her own son was taking a very forward-thinking approach to the world. Already his short reign had seen so many of the old traditions discarded that she herself was beginning to feel somewhat antiquated in her views, and yet she'd always considered herself a relatively contemporary thinker.

Pez rolled nearby, pausing to shriek hysterically at Herezah, and this dragged her from her private thoughts to the event before her. Coming through the doors now was Salmeo, looking very grand and exceptionally pleased with himself. He was holding the hand of Ana, who looked every bit the child at his side, dwarfed by his enormous stature. But although he held her hand, she walked as far from him as she could. There was little doubting how much she despised the eunuch. Above them was carried a silken canopy, embroidered with the finest gold thread.

The canopy was a bright blue — Ana's choice — and that

would now be her palace colour, untouchable by anyone else in the harem. No other woman would be permitted to wear that particular hue of aquamarine at any time, although the Zar was, should he choose to do so.

Ana was unveiled because she was in the presence of her Zar, and her arrival drew a hush of awed silence. As much as it galled her, even Herezah had to acknowledge that she had never seen a more glorious-looking woman than this one. To think they had dragged her from the river, seemingly dead, just hours previously.

Ana sparkled – every inch of her glittered and glowed and her garments had been carefully chosen to seductively reveal her diamond-encrusted shoulders and the golden-hued, flawless skin beneath. Herezah imagined the palace seamstresses' fingers were bleeding, they must have worked so hard these past few hours. The Valide jealously watched Ana kneel and then lay herself prostrate on the Throne Room's cool, magnificently tiled floor.

Herezah could not resist a searching gaze at Lazar, who, despite his own best efforts, looked disturbed or . . . she wasn't sure what the right word was to describe it . . . forsaken, she thought was the best choice. Something precious was being taken from him today – she knew it and when his own rigid stare slid from Ana to the Valide, Herezah understood that he realised she knew what he was giving up. Whether it was love, she could not tell, but his desire for this young woman was certainly obvious to her. Something was dying inside Lazar, she could sense it, and it galled her more deeply than any other wound that she was not the one who was inflicting this pain on him as he had on her for the last decade. If only he could feel one tenth of the anguish of how much she ached for him, he might come close to understanding what real envy was.

And from Lazar's forlorn appearance Herezah drew her ultimate comfort, for this day that had gone so badly wrong for her. He was suffering and it pleased her. That her son was marrying the girl she wanted dead was a severe injury but it was a balm that the impenetrable facade that Lazar had built around himself was being smashed, burned to rubble before her eyes.

She smiled at the Spur and both understood what it conveyed. He looked away, disgusted that she could read him as well as she had.

Into the hush, Salmeo spoke the traditional words. 'Zar Boaz, King of Kings, Mightiest of the Mighty, may I present your First Chosen. The harem approves the marriage and we give you Odalisque Ana to be a sparkling jewel, a treasured possession. May she please you, my Zar, and bring you fine, healthy heirs. Brothers!' His final word was the signal for everyone to offer their good wishes to the Zar and his bride. Specially crafted lightweight wooden eggs were rolled towards the couple as Ana was lifted from the floor and then guided to stand directly before her husband. The wooden eggs were symbolic, to offer blessings for a fertile marriage, and in Percherese homes the custom was for the children of the two families being brought together to paint the eggs, bought at the market. In the imperial palace it was also the custom but the eggs were studded with tiny gems for the bride to collect as a keepsake. Some women, but always First Chosen, swallowed one of the eggs as the ultimate acknowledgement of their power to bestow fertility.

Ana had already been primed by Salmeo and she did

so now, choosing a tiny egg encrusted with palest sapphires that seemed to reflect the colour of the sea that she favoured. It wasn't easy to swallow, of course, but when she opened her mouth as instructed to prove it was empty of the egg, applause exploded into the room. The only person not clapping was Lazar.

Pez was pulling at his hair with pretend joy and manoeuvred himself to be close to the Spur. 'Are you all right?'

'Not thrilled.'

'It shows. Applaud.' The dwarf began skipping around the room beaming but with a vacant look as though he didn't know what all the joy was about.

Boaz cleared his throat and the room became silent. 'Thank you, brothers. I accept this woman to be my wife, my First Chosen and Absolute Favourite, which is how she is to be known from now on. We cast away Odalisque. She is now to be addressed as Zaradine Ana.' He held out his hand and Ana, well schooled by Salmeo, stepped up one stair only so she momentarily stood above all except the Zar himself before he lowered his head and kissed her hand. From a pocket he drew a box. The box was carved, inlaid with pearl. It was too big for jewels and once again Herezah was struck that her son was breaking from custom even at the most traditional point of his wedding cere-mony, when the Zar bestows a magnificent piece of jewellery on his First Chosen.

'This is for you,' Boaz said and couldn't stop the smile from stretching widely across his face. This gift had been crafted long before that moment of tension when he'd prematurely announced his intention to summon Ana as First Chosen. He had planned this moment for so long but still he felt a tinge of hesitation and indeed disbelief that he was actually giving it to her already. 'Open it, Zaradine Ana.'

With shaking hands she took the heavy box and did as she was asked, withdrawing exquisite miniatures, perfectly rendered in stone, of her favourite statues from Percheron: Beloch and Ezram – the twin giants; Crendel and Darso – the winged lions; Iridor – the owl; and Shakar – the feared dragon.

Expecting jewellery and berating herself for thinking so little of Boaz's sensitivity, Ana could not maintain her icy composure. She opened her mouth in unfeigned delight. Whispers around the room from those who could see the gift were puzzled. Surely replicas of statues were meaningless to a beautiful woman who traditionally thrived on jewels to mark her own stature?

'Do you like them?' Boaz whispered.

'I adore them, Zar Boaz,' she replied and no-one could mistake her pleasure.

'Let the feast begin!' Boaz announced, his own delight evident.

There was more bemused clapping and smiles before Salmeo called order for the final announcement. 'Brothers, our esteemed Valide will now retire to the harem. We ask you to follow the torches out into the courtyard where the feast will be held. Our Zar and his new Zaradine will now consummate their marriage and we will provide proof shortly.' His voice took on a conspiratorial tone and the men laughed. Even Marius and Lorto seemed to understand without needing anything translated.

As Ana turned to follow Salmeo and her Zar, her gaze fell upon the Spur. There was no sense of triumph as she thought there might be within herself and she saw only deep sorrow in the look he returned. He dipped his head to her in a crisp bow and took his leave. She was sure he would not be joining the festive celebrations over food. Her mind was a whirl and it was hard to know what to think, how to think. All she knew right at this moment was intense pain – for Kett mostly but also for herself at being denied death, and for discovering that Lazar had lied. That he was alive and now she would be travelling with him. Worst of all, she knew, despite all her intentions, that she loved him harder at this painful moment than she thought possible. She hadn't forgotten her promise to Lyana either. It was an ironic turn of events. Lyana had granted her greatest prayer that Lazar somehow survive, even though death seemed so certain, and in return she had given her oath to the Goddess that she would not seek his affections. Lyana had been true and Ana intended to honour her pact with the Goddess. She hoped it would make it easier to keep her promise now that she had anger coursing through her veins but it was matched equally by the familiar pain of desire. She would have to let them go to war within and pray that anger won out. Right now the Zar would expect her to join him in his bed. She had not allowed herself to think about it until this moment and as much as she liked Boaz, it revolted her. She had never seen him as a lover, more as a brother, but she had no choice. To keep those she loved safe – and she helplessly included Lazar in this small group – she had to see this through and be a dutiful Zaradine.

The signal was given and Ana followed behind the men, carrying her box of statues, more precious than any jewels.

No-one noticed the stillness of the Grand Vizier, who was still trying to understand the meaning of the Zar's gift to his Zaradine. Maliz was utterly convinced now that, although Ana was not the Goddess, she was his guide to whom Lyana was. How Boaz could be involved intrigued him – or was it just pure coincidence? Stranger things had happened in his lifetime but he had learned to pay attention to everything, treat all potential clues as leads to the pathway he sought.

Ana and her box of statues – renditions of the very same creatures Maliz had personally turned to stone all those centuries ago – would lead him to that path.

༄ 24 ༄

Lazar did not join the festivities; instead he tried to put distance between himself and the Zar's private chambers, convincing himself that if he was physically removed it might also remove the thought of Ana and Boaz. He found himself in a lonely orange grove on the fringe of the palace complex, mercifully empty of workers or servants. He was alone with the sounds of the sea and his turbulent thoughts. His head hurt from lack of sleep, but his heart hurt far more.

Pez found him brooding.

'You didn't hide it very well.'

Lazar looked up from the ground where he had been studying an ant's labours. 'What do you mean?'

'Ana.'

'That obvious?'

'Not to Boaz, thankfully.'

'I thought I could handle it, Pez. I thought I was bigger, stronger, tougher.'

'Than what?'

'Than love,' he replied wistfully.

Pez hefted himself onto the small stone bench seat next to Lazar. He was silent for a few moments. And then he sighed. 'I hadn't realised how painful this is for you.'

'If I didn't have to keep seeing her it might ultimately be easier.'

'This is true, but you have no choice now. Not now war is coming. It seems she's our only hope. How do you think your parents will react to her?'

'I haven't known my parents in so many years it's hard to judge but I can't think of a better candidate.'

'Other than yourself, of course. Are you sure Ana has to go through this?'

'I would spare her it, Pez, I hope you know that. But there is no guarantee that they would necessarily forgive if I argued Percheron's case. Ana has as much chance as I do and they will spare her life — they have to, she is a diplomatic emissary. But with me, they could just throw me into a dungeon, kill me, do whatever they want. Except I'm no help to Boaz and Percheron in a stinking cell. I need to be able to fight this war if it's coming. I know how the Galinsean mind works.'

Pez nodded. 'Well, we shall all be there to give her confidence.'

'You've heard, then?'

The dwarf grimaced. 'Yes. But in a way, I'd rather keep my enemy close.'

'It seems all my enemies are along for the ride.'

'Herezah will certainly make it an interesting journey. I think we can count in days when she might make her move.'

Lazar groaned.

'It's probably a good thing. Keeps your mind off Ana.'

'I would not touch the wife of the Zar.'

Pez shrugged. 'That's good, then. Perhaps you can do us all a favour and keep his mother happy.'

Lazar ignored the comment. 'What about the Vizier? He's been goading me most of the afternoon.'

'What do you think he knows?'

'I have no idea. He was certainly probing, trying to make connections.'

'That's what Maliz is about. His whole reason for being is to find the clues that lead him to Lyana. He takes nothing for granted, leaves no stone unturned. There is no thread too weak for him to pull on. He will always follow each to their end.'

'And I'm one of them?'

'Of course you are, but he doesn't know that. You are simply another person to be watched or discounted as having no potential, no clues to Lyana's reality.'

'What are the clues?'

'Some have already presented themselves. Kett, for instance – he may or may not have made the connection.'

'Who was Kett?'

'I'm sorry, Lazar, I know this is all moving fast. I haven't told you this. Kett named himself the Raven a long time ago to me. He was in the haze of pain surrounding his emasculation, so the helpers would have thought he was simply ranting if they'd heard what he said. I don't think they did.'

'And who is the Raven?'

'The bird of sorrows. He lives a life of sadness, brings grave news, and if my memory serves me true, then he makes a prediction.'

'That serves what purpose?'

'Traditionally the outcome of the battle. That's why we call him the bird of sorrows. It has never been good news. This time it may be different.'

'Who does he tell?'

'It varies.'

'You think he gave his prediction to Ana?'

'Possibly. They had opportunity before he died and perhaps that's what Ellyana meant about this time being different.'

'I don't get you,' Lazar said, frowning.

'Well, to my knowledge he's never had access to Lyana before. He usually has to tell one of her supporters.'

'And you think he's told Ana—'

'Lyana.'

Lazar ignored the interruption. 'You think he's given her some important information.'

'I'm guessing. I have only the past to go on, but as I keep telling you, this time is supposed to be different.'

Something struck Lazar. 'What happens when Maliz comes into contact with the woman he hunts?'

'Ah,' Pez said conspiratorially. He paused a moment. 'Forgive, I just had to check no-one was eavesdropping.'

'The Lore?'

He nodded and continued. 'Maliz hunts down anyone he suspects – either as the Goddess or one who can lead him to her.'

'And?'

'When he finally comes face to face with Lyana herself, he comes into his true power.'

'And?'

'Well, traditionally he destroys her,' Pez said, irritably this time, frustrated a little by Lazar's dullness, couldn't understand why the Spur looked a fraction confused.

Lazar was frowning again. 'He won't waste any time. He'll kill her on the spot?'

'If he can, yes. I believe in some cycles he's done just that. More often he has to struggle a little harder. She is evasive.'

'But if he has access to her, that is to say, he comes face to face with her, he has the power to destroy her?'

Pez misunderstood. 'History shows that blow for blow, yes, he is stronger, but this time—'

Lazar shook his head. 'Then Ana is not who you think she is.'

Pez continued, talking over Lazar's soft realisation, not registering what was said. '. . . this time, being different, I have no idea how it will go. What did you just say?'

'I said, Ana is not the Goddess.'

It was Pez's turn to look dull. 'Why do you say that?'

'Because it's true, if what you've just told me holds good for all cycles.'

'What do you mean, Lazar?' The dwarf looked frightened – it was not something Lazar was used to.

'Pez,' he said gently, as if talking to a young child, 'Boaz sent the Grand Vizier to fetch Ana from the harem only hours ago. They spent a considerable amount of time together because Boaz entrusted Tariq/Maliz, whatever you want to call him, to brief Ana on the plans regarding Galinsea. And what's worse, I sense she sees the Vizier as an ally.'

Lazar watched his friend's face blanch as he revealed the news. When he had finished, Pez couldn't speak momentarily. His lips moved but no sound came out as he replayed in his mind what Lazar had just told him, how it could possibly have worked out this way. The Spur waited, knew it was a shock, understood that this news placed Pez in a situation of terrible limbo.

'Did he touch her?' the dwarf finally asked, his voice urgent.

'What difference does that make?'

'It's her touch that quickens his magic!'

Lazar looked baffled. 'I don't know. I imagine he possibly did, considering how comfortable they seemed. There was ample time to take her arm or guide her, even. They spent a lot of time talking. I'm not suggesting they're friends, but if you compare the body language of Ana and Salmeo to Ana and Tariq—'

'Maliz!' Pez spat.

Lazar nodded. '. . . it just seems more relaxed. If Ana was Lyana, she would be dead by your admission rather than pleasuring the Zar.' The words came out choked, angry.

'It can't be. This cannot be!'

'Hush, Pez,' Lazar warned.

'You don't understand. Everything I've told you is right.'

'I don't doubt—'

'No, listen! I felt her magic. It is not Lore. It is something else. It has to be of the Goddess and . . .' He reached for other clues to convince his friend. 'You've said it yourself! She knows too much about the ancients – she gave you the names of the giants, of the winged beasts, she can hear me over a mind-link, she too said this time it would be different.'

Lazar nodded but said nothing.

'She told you herself that she is an old soul. She has seen things in her dreams no goatherd's daughter would know of. You told me once she described Percheron's layout like the spread of a volcano's lava . . . as if marble has spewed out and slid down the hills to the water.'

'I did.' Again he nodded, not wanting to crush Pez's seemingly futile attempt to justify his claim.

'She's never been out of the foothills! How could she know what a volcano looks like? How can she know who Beloch and Ezram are? How come Zafira believed, as I do, and Zafira is now dead at the hands of Maliz? Don't deny that Ellyana thought Ana special.' Words were tumbling over one another.

Lazar hated to find holes in Pez's determined plan. 'Did she?'

'Ellyana gave her the statue of Iridor,' Pez replied, his anger barely contained.

'But what does that confirm?'

Pez looked as if he was going to explode.

Lazar continued softly. 'It doesn't confirm or deny anything, my friend. Perhaps all who believe have been hoodwinked.'

'Hoodwinked?' His voice squeaked in his attempt to control his anguish at what Lazar was doing. Pez looked incredulous.

'Poor choice of words, Pez, forgive me. I'm simply suggesting Ellyana, you, Zafira, have leapt onto Ana because she *is* so unique, she *does* have a curious background, she certainly shows an affinity for Lyana and . . .'

'Stop! We can settle this by finding out if he touched her.'

'If he did, she should be dead. If he did and she isn't dead, then she can't be the Goddess.' Lazar looked at Pez with deep sympathy. 'She's not Lyana.'

'He may not have touched her.'

'You said he hunts down every clue. Surely he would have tried. There is too much focus on Ana for him not to have his interest at least piqued by her.'

Now Pez looked as though he might weep.

'I'm sorry, Pez. Ana is simply a goatherd's daughter. You have to move past her, see her as nothing more than the Zar's wife.'

Lazar meant it kindly but Pez, in his sickening disappointment at the harsh truth of what his friend was saying, reacted as if stung. 'Instead of lecturing me, perhaps you should take some of your own advice!' He leapt from the seat and ran away on his short legs.

Lazar looked after him with sorrow, and understanding, not offended by Pez's response. And of course, the dwarf was right. He, too, must move on from Ana. She was no longer a forbidden odalisque – she was now the untouchable Zaradine, First Chosen and Absolute Favourite of the Zar. Death to the outsider who looked at her with any desire.

Ana was now as good as dead to him, as Shara was. Shara his first and only other love. After her he'd made a promise he would never open his heart to another woman. He would take his pleasure, enjoy the transient release that lying with a woman offered, but he would return himself to stone – just like the sculptures of Percheron he admired so much. No female would ever penetrate his facade again and get beneath his skin. He stood, renewing his promise to himself and to Lyana to relinquish Ana.

'Ana is dead to me,' he said softly, as if speaking it as a mantra sealed his oath.

A runner appeared, anxious and breathless. 'Spur Lazar,' he said, bowing.

'Yes?'

'I have been searching for you, Spur.'

'What is it?'

'The Grand Vizier. He has summoned everyone back to the Throne Room.'

Lazar knew why and felt his stomach twist in despair and hated anticipation. 'Lead the way,' he ordered, knowing full well he could not escape this, no matter how much he wanted to walk out of the palace and just keep walking.

Everyone he remembered from the wedding ceremony, save Herezah, had gathered in the Throne Room. He nodded at Marius, who smiled his response from across the room – obviously the feast had gone well and bridged the language divide. Salmeo was rocking on the balls of his slippered feet, wearing a smug expression as though his was a job well done. At the gesture of one of the mutes, Salmeo quietly excused himself, presumably to return Ana to the harem and accompany the triumphant Zar back to his guests.

Lazar could barely disguise his contempt as he stared at the eunuch's massive back. His thoughts moved sharply from Ana, from the pain of this 'marriage', to hatred for Salmeo. He couldn't prove it, but he knew, in his marrow, that Salmeo was the one responsible for the attempt on his life. Lazar had long ago dismissed Horz's involvement; he had not known the Elim well, but what he did know of him stood testimony. He had originally thought it must have been Tariq's doing – the old Tariq – but his own security measures imposed within the palace would have prevented the Vizier having any access to the harem's apothecary, or to the weapons room that only the Inflictors or the Spur's most senior men were permitted to enter. All too difficult for the old, spineless Tariq. Then there was Herezah – she had all the reasons for being behind such an intrigue, but he could not see how she gained anything from his death, other than the satisfaction of separating him from Ana – but then the harem did that rather effectively. And for all of Herezah's faults she was a pragmatist and would know how much Boaz would need to rely on his Spur. He also grimaced privately at the Valide's amorous interest in him – she preferred him alive. No, all of his suspicions this past year of convalescence rested firmly at the feet of the Grand Master Eunuch, who would have been incensed at the humiliation he received for Ana's original escape, and vicious enough to order death to the person who so painfully pointed out his failure. Salmeo was worse than a scorned woman. He possessed the cruellest of streaks and, being in a position of power, he could have coerced any number of people below him to do his bidding. And Lazar was sure Salmeo would have covered his tracks very well, cowed each person in that line of dirty deeds with so much fear that no-one would speak the truth. There were some in the Inflictors department, though, who might prove useful to Lazar in the future, but his ruminations upon this were halted as a series of gongs sounded, pulling him back to the present.

He sighed because he knew what was coming, turned, as everyone else had, towards the great doors of the Throne Room that now opened. In floated the Grand Master Eunuch above his swathes of multicoloured silks. He was beaming; the cavernous gap in his teeth was filled now and then by a bright pink tongue that seemed to taste the air. Aloft he held a silken sheet that was smeared unmistakably with blood. Not much, but enough to tell its own tale.

The clapping began and it turned into a cheer and then

a roar as a not so sheepish looking Zar entered the chamber. Lazar had anticipated a sense of embarrassment in him for this attention but Boaz was neither smiling nor serious, and he didn't strike Lazar as triumphant or, by contrast, in any way reserved. Boaz simply looked regal. He carried himself tall, proud, and now, in everyone's eyes, he could carry himself as a man. He had taken his first woman and the proof of that taking was on the pale sheet that Salmeo was rather gruesomely but delightedly showing around.

This show of the bedsheets was custom and, although it was normally reserved for between harem walls only, more for fun than anything else, Lazar could understand why today this somewhat vulgar posturing was necessary. The public presentation was not for anyone's benefit but the Galinseans'. They would not know that the blood on the satin bed linen was likely false because the Grand Master Eunuch had already prepared each new wife-to-be in a manner that effectively took her virginity. Lazar shuddered. He hoped somehow that lack of time had granted Ana an escape from this vicious trauma at the hands of Salmeo. Whether the small bloodstain on the sheets was Ana's, it mattered not. The Zar had taken a wife and their royal marriage was now consummated.

Ana may be travelling to the Galinsean capital as an emissary for the royal court of Percheron but she was so much more than a traditional envoy. Percheron was sending one of its treasures, possibly its most precious of all jewels – the woman who would bear the first potential heir to the Percherese throne. The Galinseans, as barbaric as they were believed to be, would have to take this woman's pleas seriously, for Percheron was risking its future by sending her.

That was the rationale and the Spur knew it would work. It was a clever idea to suggest the Zar marry Ana immediately, but as much as Lazar could pride himself on being the originator of the plan, he took no pleasure in his achievement. In fact he felt so empty at this moment he wasn't even sure he could hide his sour look at the stained silken sheet.

The blood of a virgin.

Ana's blood.

A virgin no more.

'Zaradine Ana,' he murmured and it rolled awkwardly, unhappily off his tongue. Now she could never be his.

The cheering was still going and Boaz was unsuccessfully trying to dampen the high spirits of those helping him celebrate not only the loss of his bride's virginity but also his own. It was obvious to all – and their knowledge certainly didn't seem to matter to Boaz – that he had just enjoyed his first experience with a mate.

'Doesn't look too flushed for someone who has just mounted his first filly,' someone muttered softly to Lazar.

Lazar didn't know anyone was standing so close to him and had to wonder how the Grand Vizier had managed to steal up without him realising it.

Maliz continued, answering his own query. 'Ah well, he's young . . . first time . . . probably all over in a blink.' He smiled conspiratorially and laid a perfectly manicured hand on Lazar's arm.

The Spur flinched as if scalded and hoped the grinding of his teeth didn't sound as loud to the Grand Vizier as it did in his own head. 'I can't remember that far back, Tariq.'

It was obvious to Lazar that Maliz noticed his over-reaction but the Grand Vizier's voice betrayed nothing more than his recently acquired sardonic tone. 'Oh come now, Spur Lazar. We all remember our first time.'

'You can?' It was meant to sound flippant but there was no tone of humour at all.

'Of course, as though it were just moments ago. She was very young, very ripe. Delicious, as I recall . . . just like Ana.'

The confronting words sounded like a test. As though the man was waiting for him to make an error, admit something, reveal a secret. Lazar felt only revulsion. 'Excuse me, Grand Vizier, I must offer my best to the Zar and go make preparations.'

'Yes, of course,' the Vizier replied and infuriated Lazar with a knowing wink.

Lazar stalked away, confused by his own internal battle over Ana, and unnerved by the Vizier's scrutiny. Knowing that beneath the newly charismatic facade lurked a demon added weightily to his discomfort. It occurred to him, as he walked towards his Zar, that perhaps Maliz suspected that he knew something about who was controlling Tariq now. But why would he jump to this conclusion? They had had little to do with one another over the years. And how would Maliz imagine Lazar was even involved in this strange struggle between gods? Not even Lazar was convinced by the claim. Since Pez had first shared his thoughts, Lazar had told himself that his involvement was purely coincidence. He was a bystander, helplessly drawn into the conflict because he happened to be friends with the person who was Iridor incarnate, and with Ana, whom Pez was so convinced would show herself to be the Goddess. But then if she was, why hadn't Maliz already tried to destroy her?

'Ah, Lazar,' Boaz said, the warmth of his smile doing nothing to penetrate the iciness of his Spur's feelings right now.

'Congratulations, my Zar.'

'Thank you. I'm not sure how to feel,' he admitted quietly between them. 'I'm married – sounds very serious and grown-up, don't you think?' He was striving to make light of his new status.

'You are a Zar. The Mightiest of the Mighty . . . that is serious enough for any man of any age.'

Boaz nodded his appreciation of Lazar's supportive words. 'And she is so lovely,' he added, a little wistfully for Lazar's jangling nerves.

'Indeed. Certainly nicer than bloating at the bottom of the river, fodder for the palace fish, Highness.'

The Zar's eyes narrowed. 'Are you all right, Lazar?'

He reined in his bitterness. 'I am, Majesty. Forgive me. None of us have had any sleep and I think I must pay attention to my recovery. I look robust, I know, but the poison took a heavy toll and I can get quite weary.'

Both knew that although the words were probably truthful, they were a barrier to distance himself from what he had actually meant. The real truth had been glimpsed but had quickly hidden itself. Lazar was now able to add severe irritation with himself to his list of grievances.

Boaz became rigidly serious. 'I feel like an enormous weight has been lifted since you returned, Lazar . . . was it only just hours ago?' He stepped down from his dais and embraced the Spur. 'I need you.'

'I know,' Lazar replied, somewhat shocked by the public gesture that no-one in the chamber had missed, and unsure of what to say.

'And I need you to keep Ana safe,' Boaz added with a fresh intensity, his dark eyes glittering.

'Of course, my Zar, she is your wife, your—' Lazar began but was cut off by Boaz shaking his head.

'She is so much more to me. I will make special sacrifices for her. I couldn't offer her protection when she was the sole property of the harem. Now I can offer her all the protection in the world because she belongs to me . . . totally.'

The words cut like a blade through flesh and muscle, through sinew and bone, straight to Lazar's soul. He took a steadying breath and replied solemnly. 'I understand, Highness,' although he had no idea what Boaz meant by saying he would make sacrifices. What sacrifice did any Zar make for any woman, wife or otherwise?

Boaz wasn't finished; determined to press his point, he moved closer still to his Spur. 'I love her,' he repeated. 'There may have to be other women in my life but there will *never* be anyone who shares my heart other than Zaradine Ana. Her son, when she gives me one – and she will . . . her womb possibly already quickening with my seed . . . is the only heir to this throne.' The words were said with fire burning around them. The intensity in Boaz's stare was almost unbearable.

Lazar had known Boaz since he was born, had always liked him as a child and had liked him even more as the boy turned into a young man. He had pledged his faith to Boaz when Zar Joreb had revealed during a private conversation that none of his other sons came close to Boaz's suitability as a leader. Lazar agreed and it was easy to give his oath to the ruler that he would lay down his life for Boaz if it was asked. He knew this boy-turned-man to be passionate, to also take all his endeavours seriously. Obviously getting married was no casual event and even though it might save them from a dire situation, Lazar suspected now that Boaz might not have agreed had he not been so smitten by the bride.

This realisation came as a shock, as though someone had punched him hard in the belly without warning – no time to brace, just a breathless wave of pain through the body. He knew all of almost everything there was to know about Boaz but he had never realised – how could he? – that the new Zar was as in love with Ana as he himself was. He had not been around the city this last year and even though Pez had tried to warn him on several occasions that the Zar was quite close to Odalisque Ana, it had never resonated fully. He was too remote from palace life to know how honest Pez had been in trying to shore up Lazar's defences for the full realisation when it came . . . when he was finally confronted, as he was now, with Boaz's infatuation with Ana.

Just standing here before the Zar was hard enough, knowing that Boaz had just tasted Ana's young, nubile body. Lazar, who loved her with every ounce of his being, had barely touched her by comparison. They had held hands – or rather she had held his – their skins had touched briefly in the Choosing Room, he had held her tightly when he raised her from the riverbed and passionately tried to breathe life back into her as their mouths had touched, but there had been nothing lingering. Nothing had he given of himself to warn Ana that he worshipped the ground she stood upon, the very sunlight that glinted off her radiant golden hair. Jumo had touched Ana more than he – Jumo had hugged and kissed Ana. Lazar, through his own remote, often awkward manner, had deliberately avoided giving anything of himself, save his helpless heart . . . and she didn't even know that he had handed it over to her in those foothills on that first night when she reached right to his core and claimed him as her own. He had given it with a sense of wonder, surprise, awe and a depth of feeling he never thought he might reach again.

Ana had become his touchstone in a matter of just a few days, his reason for living and his reason for not dying. She was his reason to be – to take a breath each day and then another and another. To go on fighting the disease that wanted him so badly and which would have been so easy to surrender to.

She had saved him because of his terrifying love for her. And here was another man claiming the same! It was impossible, it was repulsive, it was killing him. He would die at this spot if he didn't escape now. And this man had no empty claim. Not only did she belong to him as wife but she now belonged to him in body. Boaz had taken her, joined their bodies into one, might even have already sired a child on her if the gods were paying attention.

He felt dizzy. A surge of nausea overwhelmed him. The words, *there will* never *be anyone who shares my heart other than Zaradine Ana*, echoed around and around his mind, addled with angst, riddled with jealousy . . . the latter an emotion he had never experienced. He was the eldest in his family, the spoilt child, the boy who had never had to fear anyone or feel rivalled by anyone – the heir doted upon until he made his error, and even then it was his choice to leave Galinsea. Life had always been his to carve and he chose his own paths. In this timeless moment he knew he was being pushed from the chosen path. Another had the right of passage here and, save an act of high treason, there was absolutely nothing that Lazar could do to prevent his own fall by the wayside as Boaz pushed past.

There was nothing Lazar could do.

He bowed, a gesture symbolic of his acceptance of this situation. It helped cover his expression but did nothing to assist his dizziness. 'You have my word, I will lay down my life for her to keep her safe,' he managed to say.

When he looked up he was shocked again to see Boaz was misty-eyed with emotion. 'You already have once before. Thank you for offering again but this time to my wife, not a common slave.'

The words were very final – a warning. All he could do was nod before muttering his excuses to go prepare for the journey.

As he watched the retreating back of the Spur, the Grand Vizier stored away the memory of how Lazar had reacted when touched. It was as though he had been burned by a firebrand. What had startled him so? The Spur was certainly suspicious of him but Maliz believed that was because the Spur and Tariq had a historical disgust for one another. Maliz knew Tariq despised Lazar for his looks, his stature, his popularity, his disdain for the palace ways, all of which only seemed to make the old Zar, Joreb, hold the Spur in ever higher esteem – they'd been little short of blood brothers in the early years, and Tariq had burned with jealousy that the counsel that was rightly his was given by a soldier. And Maliz suspected that Lazar detested Tariq for his obsequiousness and constant desperation for acceptance and respect, to the point where he would do anything to win favour. But this overreaction to the Vizier's presence, his touch, was something else entirely, Maliz believed. Lazar clearly didn't like the Grand Vizier around him, seemed unnecessarily wary, whereas before, Maliz knew the Spur couldn't give a damn about Tariq, whether he was present or not. He simply didn't rate the Vizier as being important enough for any attention. Maliz sensed that the Spur had revealed something unintentional just now. He would have to ponder this further and he would certainly have to talk with Salazin to put Lazar beneath his watchful gaze too. He roused himself from his private thoughts with the realisation that he, too, would be a member of the party that departed Percheron city at nightfall. He, too, had preparations to make.

∽ 25 ∾

Ana was escorted back to the harem and was met by an equal amount of cheering and excitement from the girls, who had stayed up late to welcome her.

'They haven't yet grasped that she is their enemy,' Herezah murmured to Salmeo when he joined her.

'Oh, but they will, Valide. Most are still barely out of childhood, excited by the novelty.'

'How did she seem directly afterwards?'

'No weeping, if that's what you mean, Valide.'

He noticed how his news disappointed her.

'Boaz finds it hard to hurt an insect,' she retaliated. It sounded sour even to her own ears, and wrong, considering that her son was showing exemplary composure in making hard decisions that did mean injury to others. 'So, tell me, how was she?'

Salmeo took a moment to consider his response. 'Calm, dignified. There was definitely something between them.'

'Be specific, Salmeo – what?'

'It's hard to say, Valide, I only delivered and collected Ana, so my time with them both was limited to barely moments. She appeared visibly nervous on the way to the Zar's chambers but she struck me as sedate and entirely in control, with her usual sneer for me, when I reclaimed her.'

'She doesn't appear flushed or too dishevelled.'

'No, but then she did ask me for a few moments to tidy herself and I suspect one of the mutes helped.'

'One of the mutes?'

He nodded. 'That very serious one, never smiles, Salazin's his name. When I was summoned, he met me and then slipped into the chamber himself, gesturing for me to wait.' He shrugged. 'Is something amiss?'

Herezah's frown eased. 'No, I just remember my first time.' She smirked. 'Joreb made sure I could barely walk.'

'As I recall, Valide, Zar Joreb kept you for many hours. Boaz lay with Ana for less than one.'

'He's young, probably still a bit shy, unsure. The main thing is it's done. So how did they receive the bloodstained sheet in the Throne Room?' she asked, looking now to where the girls were admiring that same piece of silk. It was the harem's turn to follow its traditional custom. She watched the girls taking the four corners of the sheet, billowing it up into the air over Ana's head and dancing around her. A particular song about marriage, the spilling of blood and fertility was sung with great enthusiasm.

'Oh, it was an inspired idea of yours, Valide, with excited applause and celebration – as you can imagine – and with quiet relief for those of us who realise what's at stake.'

'And Boaz, how was he?'

'Looked rather pleased with himself, Valide,' Salmeo lied, knowing this was what she wanted to hear, even though he, too, was a bit confused by the circumspect manner of the Zar. This moment was surely any young man's greatest sense of triumph but the Zar had also carried himself with tremendous dignity and reserve.

'Excellent,' the Valide said, cutting across his thoughts. 'As much as it galls me that she is the Zaradine and Absolute Favourite, we should be glad that things have fallen into place as they have.'

This surprised the Grand Master Eunuch. 'How so, Valide?' he asked politely, knowing that things had gone so against their original intentions.

Herezah didn't mind explaining on this occasion. It helped her to carefully lay out her own thoughts that had finally sorted themselves whilst the despised Ana had lain with her son. 'Well, Salmeo, she is no longer in quite such an unpredictable position. Her duty is now directly to the Zar and I suspect our feisty Ana will not be so inclined to try any of her tricks to defy Boaz.' Salmeo thought differently, felt that Ana followed rules only with herself, but he kept his own counsel. 'But she remains very much under our control in the harem. I think if we take things slowly, carefully, we can begin to use Ana to our own ends.'

Salmeo couldn't imagine Ana would ever put a grain of faith in either of them again. He could not hide his surprise at her comment. 'Ana's not gullible enough, Valide. She knows we manipulated her towards her own demise. I can't imagine how you will use her to your own ends.'

'Can't you, Salmeo?' came the haughty reply. 'That's because you lack imagination. Ana can always be controlled. We simply have to establish what she cares about.'

'But, Valide—'

'Don't be disingenuous with me, eunuch, I know your mind is as cunning as my own,' she snarled in her soft, feline way. 'There is no undoing what is done. She lives – it is not my choice but it is how things have turned out. We move on. Because of the Galinseans – Zarab save me! – Ana is now the wife and Absolute Favourite of my son. I cannot change this but I can learn to live with it and see how best to work with her new status to achieve what I want.'

He could only admire her. Her whole careful plot had drowned, sunk into oblivion, like the black eunuch. Salmeo knew that the pain of that failure would be intense for Herezah and yet her survival instincts always emerged to restore her resilience, fuel her creative spirit to think ahead as to how she might manipulate those around her. 'What do you want, Valide?' He was careful to keep his query innocent and utterly polite.

'Nothing more than you do, Salmeo. I simply want control of the regime that is rightly mine, and I shall have it, but it may take just a bit longer. Incidentally,' she said, obviously finished with this discussion, 'whose inspired idea was it to have Boaz and Ana marry? Did the Zar come up with that clever plan?'

'From my understanding it was the Spur's, Valide. I gather Lazar suggested it when all else seemed lost. Ana speaks the language fluently but no-one would take her seriously enough as a concubine. She needs status to enter the Galinsean court.'

'I see,' Herezah said mildly, one perfectly shaped finger-nail tapping against her teeth. 'That does make it more interesting.'

'How so, Valide?'

'Because it means our Spur, so clearly besotted by the one who is now my son's wife, is planning time alone with her and out of the harem. Makes for good sport, don't you think, Salmeo?'

'But you'll be there, Valide, as chaperone,' he warned.

'Exactly. And I cannot wait for him to make his move.'

'How can you be so sure he will?'

She laughed, although it came out as a sneer. 'Intuition. I've told you before, Salmeo, you may be more woman than man but you cannot think like one of us.' With this insult, she left his side and glided elegantly towards the centre of the room where the excitement for Ana had quietened.

'Ana, my dear, how do you feel?'

Ana met her eyes with a fierce stare. 'Empowered.'

Herezah had anticipated a certain amount of defiance but was not ready for such immediate rivalry. She did not show her surprise, however, and continued in the same tone as though Ana had not said anything confronting. 'You must be a little weary . . . and sore.'

'I all but drowned today, Valide. I'm not sure I can describe precisely my physical state.'

'But you've lain with a Zar – surely you feel energised, triumphant?'

'Neither, Valide. I remain a prisoner of the harem. Until that status changes, triumph is not mine.'

There was a shocked gasp from the girls as Ana so directly challenged the woman who scared them all.

'Indeed,' said Herezah lazily, seemingly unflustered, although Salmeo believed she must be fuming beneath her calm facade at such a public rebuke. 'The Zar is young, he'll need lots of attention, unless, of course, he chooses others quickly.'

'He is free to choose whom he wishes, Valide, I'm sure

you of all people understand this.' Salmeo watched a pulse throbbing at Herezah's temple. Ana was certainly hitting a nerve with her wintry defiance and it seemed she wasn't finished. 'I for one will not fret over it. He has taken my virginity now, as you can all see – perhaps he will enjoy more virgins before he returns me to his bed. Certainly he'll have a long wait as I apparently must make a journey to help Percheron avoid war. I'd be lying if I didn't suggest that that interests me far more than the vacant pastime of being a concubine with no other role in life but to pleasure a powerful man.'

Every word of Ana's quiet but pointed speech was a deliberate note of disdain directed towards the Valide, each sentence an accusation, a sneer for the life Herezah had carved for herself. Perhaps Ana didn't feel the gathering storm or perhaps she did and pressed on regardless, determined to seek some sort of revenge for Herezah's treatment. Salmeo sensed it moments before it occurred, hardly dared breathe lest the Valide lose her normally nerveless control in front of the entire harem.

Herezah struck fast, her slap across Ana's face claiming the shocked silence at the Zaradine's words, its sound as sharp as it was surely painful to the person receiving the blow. Ana's face flew sideways from the force but she steadfastly remained on her feet and somehow found the wherewithal to turn straight back and face the Valide again. Her green eyes glittered darkly above the smile she wore openly.

'Welcome to my new world, Valide,' she uttered, loading her rival's title with as much scorn as she could achieve. 'Fate has stepped in to play her hand and we are now equals and you will never again lay a hand on me or lure me into your dark schemes. You are at the end of your power, Herezah. I am just coming into mine. Both of us enjoy this status because of your son. I wonder which one of us he would choose if he had to?' Her smile widened, lifting the cheek with its livid handmark from the slap.

No-one knew what to do. The festive atmosphere had changed entirely to something dangerous, threatening. Some of the younger girls began to weep. Herezah looked oddly bereft of any words to shape a pithy response and Ana's left cheek was turning bright red – she touched it now and nodded. There was something knowing in that gesture, Salmeo believed, and he moved as fast as his huge body would permit.

'Valide! Zaradine Ana! Enough.' His voice had lost its usual high, breathy quality. Now it sounded lower, angry. 'This behaviour is unseemly for the harem.' If he was shocked by Herezah being baited into acting so totally out of her own character, he was more stunned by Ana's equally out-of-character response. Her words had chilled him. In one day it appeared that they were no longer dealing with a broken young woman, still rather innocent, certainly naive and driven to the point of wanting to die. Before him Ana stood proud, defiant, and utterly confident in her own new status as wife of the Zar. There seemed not so much as a speck of fear reflected in those once wide, unsure eyes. Something had happened in that bedchamber with the Zar. It appeared that in taking her virginity, Boaz had given her something very precious in return. It's not that Ana ever lacked spine but she was someone clearly acting instinctively, driven by the need to be free. This new Ana – if this was how she was going to be – offered a fresh trait that suggested she was suddenly and incredibly self-possessed. How that had happened in the space of an hour baffled Salmeo, and if he had not witnessed her transformation in person, he would have scoffed at such a thing.

'Valide, we must get you prepared for travel. Zaradine Ana?'

'Yes,' she said, turning her gaze for the first time in a long time from the Valide.

'You, too, must prepare for a long journey. I shall send some slaves.'

'Do I return to my chamber?'

Salmeo almost laughed. Already Ana was, despite her carefully couched enquiry, suggesting she should be based in her own wing of the harem – as was fitting for a Zaradine and Absolute Favourite.

He cleared his throat. 'I know you can appreciate that there has been little time since this morning—'

'In preparing for a death and a wedding, you mean?' she said, her voice hard.

He nodded, determined not to be intimidated. 'Precisely. There has been no time to set up your new accommodations. And there is no point as you leave tonight anyway. I would appreciate it if you would return to your old chamber and guide the slaves in what to pack. You will need warm as well as light clothing. The desert is contrary at best.' He stopped, needing to get the Valide to her rooms. 'Come, Valide. Girls, amuse yourselves,' he said the last brightly, although no-one could take their eyes off Ana and the Valide, or let go of the cold silence that washed like a winter stream between them.

ᕗ

Boaz sighed at Bin. He was in no mood, not after this day's events. He thought again of Ana and their odd bargain made between the same satin sheets that had been so admired in the Throne Room and were no doubt now doing the rounds of the harem. 'Yes, of course, show her in. Bring some apple tea.'

The servant bowed, closed the door momentarily before it opened again and the Valide swept into the chamber. 'My Lion,' she said, affection oozing from every pore.

'Salutations, mother.' He looked at her quizzically. 'Shouldn't you be preparing for your journey?'

'Oh, I'm letting Salmeo handle all of that,' she said dismissively. 'I wanted to see you. You're sure I should be going?'

It was not like his mother to pass up any opportunity and this was by far the most generous chance she'd had in her lifetime to slough off the restrictions of the harem and taste a sense of freedom. 'Very sure. My wife needs a female chaperone. I can't think of anyone more suitable or wise.'

She ignored the compliment. '"My wife". How enchanting that sounds. How do you feel?'

Boaz felt his well-honed skills of awareness about his mother go on the alert. Her voice sounded too innocent, her tone too chatty, and there was nothing normally sickly sweet about Herezah, yet here she was displaying the breathy interest of a mother with nothing else on her mind but domestic concerns. She was here on a mission and he would just have to do the dance, as he liked to think of it, until she got to the point. He opted to be evasive. He didn't set out to irritate her but he had learned this past year of his reign that deliberately provoking the Valide tended to bring her to her point rather fast. 'About what, marriage?'

'Of course, what else could I mean? Oh,' she said, apparently startled, 'I wasn't referring to your losing your virginity.' She tinkled a laugh coquettishly.

He knew she lied. A bell sounded. 'Come,' Boaz answered, distracted by his mother's odd behaviour.

Bin ushered in a servant bearing a tray. It was delivered in silence before both servants bowed and removed themselves.

'I feel delighted,' he continued. 'She was always going to be my first choice but I'm sure you knew that. There was no surprise, surely?'

'Only in the timing. It came so suddenly.'

'Do you refer to the marriage or to the choosing, mother?'

'Both, if I'm honest. May I pour?' Her voice was light, almost carefree as if this was purely conversation and of no importance to her life. He knew differently. Boaz nodded, watched her elegant movements as she prepared the porcelain cups of apple infusion, whose soft scent now permeated the chamber. It helped to relax him.

'Then I'll be honest,' he said pointedly but not unkindly, for he needed his mother working for him now and Ana needed his mother's guidance whether she thought so or not. He took the cup and sipped before placing it before him. All of this gave him time to think on how best to respond. 'I chose Ana when I did because I was angry. The timing of your shopping trip to the grand bazaar was just too perfect – even for my normally generous tolerance levels.'

'Oh my darling boy, a mere coincidence. Had I known it would spark such a reaction—'

'Don't, mother, please. There is nothing in your life that isn't pre-planned and carefully thought through. I'm your son. I know you better than anyone in this palace, save your fat eunuch who covers your every movement.'

'And what does that imply?' She feigned her hurt with an injured tone.

'Only that he would never contradict anything you do or say.'

'That's his role, son. Grand Master Eunuch and Valide have traditionally worked closely.'

'And plotted closely, too?'

More innocent posturing. 'What does this mean, Boaz? I'm really not understanding you. I come to see you, to congratulate you, and you turn on me like an angry dog.'

'It's not like you to be quite so dull, mother. It insults me that you think I am gullible enough to believe that you didn't plan your trip to the market in order to prevent me from seeing Ana. I know you didn't want our marriage—' He raised a hand to stop her interrupting. 'Yes, she is very suitable and you were the person who picked her originally, although perhaps Lazar might have that claim,' he added and Herezah watched something cloud across her son's open face. Did he suspect something? 'But you have despised Ana since you first came to realise that she was not to be cowed by the harem and that she posed a potential threat to your superiority.'

'I think you've got me wrong,' she said, lifting the cup to her lips to cover the snarl that leapt to them. 'I've always rather admired her.'

'Possibly, but you're also jealous of her, mother, although

it has baffled me as to why. You are one of the most beautiful women the harem has seen, you have intelligence, elegance, you have status and power. It seems altogether ludicrous that you have single-mindedly made the life of a young orphan so very miserable. You've forced her into taking extraordinary risks and on both occasions her life has been threatened. You nearly won today and I was powerless this morning. But I am no longer powerless – the threat of war overrode all rules . . . even those of the harem. She may still belong to the harem but I have now bestowed upon Ana equal status as yourself. I'm presuming this is what you came to see me about?' He decided it was time to be direct.

Herezah took a deep breath, knew she had lost the fight but perhaps not the battle. She quickly took a different path as it was obvious she would get no sympathy here. 'I came only to offer my sincere congratulations to you, Boaz. I don't care much for Ana – it would be rather pointless of me to deny it – but I do admire her and I think she makes you a fine Zaradine. I just question her motives and indeed Lazar's.'

This he had not expected. 'Lazar's? What in Zarab's name are you talking about?'

'It's just, it gives them the cover they so crave. Legitimises Ana's ability to leave the harem.'

'Mother, you'd better quickly explain what you mean.'

She tried not to smile. She had him right where she needed him, enjoyed hearing his uncertainty. Once again she gave an innocent, wide-eyed shrug. 'Well, is it only me that knows Lazar is in love with Ana?'

'I'm not sure why you say such a thing.'

Herezah could see he wasn't as shocked as she'd intended

and this was confusing but she pressed on nonetheless. 'Because it's true, Boaz. Lazar might have sold Ana into the harem but he began regretting that move from the first few hours of knowing the girl. And he's never stopped grieving over her loss. You, of course, don't know any of this, but Lazar did everything he could to win her a special freedom each moon from the harem.'

Boaz blinked, always did when he was caught in a situation of deceit, and hoped his mother missed it. She must never know he was also witness to the Choosing Room. 'I had heard some rumour to that effect.'

Again she was surprised, had hoped for a stronger reaction. 'I see. Does this not trouble you, then?'

'Why should it?'

'That he would die for her doesn't surprise you?'

'He had no plans to die for her, as I understand it. Like me, he railed against a rule that could impose such a harsh sentence on a young woman. I was unable to do much but commute the sentence to a lesser penalty. He was far braver. He simply did the sort of thing my father admired him so much for, and why I feel the same way about our Spur. His poisoning was something entirely different. But to answer your question, no, I am not surprised that he would take a whipping for her. If I could have, I think I would too.'

This did unsettle Herezah. 'Oh, Boaz, please. She's a slave.'

'So are you.'

The accusation stung viciously and she wasn't quick enough to stifle her gasp but she kept her silence as they stared across porcelain cups, taking each other's measure.

Boaz continued more softly; he hadn't wanted this to

turn into a confrontation. 'She's my wife. She is Zaradine and Absolute Favourite. Please don't overlook that, mother, whilst you're away.'

Her voice remained quiet but the tone was all granite. 'Boaz, may I remind you that in the harem she is still answerable to the rules set by its internal hierarchy.'

'Yes, I have no intention – not at this stage anyway – of changing that balance . . .' and he enjoyed watching his mother blanch at his qualification. 'But for the time being, Ana is out of the harem and travelling as diplomatic envoy for the Zar. In this regard she has exceedingly high importance and her status is equal to yours. You will not exert your formidable talent at derailing her when I need Ana using all of her emotion and eloquence in bargaining a peace for us.'

'And Lazar?' Even to her ears her words sounded more like a demand.

'What about Lazar?' he roared, his patience spent.

It was the first time ever in Boaz's life that she had witnessed him shout at anyone or about anything. He had always been such an intense, almost grave child, serious about his status as potential heir; the only time she saw him truly relax and let go with laughter or immature behaviour was around the dwarf. But even those times had changed, and emotional outbursts were not part of Boaz's nature, no matter how entertained he was.

'Well,' she was unsure of her ground suddenly, stammered slightly. 'How do I handle that side of things?'

He regarded her with the expression of one in disbelief and no little disdain. 'Do you really think Lazar is going to be handled – as you put it – by anyone? You're in his domain, mother. He knows the desert better than most – he survived crossing it from west to east, as you might recall. He will not be looking to be advised by you or indeed by anyone. When this caravan leaves, there is only one person in charge . . . and it's not you. Spur Lazar will make all the decisions.'

She masked her exasperation. 'But you understand my meaning, son, I'm sure.'

'Are you asking me whether I give my authority for you to spy on Lazar and Ana? Are you asking whether I concede that I would be interested to find out if you can catch them at an indiscretion?'

'I'm asking you to take me seriously when I say that Lazar's interest in Ana is not all avuncular, as everyone seems to think!' She had not raised her voice but there was a fresh crispness to it. No longer was she the adoring lioness but speaking to a cub who still needed reminding that she was his mother and was due respect.

'I shall say this once only. I trust Ana to be true. I trust Lazar with my life, her life, your life, and the lives of all Percherese. Does that make it clear enough to you?'

Her resolve snapped. 'I will not be spoken to like this, Boaz.'

'Someone has to, mother, and I'm the only person of any real authority over you around here. You may control the harem through your clever ways, but contrary to your personal opinion, you do not control me. You haven't controlled me from the moment you kissed the emerald ring that graces my finger and hailed me as the Zar of Percheron. I know this must come as a shock, but you might as well get used to it now. You are being sent to Galinsea at my discretion as escort to my wife. That is all I ask you to do . . . guide her if she requires guidance, support her if she requires support, help choose her clothes if that's what's needed, but don't upset her by your cunning strategies. She is our only hope for peace – I cannot stress this enough. I trust you understand the delicate position we find ourselves in?'

She detested the condescension in his tone, particularly as he knew how well informed she kept herself on national security and palace politics – but she could scarcely credit her own audacity when she risked another jab. 'You say you trust Lazar. What do I do when he tries to steal private time with your precious wife? Who knows what he has in mind.'

'To lie down with her . . . is that what you mean? Come on, mother, be direct.'

'What else does any man have on his mind where a beautiful woman is concerned?'

He sighed, none of the condescension gone from his stance. 'And this just makes me sad and shows me that I must ensure the women of my harem enjoy a wide-ranging education. It's narrow thoughts like these that could set us back countless years. I want to be a Zar that people remember for his modern thinking and his dedication to change if it's a good thing for Percheron. If that's how you see men, then it shows me blatantly how damaging the harem truly is. Perhaps the Goddess was right. A return to the ancient ways of a matriarchal system where women were treated with honour, respect, where their roles as priestesses were worshipped. Look at what you've turned into, mother. Do you really see yourself as being useful only as a vessel for a man?'

'You couldn't blame me if I did.'

'No. But I can assure you that I'm not obsessed with

the notion of bedding every girl in the harem, and from what I hear, Lazar's record of being with women is discreet, to say the least.'

'And you know this how?'

'It doesn't matter, mother. Lazar is not the lascivious sort, or perhaps he would have fallen for the feminine wiles that you so blatantly used on him in the past!'

Herezah had to resist the urge to slap her son now. This really had gone too far! 'Please don't speak to me like that, Boaz. I'm due more respect from you.'

'Mother, respect works both ways – remember how my father taught my brothers and I that?' She nodded angrily. 'Well, do more than just pay lip service to your Zar. Respect me! Don't try and control me, don't try and anticipate my every move so you can be there first, don't destroy the small things that glitter in my life.'

'Like Pez?' she offered sarcastically.

He stared her down. 'Like Ana.'

Herezah was not to be completely trampled and had won some of her composure back. 'You still haven't answered me, though, Boaz, and I'm the one responsible for your new wife. What about Lazar making an attempt on her?'

'He won't.'

'Because he's honourable, you mean?' She sneered at such a sentiment.

'Yes. Also because I will have spies of my own present.'

She leapt angrily to the bait. 'Ah, the Grand Vizier. Clever Tariq. How much higher inside you can he crawl, son?'

'You are quick to assume, mother, and you would be wrong if you followed this assumption too closely. My spies will be watching you too, so behave. I want you to go safely and be returned to me safely. You are my mother, my father's Absolute Favourite, and even though you might question it right now, I do love you. But you must know your place, mother, and if I feel you trying to attach puppet strings to my back ever again, I will react accordingly. You have been well cautioned. Please heed my warnings about Ana, about Lazar, about your role in this critical event. Now I suspect Grand Master Salmeo would like your involvement in preparations for your departure – you have barely hours.'

It was a dismissal and both of them knew this as surely as they both sensed a shift in their already tenuous relationship. Herezah understood now she was no longer in a position to ever be the important woman in her son's life, and even though he was a Zar with a choice of forty-two beauties, his love was given to one alone. That was dangerous.

She hated Ana, that much was obvious . . . but although she dared not even admit it to herself yet . . . she knew that deep in her heart she hated Boaz even more for his weakness regarding the girl from the foothills.

Pez had little to pack for the journey and couldn't concentrate anyway, such was his quiet despair over Lazar's disturbing notion. His old friend was right, that was the painful truth of it. Unless by some miracle the Grand Vizier had not come into any physical contact with Ana, then, impossible though it felt to stomach, Ana was not Lyana. He felt sick at the revelation and had been sitting in a corner of his chambers lost in sorrowful thoughts since he fled from Lazar.

If not Ana, then who? It had to be her! Magic pulsed through her body — he felt it. His mind had turned the question over repeatedly. He had replayed every scrap of information he knew and he returned again and again to Ana. It was where the finger stopped pointing. She and Lyana were joined. And if he continued to believe this, then he had to believe that Maliz had not touched her, for the demon would have known and he would have destroyed her on the spot. He had to find out and be sure and there was no time like the present. He threw the last remaining items he had hurriedly pulled from his dressing room into the fabric bag and left it outside his chamber door as required. Pez made a mental note that he needed to speak with Razeen before he departed and then, crossing his eyes, he made for the harem, deliberately stumbling and bumping off the hallway walls.

No-one troubled themselves with him but by now the palace was in a state of frenzied activity to get the royal caravan away by nightfall, so it was easy to be ignored. He bounced into the main divan suite and found it filled with beautiful girls but none of them Ana.

'Ana?' he called, flapping his arms and pretending to fly around the chamber.

'She's not here, Pez,' one of the girls replied.

'Why do you bother with him?' another admonished.

'He understands sometimes.' It was Sascha who was being helpful. 'Grand Master Salmeo has sent her to her chamber to prepare.'

He didn't respond, he simply flapped his way out of the suite and made for the upstairs sleeping apartments, where he found Ana with Elza and two of the Elim.

'Oh not now, Pez,' Elza sighed when she caught sight of the dwarf apparently flying in cross-eyed and burping.

Ana smiled softly at his antics in spite of her sombre mood but it didn't hide the nasty red welt on her face. Pez noticed it instantly and it stopped his flight but he managed to keep burping through his astonishment.

'Face, face!' he called, ignoring the shooshing sounds of Elza. 'Ana's hurt just like Kett.'

It probably wasn't the best choice of words, he realised as he watched Ana's eyes cloud at the mention of her loyal friend. 'Who's hurt pretty Ana?' he enquired gleefully of the Elim. 'Was she screaming?'

'Get out, dwarf!' Elza said, exasperated, and once again the Elim came to Pez's rescue.

'We will report you if you speak with disrespect to him again.'

Elza grimaced. 'He's upsetting her.'

'He just also made Zaradine Ana smile, perhaps you've forgotten.'

'Oh, I have no time for this. How am I supposed to get a royal wife ready in such a short time?'

'You must do the best you can,' the elder Elim said and motioned to his companion. 'We will wait outside for her baggage.'

'They promised me help,' the slave wailed to their backs.

'The "they" you refer to intend to make it as difficult as possible, Elza,' Ana counselled softly. 'Did you really think they'd do much at all?'

'They should,' Elza said matter-of-factly. 'You have royal status now, Zaradine Ana.'

'And nothing's changed for it, other than title,' she said gently, leaning down to kiss Pez on the head. She was angry with him for not sharing the secret of Lazar's survival with her, but it didn't change her love towards him. 'Are you coming with us?'

He nodded his reply, waiting for the slave woman to step into the dressing room to choose more gowns. 'Who did this?' he mouthed silently, pointing to her face.

'It doesn't matter,' she replied soundlessly as well. 'I'm glad you're coming,' she mouthed.

Pez pursed his lips, perplexed at her evasion.

'Ah, so you *can* be still and quiet, Pez,' Elza said, bustling back in with a pile of silk garments in her arms. 'Well, Zaradine Ana, at least you have no end of clothes to choose from. The Valide has been generous in this regard.'

Ana sneered. 'I need comfortable travelling clothes. We'll be on horseback and then camel, don't forget. I also need clothes to stay warm with.'

'And clothes to stay cool with,' Elza followed up. 'We need more time.' She flounced back into the dressing room.

He risked a whisper. 'Ana, quick, this is important. Did the Grand Vizier touch you at all today?'

'Pardon?' she grinned helplessly at what sounded a lewd question.

'I mean it, did he at any time touch your arm or shoulder – any part of you – when he fetched you from the harem to take you to Boaz?' His gaze flicked to the dressing chamber where he could hear Elza muttering under her breath about warm clothes. 'Quickly please!'

Ana appeared baffled but she frowned and gave it the thought he pleaded for. After a few moments of consideration, whilst Pez felt tense to the core watching Elza and quietly praying that Ana gave a negative answer, she nodded. 'Yes, as I recall, he took my arm, here,' she gestured, 'and guided me through the gardens. He said we needed some time so we would take the longer way and then he could brief me properly.'

Pez felt his last glimpse of hope shrivel. 'You're quite sure?' he pleaded again, his voice choked with disappointment.

'Yes. I remember it clearly. Why?'

Elza appeared and their conversation came to an abrupt close with Pez falling to the floor in a swoon. He broke wind as he landed and even Elza cracked a smile. 'He's such a fool but it's nice to see you looking a bit brighter. How's that cheek?'

'I'll wear it with pride,' Ana said, giving a more mischievous expression.

Elza smiled wider. 'You're wicked, Miss Ana. You'll have to be extra-careful now around the Valide. She's revealed a lot today with her action.'

Ana nodded and glanced towards Pez, who had taken all of this in and understood now who had dealt the blow, although he could hardly believe that Herezah had let her infamous control slip. There would be a reckoning, he was sure, although right now his mind was too confused to allow him any room to fret over the Valide's actions in the future.

Ana was not the Goddess incarnate.

So who was?

⤳ 26 ⤳

Ana was invited to travel with her Zar in a special karak for two carried by ten Elim. Boaz was determined to see the caravan off himself at the edge of the city, so it was a colourful, almost festive party of dignitaries and servants who snaked down the hill from the palace by torchlight, following the Zar's personal cavalcade. They were still celebrating their ruler's first marriage, playing up the romance of the two virgins in their minds.

Inside the karak it was more sombre.

'I hope I won't let you down,' Ana said, breaking the silence.

Boaz took her hand, and although it was dark in the karak, he stared into the eyes he knew were the colour of the sea on a winter's evening. 'You won't. You know you don't have to veil in here?'

Ana involuntarily reached for her cheek but stopped herself from touching it. 'I know, I just think it's respectful.' There was not enough light to show the bruise that had developed but still she preferred Boaz to farewell her in a gentle frame of mind, rather than one angered. It would only mean worse treatment for her once she was out of his immediate zone of protection. She felt drained and not in the mood for any more confrontation anyway.

As it was, the knowledge that Lazar would be waiting for them was making her feel intensely nervous. She shivered, another involuntary action.

'Are you all right?'

'Of course, just thinking about what we must achieve.'

'Fret not, they will be as enchanted as I was the first time I saw you. Use that effect you have on people, Ana, to its full devastating effect.' She sensed rather than saw his smile.

She nodded, unsure of how to respond to this. 'Our bargain, Boaz—' she began but he hushed her.

'Let's not talk about it.'

She touched the soft bandage at his wrist. 'Does it hurt?'

He laughed softly remembering to pull his sleeve down. 'Not nearly as much as loving you does.'

She leaned her head on his shoulder. 'And I do love you, but . . .' Whatever she was going to say was prevented by Pez, who stuck his head in through the curtains, skipping to keep up with the moving karak. He somehow balanced a lit candle, its flame dancing insanely in time with his skipping, and throwing an unwelcome brightness into the karak.

'Forgive me,' he said, careful not to be overheard, and sensing he had interrupted something. 'I just wanted you to know we're close, my Zar.' Pez wheeled away, braying like a donkey, but the pair were grateful for the warning, for a moment later they heard the Grand Vizier clear his throat immediately outside their karak as it rocked to a stop.

'Yes, Tariq?' Boaz said.

From the other side of the silks, Grand Vizier Tariq

announced – a little unnecessarily now – that they had arrived.

'Thank you. Give me a moment of privacy, please.'

'Yes, my Zar.'

Pez had disappeared and they heard the Vizier giving orders for everyone to wait a short while.

Inside, Boaz turned again to Ana. 'What were you about to say?'

She shook her head. It didn't matter now.

'Well, may I embrace my wife farewell?'

'Seal our arrangement with a kiss?' She laced her words with levity so it didn't sound quite as pointed as it was. 'I feel I have already let you down,' she murmured.

He sighed once. 'Ana. Just go in peace and know my heart is full. I will wait for your return and for you to be at the same peace. We shall take our marriage from there.'

He was too generous, her heart felt it might break from knowing how much pain he must be in. 'You are easy to love. Kiss me, Boaz.'

In the dark, he lifted her veil and for the second time that day let his lips convey all the love and desire he felt for her. And Ana surprised herself by responding with equal ardour, knowing she needed to leave him something to cling to.

Gently he pulled away and smiled. 'I'm going to remember this moment – this feeling – until you come home to me. We'll make a son immediately.'

'And that would make you happy?'

Even in the dark she could see the glisten of his eyes, filled with emotion. 'It would. It would make me proud. It would secure the line.'

'The others—'

'Are not you,' he interrupted firmly. 'I want our son to sit on this throne in years to come.'

He was so intense, Ana had to look away, knowing that for all his declarations of love, for all his patience with her, his generosity, and especially for promising that any child of theirs would be safe, she felt every inch the traitor. For, as if attached to him by some invisible thread, Ana could feel the pull of Lazar. She knew he was out there with all the others, patiently awaiting their Zar's emergence, indulging this wish for privacy but anxious to be gone. She could imagine his face – grimacing, as usual. The lines either side of his mouth, so expressive even when he tried to hide how he was feeling, would be etched deeper, whilst his eyes would be flinty, glittering with disregard for the pomp and ceremony that now accompanied him.

None of her anger at his betrayal had dissipated but sadly her desire to be close to him was equal to that rage. Its treacherous presence seemed to mock her efforts to be immune to Lazar as well as sympathetic to Boaz, who, after all, had thrown her a lifeline. She hadn't thought she wanted to live but one look at Lazar, at that face so filled with anguish over her, and she knew she wanted life more than death – even if it did mean a life of constant sorrow and reminders of what she had lost and what she could never have.

'I must go,' she said, trying to cover the awkward silence prompted by her musing.

'Can you truly love me, Ana?'

She felt suddenly rigid with fear. Boaz was no fool and it felt as though he'd dropped in on her thoughts. 'I just need time, Boaz. I explained that.'

'I understand, and I'm giving you that time – I think you can appreciate that I have already demonstrated my sincerity in this regard.'

'Your leniency, my Zar, is cherished.'

'You must not abuse it, Ana.'

The sudden warning shocked her. She felt breathless at the cold in his voice. 'What do you mean, Majesty?' she faltered, falling back on formality to hide her uncertainty.

'I mean simply this. The time I am extending you to grieve, to come to your own peace, to find it within yourself to be my wife fully, is something I have surprised myself in giving you. My father would not have offered the same to my mother, or any of his wives, no matter how much he indulged them. And he would view this as a weakness in me.'

'Is it?' she dared ask.

'You know it is. Where you are concerned there *is* only one boundary to my love. Stay within it, Ana, and you will know nothing but generosity and gentleness from me.'

'And if I cross it?' She couldn't be sure what they were both alluding to and yet the question rushed from her lips as though she found the threat irresistible.

'No-one will save you from the death I would impose on you.'

This time Ana did lose her breath. There was not a mote of lightness in Boaz's words – he meant them as gravely as he spoke of his intense love for her. He was frightening in his black-and-white view of life. For all his intelligence and empathy, he viewed her with no shades of grey.

'What is that boundary, my Zar?'

He did not hesitate. 'Fidelity. Stay true to me and you will never come to any harm again.'

'You couldn't save me from your mother,' she risked.

'This I regret. I am aware of what happened today in the harem. Pez has informed me.'

Her alarm was obvious. 'Pez had no right—'

'Pez has every right. He and I were friends before he met you – we are lifelong friends. He is loyal to me and to you, Ana. He told me in order to protect you. Unfortunately the news reached me after I'd already had a rather stern talk with my mother.'

'She came to see you?'

'After the incident, no doubt hoping to cover her tracks. I've never seen my mother openly lose her temper – you must have said something truly fiery to provoke her. She will never dare strike you again.'

'I claimed we were equals.'

'On this journey, Ana, you may even bear a higher status in the minds of those you meet. This does not trouble me. As far as the palace generally is concerned, Zaradine and Valide are equal, perhaps my wife enjoying slightly more indulgence. Unfortunately, as far as the harem is concerned, the Valide has superiority. I cannot help this.'

'But you can change it.'

'Over years, perhaps yes. Not by the time you come back to me, however.'

She knew there was no point in arguing this. Boaz was right. And then she considered all that had changed for them. Hadn't they both had to grow up these last few moons? Boaz was already acting every inch the powerful

Zar and her behaviour in the harem today had surely shocked the witnesses. Even their odd bargain showed a new maturity – she must live up to her promise to her husband now.

'I will cope, my Zar. I will be a good Zaradine.'

'No Zaradine, to my knowledge, has ever left the sanctuary of the harem.' Again it sounded like a warning and she felt the spike of tension between them.

'These are no ordinary circumstances or neither would I,' she responded with equal care.

'There will be temptation, Ana. You need to heed what I have said.' He was treading softly, she could see this, and yet he was determined to make a point.

Ana decided to be direct for him. 'I will not try to escape, my Zar.'

'I think we shall have to let history show us your faith here, Ana. Your track record suggests otherwise, but that's not what I'm referring to.'

'You refer to my faithfulness,' she murmured.

'Yes. Temptation will present itself.'

Ana was already tired and her fatigue got the better of her. She became impatient with the innuendo that felt suddenly sinister. 'Who exactly do you think I might feel tempted by, Highness? The Grand Vizier perhaps, one of the Galinsean dignitaries, or do you already suspect me of garnering attention from one of your mutes?' Even she could hear the edge in her voice, and regretted it.

He shrugged away her sarcasm. 'I hope you'll never take that tone publicly,' he said, voice soft but firm.

'Forgive me. Dawn brought me a drowning and dusk has closed on a marriage. By this coming dawn we begin a journey to a new realm, into a lot of uncertainty, and the avoidance of a war depends on my ability to charm our centuries-old rivals. These hours I've lived through have been daunting and I'm feeling a little weary, my Zar, and I humbly apologise.'

It was well phrased with just enough emotion driving it that he could feel her own sense of the unreal. He touched her bruised cheek affectionately. 'I don't think any of us have given sufficient credit for what you've had to live through today.'

She wanted to shake away his hand but resisted, yet she remained determined to finalise this conversation with its darker undercurrent. 'Who do you keep referring to, my Zar, as being a threat to my fidelity? Please be honest with me.'

She saw the pain reflected in his eyes when he uttered the name. 'I refer to Spur Lazar.'

Ana felt dizzied, wondering again if her husband could listen to her thoughts. 'I . . .' she stammered, flustered.

Mercifully he read her discomfort differently. 'Don't fret, Ana. I know that you have done nothing to win any other man's admiration. All I'm suggesting is that other people seem to think Lazar regards you with something other than innocent care.'

'Do you believe this?'

'I don't know what I think, Ana,' and now he sounded plaintive, vulnerable. 'I'm besotted with you, that makes me jealous of any man, including the Grand Vizier, who will share any time with you.'

'Boaz,' she began, talking to him like a wife now, 'I live in the harem. The only men I meet are half-men, and then of course there's Pez. The man who spends most time with me is Salmeo and the Grand Master Eunuch is so repulsive to me that I would rather make love to a monkey from your zoo than with him.' At this Boaz barked an embarrassed laugh but allowed her to continue. 'The first time I've set eyes on the Spur in a year was today and that's because he rescued me from my watery grave. You must also remember I have thought him dead for all of this time. There has been neither opportunity nor desire on either of our parts and so I believe this warning is troublemaking, designed to make you feel unsure of me, of yourself, of the one man who is truly loyal to *you* – not your father, not Percheron, not because he has some other agenda. Lazar is loyal to you. This rumour-mongering can only have come from one source. One jealous source always looking to stir trouble. I'm presuming your caution springs from something your mother has said. Would I be right?'

'And my own good sense that any red-blooded man would find you irresistible.'

Relief flooded Ana's body that his suspicions were truly borne from jealousy and hearsay rather than looking into her soul somehow. 'Well, on the occasions I have been with Spur Lazar, both publicly and privately, he has acted towards me with the usual disdain he bestows on most. In fact I recall asking him why he disliked me so much. Spur Lazar has never let his gaze linger on me,' she lied, feeling her face flush, 'and he has certainly never laid so much as a finger on me.' She was breathing hard, hoping a sense of indignation might cover her attempt at deception. Once again she blessed her luck that it was so dark.

'We shall never speak of this again,' he said, accepting her response and her right to be vexed. 'You're right, the

Valide can provoke problems where none exist. It is her way – her method of survival from years of cunning in the harem.'

'And her own infatuation with the Spur,' Ana added.

He sighed. 'Yes, there is that too. Nevertheless, Ana, let me end this conversation by saying we are not discussing Spur Lazar or my mother but we are discussing you. It is you who is being cautioned. It is your actions that will be watched and no doubt tested.'

'I understand,' she replied, not even sure she could look at Lazar in the next few moments without revealing to both him and the Zar how treacherous her body's inclinations truly were. She wanted to tell Boaz now that her mind was willing but her heart was a traitor, that her desire to be dutiful could not match her body's desire simply to feel the touch of his Spur's skin against hers again. However fleeting it was, she knew her body would risk the danger, risk the Zar's wrath, even if her good sense told her otherwise, and still it reminded her constantly that Lazar had betrayed her.

She kissed her husband one last time and, with the help of the mute known as Salazin, she stepped out of the karak, her traitorous eyes scanning the festive crowd and instantly picking out the betrayer himself.

He stood tall on a small rise that was slightly removed from the party. He was talking to Jumo and a few of his men. Beneath the soldiers horses shifted and neighed, eager to be gone from the torches and crowd of people. And then, as if he could sense her presence, he looked up and across the distance stared directly at her, into her eyes, into that perfidious soul of hers, which was no longer true to her but a slave to him. But something deeply sorrowful about the way he hung his head soon after he locked gazes with her told her something far more revealing.

Ana knew then and there that whatever inclinations she was fighting, he was fighting them harder.

Lazar didn't need to know she had climbed out of the karak. He sensed her presence instantly and broke away from his conversation with Jumo. His friend, ever sensitive to the mood swings of his former master, quickly picked up the thread of conversation with the other men to cover Lazar's sudden absence, even though he remained standing in the same position on the crest of the small rise.

The Spur's gaze locked on hers, and even though she was far away, he knew that for all of her posturing and his careful distance, nothing had changed. And that was dangerous. He lowered his head almost immediately. He had secretly hoped Ana did hate him, would and could never forgive him for the deception of his apparent death, and even though it was not his doing, he would have accepted her hatred as the price he had to pay for her to be alive and not feeding the fish of the Faranel.

On the other side of the karak another figure, unmistakably the tall young ruler, alighted to win his attention and surprised Lazar by searching him out immediately. Lazar was dismayed to see the young man's gaze flick immediately to Ana and then back to him. The Spur held his breath – surely, surely there was no suspicion? Despite the agony of his intense love for Ana, he knew he had never revealed it to anyone, not even her. How could the Zar, of all people, have this thought in his mind, if he did have this thought at all?

He handed over the reins of his horse, muttered something to Jumo and strode down the hill, ignoring the questions and enquiries thrown at him by various people until he reached the Zar's karak.

'Zar Boaz. You grace us with your presence.'

Boaz smiled warmly and Lazar felt his shoulders relax slightly. 'I thought it appropriate to see my wife off on this great journey, Lazar.'

'Indeed, Highness.' He looked over at Ana. 'Zaradine Ana,' and bowed his head slightly. 'We have a sweet and docile filly for you to ride.'

She said nothing but inclined her head and straightaway turned to Elza, who had bustled up to take charge. Elza was clearly enjoying the sudden notoriety of being the new Zaradine's personal slave, and the chance to escape the claustrophobia of the harem was also evident by her bright smile.

Lazar returned his attention to the Zar, all crisp efficiency. 'We make for the foothills, Highness, and will camp for a few hours. My intention is that we journey in the cool of the latest hours of darkness and the early hours of dawn until the sun gets more fierce.'

'This is Samazen season, if I'm not mistaken?'

'Sadly you are not, my Zar. This is indeed the most dangerous time of the year to be anywhere near the desert.'

'But it can't be helped,' Boaz qualified.

Lazar nodded. 'We have no choice. The desert is the fastest route and I will take every precaution.'

'When can I expect news?'

'I will send Jumo ahead as soon as we know anything. I imagine you won't hear much for a couple of moons, Majesty.'

Boaz nodded. 'You take with you precious cargo, Lazar.'

'I will keep the Valide, the Grand Vizier and Pez free from harm, Majesty – on this you have my word. As far as your wife goes, I will lay down my life for her as I would you, my Zar, for she is now an extension of you.'

At this Boaz fixed Lazar with an intense stare that the Spur met head-on and did not waver from. There was a test in that long, searching look, and Lazar felt pity for the young ruler who was truly rising to his station and yet was obviously fragile where Ana was concerned. Welcome to my world, Lazar thought, and found an uneasy smile. 'I will bring her home to you safe and triumphant, my Zar.'

And he saw something relax in Boaz as he said, 'I know you will, Lazar, and for this I am in your debt once again.' He reached for the Spur and pulled him close. 'Bring her home, protect her from those who don't feel about her as you or I.'

It was an odd choice of words but, despite the clumsy expression, Lazar understood perfectly what had passed between them. 'As I stand here, Zar Boaz, you have my oath that come what may Ana will live on to bear you an heir.' He was stunned himself by his equally inept answer that smacked of something far deeper than either of them understood . . . and yet it seemed the right thing to say, it seemed to convey that Boaz's fears would not come to fruition. Lazar couldn't explain it but it was as though he didn't choose the words, they chose themselves. Whatever or whyever, they seemed to satisfy Boaz, who now grinned broadly and hugged him again.

'Perhaps she already has my heir in her belly. Go about

your duties, Spur Lazar, I don't mean to hold you from them.'

Lazar bowed, still baffled by what had passed between him and his Zar, and removed himself from the crowd of people as another karak began arriving, probably that of the Valide. He resisted the urge to cast a glance Ana's way and instead steadfastly fixed his eyes on Jumo and his mind on their departure, which would take place just as soon as they could get the women comfortable on the horses and settled within their various escorts he'd set up.

The Samazen, he decided, as he strode back up the rise, knowing she was watching him, was going to be the least of his problems.

At Jumo's wise suggestion Lazar guided the party into the foothills but in a north-westerly direction so that Ana would not feel the nearness of her family. Their small dwelling was close but not close enough that she would necessarily recognise the terrain as anything but familiar to the foothills rather than to the region she grew up in. He had doggedly resisted all contact with Ana on the slow climb into the hills, preferring instead to send Jumo on both occasions that he felt inclined to check with the royal party that all was well with their horses, the pace, their comfort.

Jumo returned now with the message he had anticipated an hour previous at least.

'The Valide wishes to speak with you.'

'And did she ask politely?'

'Something about not being of a mind to discuss her comfort with the Spur's slave.' Jumo cleared his throat as if ridding himself of something distasteful.

'Gods rot that woman!' Lazar muttered. 'I'm sorry, Jumo—'

'Don't be sorry. Her words, not yours, and I was glad to run the errand. It meant I could see Ana.'

'More luck you,' Lazar said.

'And save you the pain of it,' Jumo qualified. 'You know, Master . . .'

'Call me by my name in front of the Valide. Do not give her any ammunition. Let her see our familiarity.'

'All right. I was going to say, where Ana is concerned, I'm afraid your face, legend for its blankness, is in fact rather easy to read.'

'That bad?'

Jumo nodded. 'If you don't want to give the Valide a weapon, don't even look at the girl.'

'I haven't looked at her in thirteen moons!' he growled.

'And none of the heat has dissipated between the two of you.'

'That's ridiculous, I—'

'What is? That you both go out of your way to be so uncommunicative that it's obvious you're doing your utmost to look as though you have nothing to say to one another?'

'We don't. Not any more.' He scowled.

'Now I know that's a lie and so does the Valide. You've saved Ana's life twice now, Lazar. And knowing you as I do, I understand this is not being done just out of duty. Whether or not the Valide appreciates this is irrelevant. You both clearly have plenty to say to one another. Just act more naturally.'

'Act naturally?' It was snarled with a mixture of incredulity and sarcasm.

Jumo ignored him and continued earnestly. This was important if they were all to survive. 'Address her. Give her eye contact. Offer a few words — encouragement, enquiry, anything. Don't be afraid to be friendly. It's what they would anticipate . . . even though you're not friendly to most.' He gave a soft smile to lighten the awkward yet necessary lecture, but Lazar had never looked more grim.

'That's just the point, I am afraid to be friendly.'

'Why, Lazar?' Jumo pleaded. It seemed so simple to him, and Ana was so easy to get along with that surely the Spur could make it go lighter on all of them if he tried a bit harder. Jumo was startled when the sorrowful answer came.

'Because it will undo me, my friend. She is married now. She is Zaradine . . . more untouchable than she ever was.'

Jumo had known Lazar for so long now, shared enough to know how his friend might react in any situation. But not this time. He had never heard Lazar sound so vulnerable and it was frightening. Frightening that a man who had always seemed impervious not just to the wiles of women but to any true friendship beyond their own, could now appear so fragile where this young woman, this forbidden woman, was concerned. He could only feel the deepest pity for his friend whom he now knew was on the most dangerous of paths. No-one, absolutely no-one, could lay a hand on a Zaradine. It was one thing to covet an odalisque, a possession of the Zar, but still merely a slave amidst a myriad of other slaves. But once elevated to wife, she instantly became something more precious, and to be Absolute Favourite and likely mother to the heir meant her face would almost certainly never be looked upon by another whole man again.

Ana had always done things differently and even though this was not by her design, here she was now on a journey, not just leaving the harem – something Herezah, for instance, had never considered possible – but representing her Zar, her nation, in a desperate bid to avert war. Suddenly she had been elevated into a new status altogether – no longer just Zaradine, no longer just Absolute Favourite, no longer just woman, but diplomatic negotiator, a strategist possibly, who might just fashion the peace that Percheron wanted, needed. From today many men – strangers, foreigners, enemies – might look upon her face if need called for it.

All of that acknowledged, the truth was that in principle nothing had actually changed . . . and Lazar knew it. For all the uniqueness of this situation, this was still a royal wife – the Favourite – and to covet this one was to invite cruel death.

Jumo understood what Lazar was battling. It was etched deep into his friend's grief-stricken face. And Jumo wished, although he had suspected this forbidden love had deepened, that he hadn't assumed it would somehow be diluted over time through their absence from one another.

He had convinced himself that in not seeing each other for so long, Lazar's infatuation and what appeared a childish attachment to the Spur by Ana might have lost its potency. But Ana was not a child. She was a young woman when they had discovered her but she had the composure of one far older and obviously the maturity to match. No, their compulsion towards each other was stronger than ever and both were fighting it hard.

Lazar's inspired suggestion that Boaz marry Ana for the

sake of the nation was not just a desperate bid to secure her life and indeed possibly save Percheron, but also his skewed method of putting Ana so far out of his own reach that he could never do more than love her from a distance. And Jumo could see the price his friend was paying for that decision – undeniably the only decision he could make under the circumstances – and he also understood the debt would never be paid. Lazar would continue funding her security with his own pain; suffering seemingly a bottomless purse for this man.

'I will try,' Lazar replied finally and the forlorn nature of his promise prompted Jumo to add something, anything of a positive nature, before his friend turned his horse around to drop back to the royal party.

'I met your parents, Lazar. Perhaps you would like me to tell you about that meeting?'

It had the opposite effect to the one he'd hoped for. More darkness deepened into the shadows of the Spur's face. 'Perhaps,' he replied, and Jumo understood he was simply being polite. After all, Lazar had not even asked after the King and Queen.

Jumo looked towards the small valley ahead of them. 'That's camp. The camels will be delivered in the next few hours. I'm glad you decided to bring fewer men than the Zar originally suggested.'

Lazar nodded, said no more as he nudged his horse around and trotted unhappily back down the line of slow-moving people on horseback to the main party and to the woman who awaited him.

Attired in a midnight blue gown from head to toe, the dark eyes of the Valide flashed pure pleasure as his horse drew up next to hers.

'Valide, you wished to speak with me?'

'I do, Lazar. Why do you not travel with Zaradine Ana and myself? Surely as our guide and our chaperone, your job is to stay close?'

He knew she was playing with him but he had promised himself he would not bite at any bait she dangled on this journey. He hoped his oath was not an empty one. 'The danger, should it arise, Valide, is not here alongside you and Zaradine Ana but at the front of the column. You must forgive me but my job is actually to keep you safe by knowing precisely what is ahead of us.'

'And what is ahead of us, Lazar? I see nothing but the dark shadows of thorny bushes and the black humps of dunes.'

'And you would be right, Valide. But also, less than one league away is our stopping point for a few hours. Ahead is a small valley. Safe as a resting place so we can take delivery of our camels and both of our esteemed women might take some sleep for a while.' He looked across the Valide to where the silent Zaradine stared straight ahead into the night. He decided Jumo was right. At least he could try. 'I imagine you must be fatigued, Zaradine Ana?' His voice was gentle and he couldn't care less what Herezah read into it.

He was surprised, though, that Ana answered him so readily. Her voice was steady, clear when it came. 'I was so at the palace, Spur Lazar.'

'But no longer?' he dared, enjoying the fact that he had effectively cut Herezah out of the conversation momentarily.

'I didn't know if I would be able to stay upright on my horse, I was so exhausted, but curiously I feel refreshed to be out beneath the stars, energised to be back in the foothills. I am close to my home, I believe?' The enquiry was there, he could not avoid it.

'We are in the same region, yes.' He pointed. 'Over there, in that direction, is where your home is.'

She sighed in answer and Lazar took that sad sound to mean that she had no home. Herezah filled the void.

'So you will join us for supper, Lazar.' It was not a question but he responded as if it was.

'Thank you, but I must decline. I have to ensure the camels—'

'The camels!' She laughed at him. 'I'm sure amongst all these men someone can receive and tie down the animals for a few hours, Spur. No, I believe you make excuses.'

'Why would I do that?'

'You wish to distance yourself from us women and we are in need of some company.'

'You have the Grand Vizier—'

Again she interrupted him with a laugh and it was obvious she was enjoying this banter. Didn't she always, Lazar thought wearily to himself.

'I can engage the Grand Vizier in conversation anytime I choose – isn't that right, Tariq?'

Tariq sensibly did nothing more than dip his head gently in a meaningless acknowledgement that she had spoken.

'But supper with the Spur is far more intriguing. After all, we haven't seen you for over twelve moons, Lazar. I'm sure Zaradine Ana will enjoy the opportunity to hear precisely what you've been up to all that time that we thought you were dead.' She kept her voice breezy but her words cut like a sharp blade through him. It was all threat.

He bristled despite his promise to remain impervious to her baiting. 'I'm sure Zaradine Ana's eventful day will demand she rest, Valide. It would be irresponsible of me to have her squander precious sleeping hours in polite conversation over supper.

'We are not on a picnic, may I remind everyone. This is a journey fraught with unknown dangers and I'm afraid I must use my rank as Spur to insist everyone, hungry or otherwise, take this chance to sleep. You will hate me when I send out the call to rouse yourselves in just a few hours. You can eat on the camels in the morning and you can feast when we break for camp tomorrow but until then I will be busy with the activities entrusted to me by my Zar.' It was a slap in the face to the Valide.

'Spur Lazar. I think you forget yourself. You are here to care for our needs—'

'That's exactly what I'm doing, Valide. Forgive me if my interpretation of care is different to yours, however. As Spur I have duties. I am answerable to the Zar for your lives. I will do everything within my power to protect them . . . and that means ensuring this trip is not treated like some sort of festive event. Again, forgive my brusque words, Valide, but we are now in hostile territory.'

'Hostile? This is still Percheron, Spur—'

'The desert kills, Valide. It is hostile to all creatures and does not differentiate between Percherese or Galinsean. It will destroy us as it chooses. I am here to ensure it is never given that chance. Please excuse me.' He bowed his head to the Valide, then to the Zaradine who did not look at him. 'Tariq.'

'How long before we arrive?' the Grand Vizier enquired.

'I shall stop the caravan very shortly and then I shall return to get the royal tent up and all of you settled.'

Tariq nodded and Lazar took that as his opportunity to leave.

'Ooh, that man is so frustrating!' Herezah breathed.

The Grand Vizier shrugged. 'Only for you, Valide, it seems. Zaradine Ana had little to say to him and I can see he has no time for me.'

'It's true, our new Zaradine must be tired, after all she nearly drowned today. Tomorrow he will not be quite so slippery.'

'Why do you pursue the Spur, Valide?' Ana asked, surprising her pair of listeners by joining in. 'It's obvious neither of you care much for one another save what is necessary for formality.'

It was Herezah's turn to bristle. 'Don't question me, Ana! Please remember your place.'

'As Absolute Favourite Wife to the Zar, Valide, or as the emissary who will try and negotiate a peace treaty for Percheron?'

'I forbid you to take that tone with me, Ana.'

'You forbid me nothing, Valide.' Wintry in the control of her obvious rage, Herezah opened her mouth to retaliate but Ana made sure she closed it again. 'Out here, in the desert, we are equals. In fact I think if we were asked to survive alone I might stand a better chance. I'm from these parts, Herezah, and I haven't forgotten the harshness of the wild or how to respect it. You have never felt its sinister touch and I suspect if you were alone you would capitulate at its first fiery breath of the day or its icy night-time caress. You need the Spur, and not as an enemy.'

'I don't need him as anything!' Herezah replied, trying

to put aside Ana's lofty claims and to forget that the young woman had just addressed her by name — it was a high insult. Both of them knew it.

'Other than a supper companion,' Ana finished for her, 'or perhaps a bedmate?'

Herezah felt the compulsion to strike this girl again, hit her so hard she might tumble from her horse, but she was too wily to fall for that again. She knew Ana was playing her at her own game. The youngster was baiting her, willing her to strike, to let her son down, to bring shame on herself. She did no such thing. Instead she laughed.

'Oh my dear, you reveal too much of yourself. You are fortunate for the veil and the cover of darkness or we might all see your burning cheeks. Do you really think no-one sees through you? The Spur is not for you, child, no matter how much you covet him.'

'I am a married woman, Valide.'

'That's meaningless.'

'Are you speaking from experience?'

Maliz coughed to hide his amusement at Ana's audacity. His stolen body gave him memories of this woman of twelve moons ago. The harem had certainly matured her but perhaps not in the way Salmeo and Herezah had anticipated.

'You overstep your status,' Herezah warned, her tone so cold, Tariq was sure that Ana's face must be frozen.

'I warned you we are now equal, although I'll respect your position in the harem providing you respect my new status. Out here, however, I abide by no-one's rules but my own, Valide, and that of the Spur who is leading this journey. But as for suggesting that I am lusting for Lazar,

I see no-one panting around him like a dog in heat, save yourself.'

At this Maliz burst into laughter. He simply couldn't help himself. This journey was going to be entertaining if it continued in this vein.

His outburst startled Herezah from her fury and prevented the Valide from breaking her promise and doing something ugly to Ana that she would regret. Instead she somehow managed to join the Grand Vizier in his amusement, after which she simply dropped her voice low, menacing, and murmured only for Ana's hearing: 'There will be a reckoning for this once we return.'

'If we return,' Ana warned and nothing further could be said because the Elim were forming an escort around them once again.

'We are stopping here for a few hours, Valide,' the senior one said.

'Good,' she snapped. 'I'm weary of this company and conversation. Please get our tents set up quickly.'

The group of men, nomads, arrived with the camels at just past midnight. The camp was mostly silent; certainly the Valide, Zaradine and Grand Vizier were resting, if not asleep. The two women shared tented accommodation that could be considered grand – lavish by the visitors' awed stares – but Lazar knew that Percheron could have yielded something infinitely more breathtaking in terms of opulence had it been given sufficient time. The Grand Vizier slept in a smaller, gaudily coloured tent that would normally be used by far lesser dignitaries. Still, he had said his goodnights without complaint, and again Lazar was struck by the radical changes in the man. Tariq would have required accommodation that screamed richness and status, but not this Tariq – this Tariq couldn't have cared less where he put his head down. Whereas before Tariq simply irritated Lazar as a meaningless, syco-phantic drone, this Tariq – Maliz – gave him a constant sense of unease.

It was more than that, though. Maliz gave Lazar a feeling of dread, as though he was simply toying with everyone now, enjoying the angst within this party, not in any way involved or concerned. Coming along for the fun of it perhaps, even though his Zar expected it.

Pez materialised at this side. 'Why are you staring at his tent?'

'I'm wondering why he's here. He could have easily made legitimate excuses. There must be a reason for him coming along that suits his own agenda.'

'Ana, presumably,' Pez replied without hesitation.

'We've been through this—'

'I know. And your claims damn my beliefs all the way to hell.'

'And still you believe,' Lazar finished for him.

'I do. I feel something in Ana. She resembles plain mortal as little as I do. I don't have the answer so don't tax me with the question but I believe Ana is involved – as firmly as I believe you are.'

'He is not here for Ana, though. Whatever you believe, he has satisfied himself that she is not the Goddess incarnate.'

'I agree. Perhaps that is the difference this time. Maybe Lyana is protected.'

Lazar kept his patience. 'Tell me. What occurs to him when Lyana comes into her power?'

At this the dwarf faltered. He knew Lazar was going to trap him again. 'That, too, is confusing, Lazar, I admit. Traditionally, as soon as Maliz comes into contact with Lyana, he is endowed fully with all of his powers.'

'Magic, you mean,' Lazar qualified. He wanted none of Pez's cryptic answers.

'For want of a better word, yes.'

'Are they noticeable?'

Pez smirked. 'Does he break out in sores or suddenly grow in stature, you mean? No, Lazar, he is just equipped for the battle that will inevitably ensue between himself and Lyana.'

'And traditionally they fight – hand to hand?'

Pez shrugged. 'Not really. They use their powers against one another. She has always lost.' He pursed his lips before adding, 'but not this time.'

'I reckon he's here for you. He's keeping an eye on the person who can lead him to the real Lyana.'

Pez shook his head, determined to shore up his belief that Ana was still somehow the one. 'Perhaps he's here for neither Ana nor myself. Why not you?'

Lazar laughed grimly. 'We're going over stale ground, Pez.' The dwarf nodded sadly. 'Why can't I just go in there now and slit his throat?'

'I've explained this. He cannot die by traditional means.'

'Why not?'

'Lyana's presence gives him his powers.'

Before Lazar could argue again that Ana was not Lyana and surely that made Maliz vulnerable, Jumo arrived with the news that the purveyors of camels were ready to do business.

'We have shared kerrosh. It is time,' Jumo said.

Lazar nodded. 'I have some animals to buy, Pez. Keep an eye on his tent. I don't care that it's guarded by Elim. Everyone's tired and might get sloppy. See that he doesn't make any attempt to enter the women's accommodation.'

'I'll do one of my screams if he does.'

Lazar gave him a sad smile before following Jumo down to where the nomads sat patiently cross-legged, warming themselves around a small fire that the soldiers had built.

'Are they speaking Percherese?' Lazar asked his friend.

'No. Use Khalid.'

Lazar swapped instantly into the language of the nomads, touching his hand to his forehead and breast as he welcomed the men and thanked them for bringing the animals.

They stood and responded in kind, although this was purely formality. There was nothing resembling a smile. Instead their expressions were blank, their gazes guarded as they watched the tall foreigner seat himself in similar cross-legged fashion nearby.

Lazar got straight down to business now that the formalities were done with. 'How many?'

'We were asked to bring twenty-five,' the leader said.

Lazar nodded. 'We'll need all of them. Are they watered?'

'Yes. Several days ago but they will have water at the next well. Then they can travel for fifteen days or so without a need for drinking.'

'Good.'

'Where do you go, sir?'

'Across the desert.'

The senior man whistled through his teeth, talked to his companions in a pidgin version of the language that not even Lazar could understand. He grasped every fourth word, though, and from their body language could tell they were not impressed that their camels may not be returned. He chose to interrupt their worried conversation.

'We will buy them outright.'

'I cannot allow that. We have raised these camels from calves. They belong to the Khalid people.'

Lazar knew better than to get into any family squabble. As hostile as it was, the desert still supported several tribal families, wandering endlessly from well to well where they might soothe parched throats of man and beast. And their camels, in truth, meant more to them than each other. Camels gave them meat, milk, skins, transport, comfort, income. He'd always known asking one tribe to sell off more than two dozen of its prized family members was an optimistic notion. One or two perhaps, not that many though.

And he also knew by the man's objection that he was dealing with the right animals, too. Sometimes the wily tribes tried to sell off beasts who were used to traversing the stony plains onto unsuspecting travellers who needed to move through part of the desert. The soles of these animals were hard and shiny, unsuitable for the soft give of the sands. Jumo of course, even with limited time to make his arrangements, would not have erred on this point, he reminded himself.

'I need these camels,' he said softly to the man whose name he had found out was Salim.

'Then we will send some of our own men,' the man replied. Lazar began to shake his head. The last thing he wanted was more people in the caravan. 'Otherwise you cannot have our animals, not for any price.'

Salim sounded very final. And Lazar was running out of patience and time. He glanced towards Jumo whose almost imperceptible nod urged the Spur to take this deal. After all, what could it hurt to have some experienced desert travellers in their party?

It was probably fatigue that made him capitulate. 'I accept your terms. How many men?'

'Four.'

Lazar nodded. 'All right. What price?'

And with those two words he set off furious negotiations. Lazar understood the way of the desert. The first price was simply the starting point from which he would now barter them down as earnestly as they would argue the price back up. He ordered kerrosh, knew there would be another hour or more in this debate. Lazar would happily pay their first price – unheard-of, but his men were tired and he was exhausted. Money was not an issue either. The Zar had opened up the royal coffers and no karel would be spared in this journey. Boaz would scoff if he knew his Spur was using precious rest time in petty bargaining.

But this was the way of the desert-folk. If you didn't follow the protocol, they would take offence.

The hire price of men and camels was finally agreed upon and suddenly all the Khalid were standing, stretching, smiling and nodding. Negotiations were over, and it was time for a final serve of kerrosh.

Lazar worked hard at stifling a long yawn but lost the fight. Salim strolled over.

'You will appreciate my men. I can see from your tents that you escort important people.'

'Bit hard to miss, isn't it?'

The Khalid smirked but not unkindly. 'I would leave those tents behind if I were you, sir. Forgive my forwardness but the less attention you draw to yourselves the better in the Empty.'

The Empty. It was the first time he'd heard the desert called that. Having crossed it once, he knew the title suited it. 'Trouble?'

Salim looked thoughtful. 'Possibly. I'm presuming you're headed fully west?'

Lazar didn't really want to tell Salim much more than he had to but the Khalid was obviously intelligent and had worked out much for himself. 'Yes.'

Again the man whistled softly. 'With a royal? Has the sun boiled your brains?'

Lazar bristled but knew he must keep his temper even. He wanted those camels and he wanted to be gone in a few hours on their backs. 'What do you know?'

Salim jutted his chin towards the tent. 'The accommodation tells me plenty. The Elim guard tells me a lot more. This is precious cargo you travel with, Spur Lazar.'

'And the fewer people who know the better, Salim. What should I be fearing?'

'Apart from the scorching heat and frost at night, the lack of wells across to the west, or perhaps the Samazen?'

Lazar gritted his teeth at the man's sarcasm, recognising a similar character to his own in Salim. 'And?'

'The western quarter of the Empty is not our region. Our people have no reason to travel those lands — I don't know of any tribes who move across the Forgotten Sands, as the west is known. But we hear things. Rumours of a fortress.'

'What? In the desert?'

Salim shrugged. 'All hearsay but I'm obliged to tell you. If we lose our men and camels . . .' he trailed off, his tone sad.

'Why would you?'

Again he shrugged and it was beginning to annoy Lazar. 'What about this fortress? What rumours do you know?'

'That a madman had it built and he has assembled his own army.'

Lazar barked a laugh. 'And you believe this? An army living in the desert.'

'No ordinary army,' Salim continued. 'Men who care not for their lives on this plane.'

Lazar was tiring of this conversation. 'Salim, tell me what you know and be done. I appreciate your information and any guidance you can provide, but I wish no scaremongering of my men. We have an arduous journey ahead, fraught with all sorts of problems I don't wish to think about yet, and you are now adding to those problems.'

'I know very little. All of it based on information passed across the desert through the tribes. I have no idea if it is based on truth, nor do I know how exaggerated the information has become in each telling.'

'Go on.'

'No-one knows why they're there — if they're there. I have no name for this madman people whisper about. Rumour says he is on a personal crusade of sorts and he has over the past decade been persuading vulnerable, impressionable young men into his personal army.'

'Where does he source these men?'

'People disappear all the time in the desert. The tribes know they will lose one or two men a year to its harshness. I think, if he exists, he is using this fact to prey on those people. He steals one or two from the tribes each year, watches them go through the motion of searching for their lost one and then giving up, knowing the desert will claim lives.' Salim put his hands up in a gesture of helplessness. 'Who knows, he may even steal the people from the western cities, for all I know.'

'Is there any proof — anything real you can give me?'

At this Salim's eyes narrowed and his lips tightened to a thin line before he spoke. He nodded. 'My youngest son, Ashar. He disappeared two years ago. He was just fifteen summers. He was accompanying a party of two other Khalid. They were mapping out some new watering holes, as we have begun to open up some trading routes towards the west and—'

'Wait! This is about your son, nothing to do with our safety. Denying selling me the camels outright had nothing to do with tribal ways but so that you can implant *your* men into *my* caravan. And all that talk about the royals – you don't care, you're using the royal party as cover.' Lazar was past tired, past cranky and was moving straight into fury.

Salim had the grace to look slightly sheepish. Again he gave the gesture of helplessness. 'Have you a son of your own, Spur Lazar?'

'I have no children,' he growled, mindful of the small crowd, turning from their kerrosh and conversation to the two men arguing.

'Then you cannot begin to understand the lengths a father will go to in order to protect his child. Ashar is now seventeen—'

'If he's alive,' Lazar said heartlessly.

The man nodded sadly. 'Yes, if he's alive. I believe he is.'

'And you want to use my caravan to find him.'

'I don't believe this enclave is run by a madman. If it exists – and I believe it does – I think he is far from mad. Very sane in fact. Very calculating, too. He would have the good sense to let a royal party move unharmed through the lands he considers his. Stealing or killing royals brings nothing but damnation onto him and the might of the entire Percherese army.'

'You can bet all your camels and children on that, Salim!'

The man did not rise to the bait. 'As I say, I think he will let your caravan pass unharmed, but it will give me and my men the opportunity to get not only close enough to see whether the fortress exists but also into it if necessary.'

'You know you're the madman.'

'Perhaps. But I love my son, Lazar, and no man steals him from me.'

'You don't know that he's alive and you risk men and your own life on the chance that he is.'

Salim studied him through dark, wise eyes. 'One day I hope Zarab blesses you with a son. And then you will know the pain of parental love and the knowledge that, yes, you would die for that son on the off-chance that your life might buy his.'

Lazar shook his head in exasperation. 'I want the camels.'

'They are yours but we come with them.'

Lazar knew he was beaten. He raised a finger in the air in threatening fashion. 'You and your men are under my command. Is that understood?'

'Perfectly.'

'You go where I say. You do what I order.'

'To a point. We shall break away from your caravan should we discover the fortress.'

'Agreed.'

They locked grim stares. Salim broke it by bowing his head to the Spur, hand on heart. 'Thank you, sir. I will ready my men.'

Lazar sighed. He was not going to get any sleep this night.

❧ 28 ❧

At Jumo's insistence, Lazar tried to get some sleep, but it eluded him despite his body feeling bone-shakingly tired. Instead he dozed restlessly on a skin beneath a few goat-hair blankets. He knew he had only two hours and then they would have to rise and get the caravan moving before the heat of the day set in. This was summer and it could kill within an hour if it so chose and if the unprepared decided to gamble with it.

He turned away from the fire, and the men talking quietly around it. Lazar felt the frost near his face and acknowledged how a desert night could also murder men if they took no precaution.

He found some measure of fitful rest and amongst his frequent stirrings his dreams punished him.

Voices called to him. They urged him to set them free but he had no idea where their prison was.

Unleash us on the land, Lazar. You will need us for the battle ahead.

Who are you?

Friends.

Where are you?

But there was no response and he realised he had jolted himself awake; he could hear Jumo's voice speaking quietly with Salim and his men. He drifted off again and if the voices talked, he didn't remember hearing them. This time his thoughts were with Ana, imagining how close she was and yet how very far from him. The words of Boaz returned to haunt him, that Ana's womb might already be quickening with his heir.

He squirmed, forced himself to open his eyes and deliberately roused himself by turning back towards the fire. His gaze met Jumo's, which was full of reproach.

'You have another hour,' he said.

'I can't sleep,' Lazar replied honestly. 'Let's start.'

Jumo nodded, translated, and the men began moving as one, quietly dispersing to see to their various tasks.

Salim approached as Lazar was disentangling his long legs from the blankets.

'The water you carry in those barrels will have to go into skins.'

'They won't like it,' Lazar said, his chin jutting towards the royal tent. But it was obvious he didn't disagree. 'Go ahead. You have what you need?'

'Yes, that's the beauty of the goatskins, we can simply roll them up and carry them easily.'

Lazar nodded. 'Pick out three gentle beasts for our royal party.'

Salim nodded. 'And you?'

'Oh, the nastier the better for me,' Lazar quipped and they shared a smile – it was a smile of the desert, for most camels were cantankerous even in their most peaceful moments. The hobbled animals were already spitting and grumbling as their handlers began to get them up for the day.

'We'll give you Maharitz, then. She'll soon sort you

out,' Salim said and his normally blank face creased into a mischievous grin.

Lazar stayed well away from the royal tent but he could hear its complaints. Herezah did not appreciate being woken whilst it was still dark and she was berating the unfortunate Elim given the task. Not a word of complaint from Ana, of course, and Tariq was already dressed for the desert in simple light robes and a fashez, the turban that men favoured when travelling in the sands. Lazar was impressed as he watched the man stretching outside his humble enough tent and felt a stab of something akin to sorrow. It seemed a pity that his change into this new Tariq must end in death. The demon was a far better Vizier — a far better man, in fact — than his host had ever been. Despite his fear of what lurked beneath the shell of Tariq, Lazar rather admired the no-nonsense, direct and rather charismatic way in which the Grand Vizier carried himself these days. In a different situation perhaps the two of them might have found common ground . . . friendship even.

He shook his head free of such fanciful thoughts and reminded himself that this was a demon, not a man, and that he intended to destroy Percheron and any number of its people, if necessary, to achieve his own aims.

A smaller figure emerged beside the Grand Vizier from the royal tent and Lazar immediately looked away but not before he felt his breath sucked from him with a fresh gust of pain. It was Ana and she, too, had sensibly chosen the light-coloured, unadorned robes of the desert for their journey. She was still veiled, however, and that helped to make it feel as though she was distant, even though she was standing perhaps only fifty paces from him. He stole a glance and grimaced at the easy conversation that had instantly struck up between Zaradine and Grand Vizier. Ana was even laughing gently as she, too, stretched in the heavy atmosphere of the dewy night. A soft lightening to the east nudged at Lazar's thoughts – he must get the caravan moving. This cool was a false prelude to what the desert sun would bring once she was allowed to banish the moon and claim the skies.

Salim ambled over. 'We are ready, Spur.'

'Good. I will need to speak with the royals and they will need help mounting their beasts when the time comes,' he reminded.

The man nodded and without needing to say a word seemed to be able to give orders to his men from gestures or expressions. They were all well rehearsed in journeys such as these and required no verbal reminders of what they should do.

Lazar steadied himself and strode across to where Herezah was still ranting behind the drapes of the tent. 'Good morning, Zaradine Ana,' he said as cheerily as he could, his heart hammering as she turned her gaze fully on him. He could not see her eyes as clearly as he would have liked in the low light but it was not necessary in truth for their colour was etched brightly in his mind. 'I won't ask if you slept well,' he continued with an effort at levity, including Tariq now with a nod of his head. 'Grand Vizier.'

'Feel free to ask, Spur,' came the sardonic reply. 'Zaradine Ana was just telling me that this was her deepest, most pleasurable sleep in thirteen moons. I certainly slept like a babe at the breast.'

Lazar could believe it. Gone was the stoop of the Tariq of old, and the man standing before him belied his age of well past three score years.

'You look fit indeed, Tariq,' he said, not knowing what else to say. 'I am glad you found some rest, Zaradine,' he added, unable to turn away from her just yet. The ache in his chest did not lessen when her eyes now crinkled at their edges and he knew she smiled the smile that he held dear in his memory. Again he did not need the veil removed to know its brightness and warmth.

She spoke. 'I thought I'd become soft in my time in the harem, Spur, but I suppose one's heart never forgets what is closest to it. Memories of sleeping on a red blanket on the hard earth, beneath the stars of the foothills, are not lost to me and will remain my happiest.'

To the Grand Vizier it must have sounded like the wistful recall of sleeping in her father's home in the foothills and he smiled indulgently. 'Then you are blessed, Zaradine Ana, to experience such pleasure again.'

He said something more but Lazar didn't hear any of it. To him Ana's words provoked a distraction that left him so deeply wounded he could not have replied if she had expected one. Ana was not referring to her father's hut. No, Ana was recalling the nights travelling amongst the foothills, after leaving her family dwelling, during which she slept in the company of two men — Lazar and Jumo. They had taken their time with the journey; even in her naivety, Ana knew it didn't take so many days to reach the city. During this time Lazar had given her his own blanket to sleep on. It was red and she had commented at some point that such a hot colour did not suit the Spur's cool approach to life. And Jumo had quipped that a man's desert blanket is the truest reflection of his spirit. Even Lazar had cracked a wry smile at this.

All he could do was bow gently towards her, his throat closing with the emotion he was choking back.

'So, we leave now?' The Grand Vizier interrupted his thoughts and forced him to clear the lump from his throat.

He coughed. 'Er, yes, that's what I'm here to tell you—' Before Lazar could finish the tent flap was thrown back and the Valide stomped out.

'What time do you call this?' she demanded of everyone in her fury but especially the Spur. She looked glorious in her anger and dishevelment.

But her beauty was winter to Ana's that was all things summery – and that coldness had never held any allure for the Spur. 'This time, Valide,' he said politely, 'is what I call travelling time.'

'It's night, for Zarab's sake!'

'It's the early hours of the morning before dawn, Valide. It is cool and safe for us to begin our journey before the heat of the day. The sun will be fierce in a few hours. I explained this.'

'You explained little. You leave your servant to do all your bidding.'

'Jumo is not my servant, he is my friend.'

'He is irrelevant, as is his status! I refuse to leave my tent until I have washed, breakfasted and it's light enough for me to see which clothes I shall wear for today. Do you understand me, Spur?'

Lazar sensed the smirk on Tariq's face. He knew the Grand Vizier was enjoying watching the stand-off and looking forward to seeing how the Spur would handle the Valide's bullying tactics.

He bit back his own anger but his voice had lost the gentleness that seemed to imbue his tone when he addressed the Zaradine. Now it was as hard and cool as the marble of the Stone Palace. 'Valide, in the desert there is no status. I am sorry to enlighten you that your position in the palace carries only the weight that I allow. I permit that you are shown formal respect but you will not interrupt the progress of what is – I think you're forgetting – a diplomatic crisis.' He held up a finger. 'Firstly, there will be no washing in the desert from here on in, but I will allow you a small bowl of water as this is our first morning and water is plentiful. It won't be from tomorrow. We shall have only what we can carry and that is needed for our sustenance, not our personal pleasure.'

The second finger went up. 'Secondly, if you can eat some flatbread as you walk, that's called breakfast, and I am happy for you to do so. If you prefer not to, you will not starve but you will have to wait until we mount the camels when you can nibble on your bread with one hand and drink from a skin with the other.' If it was possible his voice became harder still. 'And if that wounds your etiquette, Valide, my personal apologies, and I shall have to ask you to wait until we have stopped for the day before you feast fully.' She opened her mouth to let fly with a new tirade but he stopped her with his third finger going up alongside its companions. 'And thirdly,' he said with a finality in his voice, 'may I suggest you dress yourself as sensibly as the Zaradine and the Grand Vizier have chosen for this day's travel. You will regret it otherwise. But it is, I might add, your choice.'

He now turned to face all three of his royal party.

'Gentle beasts have been chosen and the men are waiting for you over by the camels. Please, cover your heads now, for the sands will begin their fun.' He gave no further eye contact to the Valide, instead turning to address the waiting Elim.

'Take the tents down immediately – you have minutes to get it all packed away and onto the beasts.' He bowed to his guests and strode away.

But Herezah unwisely stalked him, stabbing at him with a manicured finger. 'How dare you speak to me like that, Lazar. You are my servant, you—'

Lazar swung around. 'In the desert I am King, Valide, I am your god, your master, your ruler. You will do as I say in order to stay alive. My job for my Zar is to get you and the royal party safely to Galinsea to broker a peace between our two realms. And then I am charged to bring you back to Percheron safely. I am *not* your servant, and something you should perhaps realise, Valide, is that I never have been. You are the slave, bought by a harem to pleasure a Zar. I choose my role for Percheron, you were sold into it.'

Her voice was a whisper when it came. 'Oh, there will be a reckoning for this when we get back to the palace, Lazar. You are never going to survive this indiscretion.'

He leant close. 'Remember who you speak to, Herezah . . . I am the heir to the enemy throne and I can keep you captive in Galinsea if I so choose.' Of course his threat was empty but she didn't know that.

Only they shared the exchange, only they knew the threats both had made to each other. And only they knew how suddenly terrified Herezah felt as the realisation hit of where she was, without a single ally. No Salmeo to do her bidding, a Grand Vizier who no longer fussed around her, no royal son to protect her with his status. Around her was controlled hostility everywhere she turned.

'Lazar!' she yelled to his retreating back.

He didn't turn, kept walking away from her, but held five fingers in the air and she knew that was the number of minutes she had before he would move the caravan out.

She returned angrily to her tent, already being expertly brought down at one end.

'Please, Valide,' a senior Elim urged, 'please let us help you dress.'

She had no choice but to meekly enter her half-crumpled tent and put on the colourless, lightweight robes already laid out.

Behind her, and out of earshot, the Grand Vizier and the Zaradine shared a conspiratorial smile.

'I think this journey is going to be very good for our Valide,' Maliz whispered to his companion. 'And highly entertaining for us.'

The caravan of two dozen camels set off not long after, with Lazar asking everyone to lead their beasts for the first couple of hours.

'When the sun is out fully,' he explained, 'we mount up.' And that was all he said before the slow-moving beasts took their first steps into the wilderness they felt so comfortable in. Herezah and Ana walked with Tariq, with Elim leading theirs and their own camels.

No-one spoke. There was not much to say after the fiery confrontation earlier. Everyone probably believed Herezah was sulking but whether she was or more likely deep in her agile thoughts, she remained sensibly quiet behind her veil. Ana wanted to enjoy the early-morning silence, which was broken only by the call of wild birds of prey. Maliz was simply relishing the building tension. He could see the dwarf skipping along ahead of them and frowned – this was the first time he'd seen Pez in ages. Where had the dwarf hidden himself all these hours? he wondered.

Jumo dropped back to offer some advice to the women and Maliz had to ignore his thoughts about Pez for the moment whilst he listened to the wiry little man.

Up ahead Pez and Lazar walked slightly apart from the others.

'What have you seen?' Lazar asked.

'A great deal of sand. Nothing stirs, apart from the odd scorpion or lizard. No problems as far as I can see, although I had to be very careful and will have to continue being watchful.' Lazar gave him a quizzical look. 'You can hear the falcon up above?' Lazar nodded. 'There were others and they'd like nothing more than to bring a large snowy owl down on the wing,' Pez explained testily.

The Spur looked towards the horizon where the sun sat on its rim; a great fiery ball, promising a furnace not too much later in the day. He looked up and saw a lone falcon, a fearsome hunter that could stalk and kill a desert bustard despite its prey's poison liquid, as easily as it could a pigeon. And then he looked across the golden wilderness as the last clumps of patchy grass lost their fight and capitulated fully to the parched sands of the Great Waste. He had survived this once before and he intended to do so again, but he felt a twist of fear in his gut at the thought that there were now so many other lives he was responsible for ensuring also survived.

'This is madness, Pez,' he murmured.

Pez could read his thoughts, shared them in fact, but still said the right words, the only words one could in this situation. 'We have no choice, Lazar. If fighting a battle of our faith is not hard enough, we now face war with our fellow man.' He shook his head with disgust.

'And it's all my fault,' Lazar muttered. 'I could have averted this.'

'How? By going yourself?'

'Of course! My reluctance means we are all under threat and this perilous journey guarantees nothing.' He sounded helpless.

'Spur Lazar, tell me what your father would do if you did appear before him.'

'There would be no war with Percheron.'

'And?'

'I would be put to death.'

'I see,' Pez said thoughtfully. He paused and then spoke again, firmly this time. 'Can you unequivocally guarantee that there would be no war with our realm?'

It was the Spur's turn to pause and consider. He took his time, so long in fact that Pez could have been forgiven for thinking he'd forgotten a question had been posed.

'I cannot give that guarantee.'

'Why?' There was satisfaction in the dwarf's tone.

'Because of all the kings of Galinsea who have resisted the temptation to invade Percheron for its riches, I believe in my heart that my father would be the weakest with regard to its seductions.'

'So, in taking full blame and presenting yourself at the palace at Galinsea we risk not only losing you to the grave but we still run equal risk of war, even after having given our lives to chance in the desert.'

'I regret that you paint an accurate picture.'

'Then stop blaming yourself. You are doing the right thing, taking the best option by keeping yourself alive to lead our men if required whilst also escorting the one person who might just be able to broker the peace we need.'

'What if my father wants war anyway and this is the best excuse he's ever had?'

'I think that has already occurred to all of us, Lazar,' Pez counselled gently. 'Boaz would have worked this out from the very first moment he met the Galinsean dignitaries but as Zar he has to leave no stone unturned to keep his people in peace. Your idea to marry him to Ana was inspired. If anyone can charm a king, Ana can.'

Lazar sneered. 'If you knew my father, you'd know that he is not prey to the usual foibles of a man.'

'I think I do know your father,' Pez said, and winked at his friend. 'I think the man I call friend well reflects his bloodline.' He wondered if Lazar might take offence, for it was obvious no love was lost between king and heir.

'Ah, well,' he said very softly, almost a sigh. 'This is probably true to some extent.'

'What happened, Lazar?' He held his breath, expecting to be told to mind his own business, but was surprised to be answered.

'I loved a woman that my parents did not approve of.'

'Not from the right family?'

'You could say that,' he said, and gave a sorry smile. 'She was . . .' He appeared lost for words.

'Special?'

Lazar nodded, and Pez could see how hard this was for him. 'I have to presume she is no longer alive for you to be unable to so much as speak her name.'

'Yes, she is dead.'

'Killed by your parents?' Pez asked, incredulous.

'I like to see them as murderers but a more generous, perhaps more realistic person might say they helped to contrive a situation that would prompt her death.'

'She killed herself?'

He nodded sadly. 'It was the only way she felt she could prevent our family being torn apart. I was the son, the heir, and my father was not having her as the next queen.'

'Her death achieved nothing, then.'

'Nothing towards healing the rift in our family, no. And nothing towards ensuring the present heir to Galinsea takes the throne. But she offered me my freedom through her act and her bravery gave me the courage not to ignore that gift. I did not look back once I fled Galinsea, for I did not look forward to kingship, to presiding over a nation that preferred to steal art – or raze it – rather than create its own. Most Galinseans are heathen when it comes to art or poetry, music and dance.'

'I'm sure you are too harsh, Lazar. Did it not occur to you to be a king who changed his people's attitude?'

'I was nineteen when I fled Galinsea.'

Pez took Lazar's hand. 'And Boaz is as good as seventeen and running his realm.'

Lazar looked abashed. 'He is a better man than me.'

'And now you speak rubbish like a true Galinsean! When will you accept that you were born to lead? You can't help yourself, you have kingship qualities in your blood – you cannot escape your line.'

'I have.'

'And yet here we go, heading back to Galinsea from where you hail, from where you fled, from where you think you can hide.'

'You're right,' he admitted. 'I can no longer hide.'

'That's right. It won't stop here. They will find you.'

'I know. I have been thinking that once this is over — if we can avert war — maybe I'll leave Percheron.'

'Run away again? We need you, Lazar. Boaz needs you and, more importantly, Percheron itself needs you — not just because you are its Spur, but I'll risk boring you again by reminding you that we are caught up in a different battle as well.'

'That one has to wait.'

'It will take its own course as and when it chooses.'

'As and when you know who the Goddess is,' Lazar reminded.

Pez ignored his jibe and left the topic of Galinsea alone for the time being. 'Have you noticed how friendly he is to her?'

Lazar didn't need to ask to whom Pez was referring. 'Yes.' He sighed. 'She is falling for his charms.' He noticed the dwarf baulk. 'Oh, I don't mean he is seducing her for her flesh. No, he is winning her as a friend, something Ana so badly needs. I can't blame her for being attracted to his charismatic ways. If we didn't know better, perhaps we might fall for them too.'

'I can't tell you how dangerous this situation becomes if Maliz has her under some sort of influence.'

'She is *not* Lyana. Her very presence here, alive and well, should assure you of that.'

'It doesn't!' Pez snapped. 'Ellyana said it would be different this time. And it is. Ana is involved. Her name suggests she is.'

'And now you're grasping at the proverbial camel's hair, Pez, and you don't have a good grip.'

'If you don't trust me, at least humour me. I have never led you down a wrong path. Please, if just for my own sanity, go along with this. Allow that I might be right and that he is preying on her.'

'For what? What can he gain?'

'If she is not Lyana, as you claim, then I have to presume he believes, as I do, that she knows who Lyana is or she can lead us to the real Goddess.'

That stopped Lazar in his tracks. 'I hadn't considered that.'

'Well, do so now. And keep walking. He watches our every move.'

'Hush,' Lazar warned as Salim approached.

Pez was already humming a nonsense song and picking his nose.

'We should mount up now,' the Khalid suggested.

Lazar nodded and held a hand up to slow the column to a halt. Pez just kept striding on, adding a skip every few steps.

Lazar could feel the sweat seeping into the back of his shirt and, as he walked towards the royals and against the soft flurry of the sands, he wrapped the desert turban around his face so that only his light eyes could be seen.

He bowed. 'Valide, Zaradine. We ride from here for the next two hours.'

'I have never ridden a camel before,' Herezah said, still sulky. These were her first words since they broke camp.

'I will show you, Valide. Come, I will get you mounted.'

He flicked a glance towards Ana and saw the soft hurt flash in her gaze. 'Zaradine Ana, Salim here will help you onto your beast. Tariq . . .'

'I can manage, thank you, Spur,' the Grand Vizier said, and shooed away any help. 'You looked as though you were in tall conversation with Pez. The Zaradine here says Pez would be talking his usual nonsense and you apparently humour him.'

Lazar did not miss a beat. 'Zaradine Ana has been quick to notice lots about the palace and to understand its ways. She appreciates the value of Pez for his humour. Yes, he is mad but sometimes his very madness can bring a strange sort of clarity to those around him. Laughter is a great tonic.'

'I didn't notice you laughing, Spur,' the Grand Vizier said, more slyly now.

'You were obviously not paying enough attention, Tariq. Pez was teaching me one of his nonsense songs. I went along with it as a way of taking my mind off the tedium of our journey.'

'Was it the song about the butterfly and the ass?'

'No, he did sing that one to me yesterday, Zaradine, but it was actually the one about smashed pomegranates that seemed to amuse him this morning.'

'Oh yes, I know that one. It's funny, even though it's so silly.'

'Quite,' Lazar said and gave her a soft smile. 'I do humour Pez, Grand Vizier, and it would be helpful if you would too. He has his place and his part to play for the palace but he is fragile and I'd rather not deal with him in one of his strange moods if I can help it.'

'I shall do my best, Spur.'

Lazar nodded his thanks and hoped Ana would notice how he included her in those as he swept his gaze by her and back to Herezah. 'Shall we go, Valide?' he said, knowing she would have felt a small stab of triumph at his sudden humility towards her. His good sense had overridden his anger for the time being and he had decided during these hours of walking not to lose his temper again with her. She would find ways to punish Ana instead and he needed everyone calm and ready for the ordeal of the desert.

Jumo waited by the Valide's camel with her handler. 'This is Masha,' he said, 'and we are assured she will not try any tricks.'

'Good,' Herezah replied, looking dubiously at the kneeling animal, which chewed indifferently, awaiting her burden.

'We won't ride like the Khalim, Valide,' Lazar said politely. 'We will seat you at the back of the camel's hump but on top of a saddle that is laden with blankets.'

'You're not trying to sell me on the idea that this is going to be comfortable are you, Spur Lazar?' she replied, a little more like the sarcastic Herezah of old.

'I wouldn't dare. But you will get used to her swinging gait quickly and my best advice is that you simply allow your body to drift with hers. Don't fight it, just go with it and by this evening you will move in tandem with her.'

Herezah pointed. 'That man – that tribal man over there – he is kneeling on his saddle.'

Lazar shook his head in some awe. 'I know, it's their way. They can go at full gallop like that and never lose their balance. I always swore I'd learn how to do that.'

'Is this why you suggested I wear the pants and robes of the desert, Lazar?' she said, a tease in her voice now.

'It is,' he joked in his deadpan way. 'You will be more comfortable for riding and, I promise you, Valide, you are far cooler in these robes than your formal wear in the palace.'

'I swear I wouldn't be comfortable in this heat even if I were naked!'

Jumo stifled a grin whilst Lazar just looked pained. Herezah was back to her flirtatious best.

She could hardly miss his grimace. 'I was making a jest, Lazar. Have you ever understood the concept of one making a jest and the listener smiling, even just to be polite?'

'Yes, Valide. As you can see, I'm not very good at it.'

'Indeed.' She rested her hand on his shoulder and gave an appreciative smile at touching him. Then she seemed to lose her footing and Lazar had to step up close to steady her, his hands unwittingly clasping her waist, and her hands more knowingly going around his neck. 'Thank you,' she breathed and loaded the words to mean so much more. 'These are certainly slippery creatures to climb aboard.'

Jumo gave Lazar a look of soft exasperation, for Masha had not so much as blinked whilst Herezah was attempting to mount her. Lazar feigned all was well and allowed her hands to linger around his neck as he ensured she was seated properly on the saddle.

'As I said,' he began, releasing himself from her embrace, 'not exactly comfortable but you should not be too sore if you don't resist the swaying.'

'I shall remember that,' Herezah said, and all three of them knew she was not referring to his advice so much as his touch. 'That's the sort of tip we give new girls in the harem,' and she pretended to stifle a playful smile.

Lazar kept his expression deliberately blank in response, whilst he turned to check that Ana and the Vizier were on their camels; as he did so, he saw the look of injury that Ana threw at him. She hadn't failed to notice Herezah's pantomime.

'Come,' Jumo said, well able to read the undercurrent swirling around him. 'The sun has no patience.'

And the caravan finally got moving, all on four legs, at a faster pace.

⅏ 29 ⅏

The first seven days passed in a monotonous routine and everyone settled into rising before dawn, walking for a few hours until the sun noticed them and threw down her fury. They would ride for another four hours, hardly wasting words, focused on nothing other than the swaying of their camels, and making it through the next hour when the skins of water would be handed around. The camels did not drink any of their water during this time but Lazar knew from Salim's urgings that on this eighth day they must make it to a well or the animals would simply stop. Everyone, including the royals, had given up eating until the cool of the evening — no-one even bothered with the flatbread of a morning any more.

Salim complained that if his men had been allowed to bring a saluki, the dog could have coursed for the desert hare and fresh meat might have been enjoyed. Fortunately he had shared this gripe only with Lazar, who kept it to himself. He didn't need anyone fantasising about roasted fresh meat when all they had was thin dried strips of goat that had been packed at the palace.

Still, it, together with the flatbread they cooked each evening, oil, dried fruits, nuts, kept them alive. He knew everyone's stomach was grinding as it began to adjust to this lean new diet and soon he imagined the gauntness that struck all desert travellers would begin to appear amongst the ranks of this party. His body was already wasted enough and he was sensible enough to take Jumo's advice seriously that he should eat more.

'We can always kill one of the camels in the future,' Jumo had urged at the outset.

Salim had come up with a solution this morning when they had woken groggily to the screech of several falcons swooping above.

'If we could catch ourselves a bird, he could hunt hare, bustard, just as easily as a saluki.'

'How?' Lazar asked, intrigued.

'If we find the well today, then we will rest the caravan and take that time to hunt a bird.'

Lazar nodded, more out of fascination at the idea of trapping and taming a falcon. 'This well, you're sure it's about two hours from here?'

Salim shook his head. 'There is no surety in The Empty, my friend.'

'Then—'

'But we have knowledge that a well should be due two hours west of here,' Salim finished.

Lazar accepted this — what else could he do but get the caravan moving in its westerly direction and hope the Khalid's 'knowledge', as Salim put it, was true?

An unspoken truce had fashioned itself around the Spur and the Valide, and most in the party, including the Elim, were feeling less tension on the journey as a result. Lazar didn't trust the easy manner of Herezah, of course — he had known her long enough to appreciate the masterful pragmatism she could demonstrate when cornered. Herezah had no doubt taken stock, realised that she had no supporters amongst this company and that to lock horns with the only person who would feel obliged to protect her was sheer madness. Lazar knew the Elim were entrusted with her care and safety, but she had punished them for so long that he was sure if it came to a choice between saving Ana or the Valide, they would choose the girl. The Spur was different. He was bound by oath allegiance to his Zar, her son. He was not so sure which way he would go if forced to make that same choice.

Herezah's good sense had prevailed during this last week and she had bit back on her own fury, swallowed her pride and allowed this uneasy peace between herself and the Spur to build. It certainly made for a less tempestuous time and she noticed that Lazar was dropping back from the head of the caravan more frequently now to talk with the royal party. He seemed ever so slightly more relaxed – that is, she thought grimly, if a stern expression and distinct lack of humour could be considered relaxed.

She noticed he paid Ana no special attention and seemed to enjoy the Grand Vizier's company, although once again, how did one tell if Lazar was enjoying anything? He certainly talked more to Tariq than either of them. Ana was saying little enough anyway. The girl had become all but mute these past few days, withdrawing entirely into herself.

'What is wrong with you, child?' Herezah finally enquired. 'Why don't you speak?'

'Forgive me, Valide, I have kept myself to myself because I haven't been feeling well.'

'What sort of unwell?' Tariq enquired gently. 'Do you need more water? I can—'

'No, I'm not overly thirsty,' Ana replied. 'I just feel slightly nauseous.'

Herezah shared a sly glance with the Grand Vizier and both knew they were wondering the same thing – whether Ana was already pregnant.

'Don't worry on my account,' Ana continued. 'I'm perfectly capable of the journey, just not in the mood for conversation.'

'That's all right, Zaradine Ana,' Maliz said, and touched her arm. He satisfied himself that he felt nothing once again. 'Just keep us informed. We're here to protect you.'

Ana gave him a small smile of thanks from behind her veil and returned to her silence. They rode on for another hour and it was Jumo who dropped back this time, smiling widely and with information that was obviously good news.

'We have found the well. We shall stop here for the rest of the day, water the camels and replenish our own stores.'

'I thought these beasts didn't require watering.'

Even Maliz laughed. 'Do you mean *ever*, Valide?' he said and bowed to show he meant no disrespect, simply some levity. 'Camels can go for long periods without water – in this case I think we've been travelling, what is it, seven full days?' Jumo nodded. 'We will no doubt plot our journey by the availability of wells. The beasts need to drink for many hours to refresh themselves and then they can last for a long time.'

Herezah didn't reply but didn't look abashed either. Camels were meaningless, smelly beasts of burden as far as she was concerned and so long as one didn't die beneath her, that was all she needed to know about them.

'So we camp here?'

'Yes, Valide. The Spur, myself and some of the Khalid are going hunting after the watering but the Elim will remain to guard you.'

'Hunting?' Herezah said, her eyebrows arching with surprise. 'What?'

'Falcons,' Jumo replied, unable on this occasion to conceal his excitement.

'Oh, I should like to see that,' the Grand Vizier said. 'Include me in the party.'

'I shall let the Spur know your wish, Grand Vizier.'

The atmosphere around the camp was almost festive as the tents went up far earlier than usual, and everyone could sense the Khalids' relief that they had found the promised well. It had been unused for a long time and half buried, but nothing that three men digging hard for an hour couldn't unearth. Before long the water was surging again, goatskins were being replenished and the camels were happily restoring themselves. Men's laughter could be heard and conversation was flowing in tandem with the water.

Lazar sipped the bitter nectar from the earth and grinned for the first time in ages, it seemed to Jumo and Pez. 'Sherem!' he said to Salim.

'Sherem!' the Khalid echoed, offering up good health to all.

Pez turned cartwheels for everyone and the Khalid laughed and clapped. They had already worked out that the dwarf was insane but it troubled them not; they seemed to like the little man who entertained them with his acrobatics and obvious problem with flatulence, which he seemed to save for whenever the royal party were near him.

'And now we hunt the falcon,' Salim said to Lazar. 'Come.'

Jumo had already mentioned to Lazar that the Vizier was keen to observe and this news had been greeted with a scowl but Lazar could hardly refuse, so the Grand Vizier, together with Lazar, Jumo, a babbling Pez and four of the Khalid, set off, having taken their leave from the women and the rest of the party.

They moved slowly on foot for the sun was scorching the sands this day. Nothing moved, other than themselves, not even a scorpion or snake, both of which seemed impervious to the desert elements. And then they heard it, the high-pitched shriek of the two falcons that had seemed to follow them on this journey.

Lazar mentioned this to Salim, who agreed. 'These birds are patient. They wait, they watch, they are opportunists who never know when something might move that they can hunt and eat.'

'So what do we lure them with?'

Salim touched his nose in a knowing way. 'Watch,' he said and pointed to one of his men, who dragged from a sack at his waist a plump pigeon.

Everyone's mouths went slack. 'He's had that with him for the whole way?' Lazar asked the question on the mind of everyone who wasn't Khalid.

Pez waddled up and stroked the pigeon's head, licking his lips in an obscene way.

'Very lucky none of us discovered that stowaway until

now,' the Vizier commented, for once agreeing with the dwarf. 'I love roasted pigeon.'

'What now?' Lazar asked.

'We make a hide. Only one man can do this bit so you will have to simply watch from a distance. It needs patience so if any of you don't think you can make it through an hour or more of absolute stillness beneath this sun, then you should return to the camp now.'

Lazar nodded. 'We understand.' He looked around at the party and translated. No-one blinked. 'I think everyone here wants to remain. We'll need some shade, though.'

Three of the Khalid unravelled fabric that had been tied around their waist. It was the same colour as the sand.

'This is what we use,' Salim said as the lengths were given to the Percherese. 'From the sky, if you remain still and upwind, the falcon will not know.'

The Khalid showed the uninitiated how to set up their shade, even how to sit. And then the Percherese watched with great interest as the men of the desert set about digging a hole into the sand to create the hide with yet more of the fabric. Once that was completed, Salim came over to remind his audience of the need for silence and stillness. As he climbed into the hole, Pez began to sing softly and Maliz watched Lazar quieten him with a gentle touch to his shoulder.

'Why is he here?' Maliz asked, his tone still with its good humour and yet there was a sense of irritation beneath the enquiry.

'For the same reason you are, Grand Vizier.'

'He's told you he wanted to witness this, did he?'

'In his way, yes. I have known Pez for almost two

decades as you have, but I understand him through his eccentricities.'

The Grand Vizier did not look convinced and was about to say so when he was interrupted.

'Hush,' Jumo murmured. 'They are ready. Do you see, they have tied a length of all-but-invisible string to the leg of the pigeon, its other end to a stone. The falcons are still here, hovering, circling. They are peregrine – shahin – and prized.'

'Do they not use the hawk?' Maliz whispered, captivated by the scene unfolding.

'They prefer the shahin for their speed, courage and tenacity. A shahin does not give up.'

'So why would they ever use a hawk? I've seen them used on the gravel plains.'

'My understanding,' Jumo whispered, wondering, as both Lazar and Pez were, when Tariq had ever visited the gravel plains two hundred miles north of Percheron, 'is that the hawk – or hurr, as the desert tribes call it – has better eyesight and is more suited to that region.'

Maliz nodded, satisfied, seemingly unaware of questions silently flying around him. Pez had been in the palace for longer than Tariq and had never heard him speak of travelling beyond the city and its regions.

Lazar believed Maliz had made his first real mistake in revealing himself. He knew for a fact that Tariq had not done much travelling beyond the city's borders and also that the Vizier – as he'd been for most of his life at the palace – would have sneered at anything connected with the desert.

'The Khalid will launch her now,' Jumo whispered.

'You know a great deal about this, my friend,' Lazar murmured. 'I'm impressed.'

Jumo shrugged. 'We hawked as youngsters but we were told stories about the desert tribes of the Great Waste and their shahin. I feel privileged to share this.'

Lazar smiled inwardly. Jumo suddenly looked like a boy again in his obvious excitement.

'Here she goes,' Jumo warned. And at his words, the pigeon was thrown aloft and with a great flapping of wings she steadied in the air and then began to ascend, the string unravelling behind her.

The falcons saw her immediately, for a pigeon is hardly silent in its bustling effort to rise. One flew behind her, banked, and then dipped its wing, shaping itself into an arrow that would swoop through a killing arc. The men watched, enthralled as the pigeon, still ascending and unaware of the danger, was hit at full force and killed in the air before both birds toppled back to the sands.

Salim cautiously appeared and stealthily made his way to the stone to which the string was still attached. Up ahead the bird of prey was tearing at feathers and flesh.

Jumo spoke softly, answering the question burning in everyone's mind except Pez's it seemed; he was unravelling a long thread from his robes, smiling at its endless length. 'The falcon always faces upwind. This means it cannot pick up the scent of the man. It is also gorging now, not paying as much attention to its surrounds as it might otherwise. It is vulnerable in these moments only. Watch.'

The string was ever so slowly reeled back in and the falcon came closer and closer until it was barely a stride away from Salim secreted in the hide. He waited patiently for the hunting bird to be so engrossed in its kill that it didn't even sense the reaching arms and only realised it was caught when the Khalid began shouting and cheering.

The group returned to camp triumphant and everyone watched with fascination as Salim threaded a piece of cotton through each of the bird's lower lids and tied the ends at the top of its head, drawing the lids up so the falcon was now blinded.

'How long does it take to train him?' Herezah asked, the most fascinated of all.

'Depending on her intelligence, she can be ready in a week.'

Sounds of surprise came from the audience.

'That fast?' Lazar asked, incredulous.

Salim nodded. 'I promise you, meat in a week.'

That night, everyone slept well and happy at the thought of fresh meat – everyone, that is, except one: Ana did not eat birds.

Pez felt unusually restless. He lay on his back, hands behind his head and looked with awe at the canopy of stars winking in concert. Pez knew it was impossible but it felt to him as if a storm was brewing; he was a person who had always been sensitive to weather changes and as a child if thunder and lightning occurred, he would start acting oddly hours beforehand. He would become agitated, unable to concentrate or be still. That's how he felt now and even though he had – in private, at least – grown out of the immature behaviour of running in circles or making a lot of noise when a lightning storm was coming, he had never lost the sensation of inward turmoil.

It had not happened that often over the years, if he was honest. Living in Percheron meant temperate weather most of the year but from time to time a storm would hit and would bring with it the fire in the sky that so excited him and yet also gave him a sense of doom . . . the sinister thunder rolls in the distance always suggested to him that something ominous was coming.

There was no lightning and certainly no thunder now – just a supremely clear and starry night that was frigidly cold despite the heat of the low fire everyone slept close to, apart from the Khalid who preferred to sleep alongside their camels and use the warmth of the beasts to heat them. Pez could see that even Lazar was snoozing – no doubt lightly – but the rhythmic rise and fall of the man's chest suggested he was asleep. He sat up and smiled to himself with the amusing thought that he might be one of the few people, ever, to see Lazar relaxed in slumber. With his face in repose, Lazar looked young, the flames of the fire smoothing out the lines of his face, the hollows in his cheeks, that had so deepened with his illness. In truth, this journey, despite all of its danger, was helping Lazar to recover better than any potion or quiet existence on an island. Lazar was a man of action. The journey would do him immense good but Pez still appreciated the untroubled, no longer grave countenance that the quiet suspension of sleep brought to Lazar. He almost wished he could wake Ana and show her how friendly Lazar could look . . . so long as he wasn't awake.

This amused him too and he silently stirred himself and climbed to his feet to stretch. The thought of Ana prompted him to get up and out of the warmth of his blankets – he had no idea why. Now that he was up he might as well move.

He glanced at Lazar and noticed his friend's eyes were suddenly wide open.

'Ah,' he whispered. 'And there was I thinking how peaceful you looked.'

No-one else stirred. Jumo was snoring and the royal tents were still. None of the Khalid moved.

'I was – you woke me.'

'I was silent,' Pez hissed.

'You're like one of the Zar's elephants moving around.' And the edge of his mouth creased in a grin but was gone as swiftly as it arrived. 'What are you doing anyway?'

'Going to relieve myself.'

Lazar nodded, closed his eyes and rolled over. 'Don't go far,' he murmured.

Pez hadn't known he was going anywhere until this moment. Pulling his blanket around his shoulders and uncaring of it dragging along the sands, he made for the closest dune but one well away from the main camp.

He turned to look back. In the tiny circle of light that the small fire threw out, everyone appeared fast asleep. He cursed his luck that he wasn't, especially as he had felt tired enough to be one of the first to snuggle beneath his blankets, singing a lullaby to himself about cranberry sherbet.

Pez slipped into the black void behind the dune and decided he might as well relieve himself now that he was here. As the stream of hot liquid brought a familiar sound of all things normal and his bladder thanked him for this unexpected comfort, a voice spoke to him and both bladder and its flow froze in fear.

'Pez, thank you for coming.'

'Who—'

She materialised beside him, her own glow giving him just sufficient light to recognise her.

'Ellyana.'

'Are you done?' she asked and smiled so kindly, he didn't even register any embarrassment as he covered himself.

'How did you—'

'Always so many questions. Come, we have things to discuss.'

'Come where? If I'm gone for more than a few moments, Lazar will—'

'He will not know. Trust me.'

She led him deeper into the desert towards a nearby dune, which, when he arrived closer, he realised held some sort of rocky cave at its base.

'Why didn't we see this when we made camp?'

'You don't have to whisper, Pez. No-one can hear us.' She smiled. 'The sands hide and the sands reveal, as they choose. There are plenty of rocky outcrops and cave systems in the desert but most are covered by the sands.'

'What are you doing here?' He had lost his initial shock and decided to be direct. Ellyana had a talent for being vague.

'I wanted to see you.'

'Why not the others?'

'Well, to begin with I suspect Jumo wishes to stick a blade into me.'

He frowned. 'You may be right.'

'Although I suspect that deep down he'd admit that he'd go through the same pain and ordeal if it meant life for Lazar.'

'I suspect he would. Jumo is loyal to the death.'

'Yes, he is. Poor Jumo,' she said, and looked at the sky, her tone wistful.

'What does that mean?'

She shrugged. 'He is a good man.'

'What do you want, Ellyana?'

'I need you to do something for me.'

'Your tasks have a way of turning nasty. You know about Zafira, presumably?' There was no friendship in his tone now as he recalled the devastating moment of discovering his old friend, impaled on her own temple's spire. All for the sake of her faith and the demon who hunted his followers.

'That was the work of Maliz.'

'Your hands have her blood on them too, Ellyana. You put her into that danger. She had nothing to fight him with, no wings, no magic, probably no idea he was even coming for her.'

'Zafira went to her death willingly, Pez. She was brave, she was old and she was ready to sacrifice herself for Lyana.'

'Lyana! I'm sick of hearing her name! She is not Ana. You have led me wrong. You have lied and cajoled and got us all to do your bidding but I'm no longer your servant, Ellyana.' In his anger and frustration he startled himself with the sensation that he might weep.

She noticed it too. 'This is a cause worth weeping over, Pez. Your memories as Iridor will tell you that lives have been lost in many ways and on so many occasions that for their sake alone – for their endeavours and their bravery – we must fight on. We have no choice, my friend. You are Iridor and you have a reason for being.'

Pez hung his head. 'She calls him friend now.'

'I know,' she replied, her voice tender again. 'But she is safe for the time being.'

'How? How can he spend time with her and touch her and not know?'

'I warned that this time it would be different,' she replied – more cautiously now, he noticed. Pez had learned that when Ellyana took this approach, she was usually not telling the full truth, using her talent to divert him.

'Why can't you just be honest and tell us?' he demanded.

'Because you must trust. The less each knows, the better . . . and Pez, I am but a servant, like you. Don't presume that I have all the answers.'

'But you never give us any answers, only questions.'

'I am not your enemy.'

'Sometimes it feels as if you are,' he grumbled, but she could see her words rang true with him.

'Please, Pez, trust me.'

'What do you want me to do?'

And as she told him, his eyes widened and his mouth opened in disbelief.

'I cannot,' he whispered. 'I will not.'

'You must!' she impressed. 'For her sake, you must. It is her protection.'

He began to look around wildly, desperate for someone to save him, ridiculously hopeful that Lazar would step around the dune now and demand to know what was going on.

'Pez, you are Iridor. You are the messenger, the go-between, the only conduit we have.' She tried to offer him something but he let it slip to the sand.

'I cannot,' he repeated.

Ellyana picked up what was dropped and pressed it into his gnarled hands. 'You must,' she urged. 'Trust me,' she now beseeched and her expression was one of such supplication, all that was Iridor within him responded and he clutched her gift to his breast, tears leaking down his misshapen face.

'Go now, my precious one. We fight this battle with stealth and cunning this time.'

'And we shall win,' he said, trying not to make it a question but a mantra to cling to.

'We will win,' she assured.

He watched Ellyana, or the vision that she could become, fade into the darkness of the desert night until he was alone, suddenly cold again. He looked at what he clutched near his heart and felt the knife of fear at what he had been charged to do.

Pez didn't know how long he stayed in that position or when he finally decided to move and pick his way back to the camp but as he pushed himself deeper into his blankets Lazar spoke.

'That was quick,' he mumbled. 'Now sleep, Pez.'

The little man wriggled closer to the fire but no amount of heat was going to smother the chill he felt in his heart at Ellyana's bidding.

∞ 30 ∞

The week passed in a slow cycle of repetitive days. Herezah
no longer complained and was one of the first to rise,
dress carefully in her desert robes and be ready to travel.
She now ate walking, on camel back, or whenever she was
hungry – there was no longer any ceremony in her life,
although Lazar had to admit she maintained a great
elegance in all that she did, even here in the desert. He
allowed them one bowl of water every three days to wash
and appreciated how hard this was for someone like
Herezah who had known daily bathing rituals since she
was a little girl. It seemed the release from the harem
that this journey afforded Herezah had offered her a
glimpse at how life could be without plotting and cunning,
without always looking ahead to where the next iota of
power could be gained over the people she was forced to
share her life with.

Lazar understood. The desert was a great equaliser. As
he had told her, there was no status out here. Survival
meant everyone helping each other, respecting one another,
sharing . . . all concepts the Valide had forgotten or had
gradually had squeezed out of her in the selfish, single-
minded existence of the harem.

Ana was quiet and eating little. Lazar asked Herezah

how the Zaradine was faring and she simply waved her hand and told him not to worry.

'All new wives become broody and introverted. She'll get over it.'

'She's not eating much.'

'Are you keeping such a close eye, Lazar?' she asked, eyebrow arched. She meant it in jest but of course Lazar wasn't used to genuine lightheartedness from the Valide. With him he bounced between viciousness and lustfulness – there had never been an in between.

'She is the reason for this perilous journey, Valide,' he answered gravely. 'Of course I'm keeping a close eye on her.' In fact it was Pez who knew Ana was not eating much, for he liked to be around the cookpot for the evening meal and the group allowed him to stir the broth or cook the flatbread – a simple enough task, even for an idiot. He shared the duties with one of the Elim, the mute called Salazin, in charge of supervising the preparation and presentation of all the royal food. Pez liked to hand the food out, too, and it annoyed Herezah no end that he always bowed rather comically to the Zaradine before handing her a bowl and bread, urging her to eat, watching her take her first ladleful or bite, but somehow managed to spill the Valide's broth on the rare occasion one was cooked, or drop the Grand Vizier's bread in the sand.

'Well, you have no reason to fret. She has complained of an upset belly but I have given her something for that. It will ease.'

'Perhaps she will brighten with some fresh meat.'

'I think we all will. This diet is excellent in preserving one's figure but it makes me feel weak. I need blood now and then, Lazar,' she said and eyed him directly.

Lazar left it at that, for the conversation was going in a direction he didn't want it to, but he intended to keep his own watch over the Zaradine who appeared to have faded these past couple of days. She no longer watched him, and he didn't believe she had spoken more than a few words in recent times. Jumo confirmed she hardly conversed with him either. If she was sickening, Lazar needed to know.

Neither the Valide nor the Grand Vizier shared with him their suspicions as to why the Zaradine was suddenly so off-colour, preferring instead to keep it a secret for now. Information was a weapon – something they both understood – and to be wielded only at the right time.

On this evening they were sitting around the usual three campfires. The Khalid sat around their own and talked in their curious language that sounded as though they were always arguing with one another. Lazar, Jumo and Pez tended to range between either the Khalid's or the royal party's fires. The Elim kept themselves entirely separate, although never far from their two female royals.

Tonight the royal fire included Lazar and Jumo. Pez was dancing a jig for the Elim, who sang for him. The royal party watched the Khalid and particularly Salim with his falcon.

'Have they named him?' Herezah asked.

'It's a female falcon. She's simply called Shahin,' Jumo answered.

'Why do they stroke her all the time? I don't think that man has been separated from the bird. He even sleeps with it tied to a post near his face.'

Jumo nodded. 'That's right, Valide. When they are training it to the lure, the person who is taming it must give every moment to that bird. He talks to it, touches it all the time, keeps it close. The bird gets used to the man in particular but also the talk of men, the movements of men and is not startled by us. They will brand it soon on the beak with Salim's mark and it will be finally his – companion, provider, friend.'

'So the falcon can definitely hunt?' Herezah asked, her eyes glittering in anticipation.

'She is magnificent on the wing.'

Both she and the Grand Vizier sighed. 'It will certainly be nice to taste some fresh meat again,' Maliz admitted, as the flatbread diet was wearing on everyone now. The cheese and fruit were dished out sparingly and had become such a treat that Herezah admitted she couldn't imagine what it would be like to sit down to a palace meal again with all of its decadence and sophistication.

'How much longer, Lazar?' she said to the Spur, who seemed deep in thought, his hollowed face even more handsome in its gauntness. His guarded expression looked more vulnerable now and the chin he no longer kept rigorously shaven had a thin close growth of hair. He was beginning to look like one of those priests they'd heard about who did a special penance by living in the desert for weeks on end.

But then Lazar always looked as though he was doing penance. Nevertheless, when he raised his eyes to her to answer, she felt the familiar thrill of being close to him and his attention given to her. In the past she would take that attention whether it was accompanied with his usual gruffness or just his disdain. Since she had realised she had no allies and was making an effort to cooperate, she had noticed a slackening of that cool aloofness he maintained.

She had discovered he was even capable of conversation and had been stunned a few days back when he had joined herself, Ana and the Grand Vizier and spent an hour talking about desert life, even reminiscing about his first experience with it when he was making his escape towards Percheron.

It had been so tempting to ask why he had needed to flee Galinsea but the truth was Herezah was, for a rare time, enjoying the simple pleasure of conversation and the even greater pleasure of seeing Lazar relaxed in her company – even smiling, praise Zarab – such that she was not prepared to risk the moment in curiosity. She knew what would have happened. He would have thrown down the shutters of his mind, his face taking on that sober, blank expression as though chiselled in stone, and he would have made some excuse to leave them. And so she had promised herself to do nothing but listen and revel in his refreshingly easy manner for however long Zarab granted it last.

Lazar replied after several moments of calculation. 'If we continue at this pace, which is relatively good, I imagine at the new moon.'

'Twenty-two more days of this?'

'I'm afraid so,' he answered her, and all noticed she didn't spit it – as the Herezah of the palace might have – it was simply a statement, accompanied by nothing more than a soft shrug. The desert was doing the Valide a power of good.

'Zaradine Ana, are you keeping up your water intake?' he asked gently.

She nodded wanly. 'Yes, of course. You gave us strict instructions.'

'You are very quiet.'

'I am fine, Spur, thank you.'

'Perhaps we can offer you some dates. The sugar will help.'

'I couldn't eat anything more,' she said softly.

Looks passed around the fire. She hadn't eaten anything of substance, barely nibbled at her bread.

'I think we should all get some sleep,' Lazar advised. 'We will get up a little earlier than usual as we'll need to give some time in the cooler hours of the day to hunting the desert bustard.'

'They're definitely here?' Herezah was obviously determined to eat well tomorrow evening.

Jumo answered. 'Yes, we have seen them and they are relatively plentiful in this region.'

'Sweet dreams, all, then,' the Grand Vizier said, rising and stretching. 'Come, Zaradine, let me escort you to your tent.'

Lazar scowled, but he covered his expression quickly and offered to walk Herezah back to the tent. She looked delighted and took his arm. Nevertheless he kept his eyes rigidly facing forward on the back of the Grand Vizier, who now put his arm around the small figure of Ana as they strolled back to the accommodation.

Tomorrow, Lazar promised himself, he would try and get some time alone with Ana. He had to know what was wrong with her.

Shahin was beautiful, Lazar decided, and so proud as she rode on the arm of Salim.

'She is tame now,' Salim told him. 'She will always enjoy a man as her companion now.'

'Is she not attached to just one man? You?'

'Only to begin with. We sell our birds all the time and so long as they are treated well, they will cleave to a new owner. This one, however, is special. There is an intensity to this falcon I have not seen in a long time and she learns so fast. She is valuable.'

'So you will not be selling her?'

'Never.'

Jumo and one of the Khalid riders arrived excited.

'They're just over the rise – at least four of them,' Jumo said.

Lazar actually smiled. He really had never seen Jumo so excited and could understand that his friend was reliving a boyhood memory with this hunt. He wondered why they had never hunted with birds before, the two of them. They would from now on.

'If we had dogs it would be easier. Dogs and falcons are invincible when they work together,' Salim bemoaned.

Lazar hadn't realised that the salukis and shahin would normally work in partnership. 'Can she kill enough?'

'Oh yes, but the bustard is a fearsome prey. It fights hard to its death but it also squirts an oily muck at its predator and it will take many days before we can fully clean a falcon of the mess on her feathers. That's why we use dogs and more than one bird.'

'How many can she take alone?'

He shrugged. 'A good one can probably kill up to eight or nine but they will take six or seven on the wing to half that on the ground.'

'So we have to get the bustards moving?'

'Yes, my friend, that's your job.'

And so with guidance from the other Khalid men,

Lazar and Jumo, with Pez flapping his arms and hobbling alongside mimicking the bustards, flushed the fat desert birds from their hollows in the sand.

It was several hours of mighty battles for Shahin. Sometimes the fight would rage over forty yards whilst she battled with her prey. The bustard was a warrior. Oil was splotched darkly over the golden ground in its attempts to thwart its attacker, but Shahin was wily and had obviously hunted this prey on many occasions when she was wild, for she nimbly avoided being coated. She was not so successful in avoiding the blow from its wings and on her third kill was stunned by one of these blows.

Salim finished off the dying bustard, breaking its neck, for he was worried about his falcon. She came around, though, and within a short while was taking her fourth, initially on the wing and killing it fully on the sands.

'A beautiful sight,' Jumo murmured, as they watched the two birds tussle in the air and then plummet behind a particularly large dune.

'Ah, if we had the dogs, this would be so much easier,' Salim sighed.

'I'll get it . . . and her,' Jumo said in high excitement and sprinted off towards the dune.

'Have you ever seen him like that?' Pez asked, out of earshot of the others, as he looked at Lazar's uncharacteristically open and grinning expression.

'Not in all the time I've known him,' Lazar said, scratching his head. 'We're definitely going to do this again, Jumo and I. We shall train our own birds and hunt regularly once this is all done.'

'And grow old together – you make a fine pair,' Pez said, with only a hint of sarcasm.

'You know what I mean. This is fun. Jumo and I spend so much time in our dutiful pursuits for the throne that we forget to stop sometimes and just do things like this.' He waved his arm at where Jumo was just scrambling over the dune, his arms cartwheeling as he reached the summit. 'Simple sport, utterly carefree.' He laughed as his friend turned and waved before disappearing at a full run down the other side.

Pez touched his arm. 'Keep that promise, it is very good for your disposition too,' he said and winked. 'I don't think I've ever seen you so relaxed.'

Lazar's smile faded. 'You know, Pez, I've never felt quite as carefree as I do at this moment. I know it won't last but right now I feel as though I have no responsibilities, no duty to anyone, no politics or diplomacies to consider . . . nothing but freedom and enjoying being amongst a companionable group. I feel closer to Salim in this short time we've known each other than I have to anyone else in Percheron in almost two decades, save yourself and Jumo.'

'That's because you let Salim in. You're so controlled all the time, Lazar, and so deliberately distant that no-one can be your friend. You let me in because I was a freak and allowed you to discover my secret; and you let Jumo in because he was different, not one of the Percherese. You seem to like underdogs. Salim is Khalid – that makes him different, exotic, and, of course, he speaks another language so that makes him entirely inaccessible to the rest of the party except yourself and Jumo. And then there's Ana—'

'Don't, Pez. It's hard enough. I need no reminding.'

The dwarf sighed. 'I'm sorry. Enjoy your light mood.

Without the Vizier around, thank Lyana he felt obliged to keep Ana company, we can all be carefree,' and he began to mimic soaring like Shahin. 'I'm going to find Jumo and our wonderful falcon,' he called behind his back, flapping his arms and struggling up the sand dune.

The other men were already excitedly running up the dune to catch Jumo, with Pez in hot pursuit, pretending to chase them down as Shahin had done her latest kill. Lazar had to admit he did feel lighthearted – he couldn't remember when last he felt this way – and he paused alone in the sands to savour this moment of pleasure.

He heard a shout go up in the distance – it was Pez, he thought – and assumed the celebrations were in full swing. They would be eating bustard tonight and perhaps Ana might brighten as well. Lazar ran up the dune feeling curiously happy, his long legs sinking into the soft golden sand, and he was still inwardly grinning, having clawed his way to the top, when he was faced with a sight more chilling than he could have ever imagined.

His mood evaporated in an instant as he stared death coldly in the face.

∽ 31 ∾

Back at the camp Ana was vomiting. She had eaten little for her first meal of the day but even that tiny amount was now staining the sands well beyond the royal tent.

'Well, if her womb has quickened – and it sounds promising – we may have begun securing your son's throne, Valide.' Maliz secretly wished he'd gone with the hunting party but he couldn't resist Ana's pleas when she had begged him to stay, frightened by her worsening state.

'I suppose I should be pleased,' Herezah sighed, fanning herself to stir the hot air beneath their canopy. 'I just wish it wasn't hers.'

'Why do you hate her so? She is good for your son.'

'No, she's not, Tariq. He is besotted with her. Boaz needs more wives if he is to truly secure his throne.'

'And you think he won't because of Ana.'

'Boaz has developed such a fascination for this girl that I don't notice him taking any interest in any of the other beautiful young women we have assembled for him. This is dangerous.'

Maliz understood more than Herezah wanted him to. He accepted her reasoning, knew what she said was right, but he also knew Herezah's main concern was how much power might be given unwittingly to Ana if she remained

Boaz's only mate. It was not so far beyond the realms of imagination that she could not only be Zaradine and Absolute Favourite but also Valide within ten moons.

'Dangerous for whom, Valide?'

'For all of us, Grand Vizier. Surely you're not naive enough to believe that one woman for the Zar is how the new regime will shape itself. It is wrong. Joreb will curse his choice of successor.'

'Joreb chose well, Valide. He chose well with his Favourite and he chose well with her son.'

Herezah eyed the Grand Vizier and felt momentarily lost for words. 'You know, Tariq, you could have said those same words to me two years ago and I would simply have sneered at you for the snivelling, self-important and oily character that you once were. Now I take them as the compliment you intended.'

'I'm glad of this. It is sincerely meant, Valide, but then I speak only the truth.'

'You never did before.'

'Before what?' he asked, amused.

'Before Joreb died, before Boaz took the throne and you went through some sort of change, emerging from your chrysalis, to give us this new sober, intelligent, charismatic Vizier.'

'Charismatic?' he echoed and smiled seductively.

'I swear you're a different man, Tariq. You didn't buy some special magic, did you, along with that magical potion you told me of that keeps you suddenly young and virile?'

'Virile?' Now he sounded disbelieving.

'Don't be coy, I see you looking at women now.'

'Why wouldn't I? Surrounded by such beauty.'

'Tariq, I have known you all of my life and not once have you looked at me in the way you look at me now. I see how you look at Ana, I see how you appreciate all women from slave to dignitaries' wives whenever they're permitted to attend formal functions. It is perfectly normal, I agree, it's just that before Joreb died, you were all but sexless.'

Maliz clapped his hands and openly laughed. 'Let's just say I hid it well, Valide. There was no room for my true personality at the palace under Joreb. The sycophant suited him.'

'He hated you.'

'But I suited you, always ready as the willing servant,' he added, seemingly unfazed by her candour.

'What changed you?'

'Boaz can benefit from me being honest.'

She felt he was speaking in riddles, giving her no clear answers, but pressed on. 'What are your intentions with Boaz?'

He became more serious, intense. 'You have nothing to fear from me, Valide. Be assured of this. My interests lie elsewhere from power and money. I do not want to be the puppeteer, simply a reliable adviser.'

'Then you truly have changed,' she said, genuinely surprised. 'Your whole life with Joreb was spent in petty power struggles with Salmeo and with gaining any little ground or notoriety for yourself out of any situation.'

'Yes, and I didn't enjoy it, Valide, but I served a purpose and I served Joreb loyally through it all.'

She acknowledged the truth of what he said with a nod. 'And now?'

'Still happy to serve.'

'Without seeking power or reward?'

'Reward comes in all shapes and sizes and all colours, Valide.' Again the shaded answer, she thought. 'With Boaz as Zar we all have the opportunity to help him shape Percheron into the single most powerful realm of the region. We are easily the richest but now we need to add strength with ships, our army, we must learn to secure our boundaries at the desert and we now have an opportunity to forge a formal peace with Galinsea that might secure the Percherese throne as a dynasty spreading many centuries. And we will all benefit in the ways we desire, I'm sure.'

'You make it sound easy.'

'It can be if people like yourself stop chasing your own little plans and simply support the Zar. You want for nothing as Valide and I know Boaz admires you tremendously – would appreciate your input frequently – but you trouble him with your desire to use him towards your own ends. If you don't mind me being frank, Valide, there should be no ends of your own. You are a woman. You cannot rule . . . not ever. But you can have a different sort of power if you'll only relent. Give up your own mission – whatever that was or is – and give yourself over entirely to Boaz's needs. I think you'll be surprised with how much he will reward you for that kind of support.'

Herezah tapped her front teeth with a fingernail that no longer shone as she liked.

He continued. 'Your association with Salmeo – and the lengths to which it has stooped,' he added, knowing she understood his meaning without him verbalising it, 'will not serve you well in the long run. Salmeo is dangerous and he himself stands on shaky ground. He has taken incredible risks because he probably believes he has your protection. I'm sure you know that Boaz has no time for him and is ever suspicious of him. If he could have pinned the Grand Master Eunuch down properly for the mystery surrounding the attempt on the Spur's life, Salmeo would no longer be drawing breath.'

'It was proven as Horz. The man admitted it,' Herezah replied.

'And you know that Horz being a murderer is as likely as me becoming a young man again.' He smiled with a wicked glint in his eye, enjoying his own jest. He had already decided that when this battle with Lyana was done and he had destroyed her once again, he would be choosing the body of a young man to inhabit, no matter what the cost to his energies. He was weary of creeping around in the bodies of old men and women, living in squalor usually and awaiting the next cycle. No, this time he planned to enjoy the time of peace in luxury and with a body that allowed him the freedom to take full advantage of such decadence. He was going to especially enjoy the pleasures of women.

In fact he had already decided on his next victim. It was too irresistible, now that he'd allowed himself to become so involved with the power merchants in the palace.

Who better than Boaz? Then he could sleep with any number of the beautiful creatures in the harem but especially he could taste the delicacy that was Ana.

It gave Maliz a warm feeling inside each time he considered this new plan of his. He would be gentle with Boaz as he died. He genuinely liked him and rather pitied that the young man must perish, but he coveted the Zar's body and his position more than any reservation that conscience would permit. His smile widened at the thought of giving lots of heirs to Percheron.

'Fret not, Valide, I will promise you something.'

'What is that?'

'Many wives for your son and plenty of heirs – in fact I think I can promise you that Boaz will lie with virtually every woman in your precious harem. What's more, I'll even let you choose the heir.'

'You will!' she echoed, incredulous.

He chuckled, cleared his throat, feigning embarrassment. 'What I meant to say is, I feel very sure that Boaz will be guided by you in his choice of heir.'

Again she felt somewhat baffled by the Grand Vizier. 'How can you guarantee me that?' she demanded.

'Just trust me, Valide, you know Boaz already does. Throw your considerable intelligence and wiles into your son. Forget everything else – join me and help me to build his power base. We can make him the most invincible Zar that has ever ruled in Percheron, and everything you desire, save ruling yourself, will come to you.'

'Trust you?'

He nodded and something in his mischievous grin intrigued her. He was certainly saying all the right words to win her over.

'Start with Ana,' he said. 'She is probably carrying your grandchild. And she and that child begin your future.'

'All right, Grand Vizier, you have my word. When this task is done with, I shall give you my trust and we shall see how well you can keep a promise.'

Maliz pulled a smile across Tariq's face. This was all so easy, he thought.

❧

As Lazar crested the dune he felt the blood drain from his veins. He was sure it was all pooling in his ankles for his legs felt too heavy to move and his body felt suddenly clammy, despite the dry intense heat.

Below him a thick silence reigned. Men looked up at him with stunned expressions of helplessness and the one who looked the most desolate of all was Jumo, already sunk to his thighs but holding Shahin carefully aloft.

'Quicksand?' Lazar croaked, incredulous.

Everyone nodded sorrowfully, even though it needed no answer, and then the silence thickened, became suffocating, as Lazar picked his way carefully to stand alongside Pez.

Tingles of fear soared through his spine, stiffening his neck and drying out his mouth. The situation looked hopeless, everyone knew it, especially Jumo, who spoke before Lazar could offer empty platitudes that he was going to survive this.

'Sorry, Master.' He shrugged. 'I should never have struggled. They say you can float on quicksand if you don't move too much. I forgot that advice in my panic.' He changed to Khalid. 'I'm going to throw Shahin. She will come to you, won't she, Salim?'

The Khalid mumbled that she would and they watched as Jumo, ever practical, launched the falcon and sank still further for his efforts. She flew directly to Salim's outstretched arm which was wrapped in fabric so her claws did not dig into his flesh. He stroked her, squeezing back his own emotion. It was never easy to lose a man to quicksand, not even a stranger, and the Khalid had come to like the wiry little man from the north.

'Salim,' Lazar barked, finding his voice. 'What can we do?'

'Nothing, Spur,' he murmured. 'Your man is lost to us.'

'Don't say that! Do we have fabric?' he asked, pointing to the men's waists, pulling at his robe to make them understand, remembering the material they had fashioned canopies from. 'Anything we can fashion a rope from?'

'We brought nothing,' Salim said, also pulling at his own robe to convey to the Spur that they had only the clothes they stood in.

'Then we use our clothes!' Lazar roared. He was stripped to a loincloth in moments.

'Lazar! Lazar!' It was Jumo, desperate to still his friend, win his attention.

Pez grabbed his arm. 'Listen to him, Lazar.' And the Khalid frowned, hearing the dwarf speak sense for the first time. Pez didn't have time to consider the implications of revealing himself, but in that moment of recognition, he felt himself safe amongst the desert people who had no reason to consult with the royals. Perhaps he could speak with them later, explain.

Lazar stopped his frantic activity, turning ashen-faced to his companion of so long. Around him the Khalid murmured softly at seeing the Spur's damaged back but Lazar heard nothing. He looked into the sad face of Jumo, who now spoke to him in soothing tones.

'It is too late, my friend. Look, I am already past my waist. You cannot pull me out – unless we had the camels, of course,' he said, 'but they are too far and instead of false hopes and you rushing off to fetch those beasts in vain, I'd rather die calmly now with your face the last I see before I go to my Goddess.'

Lazar fell to his knees. 'Jumo . . .' his voice so broken that Pez had to look away.

The dwarf looked at Salim and he understood, quietly summoning his men with a small gesture. One by one they filed past touching their hand to head, lips and heart, whispering, *May Lyana take you quietly to her breast.* Pez couldn't believe what he was hearing; the desert people had not relinquished their faith in the Goddess, not out here in the Great Waste, where no-one came to censure their spiritual devotion.

Salim was the last to offer his farewell to Jumo and then he turned to the dwarf and gave a small, sad smile. 'It seems we have both exchanged a secret, brother,' he said.

'Indeed,' Pez murmured. 'Yours is safe with me.'

Salim nodded, risked laying a hand on the Spur's bare, trembling shoulder, and squeezed gently, wincing at the sight of this man's back that was a maze of scar tissue. He could only wonder privately at such torture as he quietly moved away and over the dune, leaving the three friends and their new companion, death, to make their peace.

Jumo had almost sunk to his chest. He forced himself not to struggle. 'Forgive me for bringing this pain to you, Lazar.'

Lazar was openly weeping now, although he made not a sound. 'What can I do?' he begged in a distraught whisper.

'Let me go,' the brave man from the north beseeched. 'And know you have been loved by another who has never had a better friend.'

'Pez!' Lazar looked around wildly. 'The Lore. Surely you can—'

Pez shook his head before Lazar went off onto a new path of hopelessness. 'No,' he said sadly.

'You have magic, lift him free.'

'I cannot.'

'Then keep him alive long enough for me to fetch the camels. Hurry! We have a chance.'

Pez knew irreparable damage would be wreaked on his friendship with the Spur with his next words if he were truthful, so he lied and hated himself for it. 'The Lore does not work that way.'

'What do you mean? It's magic! Hurry, man, look, he's to his breast. Please, I beg you.' Lazar looked a broken man, tears streaming down his face, on his knees, all but naked and his arms open in supplication.

It was only the memory of Ellyana's visit that kept Pez strong and resolute. He did not falter from his path and added more weight to his lie. 'I have to be touching him for the Lore to work,' he snarled. And something broke inside him as he watched Lazar wilt, his hands cupping his weeping face, his body racked with grief.

'Lazar.' It was Jumo, his voice still firm, filled with courage. 'There is no time now. Listen to me. We never did speak of your parents. You must go on now. You must hurry and get to Galinsea. They are earnest in this war and it has nothing to do with sacking Percheron for its riches. It is about you and you alone. It is about revenge. No language barrier could prevent their understanding of my tidings. They wept at my news – I wept with them. It is over, Lazar, whatever happened between you all those years ago is finished. They lost a son. The heir to their crown.'

With much effort Lazar dragged his head up and looked at his friend again. Pez had never seen him so haggard, not even at the flogging had he looked so completely broken emotionally. During the flogging he fought back. Fought back with grim silence and by somehow holding on to life. Right now he looked ready to give up all of his spirit and let grief kill him in the sands beneath the blazing sun.

'They want forgiveness?' he asked incredulously, his voice tight as a drum.

Jumo shook his head sadly. 'You are dead, remember. No, they want Percheron to pay and they'll take that debt in blood, unless you and Ana prevent it. I am ready,' Jumo said into the thick silence. The murderous sludge was inching towards his neck — it would not be long now. 'Do not let my passing stop your mission, Lazar, or the Percherese will die, down to the last child. He didn't need to tell me, I could see it in your father's eyes. It was only your mother's urging that convinced him to send the delegation, to give Percheron a chance to prepare itself.'

Jumo was fully buried to his neck now and Pez was amazed at how calmly the man allowed himself to sink. There was not so much as a flicker of panic in his eyes. Here was a man resolved to his fate, accepting of his lot and using his last moments to build the courage of his great friend to accept as well and to go on with life. Pez felt the prick of tears at his own eyes and knew he, too, would never recover from this sad scene. Such courage and grace and the best Pez could do was lie to him. He hated himself. He could have saved Jumo, could have kept him somehow elevated in the quicksand long enough for camels to be brought and for him to be pulled free of death. But he could not risk openly using the Lore, not with Maliz so close, not with the demon paying such close scrutiny to him.

Before, he had escaped discovery because Maliz had stumbled across the Lore and not known what he was touching upon or to whom it belonged. And Pez had covered his tracks well. But out here the coincidence would be too great. If Maliz detected magic it was obvious he would put it all together amongst only a handful of people in the desert. There were only Lazar and Pez to be suspicious of and Pez knew that Maliz had probably decided that Lazar was no threat — he was certainly not Iridor. And so in his fear that Iridor would be destroyed before he even fully discovered Lyana, he kept his Lore to himself and refused to risk using it so openly. Maliz would surely come rushing back with the rescue party and everyone would demand to know how Jumo had been kept from sinking. No, no! Too many questions, too much revealed . . . too much danger to the cause that was Lyana.

'I'm so sorry, Lazar,' Pez whispered as Jumo for the first time began to struggle to keep his chin high.

'Jumo,' Lazar croaked. 'I have loved you better than any.'

'Don't waste those words on me, my friend. Give them to Ana.' The mire began to close around the back of his head, now turned to the scorching sun. 'Lyana, take me,' he said to his Goddess, 'I am ready,' and then he somehow pushed himself beneath the swallowing sands, no longer prepared to wait for death's wet kiss.

'Jumo!' Lazar roared as he leapt to his feet. 'Jumo!' He continued screaming it until his voice was hoarse and there was not so much as a mark upon the surface of the quicksand to show where his friend had been. Jumo was fully taken into the depths of the killing sands and was now in Lyana's embrace.

Lazar, his throat raw, his eyes red and angry and his cheeks wet from helpless, useless tears, slipped once more to the hot sands in a silence thick with grief. After several long minutes had passed and by which time Pez could see Lazar's naked skin burning, the dwarf rallied himself from his dark thoughts and pulled himself up the dune to fetch the others who were waiting on the other side in their own grim silence.

'He will need help,' he said, and they understood.

Whether Lazar was aware of the tenderness shown to him that sorrowful day Pez could not tell, but the Khalid gently picked him up from the burning sands and, having sensed he would not permit himself to be dressed, they made no fuss, simply threw his robe across his scarred back.

'Walk, Spur,' Salim whispered, 'he died with courage. Hold yourself proudly for him.'

They were the right words to say, it seemed, for Lazar finally straightened. He took a moment to press his hands to his face and wipe all trace of tears. Pez privately grieved that the carefree and wonder-filled expression had been cast aside and the granite-like countenance had returned. Pez wondered in that moment whether Lazar would ever let that sense of lightness enter his world again – he would remember it and similar moments of lightness only as dangerous and heartbreaking; the Galinsean love, Ana of course, and now the hunt – on each occasion he had opened himself up to their pleasures and each time he had been left broken, having lost someone precious.

No, Pez didn't think Lazar would return from this loss fully and he felt the bile gathering in this throat that he had permitted it to happen when he could have avoided the pain, saved a life . . . two lives, in fact, if he counted Lazar's that would forever suffer by this experience.

One of the men picked up the dead bustard and, with a soft murmuring of a prayer, tossed it into the quicksand where Jumo had been swallowed.

'That meat is tainted,' Salim said in explanation.

No-one said anything more. The group, with hung heads, moved out silently from the now innocent-looking patch of desert where death had come to claim a life and left no mark that the man had ever existed, and walked with a heavy tread back to their camp.

'Ah, meat!' Herezah exclaimed at the first sight of the men returning.

Ana, who had rallied these past hours, and even got a blush back into her cheeks, noticed immediately that all was not right. 'Something's wrong,' she said, 'look at Lazar.'

He wasn't difficult to pick out at the best of times but half-naked it was all the easier.

'Zarab save us!' Herezah said, startled yet secretly delighted at the same time.

'They got the birds, I can see, so the hunt's been successful,' Maliz said, frowning. 'But you're right, Zaradine, there's nothing triumphant about this arrival.'

'There's one less of them,' Ana said suddenly, having had the wherewithal to count the party.

'Probably one of the tribal men has run off or something,' Herezah said, distracted by the sight of Lazar and the promise of a good meal tonight.

Ana joined the Grand Vizier, who had stood. She squinted. 'I think it's Jumo. I can't see him.'

Her fears were confirmed as the men drew close now, sorrowfully entering the outskirts of the camp where the camels sat patiently.

Lazar strode past the royals but gave a swift glance to Ana, who saw the pain reflected and lost her breath anticipating what was coming. Salim could speak only a smattering of Percherese. He tried to explain but it was hopeless. Pez could hardly translate in present company.

'What is going on here?' Maliz demanded.

Pez realised it was up to him, even if he couldn't explain in straightforward fashion. He had arrived flapping his wings but now stood still. 'The sands swallowed Jumo,' he sang, 'the Spur has no appetite and the fat birds fell from the sky.' He began to dance before flapping off, hoping he'd said enough.

The royal party looked back at the dazed group of men before them and one of the Khalid began to mimic sinking, struggling for breath.

'Drowning?' Herezah asked. 'How do you drown in a desert?'

'Oh, this is ridiculous. Where is the Spur?' the Grand Vizier said, although he was careful enough to realise this was not a man to be pushed. He walked to where Lazar busied himself, grimly pulling on his robes and tying back his hair.

'Spur Lazar, we gather something has happened to your friend, Jumo. Would you settle our confusion, please.' His voice was low, kindly.

'Certainly,' Lazar said matter-of-factly but there was a

tone of danger in his voice now that the Grand Vizier recognised as the sign of a man on the very edge of his emotions. 'Jumo is dead. Quicksand. There was nothing we could do.'

'Spur, I can't imagine—' He reached out his hand to convey his condolences in a way that only touch can but Lazar stepped away.

'I prefer to be left alone.' It was all the courtesy he could show at this time. 'Forgive me.' He pulled on his turban and walked away, Pez crawling on all fours beside him.

The Grand Vizier did not hear Lazar's comment to the dwarf but Pez suddenly stopped, stood up and watched the tall man stride away.

The fresh meat they had all looked forward to tasted bitter in their mouths. Only the Grand Vizier, it seemed, took real pleasure in the roasted bustard. Even Herezah had the grace to dine quietly and sparingly in her tent but Salim had urged all to eat the food that the gods had provided and that Shahin had risked her life to give them.

Through gestures he managed to convey this and the Vizier took up the torch for him, insisting everyone in the royal party and all the Elim partake of this rare opportunity for freshly cooked food.

'We have a long journey ahead,' he counselled, 'with no idea of when fresh meat will come our way again.'

They ate in moody silence. Pez was nowhere to be seen and Maliz presumed he might be with the Spur, but going by the body language of both earlier, he was reluctant to fully believe the dwarf was welcome at Lazar's side. He wondered what had happened between them.

Herezah emerged and Maliz was surprised to see her thank the Khalid for their gift of meat. They bowed to her. The desert does strange things to one, Maliz decided, and then he watched intrigued as she cut herself another piece of the roasted bird and reached for some of the cooling flatbread.

'You have a good appetite, I'm pleased to see, Valide,' he said and couldn't quite mask all the sarcasm in his voice.

'I eat but little, Tariq, as you should know. This is for Lazar.'

He smirked. 'Good luck.'

'The point is, Grand Vizier, we cannot have our guide and our protector dropping dead from starvation. I'm hoping to appeal to his practical side, at least persuade him to eat for his health, if not pleasure.'

'You'd do better then to let the Zaradine take that food to him.'

Herezah bristled. 'You think her persuasive powers are greater than mine?'

He regarded her with a soft look of vexation. 'Are you truly interested in his health, Valide, or would you also appreciate his company?' He stayed the inevitable rush of insult coming his way by raising a hand. 'Forgive me. I simply mean that perhaps they can encourage each other through this sorrowful time. They are both miserable and neither are eating. We need both strong and healthy — they are our most important companions. The Spur as our guide into Galinsea and the Zaradine for the deal she must broker.'

She walked back to her tent and looked inside. A quiet exchange took place and Ana stepped out this time, pale and watchful.

'Come, Ana, you have a task to achieve,' Herezah said and led the girl away from the camp to where they knew the Spur brooded.

They found him with his head between his knees, long arms encircling all, as if by closing himself off to the rest of the world he could avoid its pain. He heard their soft footfall and raised his head. Ana winced to see the grief in his face.

'Please,' he began shaking his head.

'Lazar, you must eat something. The desert is unforgiving, I'm discovering,' Herezah began softly, conversationally, 'it makes no distinction. I gather it will happily kill without mercy, although it prefers the malnourished, I'm sure.'

He nodded, said nothing, although his expression showed a quirk of surprise. She knew what it was – he had never heard genuine gentleness in her voice previously. Perhaps the Vizier was right, she thought, that the desert makes strangers of us.

She pressed on. 'The journey ahead is perilous enough – you've warned us of this so many times – without us adding to the danger through lack of food or care for ourselves.' Herezah pushed Ana forward towards him and continued arguing her case. 'Please, eat something. I don't care whether you don't taste it or even want it. We all care that you remain strong and see us through this trial. You need this meat.'

The Spur turned his gaze fully onto Herezah now and she felt the familiar weakness that his regard could always provoke. She was used to it being loaded with disdain and felt suddenly unsettled that on this night there was nothing but vulnerability reflected.

'Imagine what a fine counsellor you could be to Boaz if only you'd . . .' He didn't finish.

'Yes,' she said, a little more brightly, 'the Grand Vizier urges the same. If I didn't know better I'd think you were in cahoots together.' She tried to laugh but it came out as a choked sound. 'But none of you men have lived in the harem to know how it shapes everything about its inhabitants. How it turns you from a happy and carefree eight-year-old into someone who knows nothing but scheming in order to protect oneself. No man can know the fear of bringing a son into this world that you know from his very first cry will probably be slaughtered – except you don't know when – and that all that stands between him and the blade is what lies between your own legs and how well you wield that weapon to achieve safety for that son.'

She was breathing hard with the emotion she was revealing to this man for the very first time . . . the only man she had ever wanted for her own – the one she hated more than any other because he wouldn't capitulate to her.

Lazar looked at the ground and Herezah had to wonder whether he felt a prickle of shame as she continued: 'No man can know what it is to fight every day of your life to secure your own and your child's longevity and that this fight means shutting yourself off to everything from friendship to pity. Compassion, care, sympathy are all emotions I have not been able to risk, Lazar, and after a lifetime of having to be strong and ruthless in order to keep all weakness at bay, you forget how to even touch again on those emotions.' She unveiled herself and he saw the movement, raised his head to look at her with the pain she provoked with her first-ever words of sincerity to him. 'I have only this,' she said, pointing to her face, 'to win favour, and this,' pointing to her head now, 'to use that favour to its best effect. I won, Lazar, because of my face, my body, my wits. My son was not slaughtered. My son is Zar.'

He watched her for several moments before he replied, Ana's presence hardly registering at this time between them. 'Then your work is done, Herezah. You have succeeded in your life's mission. Boaz is safe. You are safe. It is time to tear down the barriers and be the person you might have been had you not been attached to the palace.'

'I might say the same to you,' she replied swiftly, 'except we are creatures of habit, you and I; we are too old perhaps to change what we've become.'

'It is never too late,' he murmured.

'I shall try then, if you will,' she challenged. 'I am genuinely sorry for the loss of your companion. I didn't know him until this journey but when I bothered to notice, he was pleasant, intelligent company. You obviously had a lot more in common with him, and anyone who calls you friend clearly has something special going for them because you let virtually no-one into your life. So do the right thing by this man. Begin by eating something.'

Herezah nodded at Ana, who moved to hold the plate out to him and spoke for the first time, her soft tones touching him as tenderly as if she had used her hands. 'Don't let Jumo's life be given in vain, Lazar. From what I can gather he was chasing down this food so we could all eat well this night. Honour him, eat.'

Where Herezah's words had lifted his spirits some-what, Ana's words injured him. Her easy tenderness, her ability to touch deeply on all that troubled him, seemed to rub salt into the wound that was Jumo's death. He wanted to reach out and bury his head into her hair, hold her close. He despised that she belonged to the Zar.

He reached for the plate instead. 'I will eat, Zaradine, for Jumo's sake and in his memory, if you will too.'

It was the capitulation Herezah had been hoping for. Both women instantly moved to sit beside him, each feeling their own outpouring of emotion for this man who appeared so vulnerable and yet so determinedly closed to all, the one who sparked desire in both and yet responded with not so much as a touch to either.

Herezah risked it: she laid her cool fingers lightly on his bare arm, had to fight the urge to put her arms around his shoulders and lay her head in the warmth of his neck. 'Thank you,' she said and with effort removed her fingers swiftly for fear of him flinching. It was the first time they had ever touched meaningfully. She tried to convince herself that it was enough.

Lazar did not flinch – it was his quiet acknowledge-ment to the Valide that he understood and admired the courage it must have taken for Herezah to lay out her emotions quite so barely, to him of all people. However, as she spoke more brightly, looking out into the distance, rather than at him, to cover the fleeting awkwardness, Lazar took the plate from Ana and he deliberately allowed his own hand to brush hers. In that moment he felt the connection, saw it in her eyes, sensed it in the soft caress she returned to his palm.

❧

Later that night, mourning Jumo deeply, and nursing his sorrows over Ana — the touch that had told him she was his, had always been — his sadness intensified. He grieved again at the thought they could never be together. He needed to be alone with his thoughts, to clear them, to lay his desires to rest once and for all. Love equalled pain, and he had no more room in his heart for it. Loneliness could never get worse, a solitary life was quantifiable, and once accepted became routine, manageable and even comfortable . . . familiar as a comfy old chair or a favourite shirt.

As everyone was settling down to sleep, he drifted away from the main group unnoticed, and in cover of darkness he moved stealthily from the camp. He needed to walk, to feel the cold of the desert night, to let it chill him and cool the flames of desire that her simple touch had fanned.

It occurred to him that he could easily walk straight into quicksand as poor Jumo had, and that made him slow his urgent stride and make for a dune rather than the flat earth. The sand slipped beneath his feet, still warm in its depths, but he pushed on until he crested the dune, and there he lay, hands cushioning his head as he stared up at the bright crescent moon that had just emerged from a shadowy cloud.

It was always the moon he sought for solace and now it mocked him. *Still alone, Lazar?* it asked. *No parents, no friends, no lover?* He lost himself in sad thoughts of a life that felt unfulfilled, even though as little as fifteen moons ago he might have believed his life was full and happy. Fifteen moons ago he had not met Ana and he had a companion called Jumo. Fifteen moons ago nobody knew his identity and voices did not speak to him in his mind.

He did not hear the soft scramble of someone climbing the dune, but he did recognise the figure when it reached his eye level. He sat up, alarmed.

'What's wrong? What are *you* doing here?'

'I had to speak with you . . . alone.'

'How . . .' He was lost for words momentarily.

'No-one knows I'm gone. I told Pez – I think he understood. He's not happy, of course, but he will warn me should the need arise.'

'Ana, I—'

'May I sit beside you?'

He nodded, then thought better of it. 'Perhaps we had better sit on the other side,' he suggested.

He knew she smiled behind her veil. 'Yes, we are illuminated here on the top of the dune, aren't we?'

Lazar did not return the smile. Instead a tension, emanating from him like a tautly strung bow, stretched to the one person he least expected to find himself alone with. His throat felt too dry to talk and he cleared it nervously. 'How do you feel?'

'Happy now that I'm here.'

'Yes, the desert can offer comfort. The harem has been very cruel to you.'

'I'm not referring to the harem,' she said, releasing the veil and pulling away her head cover fully so that her golden hair could feel the touch of the night's soft, chill breeze. It blew some of the silken strands away and he could see her profile in all of its ethereal beauty beneath the moonlight. 'I mean here . . . with you.'

He had to look away from temptation. 'It's dangerous, Ana. I cannot risk you—'

'What can they do? Tell me off? Tell Boaz? Kill me?' She smirked. 'They've tried it all before and I fear none of it. I am their only hope apparently and I do this for one reason alone. You should know now that I care not for Percheron, I care not for my own life, I really don't care if war comes, save the anxiety I have for my father, brother and sisters. I was meant to be dead by now and, in truth, death suited my needs, for it would have brought closure to a life filled only by misery.'

He remained silent, guarded, sharing her sadness and wishing he could turn back time and never have visited that hut in the foothills. He was the reason for her misery.

She continued softly now, none of the passion gone from her voice but the fire of her words had settled to a more gentle glow. Ana's eyes were not turned towards his but out into the darkness where shadows of dunes hunched like ancient creatures. 'My only reason for not objecting to marriage and to this journey is because it meant I could see you, share your life for just a little longer.' She sensed him move to say something but she carried on talking, determined to say her piece. 'We have never spoken truthfully, you and I. It is time we did, before it is too late and our mission is done and I am either dead in Galinsea or returned to a living death in the harem. I feel somehow sure that we will never be allowed to see each other again once this is done with.'

He tried to sound unfazed, even though he was intimidated by her forthrightness and unsure of how to respond, so he stuck to safe territory. 'I don't see why not. They have no reason to forbid—'

'They have every reason. Herezah would no more trust me alone with you than she would herself. And Boaz kno—'

The mention of the Valide made him bristle. 'I admired the Valide's candour earlier this evening but that's where my admiration ends. Let me assure you that I can trust myself alone with her, Ana – whatever she might try, nothing would come of it,' he said sourly.

'She would find a way, Lazar, she always finds a method of getting her own way. I know this from bitter experience.'

He remained silent. She qualified her rationale. 'She would seek out some way to compromise you.'

'Herezah has nothing that can surprise me.'

'What about the fact that I might be carrying her grandchild?'

More than surprised, he was shocked, unable to form any words for several long moments. Finally she turned her gaze from the distance to focus it fully on him and even in the dark he could see the sparkle of her eyes. She waited for him to speak.

It all fell into place now. 'That's why you've been feeling so sick. Is it true?'

She shrugged. 'I do not know, yet,' she replied carefully, 'but I hear them whispering. She and Tariq have already convinced themselves I am pregnant with the next heir. They have almost convinced me.'

Lazar felt dizzy with dismay at what this meant. So many thoughts swirled around his mind, mainly selfish, angry thoughts, directed at Boaz for having tasted the pleasure of Ana's body. But he fought those back into the recesses of his already scarred heart where he would lock them deeply away, and he focused instead on the practical worries. 'We should not have you and the child endangered in the desert,' he blustered.

'Everyone was quite happy to endanger me. My child, if there is one, is hardly a problem and should not change anything. It is safe as long as I am, whether I am in the desert or imprisoned in the harem. The only suffering is done by me and there is no impact on anyone else, least of all the child. I am the tired one, the one who is constantly feeling sick. If we are to broker this peace, then it matters not whether I am with child or without. The baby would be killed anyway if war came to Percheron — don't try and tell me otherwise.' She glared at him.

'No, you're right,' he admitted. 'You and the baby would be two of the first to be dealt with. No heir to Percheron would be permitted to survive.'

'Then he's in danger whether I'm here in the desert or cocooned in my prison at the palace.'

'He?'

She hugged herself. 'Herezah thinks of it being a he.'

'When will you know if you are pregnant?'

She shrugged. 'My bleeds are unreliable at best. Another moon perhaps.'

'How did you get past Herezah anyway?'

'Pez. He organised a sleeping draught.'

Lazar gave a very half-hearted tweak of a smile in spite of his bleak mood. 'Crafty.' Then he sighed, wishing he wasn't being tested like this with Ana so close and the unique opportunity of being alone. Again he chose safe ground. 'What did you want to talk to me about?'

'I wanted to share my sorrow at the loss of Jumo, but not with an audience and one that in all truth doesn't really care. He was always so kind to me. I loved Jumo.'

'That makes two of us,' he said miserably. 'It was a terrible way to die.'

'Is there a good way?' she asked, echoing his gloom.

'In battle perhaps, or whilst one sleeps. I would take either.'

She smiled sadly. 'I also wanted to have this chance to talk about us.'

He felt the catch in his throat again, swallowed back the fear that she was moving them onto less secure ground. This is how Jumo felt, panicking, sinking further into the mire. He grappled for a hold on to something solid, something real, something irrefutable. 'There is no us, Ana,' he said, his voice betraying how hard it was for him to remain this distant, this controlled. 'You are the Zaradine, now potentially the carrier of the heir to the throne of Percheron. I am your servant. There is no us, there never was.'

'You're not very good at lying are you, Lazar? You're far better at the gruff, angry truth.'

'I do not lie.'

'Then why did you touch me so surreptitiously this evening, if not to steal a part of me for yourself? Why did you touch me fifteen moons ago when I was first being presented to the Valide, if not to hold on to me for just a little longer? Did you think I didn't feel that fleeting kiss of our skins through the sheath I was forced to wear? Did you think that because I was so young I didn't have blood pounding through my veins or the perfectly understandable desires of any young woman?'

'I . . . I . . .'

She was not going to let him off the hook now that she had him squirming at the end of her line. 'Why did you come in search of me when I escaped? Was it all about duty or was it about getting to me first, seeing me again? You could have led me from the temple – I was capable of walking – and yet you carried me. Was that sheer generosity of spirit or did you want to feel me against your body?' He hung his head and still she persisted. 'At least Boaz declares his love, you just sneak around it. You prolonged our time together in the market on the first evening we came into Percheron and on the morning of my discovery. You fought for my freedom during the Choosing Ceremony, and later, after I'd relinquished it and then brought the full might of the harem's censure upon me, you fought again, this time with your own life. You took my punishment. You died for me, or so I was told. You thought you hid your feelings so well but you are translucent to me, Lazar. You always have been. Sometimes I know you, other times you confuse me. Right now, though, I see you clearly.'

'I betrayed you.' He was desperately grasping at straws, anything to stop her from speaking the truth, and showing him so clearly for the duplicitous person he was.

She touched his long hair, a tear escaping down her cheek as he closed his eyes for fear that he might just reach for her and never be able to let go. 'I know now that the betrayal you speak of was not of your own making. Zafira and Ellyana created the deception, not you. I can see how sick you've been. Sick enough to no longer have the strength to dye your hair and keep running from the person you are. A Galinsean prince.' She shook her head, seemingly still unable to fully digest the truth. 'This colour suits you more.'

'This is dangerous, we can't,' he said, unable to finish for the rush of longing that engulfed him, rendering him helpless beneath her fingers that had now moved to caress his soft beard.

'We might never have another chance,' she said, shocking him further with her reckless, suddenly mature approach. He tried to tell himself that she was shy, reluctant, that the loneliness of her life and Jumo's death had provoked her into seeking out the one person who might understand, but the truth was he knew Ana had always been precocious and wise beyond her years. And she was not shy, far from it. She had registered his desire from the first moment they had met and although she hadn't fuelled it, she had certainly accepted and welcomed it in her quiet, guarded way.

'When you were flogged for me, do you know you told me you loved me?' she breathed near his ear, sending fresh currents of fear and lust racing through him.

'I was dying,' he groaned in a last-ditch effort of denial.

'No, you were honest. It was the one occasion I have seen your emotions bared, your expression so free of disguise. You knew you were as good as dead and so it didn't matter any more and you released the truth of what was in your mind.'

He tried once more. 'I don't remember.'

She pulled his chin around, forcing him to face her. 'I remember it so clearly I clung to it for all these moons as my touchstone. I kept my veil, spattered with your blood, as a means of keeping you alive for me. And before you succumbed I told you I loved you back, Lazar. And unlike you, I never lie to those I love,' and she leaned close and touched her soft lips to his.

Lazar, Spur of Percheron, mustered all the courage he had left inside and pushed her back. It took all of his willpower, for he wanted her so badly, he knew he could not fend her off again. 'Please, don't do this,' he beseeched. It was more of a warning.

Ana shook her head sadly. 'It is done,' she whispered and this time when she leant towards him there was no resistance. He had nothing left to ward her off with; no more weapons to fight her with, no more armour to shield himself with.

And so he yielded.

He pulled her close and returned her kiss with such passion that starry explosions winked and blinked behind his closed eyelids, his hands cupping her face in his effort to own her. And then, as the moon once again slipped behind the clouds, Lazar surrendered wholly to her warmth that banished the cold whipping at their bared bodies, and to her brightness that burned like a golden fire within him. He knew no other thought but Ana for what felt an eternity; had familiarised himself with every inch of her young, velvet-like skin, kissing it and making her laugh throatily as he mumbled, 'This bit belongs to me.' He had not heard Ana laugh like that before and would never know that neither had she. It was the sound of sunshine and calm seas, of blue skies and heavy-scented blossom. It was happiness, it was fulfilment, it was satisfaction, all in one. He told her this and she accused him of sounding like one of Pez's nonsense rhymes. And as finally their lovemaking subsided into a languorous, sensuous quiet that wrapped itself around entangled limbs, she stroked his damaged back and he lulled her off to sleep humming a Galinsean lullaby.

Lazar, however, did not sleep. He wrapped her nakedness with his robe and wanted to beg the night's frost to
kill him, for if he could not have this moment again, he
would sooner die. His melodramatic thoughts eased as
time passed slowly and he chose instead to memorise the
curves and planes of her face, so childlike in repose. She
breathed softly, a wisp of her hair rising and falling with
those breaths, and he gently touched her belly in aching
jealousy, wondering whether it carried an heir to Percheron.

She stirred at his touch, stretched slowly, sensually, and
smiled at him. 'How long have I slept?'

'Long enough here,' he murmured reluctantly. 'You
must go back to the royal tent.'

She began to object but he placed his finger over her
mouth. 'We have put Pez at risk enough. If you are missed
he must warn you.'

She nodded and sat up. 'I hadn't thought that I'd put
him in danger. You're right, Tariq sleeps lightly.'

'And Mal . . . er, Tariq, he—'

'You wanted to say Maliz, am I right? So you believe
this tale that I am Lyana?'

He shrugged and she could see no guile in his gesture.
'I don't know what to believe, Ana. Pez believes it.'

'Earnestly,' she said sadly. 'But I think he's going to
be disappointed.'

Lazar nodded. 'So do I. If you were who he thinks you
are, then the Grand Vizier would have already made his
move.'

'And how do we know that Tariq is Maliz anyway?'

'Ah, well, I think in this respect Pez has some argument. I have known Tariq for almost a decade or more.
This is not the Tariq of fifteen moons ago. This is entirely

a different man, who looks the same and has the same tone of voice but doesn't even use the same words or mannerisms that Tariq did. I am a keen observer of people and although most would not pick up on the subtle changes, I have – even in the short time I have been with the new Tariq.'

'So you believe in Maliz, his existence, I mean?'

He nodded. 'Yes, and as firmly as I believe in Iridor's existence – I have seen Pez as himself and as the owl. The magic is real.'

She frowned. 'Maliz did touch me.'

'Which is why I don't believe you are Lyana. Poor Pez.'

'He keeps telling me that you are involved too.'

He grimaced. 'I don't see how. I think once he discovers the real Lyana, he'll forget about us.'

'Who can she be?'

'If she is at all,' he warned.

'Ellyana is real. She obviously believes Lyana rises.'

'Yes, none of it makes sense,' he admitted. He sighed as he unfurled his arm from around her. 'Time will tell.'

'Lazar.'

'Yes?' he replied, distracted in pulling her robe over her shoulders, keen to get them both dressed and out of danger of discovery.

'I have loved you since you came down that incline to our hut and laid claim to me.'

'Ana, you are so young, you have—'

'Don't. Tell me the truth. There are no witnesses, just us.'

He stood, robed himself and then pulled her to her feet, taking the long pause as some precious time to formulate the words he had wanted to say to her since that same moment when his very breathing felt as though it had been arrested at the sight of her. He also remembered Jumo's dying words – owed it to his beloved friend to honour that request.

'I have known what I thought was love only once before. It brought nothing but grief. But what I feel for you I now realise is true love because it never stops hurting.' He kissed her hand. 'But if this is all we can have, then I take the pain and I thank all the gods of the world for giving me this time with you. Yes, I love you, Ana, I always have and I will continue to do so from a distance until I take my last breath. You never need to doubt me.'

He allowed her to throw herself once again into his arms and they remained in that embrace, fighting back their tears, for several minutes before he disentangled himself. 'What we have had, no-one will ever take from us. I wish I'd had more courage to resist you so that neither of us need feel such loss, but I will never regret these hours and I thank you for giving me the gift of yourself.'

Before she could speak again, he pushed her towards the camp. 'Now go, I beg you. Return as silently as you came.'

'And you?'

'Soon, I promise.'

He watched her retreat down the dune until he lost her into the darkness before he turned his back on her and wept. He had lied to her. He was not grateful, for the fleeting gift of herself was a curse and it would haunt him forever with an unrelenting taunt of what he had tasted but never would again.

And something else. The voices were back and calling

strongly to him now. He heard them more clearly at this moment than he had ever heard them previously. Until now they had sounded distant, unintelligible, as if muffled. Now, as Ana left him, they rumbled clearly in his mind.

Release us, Lazar, they called to him.

In his ire, in his understanding that Ana had given herself to him once and once only, in his fury at losing Jumo in such helpless circumstances, and at his sense that this whole journey was one of hopelessness, he asked the same question he had previously but this time he demanded an answer:

Tell me who you are or leave me alone!

He hadn't expected a response and when it came he wished he had never posed the angry question.

I am Beloch.

I am Ezram.

I am Crendel.

I am Darso.

I am . . . the list continued, all names of the mythical creatures of the Stone City of Percheron that he had always admired.

Maliz stirred. He had never been a deep sleeper but these hot days and cool desert nights, as well as all the fresh air and constant activity, were combining to ensure he slept far more soundly than he could ever remember. Still, something had disturbed him, and as he lay in his small, suffocating tent, he considered what could have woken him. There were no sounds outside, save the gentle spit and crackle of the fire. It would be out by morning and no doubt Lazar would be sending people all over to scour for anything combustible. He had already warned that they may have to live from now on without warmth at night or any heated food. The Spur had urged the Elim to cook up stocks of flatbread in case the lack of fire material became reality.

Maliz shook his head clear of the mundane – he was really beginning to think like a man, he berated himself – and focused on what had disrupted his sleep. He had been enjoying these cool desert nights of slumber but had also learned long ago to trust his instincts. If there had been no sharp noise to awaken him, what had shaken him from pleasant dreams? And now that he thought about it, he had not come to from his unconscious state gradually. He had been woken abruptly. He had simply opened his eyes in shock as if reacting to a loud noise or a nudge.

He knew it was useless trying to probe. Imprisoned so completely within Tariq he had none of his magics to call upon. He almost wished he could inhabit some old wretch again, one of those temporary, disposable hosts he used in his dormancy – simply to have the freedom to range outside of his body, just once even. But no, he had committed to the Grand Vizier and so he had to rely on wit and cunning . . . and touch, until Lyana herself had risen and provided his power.

And that's where this thought dwelled. Lyana. Had something occurred with her that had somehow fractured the status quo of the present spiritual world? She could not have risen or he would instantly feel his magic quicken within him. And yet something niggled; something he couldn't latch on to, as if it hovered at the periphery of his vision. He sat up, shaking himself fully from the dozy sense of comfort beneath his blanket, and tried to pay attention to what was ranging through his mind.

Lyana. He tracked back through past centuries. Her rising had always triggered the same response – a violent one – an arrival of his magic that made him suck in air as though gasping for his last breath or as if someone had punched him hard in the belly. But Lyana's rising had not woken him or he would be feeling the effects and the orgasmic sensation of his powers coming fully to him. And yet this disturbance had the hallmarks of Lyana. It was abrupt, it had not announced itself and now it remained hidden. He desperately wanted to believe it signalled her rising but he remained impotent, so it couldn't be.

Now he did hear a soft footfall outside and quickly pulled back his tent flap, all of his frustration poured into the action.

Ana jumped. 'Oh, you scared me, Grand Vizier.'

He frowned. 'What are you doing, Zaradine?'

'Relieving myself,' she said airily, her expression suggesting it was none of his business. 'I had hoped not to disturb anyone. I'm sorry I woke you.'

He considered. 'Did you make a noise?'

She frowned in thought.

Maliz tried to sound more friendly. 'It's just that something did wake me, and I was trying to work out what it was.'

She gave a sheepish shrug, all but her eyes hidden behind her veil. 'Forgive me, I did trip over your tent rope on my way to that dune,' she lied as she pointed to the near distance. 'I'm so sorry.'

He waved his hand towards her. 'It is nothing to forgive.' He yawned. 'I was just enjoying a nice dream, I think, and was sad to be pulled from it.'

She giggled softly in pretend amusement. 'Can you remember your dreams? I rarely can.'

'I remember everything, Zaradine. In this one I was a god, with immense power, and I had just persuaded a horde of beautiful nymphs to visit my mountain palace in the sky.'

In the dying glow of the fire, he noticed her eyes widen slightly at his words. Possibly she was shocked by the image he described, or was it the mention that he was a god? He noticed the hesitation before the smooth answer. 'And now you tease me, Grand Vizier.'

He smiled indulgently and for good measure touched her arm. Nothing! This girl was definitely not Lyana. 'I do. Actually, I was an old man, chasing after a rather lovely young creature who was understandably running with all her might from me.'

He saw her eyes reflect soft amusement now. 'I think you're far more charming and attractive than you give yourself credit, Grand Vizier. There would be plenty of women, I'm sure, who would find you irresistible.'

But only one interests me, my young Ana, he thought. *And you are not her . . . not until I become Boaz.* 'Oh, I do hope so, Zaradine, and once this mission is done with, I might try a little harder with my social life.'

She nodded her approval and then disappeared silently into her own tent.

Definitely not Lyana, his thoughts echoed. 'So who is?' he whispered to himself.

Maliz had to wonder whether his instincts had sent him a ruse. And that in chasing off after Pez, he was actually leaving behind the real trail in Percheron where Iridor existed and could lead him to the hated Goddess. He grimaced. Lyana was cunning this time. But he would find her and he would take his time killing her. His mind moved again to Ana. No. Not her. But if not Ana, who is the Goddess?

Not far away, yet distant enough not to disturb the sleepers, Pez was vomiting but with no idea why. The grief over Jumo aside, his insides had felt well enough and he had not partaken of any of the meat. The nausea had suddenly come upon him; no warning just a violent surge through his body before a darkening of the sand where he stood.

What was it? What could have disturbed his body so? His head throbbed and he sat down to lean against the dune.

'Pez,' a voice whispered.

He leapt up, startled but still dizzy from his exertions. 'Ellyana,' he murmured, 'don't creep up on me like that.'

'I cannot use magic to reach you or he will sense it. He is very alert just now.'

Pez knew to whom she referred. But not how she would know the demon's state of mind. He stole a glance around the dune to check that Ellyana could not be seen from the campsite. 'I am unwell.'

'I can see,' she said softly. 'It is not what you think.' She could see his heavy brow frowning in the moonlight. 'You are not ill. It's because you are Iridor.'

'I don't understand,' he groaned quietly.

'You will. I am here to tell you that our previous agreement regarding Ana is no longer necessary.'

He ignored his aching head to stare at Ellyana, not that he could make out her features in the darkness. 'Why?'

'Just do as I say, Pez.' She made to leave.

'Wait,' he growled in a low voice. 'Is she Lyana?'

He thought he might have caught a ghost of a smile across her face but there simply wasn't enough light tonight with the moon constantly being shrouded by clouds. 'All will be revealed.'

'Why won't you tell me?' Pez persisted.

'For your protection,' she murmured, angry now. 'Just let Ana be now. Iridor knows. Search yourself, you will find the answers you hunt.'

Pez looked to the sands, shook his head with repressed frustration, and when he looked back up, Ellyana had disappeared. So had his headache. He felt suddenly fine – the smothering pain had gone as fast as it had come, and the nausea was nothing more than a memory. He glanced over and noticed the dark patch of sand. He hadn't imagined it; he had been sick but it had passed. None of it felt natural, and Ellyana's curious arrival, timed perfectly to coincide with his disturbance, told him his nausea and headache was somehow linked to the Goddess. Something had happened . . . but what?

∽ 32 ∽

It had been two days since the loss of Jumo and although leaving the region of the quicksand and his death had helped to clear the morbid atmosphere that had pervaded everyone's waking thoughts, it had done nothing to improve Lazar's grim countenance that, if anything, had seemed to worsen into a dulled, impervious expression. Everyone assumed it was grief. But it was terror that lay behind his eyes: terror at the voices in his head; terror at his own dark thoughts of longing for the Zar's wife.

Lazar, in his withdrawn state, didn't know that Ana had begun vomiting most of the meagre bread and fruit she tried to eat in her bid to keep her side of their agreement, or that Salim was becoming decidedly nervous as they entered a part of the desert known simply as the Empty by the tribes. It took Pez and a hissing, angry exchange on this second night after Jumo's death to finally get Lazar to take notice of anything more than his camel or the horizon.

Pez found Lazar in the black of night sitting alone on the top of a dune well away from the campfires.

'I need to talk to you,' he said, anticipating hostility. They had not spoken directly to one another since Lazar had banished him from his side after Jumo's death.

He received precisely the animosity he expected. 'I have nothing to talk about.'

'Do you mean in general or with me specifically?' Pez asked, prepared to go along with the fight that was certainly due between them.

'Both.'

'Lazar, I think something's happening that we don't know about and whether you want to talk to me or not I'm the one who has to make you aware because, to all intents and purposes, you're not very aware of much at all just now.'

'Go away, Pez.'

'I will not.'

'I don't wish to discuss Iridor, Lyana, this battle, or Maliz, or anything in fact. I want to be left alone.'

'This has nothing to do with any of what you censure, Spur; this has everything to do with your job for your Zar.'

'What is it?' Lazar said through gritted teeth.

'It's Salim. He's not saying much but the language of his body and the tension he is creating amongst his own is saying plenty.'

'What is it?'

'I'm not sure, that's why I've brought it to you, but we're all feeling it. There's an uneasiness.'

'I'll need more than that to go on.'

Pez shrugged in the dark. 'It's hard to say. Salim seems overly watchful, nervous. He keeps looking this way and that. I swear he looked over his shoulder earlier today. It's certainly giving me a sense of unrest and I know the others feel similar, from eavesdropping on their conversations.'

'Have you spoken to the Khalid?'

'How can I? The Grand Vizier has nothing to focus his attention on at the moment except me, I feel.'

'Don't flatter yourself.'

'Listen, Lazar, pay attention to what I'm saying. I think something dangerous is afoot.'

'Does your big nose twitch from the Lore and tell you this, or do you have any facts to give me?'

Pez knew Lazar was being deliberately provocative, determined to goad him into the fight the Spur clearly wanted. He wouldn't bite, not yet. 'Salim senses trouble but he's not telling us anything. You need to talk to him.'

'Why should I? Simply because you feel something in the air?'

'Lazar, it's more than that.'

'Well, I don't feel anything,' he said and made it sound as though that was the end of their conversation.

'That's because you are in an Empty all of your own, Lazar,' Pez snapped, his temper no longer in check. 'You arrogant fool. Prince or not, you are all Galinsean. Don't ever say I didn't try!'

Lazar was on his feet. 'You dare talk to me like that,' he warned, turning now to stare angrily at the dwarf.

'I think I'm the only one who isn't scared of you, or that look that I can't see in the dark but I know is on your face. If you want to hit me, break my jaw again, do it. I can heal myself once again if I have to.'

'You seem quite at ease to use the Lore on yourself, or for Ana,' Lazar sneered, dropping his voice low now.

'Ah, so now we come to it. I understand what this is all about. This is not about Jumo. This is about me refusing you. And I helped Ana to have some time with you – I thought you both deserved it.' Whatever else he thought about that moonlit night he left unsaid.

Lazar was grateful for that much and hoped he could push Pez away for the time being, until his own chaotic thoughts about Ana settled. 'Go find another playmate, Pez,' Lazar urged. 'I don't wish to talk about this.'

'No, but then you never do. You run away from all things that prick at your emotions or require you to open yourself up to others. What have I done, Lazar?'

'It's what you haven't done,' he replied, almost a whisper, and there was deep sorrow in it.

Pez knew his recent lies would follow him for the rest of his life. He was glad Lazar could not see his face or the despondent expression written on it. 'I explained, I needed to touch him. How was I supposed to do that without perishing myself?'

'Well, even in my panic at that moment I could imagine you turning yourself into the owl and hovering over Jumo's head if you had to. You could have touched him easily.'

Pez had not thought of that, curiously enough, and now, feeling even more hollow – if that was possible – grasped at a fresh deception. 'I . . . I cannot use the Lore when I am Iridor.'

'I think you're lying, Pez.'

'I am not—'

'I'll tell you why I think you're lying and why you chose not to save the life of someone who could have survived with your aid. No-one should die like that, swallowed by the earth, slowly drowning in a dark mass with an audience that couldn't . . . or in this instance, wouldn't help.'

Pez felt his belly clench, praying inwardly that Lazar had not seen through him. 'Listen to me, I could not use the Lore—'

Lazar continued as though Pez had not spoken. His voice was calm but edged with ice now. No-one could hear or see them. 'I think you lied to me and to Jumo and you continue to lie to me and even yourself because you chose a dream over reality. The dream is Lyana and for her you allowed one of the best men to have ever walked at your side to die an agonising death of suffocation. He showed more courage in death than you ever could in life, Pez.' Reluctant, angry tears were rolling down his face as he pointed at the dwarf who could not see the tears but could make out his accusing finger. 'In your stifling fear of Maliz, you killed my closest friend.' Pez's expression turned from dismay to despair, his large head moving from side to side in denial. 'You might as well have, Pez. You could have saved him. You chose not to and I only worked out why on the way back to camp. You couldn't risk Maliz scenting your magic, could you? Jumo died to keep you safe from the demon.' His reasoning was right, it had hit on the truth but the accusation was unfair and he knew that too. But Lazar didn't care. He wanted someone else to suffer this pain of loss alongside him. Everyone else was carrying on as though Jumo was already something of the past, a distant memory soon to be forgotten, and of no real importance. The bile rose in his throat and he couldn't help himself: he gave back to the desert the small amount of meat that had been stolen from it a few days previous. And as he did so he swore he would never eat any bird again. He would join Ana in her idiosyncrasy of not eating a creature that flies. His reason was different — his best friend had died chasing down the meat of the sky.

Pez was breathless from the pain of Lazar's words. They stung because for the most part they were true, but he refuted that he actually killed Jumo; he just hadn't felt in a position to save him. It was too dangerous for him, for Ana, for Lazar even . . . for all of them connected with the rising of Iridor and the ultimate battle ahead. None understood how their very lives hung on the fragile thread of secrecy. He could almost hate Lazar in this moment for making him feel so responsible for Jumo's demise.

He took a deep, steadying breath. 'Yes, there is some truth in what you say but I didn't withhold my magic to save myself, Lazar. In this you are unjust, for my life as Iridor is forfeit. No, I made the hardest choice without much more than a second to reach that decision in order to save your life and especially Ana's. Over the centuries Maliz has chosen a variety of ways to destroy Lyana once he has her at his mercy. I thank my Goddess that I have never had to witness it but I have learned about it all the same. He once physically tore her limb from limb, until she lay scattered in pieces; another time he disembowelled her but kept her alive for an hour or more — and I can't tell you what a slow, agonising death that would have been for her. Jumo's, if you'll forgive me, was swift by comparison.'

'Stop.'

'Then there was the time he ate her. Roasted her alive over hot coals and carved her up to consume at his leisure. She took a long time to die that day too, as I understand. My personal favourite, though,' he said sarcastically, 'was learning how he slowly bled her to death. Each day he would drain some more. It took her many days of suffering, witnessing her own demise as he drank the blood he drained from her.'

'I said stop,' Lazar commanded.

'Another time – I think it's the occasion Maliz enjoyed the most – he raped her over and over. And when he was spent, he forced other helpless individuals to line up and rape her until she died. Again she suffered with courage – it took her a day and half of endless rutting, her arms and legs pinned out by stakes in the ground, to capitulate.'

'Stop, I said!' Lazar roared and both of them knew he could be heard for miles. Pez, against his own desires, but for the sake of appearances, began to do a jig, hoping that the audience from afar would assume his endless chatter and movement had so infuriated Lazar in his despair that he had reacted with anger. 'Please, I beg you,' Lazar whispered.

'You need to understand what we are dealing with here. He takes pleasure in injury, pain, suffering. He never lets her die easily – once, perhaps, was swift, but for the most part he prolongs her agony, enjoys her slow death. He will do this to Ana and I know him so well, I believe he will keep you alive and make you watch. You see, I think our Grand Vizier has worked out your weakness, Lazar, and whether you believe that Ana is Lyana or not is irrelevant – just as a simple woman she makes you vulnerable. He has seen this and he will make you pay the price for that helplessness where Ana is concerned. He will dream up something even more spectacular with you as audience and you will share her every groan, her every plea to die. This is why I had to choose. There was no surety that I could save Jumo but there was a guarantee that I would not reveal myself and thus endanger Ana and you. Believe me, I have not lived easily with myself these past two days and nights. If it was only my life to jeopardise, I would have risked it gladly for Jumo, but there were too many lives at stake, Lazar. The price was too high.'

'Would the Lore have saved him?' he demanded.

Pez shook his head with a sense of hopelessness. 'I cannot say. I could have tried, that's all, and perhaps we would have won but Maliz would have worked it out. Apart from sensing the magic, not just he but others would have had to wonder how we kept Jumo aloft long enough in the quicksand for the camels. So much risk.'

Lazar hung his head. 'We cannot bring him back.'

'That's right. I made a decision for the greater good and I cannot bring him back even if you deem that decision wrong. I stand by it. Ana is safe for the time being and soon I will prove to you why we have suffered this loss, why her life is so important to us.'

'If she survives.'

'She will survive, I promise,' and his certainty made Lazar turn towards him sharply.

'How can you be so sure?'

'Instinct,' Pez said, too quickly, and Lazar heard the catch in his throat as if Pez realised he was wrong to have shared his thoughts openly. They had argued enough, though. There was no point in opening a fresh wound. 'Will you forgive me?'

'I cannot bring him back,' he repeated.

'That is not an answer to my question. We have been great friends over the years. We know much about one another, especially each other's deepest secrets. We have trust. I don't want to lose that.'

Lazar stared out towards the moon that was shrouded by clouds this night and shivered against the chill. 'Prove me wrong, Pez. That's all I ask of you. I doubt Lyana, I doubt Iridor . . . prove me wrong and let my friend's death count for something.'

Pez nodded. 'I will do that, my friend – may I still call you that?'

'Of course, Pez, I—' Lazar never did finish what he was going to say as he was knocked sideways with a powerful shove.

There was a pressure at the top of his arm and in the darkness of night he couldn't see much, but when he clutched at where the sensation was, he felt a new feeling. This time it was pain and there was a sticky wetness on his palm, and impossible though it seemed, there was an arrow sticking out of his arm.

'Pez,' he began, incredulous, now wavering on his knees.

'I am gone to fetch your sword,' he said. 'Get that arrow from you. We are under attack.'

Lazar ignored the pain, growled as he broke the arrow as far down the shaft as he could, and got himself quickly back to his feet. I *can't see anything*, he thought anxiously, praying that Pez would change into Iridor and make a reconnaissance flight to locate the enemy with his sharp owl night sight.

He waited for what felt an interminable length of time, his frustration increasing to the point of wanting to shout to the heavens. Lazar heard scrabbling nearby and prepared to throw himself down the dune, for without a weapon he was useless to his group.

'It's me,' the breathless reply came. Pez crawled up on his belly, two swords somehow in tow. 'Don't ask me how I did that.'

Lazar took the swords and automatically felt their weight by swinging them in the air. 'Tell me.'

'A small army, you could say. There is no indication who they are or why they've attacked us. The Elim are making a good fist of it, but they are dying. There is no rallying point – they need you. It's each man to himself but all fighting to keep the royal tent unbreached.'

'Salim?'

'The Khalid have fled, I think, although they could be dead, Lazar, I didn't have time.'

'Stay out of sight, you're no use to us in the fray and I'd rather you kept alive.'

'I'll watch and keep you briefed.'

'You risk much?'

'This time I can save many lives with my magic – I am obliged to take the risk because you and Ana are involved, and I think Maliz is hopefully too occupied to be sensing Iridor.'

'Thank you,' Lazar said and although it hadn't been mentioned, Pez knew that was thanks for the time with Ana. At least it sounded reassuring that their friendship was back on solid ground again. As he watched the Spur run nimbly and silently down the dune, he felt a momentary guilt that he hadn't asked after Lazar's arm but then Lazar didn't seem to care much anyway that blood was flowing down to his wrist; thank goodness the arrowhead was still buried, Pez thought, preventing the open wound from spouting too much blood at this stage. Pez cast a silent prayer to Lyana to protect Ana and Lazar and then he changed into Iridor to try to scout for a particular member of the Elim, one he hoped would not lose his life here this night.

Lazar hit the bottom of the dune at a full run and with such force his sheer momentum, together with wheeling swords, killed five men before they even realised they were being attacked.

He was shocked at how many men were in their camp and he had no idea who was foe or friend in the dark; he had to hope anyone from their own group would scream quickly or somehow recognise him before he dealt a killing blow.

After a momentary pause to take in the stupefying scene – many of the Elim already dead and only a few courageously fighting on, holding the royal tent secure – he settled himself into the serious business of maiming. Lazar had never been a fan of slaughter. He held true to his creed that the single most important task in any battle is not to kill but to disable your enemies so that they can no longer kill you. He was only one man but he had the benefit of surprise and coming from the rear, so he used it to best advantage as he set about his subtle art of slashing through Achilles tendons, hacking off sword arms, chopping at knees or hands. Fighting with two swords was his speciality – a Galinsean skill – and he had been one of his nation's leading talents. Since he was old enough to support his own weight his father had thrust a practice sword into each hand. Lucien had learned from this tender age the beauty of being ambidextrous. As he grew older he understood and mastered the art of separating himself mentally into two fighting sides, working as independently as they could of each other. It was no mean skill.

If any had been capable of taking time away from their own fight to watch him now, they would have been fascinated. Twenty-five men he dispatched single-handedly, in what seemed merely moments. But someone was observing him. A man on a camel, shrouded in black, so like a shadow that if not for the beast, Lazar would not have seen him.

The man in black robes silently applauded. He'd never seen such a magnificent display of ferocity. Such single-mindedness, such devotion to the cause. This fighter was a man to admire.

A rough count told him thirty of his men now lay mortally wounded or incapacitated. He worried not for any of them. Their lives were given years ago. This was the culmination of their faith, when they proved their devotion. On the warrior's side, they were down to one brave Elim, holding off several of the watcher's men, but he could not last, for there was a queue of others to take any of his enemies' place as soon as they fell. It was simply a matter of time.

Perhaps these two were worth saving.

'Shaba!' The command was heard and the fighters, all shrouded in dark robes with only their eyes visible, obeyed that instruction and stopped.

Salazin, bleeding from several slashes, was breathing hard and looked to Lazar now for his lead. Lazar had barely broken a sweat but none of the intensity of his fighting rage had left him. He had eyes only for the leader on the camel.

'Who are you?' he demanded.

The man responded in perfect Percherese. 'I think I'm your saviour.'

Lazar ignored the facetious response. 'Why have you attacked us?'

'Why not? You enter my land without permission, steal my fowl – although I understand a debt was paid, as is right, and—'

'Your land? This is desert!'

'My desert,' the stranger replied, unruffled. 'The Empty belongs to me.'

'Where? What do you own in this wilderness,' Lazar asked, 'that you are permitted to slaughter for it?'

'That is my business.'

'No warning, no messengers?'

'You should not be here. You entered the region of my fortress and you—'

'Fortress!' Lazar's anger turned to cold rage. 'What have you killed these innocent travellers for?' he yelled, incensed that only one of the Elim remained alive.

'Trespass,' the shrouded one replied. In the burning torchlight, Lazar looked lost for a response. 'And the fact that I hate the Percherese,' the man added. 'I'm hoping your Zar is behind that tent flap. It would give me great pleasure to kill him, especially as I understand he is child-less.'

Lazar's fury was now ice. Over his dead body only would this murderer take what stood behind that tent flap. 'I am Lazar, Spur of Percheron, I—'

'I know who you are. Bring out the royals,' he commanded.

Salazin, the remaining Elim, raised his sword. It was useless. Lazar gave a hand signal to the mute that in any language meant 'stay your hand'. They were hopelessly outnumbered and he was going to have to risk that this madman had no interest in lesser royals. It was a big risk — these were men, after all, and the people about to be presented were women. Fair game.

Maliz, Herezah and Ana were dragged out. Lazar looked to Herezah and shook his head slightly. He knew he could count on her to understand. More torches were lit so their enemies could see their captives more clearly.

'Ah, no young Zar. Who are these people?'

He addressed them but Lazar answered. 'Vizier Tariq is making a diplomatic journey to Galinsea. He brings with him his wife and daughter.' To her credit Herezah didn't flinch, although Lazar knew what insult he had just given. He silently thanked her with his eyes for understanding and co-operating. She bowed her head, as did Ana.

'I don't know much about you, Tariq, but for some reason I thought the Percherese Vizier was unmarried, childless.'

Maliz bowed. 'Sir, so did I.' Lazar felt his insides do a flip. So the coward finally emerges. 'Until my beautiful Farim came to me.'

'Farim?' the man queried.

'My new wife.' He gave a soft conspiratorial sigh. 'I lay with this woman when I was a younger man. I did not know that my seed had quickened her womb and she had given birth to our beautiful Ana here. Farim came to me when Ana was turning fifteen and told me the truth. She needed help securing a good husband, a good life for our daughter. She had never asked for my assistance before. I had forgotten about her entirely, in truth. But Farim is persuasive and far more handsome in these older years than the gangly young creature I recall having bedded. And Ana is a beauty, I could not resist her needs.'

'And you take the word of a woman you have not known for so many years that this is your child?'

Maliz shrugged, did not skip a beat. 'Would you not if this pair were presented to you, sir? I am old, I am wealthy, I have nothing in my life. Farim and Ana have given me reason to wake up and bless my stars. Whether Ana is mine or not, it is irrelevant. These women are mine now.'

'Very admirable,' the man said, his head to one side. 'Bring the girl closer.'

Lazar had silently revelled in the Grand Vizier's supremely crafted lies but now his heart lurched as Ana became the focus of the stranger's attention. In a shocking move, the man pulled away her veil.

'You need never do this for any man,' he growled. 'Choose it only if you do so for your own modesty or your faith.' He pulled her further aside, and gave a warning finger to Lazar and to the Vizier, not that Maliz was about to do anything heroic—

'Come, child.'

'Where do you take her?' Lazar demanded, fear thrilling through him.

'I wish to speak with this girl who stares at me so defiantly.' He withdrew Ana behind his camel and then closer to some dunes before he spoke directly to her. 'Any other Percherese woman would have screamed, or covered her face with her hands if I'd done that to them.'

'I am not any other Percherese woman, sir. I follow no man's rules.'

He removed his own face covering but in the dark she

could not make out his features. 'If you follow no man, who do you follow?'

'Only my god, sir.'

'Zarab is not a worthy—'

'I spit on Zarab, sir,' she said for his hearing only, and felt rather than noticed the tension she provoked within him. 'I follow Lyana alone. And if that curses me in your eyes, I am not afraid of you.'

He brought his hands together in a gesture akin to prayer, rested his fingertips against his mouth as he considered her. 'Lyana. Do you believe she will come again?'

'I believe she is rising, sir. She will be amongst us very shortly.'

He gave a deep chuckle. 'You intrigue me, Ana.'

'And what of the others . . . my parents, the Spur?' She carefully omitted Pez, for he had not been seen. Hopefully he might raise some alarm, perhaps persuade the Khalid to rally and fight.

'They do not intrigue me.'

'You're going to kill them?'

He cocked his head to one side again. 'The Spur is an extraordinary fighter. He certainly has a keen interest in you.'

'What do you mean?' she stammered, the first time she had dropped her confident countenance.

It amused him. 'I mean he has revealed himself to me. Throughout the entire monologue from your father, the Spur's eyes never left you.'

'That's not true,' she whispered.

'How would you know? Your head was bowed. He briefly gave attention to your mother but his concern is for you alone. Does he love you, Ana?'

'I . . . I hardly know him,' she answered, flustered, frightened for Lazar.

'Well, because you mean something to this proud man, whose fighting prowess I can only admire, I shall give them a sporting chance. And I shall give him a choice.'

'What choice?'

'Heart over duty. Which do you think he'll choose?'

She shook her head. 'I don't understand.'

'Let me give you a demonstration, then,' he whispered close to her ear. 'I'm thinking the very proud and honourable Spur of Percheron will choose duty . . . very sad, because I think you would like otherwise. Come, child, watch.'

Ana and her captor re-emerged, much to Lazar's relief, but the pause that followed felt too sinister for him to trust this stranger, who had already killed on a whim. The metallic smell of blood clung like a death shroud about him and warned of more to come. The first streaks of dawn were slashing across the wide desert sky. It was hardly light but he could now finally pick out the ghostly face of their oppressor, who was smiling.

'Brothers, sisters, a decision has been reached. It is because of this beautiful creature who stands beside me that I have decided to spare your lives . . .' Visible relief was shown amongst the captives – their shoulders relaxing, worried, thin lips parting, and glances of ease shared. '. . . for the time being,' he continued. 'What happens next is entirely up to your Spur.'

Now all of them looked baffled. Salazin firmed his sword in his hand and Lazar tensed. The stranger was certainly not done with them as he'd hoped.

'You have two fighters with you,' the man explained to Maliz and Herezah. 'Both formidable, especially your Spur. He is surely worth ten of mine.' He rapidly spoke in his own tongue. They watched as a dozen of his warriors stood to attention and walked to stand in a line not far from the royal tents. Lazar didn't need to be told what would happen next. He dropped his angry gaze to the ground, marshalling his strength, turning his fury into focus, readying himself for battle and the inevitable grief that he knew was coming.

The man said something else to his men and as one they answered, presumably in the affirmative, that they understood his instructions.

He returned his attention to the captives. 'On my signal my men will hunt you down and kill you as they choose. What stands between you and death is this man over here,' he said, pointing to Salazin, 'and your Spur who has a rather nasty decision to make.' He chuckled.

'Wait!' Maliz cried out. 'This is barbaric.'

'Then we are brothers in arms, Vizier. I have never thought your precious Zars over the years, or the god you pray to, have shown any mercy.'

'To whom?' Maliz beseeched. The man was speaking in riddles.

'I'm sure you'll work it out, Vizier, when the hour is upon you. And it's coming; that, I promise you.'

Maliz began to jabber. 'What are we expected to do, unarmed, without mounts?'

'Run, I think, would be my first suggestion. My second would be that you leave right now,' and they could tell he did not jest. There was no longer any amusement in his voice.

Maliz looked at Herezah and she in turn looked to
Lazar. They both looked terrified. Salazin was the first to
move, silently ushering the pair, pushing them into a trot.
Herezah tripped on a tent rope, stumbling slightly, but
Salazin grabbed her, kept her upright, pushed her forward.
Maliz didn't bother to wait for the Valide, he was already
running as hard as his legs would allow. Lazar gritted his
teeth, felt sure he would run through the cowardly Vizier
with his blade if he got the chance. He looked back at
the man who taunted them.

'Give me Ana,' he demanded.

'No, Spur. She is mine. As I said, I find her intriguing
and her life alone is safe, although you can secure the
Vizier's . . . and the Valide's. Did you think I would fall
for those lies? They were nicely done, too, and if not for
my reliable information I might have fallen for them. But
no, I know who that man is and I know that his companion
is the Zar's mother and I know that beside me stands his
new Zaradine and Absolute Favourite. I also know that
you and she have a special understanding, shall we say.'

'I'm warning you, whoever you are, not to lay a finger
on Ana.'

He laughed. 'You are not in a position to threaten me,
Lazar. I still have twenty men ready to cut you down and,
as good as you are with both of those blades, you will not
make it as far as me. But you can try. I know you want
to.' He shouted a command and Lazar looked in horror
as the men who were lined up yelled some sort of war cry
and began their pursuit of the desperately retreating trio.

'Here is my camel, saddled and ready,' the man offered.
'Take it, and hunt my men down as they hunt your people.
You have a duty, Spur, to your Zar. His wife is safe – I

give you my absolute word — but his mother is not. She will die a horrible death, for my men have not had a woman in a long time.'

Lazar felt the grip of panic around his insides. The despair of choice.

'Heart or duty, Spur? Choose.'

Lazar looked out towards where Herezah had fallen over. Her pursuers were still some distance away and Salazin had turned to help her, stood by her, sword raised and would no doubt fight to his own death to keep her safe for a few minutes more. But the men would be upon them soon. He returned a sad gaze to Ana.

'Ah, duty calls,' the man said and laughed delightedly. 'Say farewell to Ana, Spur. It's unlikely the two of you will ever see one another again.'

'Ana,' Lazar said, ignoring his tormentor. 'I shall come for you.'

Howling laughter followed his promise but Lazar met it with the disdain it deserved. He bowed to the woman he loved. 'Wait for me,' he impressed upon her and before the man could taunt him further, he addressed him. 'She is with child. The heir to Percheron. Harm her not.'

'I will not harm Ana, but I cannot say the same for the child.'

'Heed my warning, stranger, I will come for you and I will have your blood.'

'Hurry, Lazar, they are almost upon the Valide,' he warned.

Lazar ran and leapt upon the camel that had been cajoled to its knees for the purposes. The handler let go of the rope that held the beast and it instantly pushed itself to its feet.

'What is your name?' Lazar demanded.

'I am Arafanz, of the Razaqin. May you and your kind never forget it.'

Lazar urged the camel forward, then gave a final glance to Ana, whilst a slap on the animal's rump from the handler spurred it into an almost instant gallop. Lazar gave a bloodcurdling howl of his own, loading it with all of his hate, every ounce of fury he had ever felt at the world. He became a rampant killing device on four legs. The camel, trained for battle, ran the men down easily, and from his vantage, Lazar no longer gave any quarter. He beheaded his foe, one after another, until some of them brought the camel down, at which point he leapt nimbly from the dying beast before it crushed him. Without breaking pace, he fought in a haze of bloodlust he had never felt before.

The remaining enemy kept backing them further and further from their camp. Herezah was hurt. Her ankle was probably twisted and Lazar could see she had been cut, blood blooming at various sites on her body. The men had already deduced that attacking the Spur was useless – he was too good for all of them, so they concentrated their efforts on tormenting the helpless woman, hoping to draw Lazar into their midst and best him that way. Salazin, realising their intent, immediately stopped trying to defend, and dragged Herezah from the fray.

The warriors knew they were likely to die this day but it mattered not. Their souls were already given and harboured in a secret, beautiful place. What remained were shells and those, too, would give up their lives gladly for their cause and join their souls in the Garden.

And so they fought bravely, ferociously. If Lazar had

had the opportunity, he would have marvelled at their desire to die. As it was, he had never encountered such lack of care for life and so he dispatched them as efficiently as he could. At each given chance he took it. They were no match for his whirling swords. Salazin ran back and with one swing of his curved scimitar took a man's head off, as Lazar finished off the final two with a series of concerted blows.

He did not speak but he bent over to breathe. It was too soon after his illness for this sort of exertion. He sucked in the air, used the time to gather his wits, to calm the berserker within him. He glanced at the dying camel with a sense of hopelessness, realising it was useless to him, and in the distance he could see that the camp was deserted. He also understood that Arafanz would have disappeared with Ana the moment he himself charged across the sands to fight.

'How is the Valide?' he asked, straightening.

'She needs the help of physics.' Salazin's voice sounded gritty from lack of use and from his own exertions.

Lazar nodded, the full sense of despair laying itself across him. He needed to get the Valide back to Percheron. The journey to Galinsea was lost anyway without their royal emissary, and he could hardly go on alone, even if he'd wanted to, and leave the Valide, potentially to die.

No, his duty called. He could hear the laughter of Arafanz still echoing in his mind. How well the man had played him.

'Tariq?'

'Cowering somewhere,' Salazin replied in a hiss.

'Find him. I will take the Valide.'

The last of the Mute Guard nodded and jogged off in

search of the Grand Vizier. Lazar trudged to where the Valide lay panting in the distance, bleeding in the sand. Dawn had broken fully and although it was still cool, it would not remain so for long. He hoped she had not heard his murmured conversation with the 'mute'.

'Put your arms around my neck, Herezah,' he said, and surprised himself with the gentleness in his voice. She opened her eyes, looked at him with a frown. Lazar knew it was because she was unsure of why he was here instead of with Ana. He lifted her easily and settled her into his arms. 'I'm taking you home, Valide. Please don't die, for all our sakes.'

Herezah didn't smile but even injury had not cowed her biting wit. 'And waste this chance to be this close to you for the first time in my life, Lazar? You jest.' She breathed shallowly, her face pale. 'No, I will not die. I think I will savour every moment.' He would not look at her but he realised she knew he battled his emotions, understood that it must have taken every ounce of his strength to run towards her and not Ana.

'Thank you, Lazar,' she said, and meant it.

There was nothing more to say, although inwardly he set his promise in stone, carving it mentally on his heart, burning it into his flesh. He would return for Ana.

ᴄᴏ EPILOGUE ᴏᴄ

Pez had watched it all unfold with increasing horror. He could not hear what was being said, but it didn't take much expertise to work out what was happening once the man in black robes brought Ana back from behind the camel.

He had seen the intruders line up, had watched the heated exchange between Maliz and his captor, and then felt frustrated, helpless when suddenly the Grand Vizier, Herezah and Salazin had set off running. He knew what would come next.

Rightly enough, Lazar was wavering between giving chase and staying with Ana, who was encircled by the stranger's arm. That embrace looked all too proprietary. Pez knew he was keeping Ana and that explained Lazar's reluctance to leave. He wanted to save her but presumably she didn't need saving as such. The man looked relaxed – he would not hurt her. But he would hurt the others and that's where Lazar's duty lay. He was compelled to save the lives of the Grand Vizier and, especially, the Valide. She in particular was his responsibility. Ana was not under threat, Pez guessed.

And then he watched with shared despair as Lazar jumped onto the camel and gave chase. He would kill all the attackers, of that Pez was sure, but he could not be in two places at once, and Pez was also sure, as the stranger urged Ana onto another camel, that Lazar would never know where she was being taken. And in the desert, how would he ever find her again?

Ellyana gave him no clues, curse her, but she persisted in making him believe Ana was vital to Lyana's rising. She was evasive, would never answer his questions directly, and yet she had given him instructions so horrible that he had not wanted to carry them out. He had resisted, argued, but she had also calmly impressed upon him that without this deed, all could be lost. And so he had conscripted the help of Salazin and together they had followed her bidding, hating it as they went about their secret task. And then on the night he had felt so ill, Ellyana had reversed her instructions. It baffled Pez but it still did not divert him from his duty as Iridor.

His duty remained with Ana – he was none the wiser as to whether she was the physical embodiment of the Mother Goddess or just another pawn. But he had no choice. He would follow her captor. Iridor would be Lazar's eyes.

He cast a final glance towards the Spur in the distance, watched him cutting down the enemy expertly from behind, his camel reaching them with relative ease before they could see off the Grand Vizier and Herezah.

He had no time to reach Lazar to tell him what he was doing, and he would not risk a link through the Lore that could alert the Vizier, or worse, at this stage, alarm or stop Lazar. Already the men and Ana were well into the distance, all mounted, moving fast, the black-robed man in their midst. The shifting sands would cover their tracks quickly enough, and without a beast of his own, Lazar could never give chase.

Pez transformed into Iridor. Then he flew. Harder, faster, than ever before, giving chase to an unknown enemy into the Empty Quarter of the Great Waste.

An extract from

GODDESS

◌ PERCHERON ◌
BOOK THREE

Blinking beneath the ferocity of the sun's brightness, Ana was struck by the irony of her situation. Isn't this what she had craved? Wasn't the tantalising lure of freedom a drug for her . . . something she had risked her life for in the past? And yet here she was, free from all Palace constraints for the first time in more than a year of her young life and she was trembling. But not with joy. No, she was trembling with fear as the mysterious Arafanz led her out on the rooftop of his fortress.

She felt the dry caress of the breathless desert heat kiss her grubbied skin whilst reminding her that it did not love her, did not love anyone. The desert's treacherous welcome was one of death if you were naive or careless, as they had surely been when Arafanz and his men had stormed their camp. She realised now that she had always been their target – Arafanz and his Razaqin had intended to abduct her; the killing and the humiliation of the royal party and especially Spur Lazar had been nothing more than sport. She remembered how many of Arafanz's own men had died and from her recollection of that night he had not so much as blinked in sympathy. Clearly this man was ruthless, so there would be no escape; not into this seemingly endless panorama of parched emptiness.

It was as if he could read her thoughts written across her open, unveiled face. 'Look out here, Ana,' he said in flawless Percherese, his free arm sweeping in a wide arc to encompass the wilderness stretching out before them. 'Isn't this what you have hungered after for so long?'

'I have craved freedom, this is true,' she said with care, tearing her gaze from the sweltering landscape to focus on the narrow, softly lined face of her captor. He was hard to age behind that closely shorn beard but a glance at his unblemished hands told her he was likely of an age with Lazar, perhaps slightly older. A bead of perspiration slipped down her back and she couldn't be sure whether it was only the heat that provoked it. Fear was coursing through her.

His gaze, dark and rarely still, briefly danced upon her before moving to another point over her shoulder, returning in an instant. 'I give you this,' he said, 'I have freed you from the entrapment of the corrupt royals and their debauched ways.'

'But I am not free, sir,' she said, 'I am as much your prisoner as I am of the palace.'

'No one here will force you to lie down with a man.'

'But you do oppose my will.'

'I ask only your obedience.'

'Then are you so different from Zar Boaz, sir? He asks nothing more from me.'

Beneath the beard a smile ghosted across his surprisingly generous mouth and she was struck instantly by how that small gesture changed his intense expression from severe to almost welcoming . . . almost. It left as quickly as it came, however. 'Perhaps not, except that I win absolute loyalty from those who surround me, unlike your precious Zar.'

'He is not mine, although we are married. He belongs to his people and they are all loyal.'

'To the death?'

'Who can say until they face it?'

Now the creases in his face deepened as genuine amusement touched his restless gaze. 'Well done, Ana. That was truly the right answer. Come. I wish to show you something.' He walked her to the very edge of the rooftop and Ana looked down, not to the sand as she expected, but to another rocky roof below them. Twenty or so men were assembled in neat, silent rows. They wore the dark robes she remembered from the time his men had attacked the royal camp and again she could not see their faces. 'These are some of my loyal subjects,' he said.

Ana remained quiet but felt a fresh tingle of fear climb up her spine. Arafanz continued. 'I wish to demonstrate what true loyalty is.'

She didn't know what to say, had no idea where this conversation was leading her.

'Choose one of these men, Ana.'

'Why?' Her voice shook.

He shrugged. 'I want to explain something.'

'Can you not simply tell me?'

He gave a short laugh. 'I was told you were clever with words.'

Ana swallowed, hoping to steady her voice. 'Forgive me, sir, I wish only to understand.'

His eyes glittered now, their gaze finally resting upon her at length, turning into an intense, unsettling stare. 'I want you to understand and in a way only something visual can explain. Choose one of these men, Ana.'

She shook her head slowly. 'I cannot.'

'Give me a reason.'

Ana knew there was no rational explanation, for hers was an irrational fear. She gave an excuse instead. 'I do not know them. I cannot even see them.'

'Would it make it easier if you did or if you could look them in the eye?' Aranfanz didn't wait for her answer, instead he barked a harsh order in a language Ana recognised and chilled her despite the heat. She watched the men instantly move at his command.

Ana waited in awkward silence during the minute or so that it took before the men emerged onto the same rooftop that she and Arafanz shared, and arranged themselves once again in straight rows.

'I will have them take off their headdresses.'

'No. Do not.'

'But you said –'

'What do you want of me?'

'I want you to choose a man,' he said smoothly, his tone untroubled by her capriciousness. 'Walk toward one, pick one. He will thank you for it, I assure you.'

Ana felt hope flare inside. She looked away from Arafanz to the gathered men, anonymous behind their head to toe robes. She moved hesitantly.

'Take your time, walk amongst them. One will call to you for one reason or another,' he urged. 'The choice is yours alone.'

Did she hear cunning in his voice? It mattered not, she was on a path now that she couldn't step aside from. If she refused she was sure there would be recriminations – Salmeo had taught her this, if nothing else – and it was clear she was not the one in a position to make demands, deny Arafanz anything.

She passed down two of the rows of men before a flash of brightness caught her notice. It was sunlight, she realised, glinting off a curved blade at his hip as one of the men lifted his chin on her approach. In that small movement he had drawn her attention, unwittingly committed himself to her.

Ana stood before him, stared up into dark eyes that did not see her, would not look at her and with a heart filled with dread, Ana raised her hand and lay it against his hard chest, hoping somehow to reach his heart through her touch. 'I choose you,' she said, feeling faint with fright.

'Return to my side, Ana,' Arafanz said and she did as she was asked. He swapped to the ancient language. 'Are you prepared?' he said now to the chosen one, his voice taking a more sonorous timbre.

'I am, Master,' the man answered.

'Show yourself, then!'

The man emerged from the rows and peeled away the linens that covered his face and body. He undressed to billowy dark pants and soft boots. His hair was tied loosely back to accentuate a face of youth that was not very well disguised behind a gauzy moustache. His lean, hard worked body, burnished from the sun, he displayed proudly.

He undid the scimitar from his side and handed it to Arafanz with a reverential bow. 'What is your command?'

'Do you see that blade, wedged between those rocks in the distance?'

The man squinted slightly to pick out the weapon and Ana swallowed hard, her legs shaking as she too followed his line of sight to where Arafanz had pointed. She could see the blade winking at them ominously.

'I do,' the man said.

'Good. I wish you to impale yourself upon it.'

'It is done, Master,' the man said, turning briefly toward Ana and bowing. 'Thank you,' he said before striding away across the rooftop from where the men had first come.

'What?' Ana screamed, using the ancient tongue. 'He's to kill himself?'

Arafanz did not look at her. 'I am impressed that you understand. We shall discuss that later. Now, watch, Ana.'

'No! This is madness.' She ran to her captor, beat at his chest. 'Stop this! You cannot do this.'

Aranfanz was unmoved. She could feel how strong and wiry he was beneath her fists. He turned to her. 'As he said, it is done. And as I promised you he knows only gratitude to you. Look.'

And Ana wheeled around, desperately wishing she could shield her eyes but knowing a man was about to give his life and respect was the least she could give him. She watched, nausea threatening to overwhelm her, as she saw the man running blindly at the blade, howling a warcry not dissimilar to a chant of prayer. His devotion to Arafanz became complete as he thrust himself as hard as he could at the vicious blade, its tip expertly parting flesh, bone, sinew and organs on its cruel passage through his body, breaking through the skin of his once strong, flawlessly sculpted back.

His body halted against the boulders but it didn't rest, trembling and twitching for an agonising few moments until his brain accepted that his heart had stopped beating and life was over. The initial burst of blood slowed to a trickle, its stain already bright against the golden sand as the young man slumped forward.

Ana choked back a sob. 'What was his name?'

'What does it matter?' Arafanz replied. 'He is happy. He has gone to Glory.'

'Glory?' The despair was still evident on her pale, unveiled face, despite her contemptuous tone. 'Glory did you say? I think not, Master.' Ana loaded his title with every ounce of derision she could pull together. 'I think he has gone nowhere but to hell, on your orders. There he is, heaped against the unforgiving rock. He has gone nowhere, you make a mockery of his young, beautiful life, whoever he was.' She was breathing hard with the emotion driving her angry words. She knew she must sound as if she were babbling.

Calmly he turned to her. 'He didn't think so.'

'How would you—'

'Choose another!'

She stared at him, mouth agape now. Ana could feel a ringing in her ears and the blood pounding through her head. She glanced over at the corpse. The man's helplessness as much as his courage reminded her of Lazar after his whipping and she felt the rage of a year ago rise within her. It quashed her fear and it steadied her nerve. She turned back to Arafanz. 'No. I refuse you.'

'Then you shall die.'

✑

Fiona McIntosh was born and raised in Sussex in the UK, but spent her early childhood commuting with her family between England and Ghana in West Africa where her father worked. She left a PR career in London to travel and found herself in Australia where she fell in love with the country, its people and one person in particular. She has since roamed the world working for her own travel publishing company, which she runs with her husband. Fiona lives with her young family in South Australia.

Read about Fiona or chat to her on the bulletin board via her website: www.fionamcintosh.com

Find out more about Fiona McIntosh and other Orbit authors by registering for the free monthly newsletter at www.orbitbooks.net